T0283564

# HIDDEN ROOMS

# HIDDEN ROOMS

KATE MICHAELSON

CamCat Publishing, LLC
Fort Collins, Colorado 80524
camcatpublishing.com



Hardcover ISBN 9780744310153
Paperback ISBN 9780744310160
Large-Print Paperback ISBN 9780744310191
eBook ISBN 9780744310184
Audiobook ISBN 9780744310214

Library of Congress Control Number: 2023945544

Book and cover design by Maryann Appel

Artwork by David Goh, George Peters, Jklr

5 3 1 2 4

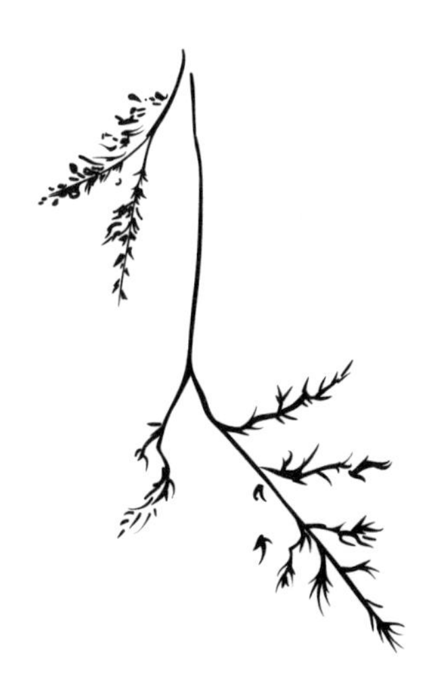

*To my parents:*

*For raising me in a place so special*

*I had to write about it.*

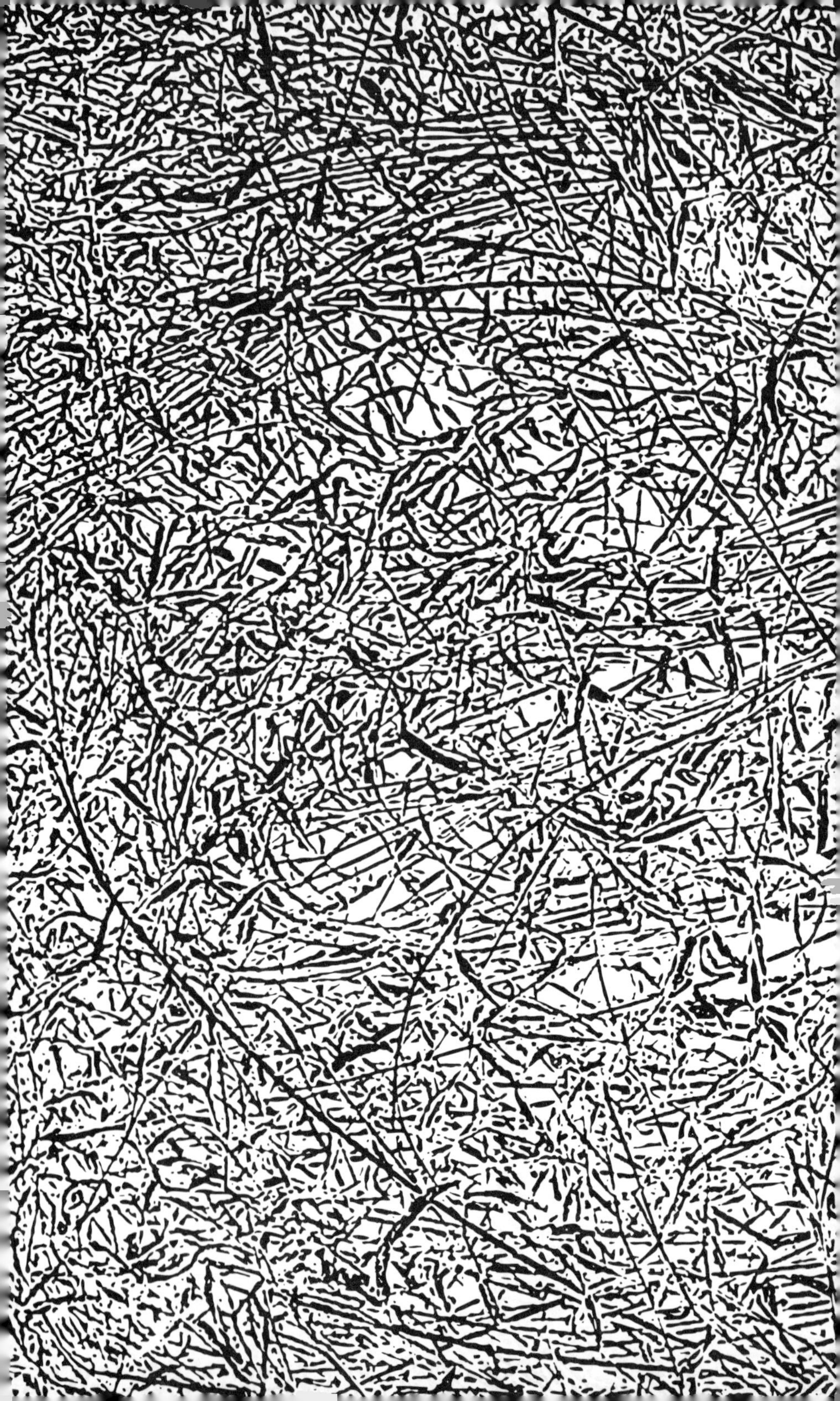

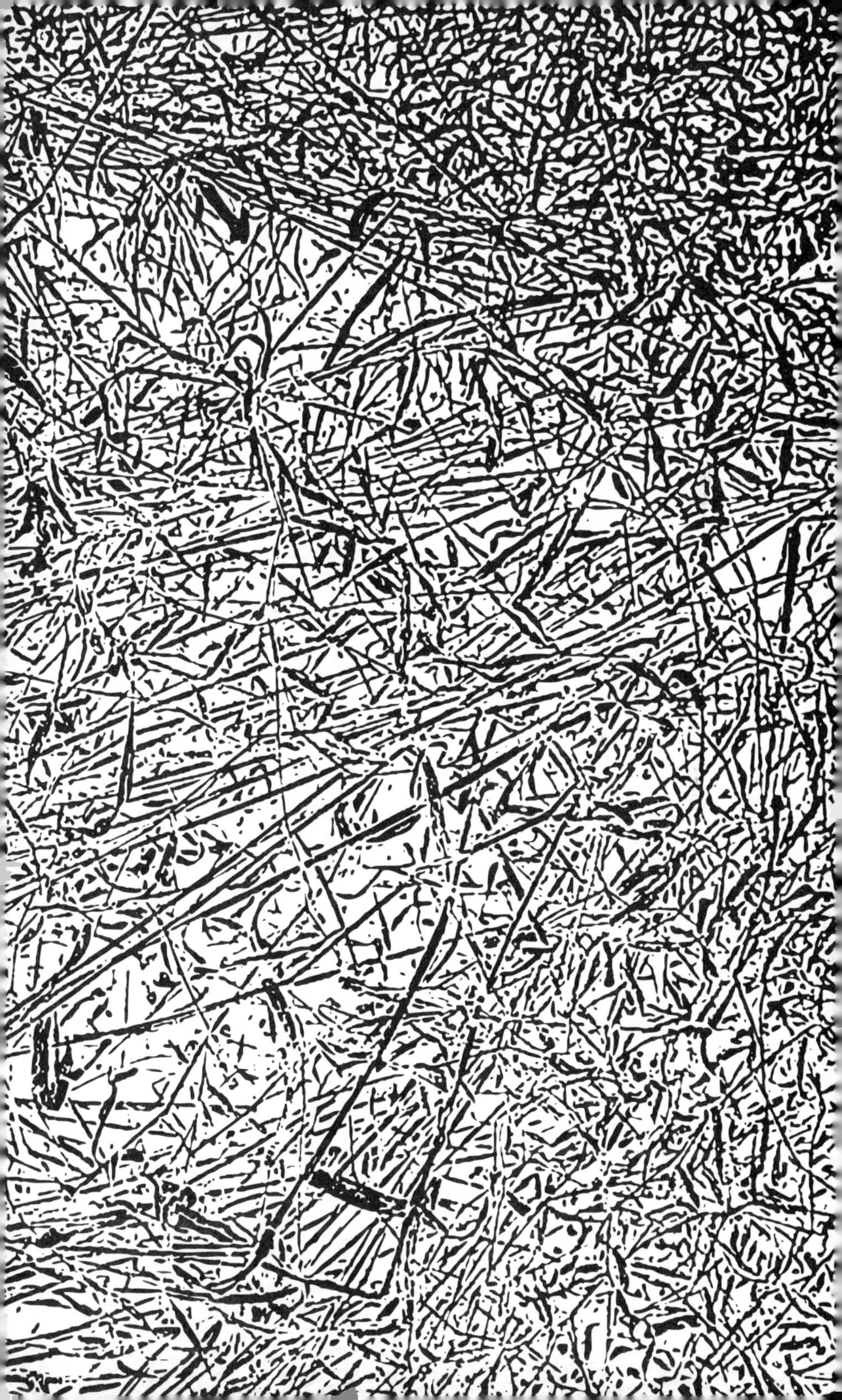

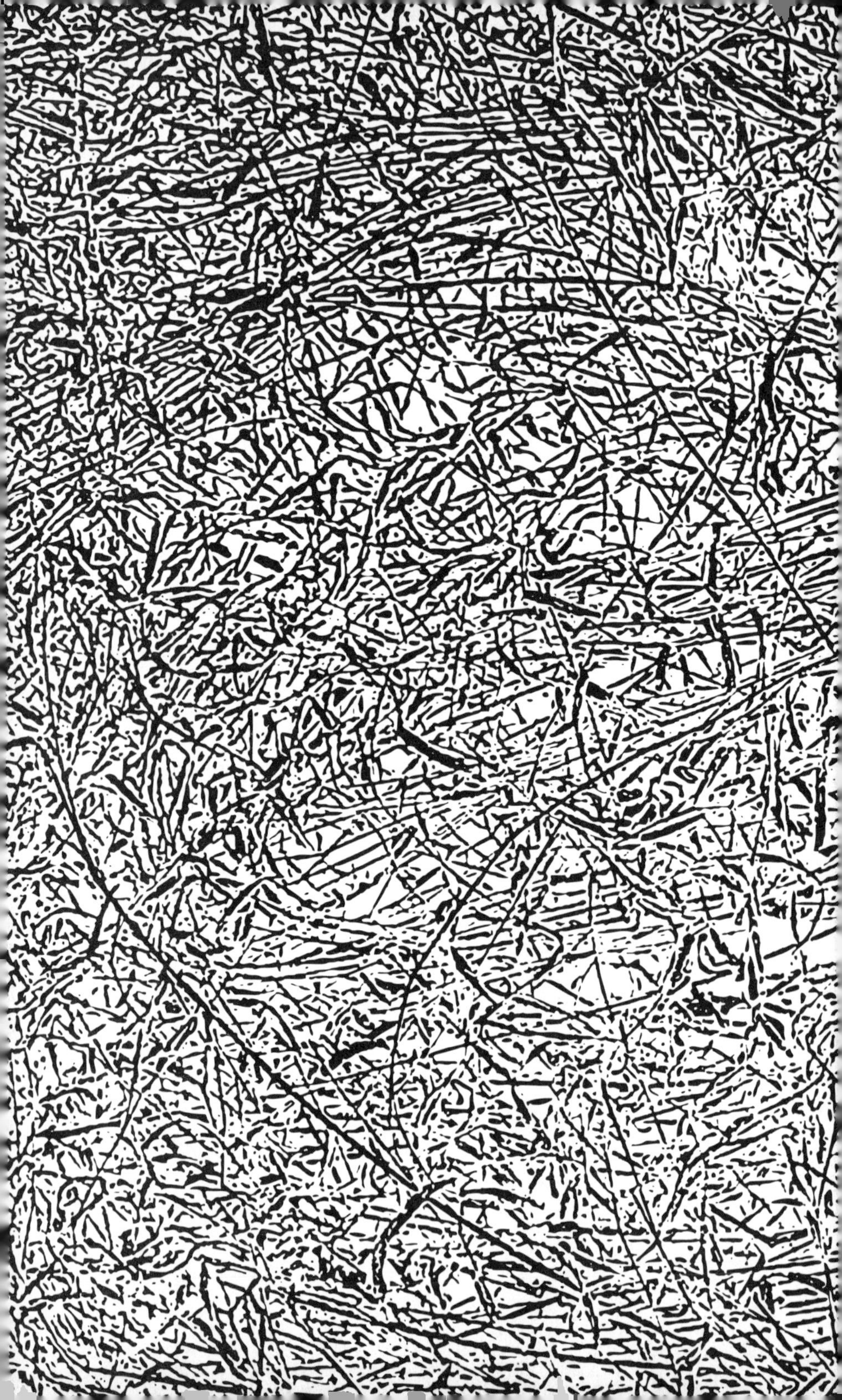

# PART ONE

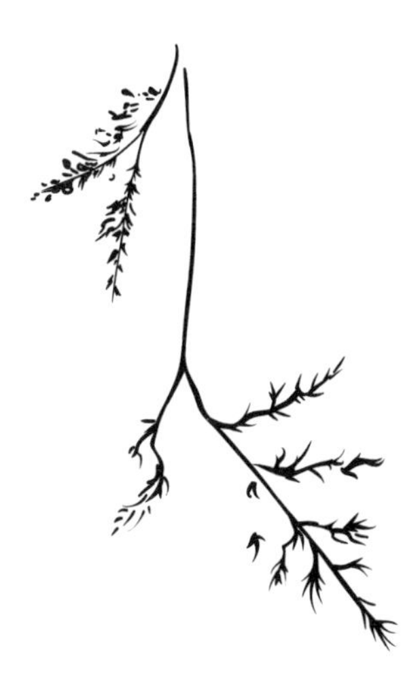

# CHAPTER ONE

*September 23, 2022*

I grew up inside a lightning bolt, in a family of pure momentum. My siblings and I were young, stupid, and fearless in our white gingerbread house, surrounded by dark earth, green shoots, and wild woods—untamed beasts running loose from morning to night. We snarled and bucked, more a pack than a family.

Born less than a year apart, my brother Ethan and I spent most of our lives scrapping after the same few things, pinching each other where we knew it would hurt the most. But we also protected each other. When Trevor Paltree shoved Ethan off the tall metal slide the first day of preschool, I kicked Trevor's little ass, and I'd do it again.

Only, now, I didn't know what protecting my brother looked like, though I felt fairly certain that kicking his fiancée's ass was not it. Besides, I couldn't even say what exactly Beth was up to, which (admittedly) undermined my argument. Putting my head down and going along with the wedding might feel cowardly, but it also seemed like the least destructive path forward.

So, that's how I found myself pulling up to Ethan and Beth's house to pick up my puce monstrosity of a bridesmaid's dress with Beth's recent words still replaying in my mind: *Riley, you know I'd never do anything to hurt Ethan.* The problem was that she also once said with a wink and a smile that what Ethan didn't know couldn't hurt him. I parked in the shade of a low-limbed oak and got out, lifting my hair off my neck to catch the breeze. The autumn sun had built throughout the afternoon into the kind of fleetingly gorgeous day that makes up for Ohio's multitude of weather sins: one last warm postscript to summer. Rain loomed in the low shelf of clouds to the north. I crossed my fingers that it would hold off until I could get home to walk Bruno. Maybe I could even get a run in if my energy held out.

My phone buzzed, and I knew without looking it would be Audra. She called most days and knew that just the previous night, I'd finally worked up the nerve to have a conversation with Ethan about Beth. She would want the details. I was amazed she had waited this long.

"How'd it go with Ethan?" Her melodious voice skipped along briskly. People usually went with what Audra said simply because they were so swept up with how she said it. As her sister, I was an exception.

"Hello to you too." I continued toward the house but slowed my pace. "I'll give you one guess how it went."

"Hello, *dearest* Riley. I guess he got mad."

"Not just mad. He guilt-tripped me. I asked him if he'd noticed anything wrong with Beth, and he acted all injured about it. He told me, 'She thinks you're her friend.'" I mimicked Ethan's self-righteous tone. The jab still stung. "I told him I think of her as a friend too, which is how I know she's hiding something." Granted, I couldn't untangle what it was. It was something I sensed more than saw—a shift in posture or flicker behind an expression. The past few weeks she'd become more self-contained than ever, which was saying something for her.

"Yeah, but can you really be friends with someone who has no personality? It's like being friends with a mannequin. I don't know how you can tell if she's hiding something when she never shares anything—"

"Look, I can't talk about it now." I lowered my voice as I neared the house. "I'm at their place getting my dress. I'll call you later."

I climbed the porch steps, the front of their house looking so Instagram-perfect that I wondered whether I'd been seeing problems that weren't there. The afternoon light slanted across the pumpkins and yellow chrysanthemums that Beth had arranged just so. Dried bundles of corn rattled in the breeze. Beneath the pale-blue porch swing, Beth had set out a matching ceramic bowl full of kibble for Bibbs, the half-feral cat that had adopted her and Ethan.

The only thing amiss was the open door of the old-fashioned cast-iron mailbox nestled amid the pumpkins and flowers. Beth would kill the mail carrier for ruining the ambience. I grabbed the few pieces of mail in the box and shut the little door obligingly, like a good future sister-in-law.

Careful not to disturb a precarious wreath of orange berries, I knocked on the screen door and tapped my foot, ready to grab my puffy dress and go. I had been a whirl of motion all day, zipping through work and crossing items off my to-do list. I worked for Wicks, an oversized candle company that sold overpriced candles. Today was my last day in the office before a trip to England to set up the IT network at our new British headquarters.

For months, I'd been fighting some kind of long-term bug my doctors couldn't figure out, but today I felt a glimmer of my former self, twitchy with energy and moving at a clip to get everything done.

Deep down, I sensed that rather than a sudden return to health, my energy was more of a fizz of nerves, arising from the uneasy note I'd ended on with Ethan the night before. Our squabble had nagged at me throughout the day, like an ache that couldn't settle in my joints as long as I kept moving.

I rapped on the door once more, and when no one answered, I tried the handle. Unlocked. This was not unusual in a town where nobody locked their doors, but Beth wasn't from here. She'd moved to North Haven her senior year of high school and, thus, hadn't lived here long enough for people to think of her as a local. But to be fair, that usually took a lifetime.

I plastered a smile on my face and stepped into the house—immaculate as usual and smelling faintly of cinnamon. I couldn't tell if the homey scent came from something baking or wafted from a candle. I liked to tease a copywriter friend from Wicks with terrible ideas for candle taglines. My brain began composing a homespun blurb about the charms of cinnamon. *Nothing welcomes 'em in like cinnamon!*

Appalling. I'd write it down later.

"Beth?" I called out. The only reply came from the ticking of the grandfather clock down the hall. I peeked into the small kitchen, where the pale-blue vintage-style fridge rattled and groaned inefficiently in the corner. My mom once described it as looking cute and sucking up energy, much like Beth. I had snorted, mostly relieved my mom had directed her acidity at someone other than me.

I poked my head into each room downstairs: each as spotless and Bethless as the last. Checking my phone, I sighed. Nothing. I replied to her last text with *At the house to get my dress. Where are you?*

It seemed fair to look in the back yard and then leave in good conscience. The moment I stepped into the small kitchen again, I noticed that the door to the back yard stood open a few inches. I pushed it wide open and descended the steps off the back porch.

Ethan and Beth lived on ten acres, and the smells of sweet, smoky autumn air and sun-warmed fields hit me as I walked into the yard. Unlike the front of the house, the back was still a work in progress, with a cracked concrete patio jutting up unevenly and half-finished projects littering the yard, but the view of the fields and, beyond that, the forest ramping up for fall, lent the mess a pastoral charm.

Laundry billowed on the clothesline, the edge of a sheet skimming the top of the soft green grass. I imagined Beth reveling in her homemaker image as she hung the laundry out to dry and took pictures of her bedding wafting in the breeze, poised to post.

The clouds to the north had bloomed from gray into a more ominous purple while I'd been inside, and a cooler breeze had picked up. With the serene blue on one side and clouds heavy with rain on the other, the sky seemed to be of two minds.

Something about Beth's absence struck me as wrong. For one, why would she leave clothes drying on the line with rain coming? But beyond that, her behavior had worried me lately, like the way she hid her phone with a startled expression the moment I walked into a room and then offered some flimsy explanation about wedding plans. I wasn't sure if I should be concerned for her or for Ethan, or if I was worrying over nothing. Yet, for all her odd behavior, disappearing in the middle of the day felt unlike her. If anything, she was the opposite—staying close to home and fastidious about her routine and the wedding. The hairs on my arms prickled in the breeze.

Passing the clothesline, I had just decided to text Ethan when a sheet caught a gust of wind and billowed into my face. As I struggled to grab its fluttering edges, I felt a wet stickiness. Finally grasping it, I pulled the fabric taut. A pattern of little yellow fleurs-de-lis dotted the white cotton, but it was the irregular dark red splotches that caught my attention. The marks trailed across the lower corner, where they became more saturated, coalescing into the shape of a hand. My scalp tingled, and my ears began to ring. A dozen scenarios flashed through my mind, all ending in fresh blood and a missing Beth. Cold logic told me to calm down. Stop overreacting. But some instinctual part of my brain roared, telling me that whatever Beth had been hiding—that wrongness I had sensed and then brushed off—had led to this.

I tried to slow my breath. *That doesn't seem good.* My head swam and my vision tunneled as I reached for my phone.

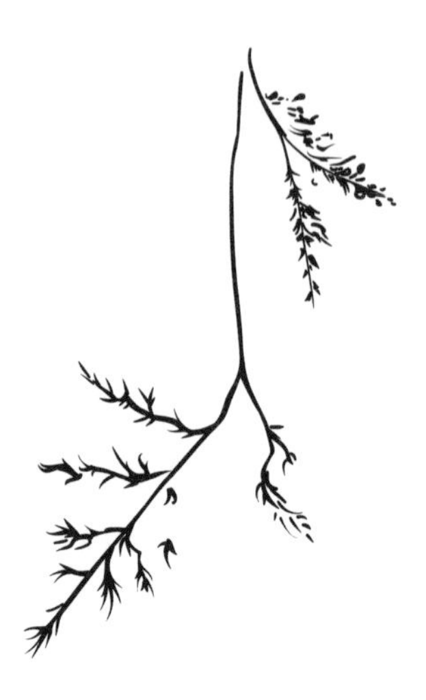

# CHAPTER TWO

*Eight Months Earlier—February 20, 2022*

The engagement party Mom held for Ethan and Beth was elegant, hearty, and vibrating with unexpressed anger in a way that only my family could pull off. I arrived early to mash the potatoes, frost the cake, set the table, and listen to Mom vent about how Beth "couldn't lift a dainty finger to help us out." But by the time our aunts, uncles, and friends poured in the front door, creaking the floors of our family's hundred-year-old Gothic Revival, Mom had her game face on, all cheek kisses and hugs.

Unbundling their thick coats, people blew on their hands and—since most of them had been married and had kids before twenty—laughed about the miracle that at the ripe old age of twenty-seven, Ethan and Beth were finally settling down. Beth's only guest, her father, arrived a half hour late, and unintentionally caused more laughter when he blamed traffic, which, aside from the occasional slow-moving tractor, everyone knew was nonexistent.

Over dinner, I sat at the end of the long dining-room table with Beth and Ethan. The adults' laughter and kids' high voices merged in one continuous hum, like a chorus of giddy birds. Cutlery clinked against china, and

the scents of roast chicken and rosemary filled the room. Amid the buzz, I picked at my food. I'd felt awful since the previous day, when I'd run a ten-mile race outside of Cleveland. I'd broken a record, but not in a good way, recording my slowest time since junior high, when I'd begun running cross-country. I attributed it to the flu I'd had a few weeks earlier. My head throbbed like my skull had been filled to the brim. I'd zoned out and was staring at my green beans, when Ethan's words caught my attention.

"You didn't know our great-great-grandfather was an axe murderer?" Ethan was looking at Beth, his jaw dropped, like he was sure he must have mentioned this juicy tidbit at one point or another. Beth forked a green bean and regarded him with a blank look.

Ethan pivoted to me for backup. "Tell her, Riley."

I blinked and focused on Beth, her shining auburn hair and cinnamon-brown eyes. "It's true," I told her. Wondering if she would find the story as darkly amusing as we did, I scanned her face: unreadable other than a little crease between her delicate brows. "Don't worry. Aside from that, he was a great guy. And it was just the one time."

Ethan grinned and she cracked a smile. "Oh, well, if it was just the once . . ." From down the table, a loud burst of laughter erupted from my sister Audra and her friend Polly as they teased my brother-in-law, Marco, about his new winter beard.

Beth side-eyed the commotion and then tilted her head at Ethan. "Are you joking?"

"No, Riley found it in an old newspaper." Ethan pushed his empty plate away and leaned his elbows on the scarred oak table. "Should I have mentioned this before I proposed? I thought it might dampen the mood." He smiled his wide, dimpled grin. His face flushed beneath his tan, and he looked so dopily happy that I wanted to slap him and hug him in equal measures.

"Yeah," I recalled the headline I'd found. "'Harald Svenson of North Haven killed his wealthy neighbor with an axe.' Dad only told me about it after I asked." I paused, remembering how he had avoided my eyes as he explained. I'd discovered the story when I'd completed a genealogy project for school. Tracing my mom's side had been easy. Her father, the town mayor, had brought over reams of paper with a calligraphy family tree listing generations of educated abolitionists who came from the northeast to the Firelands of northern Ohio. Pictures from the early 1900s showed them dressed in white and lounging on smooth lawns in front of charming homes.

When it came time to look at my dad's side, I found next to nothing. In the one old picture I dug up online, a family of eight crowded together on a rickety porch with grim expressions, looking like they wanted to kill each other. As it turned out, they only killed outside the family.

My siblings and I always joked about our unsavory family history. To our minds, time plus tragedy equaled comedy. My dad—one generation closer to the event—hadn't found it so funny. Almost four months had passed since his death, and the same wave of anguish and fondness still smacked me in the chest when I thought of him.

I cleared my throat. "The guy he killed, something Aldridge, hired him and his kids to clear some fields. Then, I guess one day Harald brought his little girl along and caught this guy messing with her and *whack*—" I made a slashing motion across my neck. "That's why people don't mess with the Svensons. Or if they do, they only do it once."

Beth ignored my feeble joke and leaned forward. "The Aldridges that owned our place?" Ethan had purchased the Aldridge estate at auction a few months ago after it had fallen into bankruptcy. He and Beth were in the process of resuscitating it from decades of neglect.

"Same family." Ethan squeezed Beth's hand. "But hardly anyone knows the story anymore, except for our family." He shrugged. "And now you."

"And now you also know why Ethan is such a brute," I added. "It's in his blood."

Beth laughed, just a sigh and crook of her mouth. Ethan turned sharply toward me. "Well, we can't all be as refined as you, Riley." His tone was light, but annoyance flared off of him.

I tensed, realizing I'd hit a sore spot. Growing up, he and I had teased as easily as we had breathed—our jabs a form of affection that didn't require us to *say* the mushy things that would have made us roll our eyes. But as adults—living very different lives in different states until recently—we'd lost the easiness, with Ethan extra sensitive to anything resembling snobbery.

I was considering what words might mend the damage when Audra interrupted, ringing her fork against her wineglass with such vigor that I tensed, waiting for it to shatter.

"Toast, toast! Riiiileeeey," she drew out my name for a full breath. "Let's hear from you." Her nose was pink from a cold, but she looked as radiant as ever in a deep-red wrap dress with her honey-colored hair and bright blue eyes. I looked shabby by comparison in my worn jeans and a gray sweater, but there had never been any point in trying to compete with Audra when it came to looks.

Glancing around, I stood and picked up my water glass. The progeny of Harald the axe murderer was gathered around the dining-room table. Oddly, with all the axe-murdering blood mingling in the room, it was my mom, with her fancy non-murdering ancestors, who looked ready to kill, brandishing a cake knife in her white-knuckle grip.

I held out my glass. "To the future of two of my favorite people in the world, Beth and Ethan. I know you will be happy together. Now that you're making it official, we shall henceforth call you *Bethan*."

Everyone clapped politely, and Audra echoed, "To Bethan! It's so much more efficient."

"Awww." Ethan grinned as I sat back down. "We're two of your favorite people?"

I clinked glasses with him and returned his smile. "Don't get too excited. I don't know that many people." I winked, and he laughed, his irritation from a moment ago forgotten and our easy connection restored. He was like that, flashing from amiable to prickly and back again with the speed of a thought. In some ways, he still reminded me of the Ethan he'd once been, the enthusiastic kid who never grew out of asking a million questions. But the problem was that he'd never grown out of his tantrums either.

Glasses clinked in chorus around the table. My mom acknowledged us with an eye roll and then turned toward her masterpiece: a heart-shaped layer cake she'd made for the occasion. Her smile stiffened as she passed a slice to Beth. Since my dad's death, she'd not only lost her partner of forty years but also inherited a farm she had zero interest in running. She'd been forced to rely on Ethan to manage the business—and here he was, her favorite, moving on to start his life with Beth. Behind her barbs and complaints, I sensed her terror that the life she'd built had been upended, and she'd been given no say in the matter.

I got up to grab the pot of coffee from the kitchen, my knees, which had been stiff and swollen for the past week, protesting along the way. From the doorway of the kitchen, I paused to savor the scene around the table. The dining room glowed with crystal, candles, and silver, sparkling against the blue-black dusk at the windows. Beth and Ethan held hands and stole quick glances to smile at each other, both apple-cheeked and beautiful. Audra approached Beth and grasped her arm to congratulate her. Whether to avoid the germs or just to reclaim a little personal space, Beth widened her eyes and leaned back from her. My niece Sophie peppered Ethan with questions about wedding colors, whether she would be a flower girl or a bridesmaid, and did he know that junior bridesmaids were a thing too, and that she was definitely old enough for that? Ethan nodded along gamely, his cheeks dimpling, and asked what colors she would choose when she got married one day.

As I approached the table with the carafe of coffee, I caught my three-year-old nephew Franky grinding a handful of frosting into the side of his head. "Franky, no." I set the carafe down and wiped his fingers with a napkin as he scrunched his fine eyebrows at me.

Aside from Mom, the only one who did not take part in the swirl of sugar-charged elation was Doug, Beth's father, who leaned back in his chair with one foot resting on his knee. He had the artfully raked-back hair and bronzed look of someone who had just returned from sailing. Between sips of coffee, he scanned the room, the real-estate developer in him pausing on the elaborate crown molding and wainscoting with a distant look like he might be calculating what this place could go for in the right market. Doug and Beth had relocated to North Haven from Austin her senior year—according to the rumor mill, on the heels of a scandal, but the gossips struggled to settle on what *kind* of scandal, and the rumors had fizzled.

Suddenly, as if he'd sensed my gaze, Doug turned to me, his dark eyes locking with mine. Caught off guard, I floundered around for a topic of conversation. "So, tell me about work—" I thought about the last time I'd seen him. "Oh, the townhome project. How's that coming along?" The second the words left my mouth, I regretted it. Roughly half the town objected to Doug's plans to develop the strip of scenic wilderness along the Vermillion River, which wound through North Haven.

Doug flashed a wry, white smile. "Slowly. Nearly the entire parcel I'm looking at is part of the Carlton Castle Trust, and the association hasn't been too keen on the idea of townhomes going in so close to their historic site." Doug chuckled, as if cultural preservation were a quaint idea. "But I asked them, what good is a historic site if there's no one around to appreciate it?"

I didn't say it, but plenty of people living in North Haven—including his own daughter, who stared at her father with her lips pursed—already appreciated the wooded grounds and the grand mansion that had been a stop on the Underground Railroad.

Across the table, Audra's husband, Marco, picked up on our conversation. "I know a lot of people who would love a little townhome along the river."

Doug cleared his throat. "Well, the price point I'm looking at might be a little steep for most people in this area. The hope is to attract some fresh blood."

Audra narrowed her eyes at Doug and said dryly, "Ah, I get it. You're going to tap into all those millennials who want to work remotely and enjoy our untouched wilderness and Dollar Stores?"

Ethan huffed a laugh. "Didn't you lose your vote when you moved away from North Haven?" Audra flushed and my stomach tightened.

Doug managed to keep the smile on his face. "Well, you may not share my vision, Audra, but I see something special here. Something . . ." He searched for the word. "Untapped. Just one or two new businesses could change the image of this place and draw people in. Not to mention, help out the people who live here already." He glanced at Ethan, who returned his smile.

Audra smirked, but beside her, her best friend Polly, a sheriff's deputy, nodded, probably welcoming the idea of something in town to keep people entertained and give kids something to do other than drugs.

Audra and Polly both drew in their breath like they were about to speak—and probably on opposite sides.

"Anyone want more coffee?" I interjected and reached for the carafe. "Coffee?"

Marco held out his mug. "I'll take a little more. Talking of new businesses, has anyone tried the new diner on Route 13? I heard it's good."

The conversation turned to whether the diner served homemade or store-bought pies and my stomach unclenched. I mouthed my thanks to Marco, who gave me a conspiratorial wink.

As I circulated with the coffee, Beth excused herself from the table and Ethan moved his chair next to Marco, where the two began discussing what to do with Liam, a longtime employee who never seemed to make it to work on time or show up where he was supposed to be. Ethan leaned toward Marco and said in a low voice, "Called in sick again this morning. Probably has an infected hangnail."

With Dad gone, Marco and Ethan were left in the nebulous position of deciding who was in charge of filling his shoes, which meant managing everything from the herd and crops to staffing. When I'd gotten the punch bowl down from the office closet earlier in the evening, I'd glimpsed a pile of paperwork from the family attorney. Curiosity had drawn me toward the cover letter that rested atop the thick stack of documents.

My breath caught as I'd read.

The attorney explained that Mom could, indeed, transfer the farm into Ethan's name while she still lived and leave the monetary equivalent to Audra and me in her will. I skimmed the explanation that this was a common approach for family farms where one child was interested in taking over the business but the siblings were not. I was glad I'd set the punch bowl down, or I would likely have dropped it. Marco may not be a sibling, but he was family and had worked at the farm since he was a teenager. I shuffled through the papers, relieved to see Mom hadn't yet signed anything.

All night, I'd watched Marco and Ethan for clues that either one of them knew about the arrangement, but they seemed as warm with each other as always. Still, my hands trembled as I set the carafe back on the table. I sank into my chair and looked around. While I studied everyone around the table, no one studied me. Even Franky had gone back to his frosting. Still, I knew I'd be hearing from a few of them after dinner. I may not be the one they look at, but I have always been the one they come to with their secrets.

At least, that's what I believed at the time.

After the guests drifted off into the snowy night, Audra, Mom, and I convened in the kitchen over a sink of dishes. Mom washed, I rinsed and dried, and Audra put everything away. Mom sponged at the thickened frosting on the cake knife and turned to me.

"Well, I guess Beth got what she was after at last, didn't she?" She stated this with the long-suffering air of someone who had seen this coming and sounded the alarms to no avail.

The hot water in the sink fogged up the kitchen window, creeping up from the bottom panes. Through the steam, Beth and Ethan's taillights still receded as blurred red dots down the long, icy driveway.

"Oh, Mom." I nodded at the taillights. "So soon with this?"

Audra rolled her eyes at me as I handed her a stack of clean dishes.

"I don't *dislike* Beth. You know that." Mom turned the power of her pewter-blue eyes on me to sell it. I knew she loathed Beth, but I also knew she didn't want to be the kind of woman who disapproved of her future daughter-in-law.

That caveat out of the way, she began detailing all the ways she disliked Beth. "I just don't understand what Ethan sees . . . I mean, yes, she's pretty—she's very pretty—but so are a lot of girls, and those girls have personalities and *careers*." She shook her sponge to emphasize the last point. "I don't think Beth even wants a career. First, she quit the bank because all the time on her feet hurt her back. Then, she had to stop working at Earl's because sitting hurt her back." Mom scoffed, apparently finding it ridiculous that someone could possibly experience back pain in more than one position. "I guess the only thing that doesn't hurt her back is lying flat on it."

Audra wrinkled her nose at the insinuation.

I groaned. "She *did* break her back, for God's sake." Mom liked to gloss over the horrific car accident that had put Beth in the hospital for months. *That was six years ago*, she'd said when I'd mentioned it recently, as if Beth could overcome her chronic injuries if she'd just try a little. "She's still in more pain than she lets on."

Mom waved my comment away. "Well, the worst thing is it's impossible to carry on a conversation with her. It's like there's not even a person in there, and it's only gotten worse. I feel like somehow I know her less the more I talk to her. You know what I mean, Audra."

Audra deposited a stack of plates in a cupboard as she answered. "Well, I may not be her closest confidante, but I don't need to be." She turned and winked at me. "She's got her maid of honor, Riley, for that."

I rewarded Audra with my most insincere smile.

"Well, of course Riley will be her maid of honor!" Mom exclaimed. "She's Beth's only girlfriend. You notice she didn't have a single friend here tonight." I took the soapy steak knife that she waved in my direction. "You spend as much time with them as anyone, Riley. What does Ethan say to you?"

I blew out a breath. All our lives, people had asked Ethan and me what the other thought, as if we were one person, not seeming to notice that we'd moved in diametrically opposite directions over the past decade. Ethan had wanted to farm since he was old enough to toddle around in Dad's shadow with his green hat falling over his ears, while I had wanted to get as far away from home as in-state tuition and work would allow. But I considered how long it had been since Ethan had come home from a concert with a split lip and skinned-up knuckles and how being with Beth seemed to calm him in a way he needed.

I could feel my mom's impatience building like a geyser, almost hear the ticking of the pressure. Finally, I shrugged. "Ethan's happy when he's with her . . . and calmer. They take care of each other."

"Well, how long will that last? And how long will she be happy living here?" She gestured out the window with her sponge, *here* being middle-of-nowhere Ohio and the sprawling thousand-acre farm.

"She likes it here." I looked out the kitchen window where only the tops of the bare, waving branches showed through the steam, black against the navy sky. Our area offered little beyond history and trees, especially this time of year, when everything iced over. "She loves the old houses . . . the woods. She's doing just as much as Ethan to restore their place and working with Mr. Perry to get the Castle in shape for their wedding. Then she wants to manage it as an event venue once it's up and running." The more I defended Beth, the more my head throbbed. But I saw her laying the foundation for a life here and trying to find a way to balance what she wanted with what Ethan needed.

Mom tried a different tack. "Well, how many 'breaks' have they taken over the years?" Suds spattered the backsplash as she made air quotes. "You don't get to take breaks once you're married."

"It's not like it was constant bliss with you and Dad," Audra shot in. "You wanted to kill each other half the time."

"Of course we wanted to kill each other. We were together for almost forty years. But we *didn't*, and that's a sign of a strong marriage." She glanced at me to make sure I was soaking up her valuable life lessons. Her voice had been rising with each breath. "What happens once the house is fixed up? She has no ties here. She'll want to sell it for the profits and move. Then what? Cleveland, Chicago, or back to Austin? Did you hear her dropping hints about how great Ethan would be in finance? She gave him cuff links for Christmas! What farmer wears cuff links?"

"A fancy one?" I ventured.

Audra snorted, but Mom slammed a plate onto the counter with a crack. Shards of white porcelain skidded across the dark granite. We all jumped, Mom included. Then she snapped.

"It isn't a joke, Riley! You, Audra, and the kids are in Wicksburg. You're traveling half the time, and Ethan has one foot out the door." She didn't mention Dad's absence, but we felt it in the empty living room. She leaned over the sink, head down and her eyes clamped shut.

Audra had frozen with a handful of silverware in her hand, her mouth hanging open. I had seen Mom shed tears only a few times in my life; her drama was usually more combative than vulnerable. The whole last month that Dad had lain in the hospital, she'd only cried when the nurses removed the ventilator.

She didn't cry now, but turned to me, her eyes still closed and a heavy slump to her shoulders.

My throat tightened, and I felt the familiar tangle of emotions flood my chest. Looking at my mom, I saw the woman who used to give us kids the silent treatment for days, letting us creep around, wondering what we'd done wrong and how to fix it. She was the woman who told me the summer I turned twelve and stopped eating that I was "starting to look better" but should still be careful to suck in my tummy when I wore my bathing suit. But she was also the woman who, on other days, got up at five to pack our lunches and slip sparkly stickers or little notes inside telling us that we meant the world to her.

I put my hand on her arm and whispered, "I'm sorry, Mom." As was often the case, I wasn't sure why I apologized; I only knew these were the magic words to ease us through the moment. She turned and put her arms around me, her warm, wet hands soaking my sweater.

"No one else is going anywhere," I murmured into her shoulder. Audra stayed quiet across the room.

Mom rested her chin on my shoulder, and her breath slowed near my ear. After a minute, Audra blew her nose and Mom straightened up without another word on the subject and squeezed my hand. She wiggled her shoulders, as if working the unpleasantness out of her system, and gave me an appraising look.

"All that travel is wearing you down, Riley. You look pale, even for you." She brushed my cheek with the backs of her fingers.

With that, we went back to cleaning up. Audra palmed the jagged pieces of the plate with a paper towel and dropped them in the trash. In the quiet of the kitchen, we could hear joyful cries from Marco and Audra's kids playing outside in the snow and the tinkling crash of icicles falling from the eaves.

"Wow, Riley." Audra turned to look at me as soon as she slammed the car door. "Do you regret moving back yet?"

I'd caught a ride back to Wicksburg with Audra, Marco, and their kids after dinner. I glanced at Sophie next to me in the back seat to make sure she couldn't hear me through her headphones. She drew shapes with her pinkie finger on the frosty window, showing no interest in what the adults had to say. Worn out from playing in the snow, Franky slumped in his car seat. I hoped he would sleep through his mother's dissection of his grandma's pathology.

"Do you remember how she gave me bus tickets for my graduation?" Audra continued. "It used to be that she couldn't wait to get rid of us, and now she acts like she needs us all within half a mile of her forever. Did you know that when you're working overseas, she looks up the leading cause of death wherever you are? It's ischemic heart disease in Wales, by the way. I didn't need to know that, but I do now. You'd better not mention the possibility of moving to Bath or I'll have to hear about the crime rate there next."

"Well, I wouldn't go anywhere until after the wedding." I allowed myself to think about the prospect of relocating to England, the promotion, and then put the idea away, like a treat for later. "Mom just has a lot on her mind, managing the farm without Dad, and wants to keep us together." It had become a force of habit to explain what passed for Mom's logic to Audra.

"She never used to care. I almost prefer the indifferent woman who raised us to this . . . whatever this is." Audra sighed. "I don't know how I turned out so normal."

At that, Marco laughed. Audra lightly punched his arm but then laughed too.

We all quieted, and I watched the familiar snow-covered fields and bare trees whip past outside my window, but Audra's question about whether I regretted moving home lingered. After college, I'd taken a job as a cybersecurity analyst at a financial services firm in Seattle. The first evening after work, I'd run the mossy, wooded trails of Ravenna Park and felt that I was exactly where I'd always wanted to be. I'd spent five years in Washington, but when Dad got sick, my priorities changed. Wicks offered me the position as the network team leader, and I'd given notice at my old job that same day.

A mix of coziness and sadness settled over me as I realized I recognized every house we passed. I could picture what each place would look like and the people who lived there before we even reached it. Catching my own reflection in the dark window, I looked like Audra and Marco's overgrown child bundled into their back seat between their kids. For all my efforts to get away, I'd ended up right back where I'd always been, mending rifts between Audra and Mom and answering for Ethan.

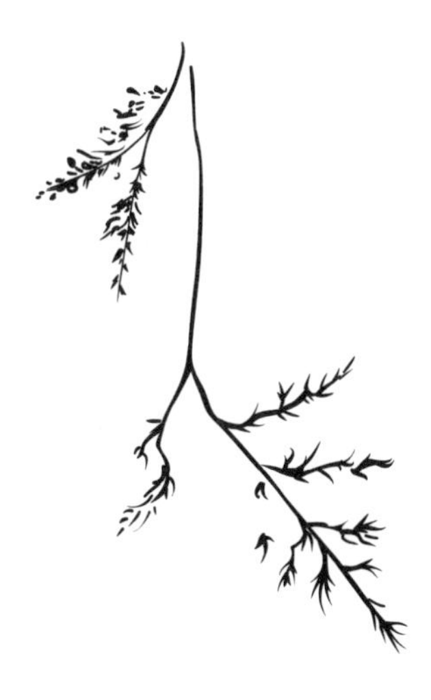

# CHAPTER THREE

*September 23, 2022*

I don't know how long I spent gaping at the bloodstained sheet before my brain sputtered back to life. The rain closed over the field in a wide gray curtain, and I raced toward the shelter of the back porch. There, with the heavy drops drumming the roof, I dialed Ethan and then the police.

As I waited on Ethan's porch, I tried to keep calm—to convince myself I was overreacting. I paced, I sat, I stood, paced some more, and then leaned against the railing, staring out at the bloodstained sheet. The steady rain had soaked it through until it bowed the clothesline with its sodden weight. Then, from the vantage point of the porch, I spotted something I hadn't noticed earlier: a dark splotch, about two feet across, on the uneven concrete patio. *Oh no.* Squinting at it through the rain, I tried to think of explanations that didn't involve Beth. After conjuring a few unlikely scenarios involving their cat and a very large rodent, I gave up.

I tried Beth's phone a dozen times with no answer and was looking up the number for the hospital when a sheriff's SUV pulled up the driveway, and Deputy Polly Nesbeth stepped out. Polly and Audra had been friends

since they had learned to walk. Polly was the embodiment of reason and competence. The sight of her familiar slim figure lowered my blood pressure a notch. She would know what to do.

Polly jogged toward me. By the time she reached the porch, she was already soaked, and her pant legs were spattered with mud. Her sharp gaze met mine. "Tell me what happened."

As I described looking for Beth and finding the blood on the sheet, Polly's even features stayed immobile, but her hazel eyes roamed the back yard as she listened. When she turned her head, rain dripped from the end of her long brown braid.

"Stay put," she instructed after I'd finished. "I'll take a look around."

"What should I do?"

"Stay put," she repeated firmly.

With long strides, Polly approached the sheet, bent forward to examine it, and then circled the house. By the dark splotch on the patio, she paused and squatted for a closer look. I didn't know much about forensics, but I'd watched enough CSI to speculate that the soaking rain was not the ideal environment for preserving evidence. I scanned the porch for something I might throw over the splotch and found an old wool blanket folded over a chair, but I feared the blanket might do more harm than good by contaminating whatever the rain had not yet destroyed.

From the patio, Polly headed toward the barn, keeping her hand poised near the gun on her hip. Minutes later, she jogged back to me on the porch. She frowned and shook her head, flipping her braid behind her. That was about as agitated as Polly got.

During Polly's search of the property, another police car had arrived, its siren growing louder through the patter of rain until it blared up the gravel driveway. Soon after, Ethan arrived.

He jumped out of his truck almost before it stopped moving and jogged toward the porch. A friend of mine had once described Ethan as walking charisma—tall, broad-shouldered, and handsome. But more than that, he was the guy whose attention warmed you like the sun, as if for that instant you were the most riveting person in existence. But as he approached through the rain, all his attention turned inward, blue eyes downcast and shuttered.

Polly shepherded him to the porch, where I wrapped him in a hug. "Have you heard anything from her?" I asked and he shook his head.

Polly pulled a notebook from her pocket, and brought him up to speed before shifting into questions. Ethan stood with his hands in his pockets looking at the porch floor, his jaw set tightly.

"What did Beth tell you about her plans today?" Polly kept her voice unhurried as she focused on Ethan.

Ethan gestured toward the house. "She was spending the day here, taking wallpaper off in the back bedroom. And she was waiting for Charlotte to drop off the dresses." He had come directly from the farm and wore a black T-shirt, jeans, and his work boots, which left chunks of mud on the porch floorboards. "Charlotte was supposed to do another fitting on her gown too. Did you talk to her?"

Charlotte, the town seamstress, had fitted bridesmaids' dresses on seemingly every woman in North Haven. Everyone knew Charlotte and had no option but to trust her with their measurements and whatever gossip she extricated during their fittings.

"Yeah, we'll talk to Charlotte." Polly kept her eyes on her notebook as she wrote. "Was she expecting anyone else that you know of? For the wedding or someone working on the house?"

Ethan rubbed his forehead with one hand. "No, no one else that I know of. I told her that Mom could help her with the wallpaper, but she wanted to take care of it herself."

I could only imagine Beth preferring her own company to Mom's probing chatter.

"When did you last speak with Beth?" Polly looked at Ethan.

He looked down at the porch floor. "This morning—when she told me she'd be home working on the house. She was redoing the spare bedroom and taking pictures to post for her portfolio. I've been trying to get the corn in on Old Bridge Road before the rain, so I've either been hauling grain or fixing the conveyor belt for the silos. Marco was in Wicksburg getting parts, so I had to cover part of the milking too. I couldn't even come home for lunch." His voice broke. He turned from us and looked toward the window into the dining room. Polly had told us in no uncertain terms to stay out of the house.

I scanned the driveway. While we'd spoken, the police had begun clustering in an open area in the back yard. One officer was finally putting a clear tarp over the splotch on the patio. Karl, an enthusiastic volunteer firefighter, who was never far from his police scanner, roared up the drive in a truck that sported a rack of lights worth more than the vehicle itself. He jumped out with his fire helmet on, and his German shepherd leaped out behind him. The dog wore a blue vest like an official search-and-rescue dog, though I was pretty sure he had never rescued anything more significant than a tennis ball from a pond.

Polly drew my attention back to Beth's whereabouts. "Does she have a car?"

I nodded, realizing now that I hadn't seen her car in its usual spot by the barn.

Ethan had turned back to us and spoke up. "Yeah, but it's at Stan's for the alternator. I'm supposed to take her over to pick it up tonight." I saw that his eyelashes were wet.

"And who'd she talk to on a regular basis besides you and Riley?"

Ethan hooked his thumb in my direction. "Riley is her closest friend. She doesn't hang out with too many other people. I mean, she is friendly, but she keeps to herself."

Polly glanced at me. "Anyone else you know of?"

I shivered and crossed my arms over my chest. "She still talks with some of her friends from the bank. I'm her only bridesmaid. Sophie is a junior bridesmaid." Despite Beth's desire to keep the wedding small, she had given in to our niece Sophie's fervent desire to wear a fancy dress and play a role on the big day.

Polly ripped a piece of paper from her notebook and handed it to me, along with a pen. "Okay, the two of you write down any names you know from the bank. And, Ethan, jot down people for the wedding. Now, did she mention anyone she had trouble with? To either of you?"

"No, nothing like that." Ethan shook his head.

"No," I answered a beat after Ethan. The type of trouble Beth had with people wasn't the kind that Polly meant. People just didn't like her all that much.

Ethan kicked at a chunk of mud on the porch floor. I could see his agitation rising, the line between his eyebrows pinching deeper with every question. "What is this, Polly? Can't we get out and look for her? Obviously she needs help." He gestured at the clothesline where an officer in a protective white suit was struggling to arrange a plastic tarp over the blood-spattered sheet to protect it from the rain that continued to fall. None of us had ventured to theorize where the blood might have come from. We'd carefully talked around it.

"We're working on that, Ethan, but we need to find out what we know first. We don't want to get a search going and come to find that Beth cut herself and has been at urgent care getting stitched up this whole time."

"How would she get there without her car? And wouldn't she have answered her phone by now or texted back?" Ethan raised his shoulders in a frustrated shrug.

I only half heard Polly's response about Ubers and cell phones running out of juice. I looked where Ethan had gestured, at the clothesline where officers had removed the tarp and begun bagging up the sheet. From the vantage point of the porch I noticed a gap of about six feet between the sheet and the two pillowcases.

The sheet with the blood had been a flat sheet, but there was no fitted sheet on the line. As I considered this, Polly was wrapping up: ". . . do a thorough search if it's warranted. We're checking the hospitals in Wicksburg and Sandusky. We just need to figure out what's going on before we head out. That's what we're doing."

Tucking her notebook into her shirt pocket with finality, she left us to join the other police, who were now assembling a tent with a white awning. Some faces I knew, and some I didn't. An unfamiliar officer walked past us, avoiding our eyes as she stretched plastic booties over her shoes and entered the house.

With Polly gone, Ethan pivoted and peered into the house through the window. We'd been warned to remain outside. Without looking at me, he asked, "What's going on here, Riley? Did Beth say anything to you?" He kept his voice low, as if I might know something I wouldn't want others to hear.

I looked up from writing names on the paper Polly had given me. Seeing the helplessness on his face, I wished I had something to tell him.

"I don't know." I paused. "I told you I thought something was going on with her," I said, thinking of how he had brushed me off the previous night.

"You said yourself that you didn't *know* anything. You only had a feeling." The muscles in his neck tensed. "Was I supposed to call off the wedding over a feeling?"

I shook my head in frustration. "I never told you to call off the wedding. I just said to *talk* to her."

"Well, I already do that. Every day. Besides—" He flicked his eyes from mine.

"What?"

He lifted his eyes back to mine and kept his voice gentle. "You just worry lately, whether there's a reason or not. I thought maybe you were making something out of nothing."

I flinched. I knew exactly what "things" he meant—the fatigue, the mysterious pain, all those pointless tests. So that was why he hadn't believed me. If he'd snapped or made a smartass remark, it would have hurt less than the delicate tone he used, like I was some hysterical creature he had to handle with care.

I shoved the pen and paper into his hands. "Write down the names Polly wants." Tears started in my eyes, and I turned away. With the rain, the temperature had dropped at least ten degrees and I shivered. Pulling my sleeves over my hands for warmth, I sank into an Adirondack chair along the back wall of the porch.

The rain pounding on the porch roof only added to the noise inside my brain as I replayed my last conversation with Beth. I tried to tease out what had made me so uneasy. The memory grew hazier each time I conjured it, and I was beginning to question what I'd seen versus what I *thought* I'd seen. On the surface, there was nothing remarkable about the encounter, so I'd not said anything about it to Polly, and I hadn't told Ethan the full story—for different reasons.

It had been Wednesday evening—two nights ago—when I'd stopped by to drop off a sample bouquet that Beth had asked me to pick up from the florist in Wicksburg. I'd felt unsteady that day and had pulled around to the back of the house to have a shorter walk with the awkward vase. That was where I saw a familiar black truck with a dented fender parked in the drive.

As I got out of my car, the back door of the house opened. Out stepped Beth and Liam, heads tilted toward each other in conversation. Liam was a few years younger than me and had worked at the farm since high school. I'd never known him to be close with Beth, but it wasn't his presence that bothered me; it was the intensity of their expressions as they talked. I couldn't imagine a single thing the two of them would have to say to each other that could be so engrossing. Turning toward the drive, Liam saw me and took a startled step back. The alarm in his expression and body language told me he hadn't wanted to be seen. He carried a duffel bag, which he slung over his shoulder before giving me a quick nod and slinking off to his truck.

As he pulled away, I approached Beth. She stood on the uneven patio, her hair flying around in the wind and her arms crossed over her chest. A flowered A-line skirt blew around her legs, the zipper twisted out of place around to her hip. Her dark eyes were hooded as she watched me.

"What was Liam doing here?" I asked casually.

She turned her back to me and walked toward the kitchen. "Dropping off rent."

Liam rented Ethan's old house, but the explanation didn't ring true. Beth's tone had a forced nonchalance. "In the middle of the month?"

She waved a hand. "You know Liam. We're lenient as long as he doesn't fall too far behind." Her words came slower than normal, the edges faintly slurred. She leaned heavily against the kitchen door to hold it open and nodded at the bouquet. "Will you bring that in here?"

I stepped into the kitchen and set the vase on the counter. Turning her back to me, Beth examined the bouquet, fiddling with each flower as I watched. "Do you think the lisianthus are too dull?" she asked, flicking at some faded pink flowers.

"They're fine," I replied, my mind still on Liam. "Why'd he have a duffel bag?"

With her back still to me, Beth shrugged and continued fussing with the bouquet, straightening some limp greenery. "These are kind of droopy." A burst of laughter erupted from her that petered out into a sigh. "How long'd this sit in your car?"

"Just from Wicksburg to here. What are you up to today?"

She ignored me, dreamily twirling a length of ribbon from the bouquet around her finger and then letting it unfurl.

"Are you okay?"

"Yeah, I'm great." It came out as a contented sigh.

I took a deep breath and moved a step closer. "Look, I'm not sure how to ask this, so I'm just going to ask. Is something going on? Why was Liam here?"

The startled expression when she turned looked real enough. Her cheeks were flushed and her irises tiny pinpricks, even in the dim light of the kitchen.

"Are you insane? What would be going on?" She lowered her brows as she studied my face. Then her expression softened, dissolving into a drowsy smile. "Riley, you know I would never do anything to hurt Ethan. I promise."

Despite her smile, the sadness in her voice left me doubting.

People had been projecting their own issues onto Beth since she had arrived in North Haven at the start of our senior year. I'd been sitting in AP History when my best friend Sydney slid into a desk beside me and pointed across the room.

"Have you met her yet?"

I'd looked at Beth then, sitting with her ankles crossed and her head bent over her notebook, doodling. Her hair fell over her shoulder in coppery ringlets. She wore a brown dress with white polka dots and red lipstick. In the sea of jeans and T-shirts, she stuck out like a charming anachronism. As I studied her, she looked up and caught me staring; I smiled instinctively. With her big brown eyes and little nose, she reminded me of a cartoon forest animal.

I looked back to Sydney. "Never seen her before."

"Well, you know how Harmony's mom is a realtor? Harmony told me that she moved here with her dad. Apparently they're loaded, and I guess he was really picky about buying a house. They showed them twenty places and he didn't like any of them. He finally bought that house on Ridge Crest on the river. It's not even ten years old and now he's redoing *all* of it." Sydney widened her eyes at the wastefulness. Resting her elbows on her desk, she leaned a little closer. "Of course, since it comes from Harmony and her mom, you can only believe about half of it."

I flicked a glance at Harmony, who was gazing at her reflection in her phone and arranging her silky blond hair. "Maybe only a quarter of it if it's been filtered through both of them."

I'd thought no more about Beth until lunch when I found her sitting at a table with my circle of friends. By the time I sat down, I could tell that Harmony had been peppering her with questions. Harmony was starting to show signs of frustration, saying with uncharacteristic fluster, "Well, if you don't want to talk about it, that's fine. I was just trying to be *friendly*." She spat out the last word. "I mean, people don't move here that often, let alone from across the country, so I just wondered." She tossed her hair over her shoulder with a huff.

I studied Beth for a reaction. Blandly chewing her carrot sticks, she didn't seem to realize she was getting off on the wrong foot. North Haven ran on a Byzantine system of unspoken rules that all of us internalized growing up. The most sacred of all the rules was a simple one: just try to fit in. Beth, in no way, seemed to grasp this.

It didn't help that when my friends and I invited her to join our typical Friday-night entertainment at the Pizza Barn, she claimed to have plans. Every time. In those days, I never knew if her detachment stemmed from shyness, snobbery, or a not-unwarranted aversion to the Pizza Barn. Whatever the reason, the effect was the same: it kept people at arm's length. With her reserve, her retro girly dresses, rich dad, and outside roots, it quickly became doctrine that she thought she was *too good for us*, *full of herself*, and *better than this town*.

Without much of her own doing, she made enemies from the start.

My family arrived at Ethan's in waves. A few minutes after we finished speaking with Polly, I spotted Mom trotting toward us with her hands over her head to block the rain. Beneath the porch roof she shook once like a wet cat and wrapped Ethan in a smothering hug. Her soft brown hair poked out from a black, broad-brimmed hat. I wondered if it was a coincidence that on her way out the door she'd chosen a hat that was both stylish and sensible.

Audra arrived next, crowding onto the porch with us and hugging Ethan. Marco, who had paused to talk with the police, headed our way as well. He ducked his head under the porch roof and looked at Ethan. "Polly says Beth's purse and meds are still here. With that and all the blood, they have reason to expedite the search." Not many people could reference a pool of blood without ratcheting up the tension, but somehow Marco did it. His tall, loose-limbed frame filled the porch with an ironclad sense of what to do next. He gestured toward the field. "The rain is letting up. We should get out there."

Ethan swallowed hard and nodded.

People continued streaming in, neighbors from down the road and workers from the farm. The bad news had spread its dark tendrils. Cars and trucks parked along the roadside, tilting into the deep ditch. Somehow people walking up the drive were already arriving with food, as if they'd kept casseroles at the ready for such an occasion. It seemed as if half of North Haven buzzed around the house like an agitated hive of bees. People took turns touching Ethan's shoulder and shaking their heads. The air, which had been sweet and smoky when I'd arrived only hours before, had turned damp and thick, and cutting through it all was a flurry of motion this town seldom saw.

This atmosphere of morbid excitement made the reality of the situation sink in. Something bad was moving toward us; no matter how this turned out—whether Beth turned up okay or not—I didn't see things going back to how they were before.

Liam, my mom, and I were grouped together and tasked with searching a hundred-foot swath of the cornfield to the northwest of Ethan's house and into the woods, or as far as we could get before dark. On either side, neighbors and friends in their Carhartts and colorful raincoats dotted the fields through a filter of gray mist. Hearing a faint hum, I craned my neck toward the woods. Above the treetops, a drone hovered and zoomed.

Liam had avoided my eyes when Polly had grouped him with me, but that allowed me to study him. Slouchy and lean, he was handsome in a way that differed from Ethan, with fine features and dark eyes in contrast to Ethan's square-jawed solidity.

I couldn't imagine Beth being interested in him romantically, but also couldn't shake the feeling that there had been more to his visit than she had told me.

I scanned my surroundings for any spot of color, anything unusual that might offer some clue as to where Beth had gone. The even rows of chopped corn spread out like lines of draped tweed to the west, and to the north, thick woods extended as far back as the Vermillion River. Our childhood home and the farm lay beyond that, through a patchwork of woods, streams, and fields less than a mile from Ethan's.

As we trudged across the field, my mom drifted much closer to me than the designated twenty feet apart. She hopped through the stubble on the uneven field, swiveling her head between me and our surroundings. Calling across the distance, she stage-whispered, "This is just terrible." She shook her head and frowned, but something in the way she held my eyes conveyed a general criticism of Beth for causing all this fuss.

I nodded but looked away. Her tone had the probing quality of an opening gambit. I could sense her testing the waters and knew what was coming. I just didn't know how to stop her and never had.

Mom edged still closer. "What do you suppose she got herself involved in?"

Liam had wandered about fifty feet beyond us, probably assuming it would be his job to cover at least half of our assigned area since my mom had already abandoned hers. Realizing I had no escape, I held out my palms. "We don't know that she *got into* anything, Mom. I don't think she intentionally went missing and left her blood behind."

She gave me a look that said, clearly, I still had a lot left to learn about the world and she was disappointed to have raised such a rube. "Well, I'm not saying she did it intentionally, Riley, but how often do completely innocent people go missing?" Her expression shifted abruptly. I could almost hear the lightbulb ding above her head. "Or maybe it *was* intentional? She wanted Ethan off the farm and working in some bank in Cleveland. Maybe she got tired of waiting." Her tone told me this should be painfully obvious to anyone who's ever watched a single Lifetime movie. She lowered her voice. "People stage their disappearances, honey. It happens."

"Do you even believe what you're saying?" My voice shook. "If Beth was planning to run off, then why was she working on the house and building up her portfolio online? I don't think too many people spend their last hours stripping wallpaper before staging their own disappearance. She could be hurt or dead, and you're . . ." I couldn't finish, horrified at what I'd put into words.

"Now, don't say that. I'm sure she'll turn up, honey. Don't get yourself worked up." But her tone was chastened.

I sped up my pace, unsteady on the uneven ground, and pulled ahead of Mom. She had never had much nice to say about Beth, even before she and Ethan had gotten engaged. Anyone with an inner world not readily apparent to her immediately roused suspicion, but she hadn't been alone in that way of thinking.

The rumors swirled around Beth and her father from the start: the pretty, rich girl who kept to herself. When classmates eagerly approached her with questions about where she came from, what it was like there, and why she'd moved here, she would answer them pleasantly, with the fewest words possible, and turn back to her book. I initially thought Beth just didn't want to try, but over time I began to think that maybe she didn't know she was supposed to try. Maybe, misguidedly, she thought that she could just show up, be herself, and that would be enough.

Unlike the girls in my class, Ethan had never minded Beth's reticence. When she and I were paired up for a year-long project in AP History, she began spending time at our house after school. One day, Ethan looked at her in a floaty, flower-sprigged dress and commented that that was how a woman should look. I'd made a gagging sound and told him he was gross, but I didn't mind when he started dating her.

As she spent more time at our house, everyone laughed about "Beth, Riley's new best friend," but just from the sheer hours spent in each other's presence, she and I became about as close as two people can without exchanging many meaningful words. With Beth, I never felt the need to fill silences. Through short asides, I discovered that she sewed, collected antiques, wrote poetry, and wanted to get out of North Haven at the first opportunity.

A trickle of rain down my neck brought me back to the muddy field and the grim search. I looked over my shoulder at my mom, who had settled into a steady pace a ways back. As she walked, she kept her head down, and I could see she was twisting the wedding band she still wore. I wondered if she was missing Dad at this moment as much as I was. Behind her, I was relieved to see that another team of searchers were following us to ensure nothing had been overlooked.

Up ahead at the edge of the woods, yellow leaves plastered the dark earth. The light was fading, and against the orange and chrome of the western sky, black wavering limbs stood out in stark relief. Since finding the sheet, I'd had a heavy feeling in my chest, a jammed-up mix of worry, sadness, and guilt. I couldn't help thinking I'd made a misstep somewhere along the way.

As I wove my way through corn stubble up a hill, a familiar wave of nausea and faintness rippled through me. Focusing on my feet, I trudged up the hill, my breath coming hard.

At the edge of the woods, I stopped to catch my breath. In the dim light, a shower of wet leaves whirled down around me. I steadied myself against a beech tree, its bark smooth against my palm, and peered through the briars and thin undergrowth. I squinted in the gloom. Then I saw it.

About twenty feet into the woods, not far from the river, a white sheet with a pale-yellow pattern, camouflaged among the falling leaves, wrapped around a form. She was turned away from me, her streaming auburn hair wet and matted darker around the crown of her head.

I called her name but she didn't move. I knew she wouldn't.

As I stumbled back toward the open field to call for help, the wave of spinning crested. A tinny noise echoed in my ears. Blackness cut across my vision and my knees buckled, I heard my mom's startled tone. "What on earth are you *doing*, Riley?" Then I hit the wet ground.

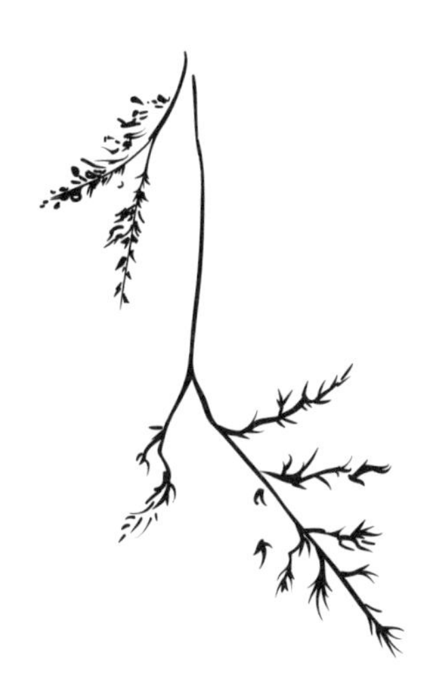

# CHAPTER FOUR

*September 23, 2022*

Gradually it dawned on me that I was lying on wet, furrowed earth, corn stubble jabbing into my back. When I opened my eyes, a man I'd never seen before, with dark hair and concerned brown eyes, leaned over me. Nearby, I heard my mom apologizing. "She's not usually like this."

The man leaning over me asked, "Can you hear me?" Staring up at him, I realized that the outer corners of his eyes naturally tilted down a bit, giving him that perpetually concerned look. His brisk tone didn't match.

"Yes." I cleared my throat. "I'm okay." The weakness of my voice embarrassed me. I sat up, a high ringing in my ears. Fog shrouded my thoughts, but the same heaviness hung over me as the morning after Dad's death—the same sense that something had gone irrevocably wrong.

"You sure you're okay to sit up? You're still awfully pale."

My mom had joined us and leaned over me too. "Oh no, Riley's always pale. That's how she looks." She squeezed my arm. "You okay now, honey?"

I nodded, but Mom swam across my field of vision. I remembered seeing something—or had I? I couldn't pull my thoughts together or even hear

them over the keening in my ears. I was sitting up fully now, waiting for my equilibrium to settle back into place.

"Let's get you up off the ground then." The man said it like someone might talk about towing an old car out of a ditch. He held out his hand to help me. I took it and stood, the muscles in my legs quivering but holding. Assured that I was up and not going back down, he took a step back and put his hands in his pockets. Now that he stood a few feet from me, I noticed the yellow sheriff's insignia on the front of his dark jacket and I remembered. *Beth.*

What I'd seen in the woods hit me with the force of a blow, and I clutched the detective's arm. In the commotion I'd caused, no one else had noticed. I swayed and pointed in the direction of the river.

"I saw something." My voice came from far away. I cleared my throat again. "Farther into the woods."

The detective's brown eyes bored into me for a split second before he turned. My mom swiveled her head in the same direction. For a moment, time hovered, suspended like a cloth unfurled and caught in the air. My mom let out a rough cry and brought her hand to her mouth.

Then everything happened at once. The detective put his arm out to restrain my mom from stepping forward and pulled out a radio.

"Don't move," he ordered and walked in the direction I'd pointed, stepping over briars and dodging saplings. He stopped near the wrapped-up figure and brought the radio to his mouth. I couldn't hear what he said, only the clipped tone and a sharp flare of static. Seconds later an air horn sounded from behind us, in the direction of the house.

The man knelt, placed his hand on the figure's neck, and then rose. When he turned back to us, his face in the dusk was as pale as mine. He pushed his hands toward us, motioning us to step back. I grabbed Mom's arm and backed up.

Again, the air horn blasted. Someone with a bullhorn was bellowing, "Please reconvene, return to the house." Over and over.

As the man neared us, I said, "It's her, isn't it?"

He pressed his lips tight and took my elbow, turning me toward the house. "I'm sorry."

The words hit my chest with a dull, heavy thud, reverberating to the soles of my feet. My arms went numb, then cold. My legs moved mechanically as the man ushered me toward the house. Next to me, my mom moaned and clung to my arm.

Dusk was rapidly turning to full-on darkness. On a rise in Ethan's back yard, a white police tent had been erected in our absence, lit brightly from within and shining in the gloom like a paper lantern. It gave the scene a look of permanency.

From all sides of the house, illuminated by their flashlights and phones, our neighbors, family, and friends were turning, making their way toward the white glow of the tent, disheartened lines trodding, not yet knowing how bad the news would be.

The police sequestered my family in Ethan's small formal living room, ushering us out of the way of the investigators who were still combing the woods and processing other rooms. Audra cried into her hand, and Marco gathered her in, comforting her in a low voice. Ethan pressed his hands to his eyes and paced. His chest rose and sank in heaves.

Watching them, I wondered why I wasn't crying. Maybe this dullness creeping down my limbs and up my neck was shock. My thoughts kept circling, trying to explain what happened, finding no answer, and going around again. Ethan stopped pacing abruptly and sank down next to me on the deep couch. It was a hand-me-down from my parents, and the worn cushions sank toward the center and tilted us toward each other. I grabbed his hand and held it. Arranged on the sofa and high-backed chairs, my family formed a tight semicircle in the soft lamplight. No one spoke.

I heard Polly and the dark-haired detective before I saw them, the wood floors creaking with their footfalls. They both paused, framed by the doorway and unmoving in their dark jackets like subjects in an old Dutch painting.

Ethan jumped to his feet. The rest of us sat up, looking toward them for answers.

Polly broke the heavy silence. "Ethan, can you come with us?"

Ethan took a step forward and then halted. "What is it? Can you just tell us all? Please."

Polly and the detective from the woods exchanged a look, and he shrugged. Everyone leaned forward, the tension connecting us all as palpable as a thick web woven across the room.

Polly looked at us all but settled her eyes on Ethan. "As you know, Beth was found not far from here. I'm very sorry. We're going to need to talk with everyone here."

Ethan's face took on a hanging, gray look, as if the reality of the situation hit him anew, and sank into the couch. I put my hand on his back. He rocked slightly back and forth.

Looking up at Polly, he asked, "Does Doug know?"

"Yes, we've called Beth's father. He knows. He's traveling back from business in Chicago and should get here shortly."

Ethan nodded. In a strangled voice, he asked what we all wanted to know: "What happened to her?"

"We're not sure yet," Polly answered. "We're all looking into that. This is Detective Osborne." The brown-haired man nodded. "He and I will take statements from all of you. We're going to need everyone to stay nearby so that we can talk with you and start sorting this out."

"What do you need from us?" Ethan raised his hands to encompass everyone in the room. "We don't know anything."

Though I couldn't fathom what may have unfolded, looking around, I had to agree with Ethan that no one in this room would know anything.

Osborne moved toward Ethan. "I know you spoke with Polly earlier, Ethan, but anything you can tell us might be helpful. We're combing the scene and looking at anyone in the area with a history of violence, but we need to talk with the people who knew her best so you can point us in the right direction."

"Then ask." Ethan reeled his hand in a prompting motion.

"We'll want to talk with each of you individually," Detective Osborne answered, looking only at Ethan. "If you'll come with us first, Mr. Svenson, we can start."

Ethan took a deep breath, straightened up, and followed the officers from the room.

Not long after Ethan left, Dr. Thorpe double-knocked on the doorframe, cleared his throat, and entered the living room. In his early sixties with sandy hair fading to gray, Thorpe was a North Haven fixture. He'd been my childhood doctor and, in more recent months, I'd had a few distinctly unhelpful appointments with him.

After offering his condolences to the room, he approached and bent down to address me. "I heard from the detective you had another spell, Riley. He wanted me to look you over." Thorpe had a warm, deep voice, like he should be selling Werther's Originals, but I detected the skepticism in the purse of his lips around "another spell."

I'd visited him in March when the dizziness and fatigue that I'd had since February had worsened and I'd started having intense neck pain and weakness in my hands. He'd run some standard blood work and suggested that I cut out sugar, dairy, and gluten. A month later, a lightning-bolt pain had erupted into my cheek and electrical shocks had begun shooting down my left arm when I turned my head. After passing out at work one morning, I'd made another appointment. At that point, Dr. Thorpe had suggested a CT scan, "to make sure you don't have a brain tumor or something," as he put it, and ordered more blood tests. Everything came back normal aside from high levels of COVID antibodies, likely from my vaccinations. When he told me the results, he'd raised his hands out to his sides. "I don't know what to tell you, Riley. There's nothing there. Some people want to find something physically wrong to explain *other* kinds of problems. Others just like the fuss." He gazed at me as if still deciding which category I fell into. I'd made it to the car before breaking into tears of frustration.

Now Thorpe sat down next to me in the seat Ethan had just vacated and pulled a stethoscope out of his bag. I shivered, wondering if he'd been the one to check Beth's body for a pulse.

He put the stethoscope to my chest. "I'm okay now—" I started.

"Shhh, deep breaths."

I filled my lungs as much as I could, but it felt as if a tight iron band had wrapped around my chest over the past few hours. Audra, Marco, and Mom stole glances my way but gave us as much privacy as the small space allowed.

After listening to my lungs, Thorpe checked my heart and then wrapped a portable blood pressure cuff around my wrist. The cuff constricted with a series of clicks, loosened with a little sigh, and the numbers 88/54 appeared on the display.

He nodded, which he did a lot, as if he expected that whatever he found, it would confirm what he'd thought initially. "Little low, but could just be that the cuff is wrong. You're dehydrated and, of course, you've had a shock." He patted my hand. "Have you been drinking water?"

I pointed to a glass on the end table next to me that a deputy had brought in earlier and, since Thorpe continued watching me, picked it up and drained it.

A satisfied smile spread across his face and he patted me again. "Good girl. Now, I recall you were having a few other issues." He zipped his bag up and leaned closer, as though he had a secret for me. "I should have told you when you came in before, there's no shame in talking with someone about it. The mind can play all kinds of tricks on us." He patted my shoulder.

I looked down at my red, swollen knuckles, wanting to ask what trick of the mind caused that. But now was not the time to get into it. For the briefest moment, I imagined how I'd later tell Beth about this encounter. Then I remembered, and the iron band around my chest tightened another notch.

I sank back into the couch as Thorpe left the room. Over the last six months, Beth had been one of the few people who would ask how I was doing and seemed able to accept that I still felt bad and didn't know why. Most times, if I told someone about my numb hands, they would ask me what was causing it—a natural enough question. But not knowing the answer to this myself would set me off jabbering about all the possible causes for numb extremities, wondering the whole time if I sounded like a hypochondriac. My inability to explain *why* I felt bad compounded the stress of feeling bad. By contrast, when I'd told Beth this past weekend that my feet were numb, that my face and joints throbbed, and that I was tired as always and couldn't explain why, she had just nodded. To her, it wasn't strange, maybe because it mirrored her own experience.

I thought about the accident Beth had survived when, on the way home from Oberlin for winter break, a semi had sent her Mini Cooper tumbling into oncoming traffic. She didn't remember it, which was fortunate since she fractured both arms, her pelvis, and several vertebrae. I'd never forget seeing her in the hospital with her eyes closed and blackened. Ethan visited every day and carefully held her fingers where they poked out from one of the casts. Her recovery and physical therapy took ages. Little by little she sat up, began to feed herself, and walked again. And little by little, without talking about it, she and Ethan got closer. Beth never went back to Oberlin. If she regretted it, she never said so.

I closed my burning eyes and rubbed them. The couch cushion next to me sank and I opened my eyes to see Mom beside me. Her mascara was smudged, and she'd lost her jaunty hat somewhere along the way. She leaned back into the well-worn cushions with me. We let gravity pull us together, and sat there shoulder to shoulder.

Although it felt like days, the grandfather clock showed Ethan had been gone for less than an hour when a door slammed at the front of the house. I heard a tense exchange of raised voices. A second later, Doug burst into the room as if a strong wind carried him, his silver hair wild around his head.

"Where is she?" He looked straight at me. "They said she's dead."

I couldn't form words. I nodded.

Doug looked up at the ceiling but not before I saw his face crumple. He put his hands on his hips and dropped his head. He stood that way for a minute, his eyes closed and his breath rough. As suddenly as he had arrived, he turned and left the room. Seconds later, the exterior door banged again, sending a tremor through the entire old house.

Close on the heels of Doug's exit, Ethan returned, every muscle in his face tight yet somehow slack.

"You're next, Riley," he said, his voice flat.

# CHAPTER FIVE

*September 23, 2022*

"What did they say?" I asked Ethan, but Detective Osborne and Polly followed close behind him, already waiting for me.

When I rose, my vision tunneled. I leaned over with my hands on my knees and looked back at my family through the pinhole of my view, all of them staring at me like I was leaving on a long journey.

Polly steadied me.

Straightening up, I walked with her and Osborne. As we passed the kitchen, I glimpsed investigators suited up and spreading black powder across the countertop and another crouching and shining a light over the bottom of the back door I'd gone out earlier that afternoon.

They led me into the formal dining room, the first room that Beth had fixed up once she and Ethan moved in together. She had taken down the avocado-green wallpaper, peeled back the shag carpet, and refinished the scarred oak table that had been left behind. She had painted the chairs an antique white and reupholstered the seats in a floral pattern. Polly pulled one out for me and motioned for me to sit.

They arranged themselves across from me, and Detective Osborne opened up a laptop that sat on the table. I settled my shaking hands in my lap.

"How are you holding up, Riley?" Polly asked. "I know you and Beth were close." Again, her familiar presence comforted me. Even though she was only in her early thirties, Polly moved and spoke with the steadiness of an old soul who had seen the world at its worst and could no longer be shocked.

Part of it may have stemmed from her difficult upbringing; when Polly was just eleven, her mom had mixed the wrong pills with her daily dose of booze, and Polly had driven her to the ER. She hadn't sounded all that happy afterward when she'd told Audra her mom was going to make it. After years of keeping her chaotic family from going off the rails, managing the crises of a small town was second nature.

"I'm okay," I told Polly, as my hands shook. "It doesn't seem real."

She nodded. Next to her, Osborne was all business. "Can you please tell us how you knew Beth Lauderdale, Ms. Svenson?"

"She's my brother's fiancée. But she and I have been friends since high school," I added.

"Tell us about your friendship," Polly prompted.

I paused, unsure where to begin. "Well, our senior year of high school, she and I worked together on this year-long capstone project. We got to be friends through that. She came to our house a lot to work on it. Or sometimes we went out to the Castle to look around and take photos. The project was on Carlton Castle. We made a website about it," I explained to Osborne. "Then, when she and Ethan started dating, we spent quite a lot of time together. Ethan and I have always been close." I shrugged, hoping I'd said enough but not too much.

"You, Beth, and your brother were all in the same class?"

"Yeah, Ethan and I are only eleven months apart. I was on the older side and he was the youngest in our class. Mom thought it would be good for us to start school together." I didn't add that this was more for her benefit than ours. Almost a year younger than many of the kids, Ethan had always been the smallest until he hit a growth spurt in high school, but as early as kindergarten he'd learned to use his fists to compensate for his stature.

Polly again: "Did Beth have any problems with anyone? Disagreements?"

Since Ethan and I had spoken with Polly earlier, I'd had time to think. "Maybe Simon Aldridge." Polly's grimace told me she knew Simon well. "He lost the house to bankruptcy. It had been his family's home for generations, but he hadn't paid the taxes in years. When Ethan bought it, he didn't want to leave. There's even an Aldridge family cemetery on the property." I left out the part about my great-great-grandfather putting one of the Aldridges there.

"After Ethan and Beth moved in, Simon kept stopping in at the cemetery. He'd walk around the yard and go into the barn when Beth was here by herself. He doesn't like Ethan. Actually, he doesn't really like any of our family," I admitted. "He sold off his land little by little over the years, and my dad bought most of it."

"Did Ethan or Beth report Simon's trespassing?" Polly asked

"Ethan told him to stop coming into the yard, but he wanted to handle it himself. I don't think he wanted to agitate Simon any further. He's kind of a . . . volatile person, I guess." If anyone I knew carried around enough hatred to kill someone, it would be Simon. A shiver ran through me as I pictured his haughty scowl and the glint in his eyes.

"Do you know when these incidents happened, or if Simon actually approached Beth?" Polly's pen hovered over her notepad.

"I don't know if he talked to Beth, but I know he came around last spring because Ethan told me about it at Easter. Then it stopped for a while over the summer, maybe because Simon was sick with COVID for a long time and couldn't do much. I think he's doing better now—at least I've seen him riding his Ranger around—so he could have been at it again."

"Can you think of anyone else who might have been giving Beth problems?"

Liam's name was in my mouth, but I paused. "No," I answered. I hadn't told Ethan about his visit yet and didn't want the police to spring the news on him.

Polly scribbled notes in a yellow pad, and Osborne shifted in his chair. "How would you describe her relationship with Ethan?"

My face warmed, but I told myself it was natural they would ask about Ethan. "It was good. I mean, they were getting married in less than a month," I answered. "They'd dated on and off for about eight years. In the past year, they were as happy together as I'd ever seen them. Excited about working on the house and fixing up the Castle for their wedding." Osborne gave me a questioning look. "That's the old mansion on the river. Beth and some others were working on turning it into an event venue."

Something caught in Osborne's eyes. "Where on the river is this? I'm still new around here," he said.

I described its location, a couple miles east on the other side of the Vermillion River. "Polly knows it. It's a landmark."

"What did Beth do there?" Osborne prompted.

"She and Mr. Perry—that's one of our teachers from high school—they led the restoration. They were getting the exterior and first floor in shape for the wedding, but in the long run, they wanted to turn it into a historical attraction and event venue."

Osborne kept his head bent over his pen and notepad. "How much time did Beth spend there?"

I paused, suddenly wondering what it could possibly have to do with her death. I threw a questioning look at Polly, wondering if she knew where Osborne was going with this.

"I have no idea. Ethan and I volunteered with her some weekends, but she was there during the week too."

Osborne looked at his notebook. "You said that Ethan and Beth dated on and off." He repeated my words and looked up at me, his tone suddenly friendlier. "Why was that? Did they have a rocky relationship?" He tilted his head like he was just curious, like I could confide in him.

The subtle switch in his demeanor set off alarms and I felt the flush creeping up my neck. "Not at all," I said, hearing my voice rise. "Why would you say that?" I paused, fighting for composure. I needed Osborne to understand that their long on-and-off relationship had never been a sign of something wrong—it showed their determination to make it work. "Sometimes Beth thought about going back to school, but their relationship was fine. They just wanted to make sure they wanted the same things before they settled down."

He tapped his pen and watched me. "Would you say that he and Beth wanted the same things now?"

My lips stuck to my teeth and I swallowed. A ball of tension had built steadily in my chest. I squirmed in my chair, then thought about how my squirming must look and stilled.

"Yes, obviously I think that since they were about to get married. Now, can you tell me what's happened? Because if someone killed her, you need to look somewhere else."

Polly leaned her elbows on the table. Her eyes were glassy and her tone weary. Wisps of hair had escaped her braid. A long night probably lay ahead of her. "It's looking very likely that there was foul play, Riley, specifically because of the way Beth was found. She was wrapped up with care. We'll need the autopsy results for cause of death, but it looks like, at the very least, someone moved her to where she was found."

As Polly spoke, an image sprang into my head: the many cold afternoons I'd spent with Ethan and Beth in the drafty old house this past winter, Beth lying on the couch and Ethan wrapping a quilt around her. She would smile up at him.

Tears burned at the edges of my eyes and I looked into my lap, as if the image in my mind might show in my eyes. Osborne pushed some tissues toward me in a pink-and-blue box with a loud geometric design. It didn't look like something Beth would have picked out. My eyes blurred as I wondered if homicide detectives traveled with their own supply of tissues for occasions like this.

"Are you okay, Ms. Svenson?" Osborne watched me. "Could we get you some water? She fainted earlier," he explained to Polly.

"Yeah, I'm sorry," I managed to reply. "Water would be good, thank you."

Polly glanced from him to me and then rose. "Let me get that for you." Knowing her, I detected a hint of iciness that Osborne had left it to her to fetch a drink. She pushed her chair in roughly and headed toward the kitchen.

Osborne's eyes stayed on me as we sat in silence for a moment. "I know you were close to Beth," he finally said. "This is as much about eliminating suspects as it is about finding them. When something like this happens, it's usually someone the victim knew. In this case, the consideration that was taken to cover her up indicates it was someone who cared about Beth."

*Someone who cared.* I searched his face but couldn't tell if he meant Ethan. Maybe he meant me. I dropped my eyes to the table, studying the waves of gold-and-brown wood grain that Beth had sanded and polished as I tried to catch my breath. "Polly said foul play. Is that any different than murder? If she was wrapped up in a sheet and moved, how could it be anything else?"

Osborne cocked his head, as if surprised by the sharpness in my voice. "She suffered blunt-force trauma to the head, but we'll need an autopsy to confirm the cause of death and how it was inflicted. We're treating it as a suspicious death, given how she was found." He clipped off his last words, and I waited for more.

Polly returned, plopped the glass of water on the table for me, and sat down again. I could feel her studying me. It felt like all the blood in my body was pumping through my hands, and I wrapped them around the cool glass.

Osborne continued, "I understand Beth has had some health issues in the past. Can you tell me more about that? Do you have any idea what doctors she was seeing to treat these issues? Your brother mentioned a Dr. Maclean in Wicksburg."

"Is that the *refrain from pain* lady?" Polly asked and glanced at Osborne. I wasn't sure if I imagined a fleeting smirk.

I felt the flush rise again and hesitated. At Beth's recommendation, I'd been seeing Dr. Maclean as well and didn't relish dragging her into this mess. "Yeah, that's her. She was Beth's primary doctor. But she saw an orthopedic surgeon too. Why would any of that matter? You should be talking to Simon, not wasting time delving into Beth's medical history." I couldn't keep the frustration out of my voice.

Polly folded her hands on the table. "It's helpful for us to get a sense of her health issues and what medications she may have been taking. Just to get an idea of her state leading up to this." Polly nodded as she spoke and gave me a smile that looked like it was meant to be encouraging, to tell me I couldn't help but see the logic in this. I could tell she was trying to placate me.

I told my face to smile, but my lips felt tight.

"I wouldn't know much more about that," I said and sipped my water.

By the time Polly and Osborne wrapped up, my eyes were so heavy that I contemplated whether it was wise to drive home. Doug must have returned during my interview. From the living room, I heard his deep voice alternating with my mom's quavering tones. I didn't hear Ethan, but I had an idea where I would find him.

No one stopped me from entering the kitchen. The techs had finished, but black fingerprint powder still clung to the surfaces like a layer of fine soot. I went straight out the back door into the cold night air.

Ethan sat on the stone step of the back porch with his head in his hands. Sinking down next to him, I leaned my head on his shoulder. It was after midnight, but it seemed like years had passed since I'd arrived to pick up my bridesmaid's dress. Out of all the cars that had poured in, only a few remained around the back of the house.

"Hey," I said—that one syllable, shaded with tone and context, that he and I used to communicate the things we had trouble saying. "What can I do?"

He placed his hand on mine, his fingers icy. He stared straight ahead and didn't respond at first. After a minute he said, "There's nothing anyone can do now." The words came out flat. I straightened up to look at him. The porch light above cast his eyes in shadow. He gave an almost imperceptible shake of his head. "She should have just—"

Behind us, the door swung open, and I turned to see Mom. She held the broad hat she'd worn earlier.

"You ready, honey?" she asked Ethan in a soft voice.

We both stood and I steadied myself on his arm until my dizziness passed. He patted my shoulder and then hugged me. "I'm staying at Mom's until they finish with the rest of the house," he explained. He released me and the two of them moved off together, Mom's arm around Ethan's waist.

As I watched their taillights recede down the driveway, I suddenly felt the need to move. My legs carried me in the direction of the barn, each heavy step putting distance between myself and the house.

Ethan's voice replayed in my mind. *There's nothing anyone can do. She should have just*—what?

Despite the familiar surroundings, a feeling of menace hung in the night so close to where Beth had died just hours ago. It struck me how alone I was in the dark. Would Polly or Osborne hear me in the house if I called out? I softened my breath to listen but heard only crickets and the far-off rumble of a passing train.

The weather had lifted and the nearly full moon lit the side of the old stone barn, glinting on the vines that climbed the crumbling walls. Suddenly, a shadow darkened one window frame, and I flinched.

Then, heart thudding, I recognized the lean silhouette. Bibbs the cat. She thumped her tail and cocked her skinny head in my direction. I stopped and watched her.

Bibbs had started out so wild that no one could get within thirty feet without her crouching her belly down to the ground and darting off. After months of Beth's feeding and coaxing, Bibbs crept nearer, still poised to flee but less fearful. Ethan had objected, not wanting to encourage the sickly thing to hang around, but Bibbs seemed to consider this home now. Her eyes glimmered and winked as she tilted her head to examine me, probably hoping I'd brought food. I wished I had.

That was when I cried, staring at the poor hungry cat sitting there patiently, waiting for a kindness that would never return.

# CHAPTER SIX

*Four Months Earlier—May 27, 2022*

The hand-painted sign on the wall of Dr. Maclean's office advised me to *Refrain from pain.* Next to that, a light-green piece of printer paper taped to the wall reminded me that co-payments were due at the time of service.

In one corner of the exam room, a relaxation fountain bubbled, and a tall plant with round, tropical leaves encroached at my elbow. When I'd told Sydney that I'd scheduled an appointment with Dr. Maclean, she'd laughed. "The *refrain from pain* lady? I thought that was a pill mill."

Granted I didn't know what a pill mill looked like, but I didn't picture this many potted plants.

Almost half an hour had passed since I'd had my blood pressure taken and completed a ream of new-patient paperwork. The header on the forms had echoed the mantra to *refrain from pain* and then instructed me to circle all my areas of pain.

Under the question that asked how I'd heard about the clinic, I wrote Beth's name. When she had suggested Dr. Maclean to me, I'd resisted at first. "I don't think I can stand telling the whole story again and having

someone look at me like I'm crazy," I'd told her. But she had been unusually insistent. *Just try her.*

Next to me, Audra's foot tapping grated on my nerves. She had insisted on accompanying me for moral support, but I wondered if she regretted it now. She was stretching her arms and yawning ostentatiously when two sharp knocks sounded on the exam-room door. A second later it flew open.

The first thing that surprised me about Dr. Maclean was her height—she was easily six feet and she moved like an athlete. There was something fluid and powerful in the way she strode into the room, despite the bulky brace that hinged at her knee with each step. I realized that when Beth had described Dr. Maclean as caring, I'd conjured up a little old lady in sensible shoes and a knitted cardigan. Other than sensible shoes, Dr. Maclean didn't fit my expectations.

Next to me, Audra sat up straighter. I realized I had straightened up as well.

"Riley?" Dr. Maclean leaned over me, waiting for confirmation. Behind her black-framed glasses, her eyes bored into me, like she might be able to see the seeds of thoughts forming and blossoming in my brain.

I nodded. She pumped my hand in her firm grip. "Nice to meet you." She pivoted to Audra. "And you are?"

"Audra—Riley's sister," Audra answered cautiously as if she feared the wrong answer might get her booted from the room.

"Nice to meet you as well," she said and flashed a smile at us both before sitting at a small desk. The hinges of her big brace sighed as she bent her knee. She arranged her white coat around her and brushed her bangs back. Her whole bearing spoke of vigor and efficiency. Although I should have been comforted, I felt intimidated.

She held what I assumed was my file in her hand. "It looks like you've been having quite a few problems recently. Tell me more about how all of this started," she prompted, her tone brisk.

I shifted, crinkling the sheet of white paper I sat on, and took a deep breath as I began recounting my past five months. Three doctors, a CT scan, an MRI, three rounds of blood tests, one depleted health savings account. No diagnosis. Dr. Maclean's fingers clattered on the keyboard as she took notes. Each time I paused, she encouraged me to continue, asking "and what else?" Her prompting kept me talking long past the point where I would normally have stopped. I found myself confessing other new symptoms I hadn't mentioned to other doctors, from unusually painful periods to episodes of double vision. When I told her I'd never tested positive for COVID, she paused her note-taking and looked up. "Do you think there's a chance you may have had it at any point?"

"Not that I know of." I told her how my dad had passed away from it after chemotherapy had weakened his immune system but that the rest of us had tested negative at the time.

She looked up from her keyboard. "I'm very sorry about your father." She did look sorry in her own highly intense way.

As she rose and approached me with a flashlight and tongue depressor, I tried not to cower. She studied my eyes with the light, tested my hand and arm strength, and examined my fingernails.

"All right, Riley. Can you stand here? Put your feet close together. Good." I stood, and she put her arms on either side of me. "Now close your eyes." I did as instructed and promptly teetered over to my right. I took a step to catch myself, and Dr. Maclean steadied me with a firm hand on my arm.

Dr. Maclean told me to sit and went back to typing. As she communed with her computer, I scanned the list of symptoms and previous tests that I had prepared to make sure I didn't miss anything. When I had brought a similar list to a neurologist on my first visit, he had glanced at it and smirked. "Wow, headers and everything. Are you planning to publish a journal article?" Later in the appointment, when I had asked about different possibilities, like chronic fatigue and Lyme, he'd eyed me over his glasses and told me he knew those were fashionable diseases right now but that I shouldn't believe everything I read online. That was when I realized that what I saw as being prepared and informed looked like hypochondria from the outside.

Next to me, Audra was shifting in her hard plastic chair and stretching again. I hadn't said so, but her presence meant a lot, especially given the attitude I'd been sensing from Ethan. When I'd mentioned to him how achy and exhausted I'd been, he'd told me, "Everyone is tired, Riley. I worked ninety hours last week to get the corn planted. I don't know why you'd be any worse off."

With Mom, on the other hand, I'd done my best to hide the extent of my illness. I knew from her questions—mostly about my weight loss and pallor—that she could sense something was wrong, but she worried enough without me giving her another reason.

Dr. Maclean punched a button, pushed her keyboard in, and swiveled on her stool to face me.

"Okay, Riley. Here's the plan. We're going to run some lab work. Your symptoms could fit with various diagnoses, but until we know what's happening in your body, we can't really make an informed decision on what to do." As Dr. Maclean spoke, she shoved a list of tests she'd printed out into my hands.

"Those results will take a few weeks, but one thing I can tell you now is that you're having issues with proprioception—that's your sense of where your body is in space. When you close your eyes, you lose that visual reference, but your body should still be able to maintain balance. Then, another thing I'm seeing is some autonomic dysfunction and orthostatic hypotension, but there can be a lot of reasons behind that. I'm sorry that I can't tell you more right now." A smile softened her intensity. "I know you've been through a lot and that not knowing what's going on must be frustrating. Now, you talked to me about a few sources of chronic pain. How are you managing that?"

I felt her studying me, and without warning, I teared up. I looked down at my lap. It was the first time a doctor had acknowledged the stress of not only feeling awful, but not knowing what was wrong. Still, I didn't want to start bawling and blow it with a new doctor who would see my tears and attribute my symptoms to hysterics.

I swallowed and recalled her question. *Pain management.*

"Just over-the-counter medication, like ibuprofen," I answered.

"Is that helping?" she asked.

"Not much, at least not with the pain in my . . ." The words I needed hovered just out of reach. I pointed to my cheek and neck.

"Your cheek and neck?" Dr. Maclean supplied and studied me. "Does that happen often? Having trouble finding words?"

"More than it used to."

She nodded. "Right, nothing stronger than over-the-counter NSAIDs? What are your thoughts on opioids and prescription painkillers?" Her eyes scoured my face as if she were searching for something.

I wasn't quite sure what she was asking—or why. Did she suspect I was taking something since I'd stumbled over my words? The pill-mill conversation with Sydney flashed through my mind, but Beth wouldn't send me in that direction. She had gone through hell with doctors over the years too, and I trusted her to steer me right. "Uh, I don't know. I've never taken anything like that."

She shifted on her stool. "Good to hear. We always want to watch out for that, though they can be warranted in some cases. And how do you feel about *alternative* pain treatments?"

Again, I wasn't sure where she was headed. I glanced at Audra, who shrugged.

"Like marijuana?" I ventured.

"Among other things." I waited for her to elaborate. She didn't. "Once we have a diagnosis, we can look into more options. We may be able to get you a card for cannabis if you'd be interested. Now, in the meantime, you could try CBD, or if you know somewhere you can get your hands on some cannabis without too much trouble, you might try that route. Just don't get yourself arrested in the process. Going to jail will do nothing for your health."

Audra barked a laugh, but Dr. Maclean had the kind of face where I couldn't tell if she was joking or not.

The morning after my appointment with Dr. Maclean, I pulled into the Castle drive for the annual Castle Cleanup. The old trees on either side arched into a lush cathedral over the driveway and quickly enveloped any car that turned off the main road to make the secluded climb up the hill. I realized why, for so many decades, this location had been the site of choice for activities where people wanted to remain unseen.

Set back about a hundred yards behind a thick stand of cedars, the Castle itself sat on high ground with a view of its surroundings, almost the way real castles had been built along the waterways in defensive positions with lookout towers. The privacy had once served a noble purpose, allowing the property to serve as a stop on the Underground Railroad. In recent years, the secluded site had served less virtuous purposes, mainly revolving around drugs and hookups. However, as I drove up the drive that morning, I'd realized that, despite the years of neglect, the Castle was beginning to live up to its name again.

It was the kind of spring day when everything that had been dormant for months seemed to have turned green, leafed out, or flowered overnight, and the cool May air smelled like licorice. At the end of the long drive, a tunnel of locust and redbud trees opened up to reveal the imposing Second Empire mansion plunked incongruously down on a green hill in the middle of Ohio. The mansard roof sloped down with a graceful swoop along the four sides, with arched dormers peeking through the blue-and-gray-patterned slate. Over the last decade, pieces of plywood filling the tall, rounded windows had been replaced with sparkling glass. In the middle of the structure, the tower that gave Carlton Castle its name rose four stories and was topped by spiky cast-iron cresting. Situated against the sky at the crown of the hill—the tower falling away to the sloping roof on either side—the silhouette had always reminded me of a plumed and brooding bird.

Mr. Perry, our high-school history teacher, traced his ancestry back to the Carltons who had owned the estate and had long led the restoration efforts. Tall, fair-haired, and clad in an inexhaustible supply of Columbia sportswear, he speed walked around the complex of buildings and chugged coffee. As chair of the Carlton Castle Association, which owned the property, he ran the show, with Beth as his first lieutenant. Each year, more and more of North Haven turned out for the spring workday as the efforts had started to pay off and show the promise of the place.

In high school, Mr. Perry had brought us on field trips here, even when the place had been a hazardous maze of mold, broken glass, and discarded needles. Despite—or perhaps because of—his earnest enthusiasm, he won over the town's cynical teens. His in-class tangents about ghosts, UFOs, and his ex-wife may have helped. On field trips, he would guide us through the ruins, explaining what little was known about its use in the Underground Railroad and painting the former splendor of the mansion for us in minute detail, from its two-story ballroom to the tower that marked the highest point in the county. Discovering their mutual obsession with the glorious ruins, he and Beth had formed the North Haven Historical Society with a shared vision of bringing the Castle and the town back to what they thought it could be.

As the volunteers set to work, Mr. Perry bounced from group to group like a kid at a carnival trying to play every game at once, first monitoring Ethan, who was restoring trim on the back of the wraparound porch, to another group putting up drywall in the entryway, and then to Charlotte, Harmony, and Harmony's mom, who were planting annuals and mulching beds.

He flashed a thumbs-up to Audra and Polly, who worked on taming the boxwoods and yews that grew along the foundation.

Given our physical limitations, Beth and I had been assigned the less-demanding task of painting the gingerbread trim on the new gazebo. It seemed appropriate since it was the spot where she and Ethan would exchange their vows that October. The wind blew loose strands of Beth's hair and she smiled as she brushed white paint onto the trim. I'd been catching her up on my appointment with Dr. Maclean.

"Did she tell you to buy some weed?" Beth asked after I'd told her about the tests Dr. Maclean had ordered.

I snorted in surprise. "She did. I'd get some if I didn't think it would just make me dizzier."

"I tried it, actually, like a cannabis tincture." She added, "I qualify for it because of chronic pain. Dr. Maclean helped me get the card." She glanced at me. "Don't mention it to Ethan. You know how he is about that sort of thing, even if it's perfectly legal. What he doesn't know won't hurt him." She winked and smiled again.

I stared at her. I didn't know why Ethan would care about her using medicinal weed, but what surprised me more than her words was the playful wink. Beth looked more animated than I'd seen her in a long time. Even though she grimaced now and then as she bent, she looked like she was in her element.

"Did it help?" I asked.

She shrugged. "It took the edge off a little, but it made me tired. The whole point of taking it was to be able to work, but I couldn't use it at the bank, obviously. I take it when I work around the house sometimes or at night if the pain keeps me up."

Beth seldom spoke of her pain so directly. When Mom or Audra asked about her back and hip, she would typically answer that she was "okay" and leave it at that. One time when Audra had pressed her further, Beth had told her flat out that she didn't want to talk about it. Her habit of minimizing her pain gave my mom the impression that it was just an excuse to quit working, but Mom didn't spend the time with her that I did. I witnessed all of the contraptions and strategies Beth used to avoid bending when she worked on the house, the physical therapy apparatuses that she hid away in the hall closet when guests came over, and the orthopedic pillow on the driver's seat of her car. I knew that coping with pain on a daily basis was a job in itself, even if she didn't talk about it. Whether it was a reluctance to show vulnerability or a desire to ignore something as depressing as chronic suffering, I could identify with not wanting to talk about it.

"What about the other treatment you told me about?" I asked. "The radio thing?"

Beth brushed a loose strand of hair back into her messy bun and squinted into the sun. "Radiofrequency ablation. It's the next option since the surgeries and epidurals haven't helped. But I have a huge deductible, so insurance wouldn't pay anything. And I already have so much medical debt."

I knew her lack of income was a sensitive topic. Even though people around town labeled her a gold digger, I'd seen how she sewed most of her own dresses now and squeezed every cent, as if painfully aware that the money coming in was Ethan's and not hers. Depending on which rumors you believed, her dad had plenty of money, but she didn't appear to want his help. I considered how to phrase what I said next. "You and Ethan are practically married, I'm sure he—"

"Ladies, it's looking fit for a wedding!" Mr. Perry called out to us as he strode across the lawn, pumping his arms for speed. He gestured at the gazebo, which was looking nice with the fresh white paint on the ornate trim. He smiled broadly, his eyelashes and brows chalky with drywall dust. "I knew you two would do a careful job. Helen and her boys would have made a slop of it," he confided, inclining his head toward some juvenile delinquents putting in their community service hours. "It will be beautiful inside and out by this fall. At least the downstairs will be."

He motioned to the trees and river. "And look out there. You can't improve on that." Robins hopped across the lawn that extended down to the Vermillion River, and swallows zipped in arabesques across the sparkling water.

Instead of looking at the river, Beth looked toward the house, where Ethan fired nails into a piece of trim. "I just hope no one messes it up." She turned to me. "People have been poking around when we're not here. There was mud all over the ballroom last week when we had the French doors off to repair the glass. People go in and out like they own the place." There was a note of resentment in her voice, that people still saw the Castle as a communal dump and a place to get high, rather than the grand venue Beth envisioned.

Mr. Perry's smile wavered and then returned at double strength. "It's a compliment, Beth. People want to look at what we're doing. No one has vandalized anything. People aren't leaving needles and the like anymore. A little mud can be cleaned up." He turned to me and gestured toward a gap in the tall grasses by the riverbank. "I'd say it's just fishermen who pulled their boat up there where the grasses are tramped down. Besides, it's all locked up now that we have the doors back on."

Beth raised a carefully groomed eyebrow at Mr. Perry. "Well, we can't lock them out of the gazebo. We should put up cameras to discourage people, especially after all this work."

Mr. Perry patted her shoulder. "Still a city girl. People just want to look around, you'll see. Maybe we could put up a trap camera or see if Polly would patrol here. It would be good to know who's coming and going, but you're going to have to get used to sharing the place. Speaking of which"—he pointed a finger at Beth—"I'm going to need your good taste to get the paint colors and the furniture moved in now that we're getting the drywall up. Could you come with me to see Mrs. Meade after school next Tuesday? She has a whole barn full of furniture and antiques she's letting us use. I think she joined the association just to find a home for all that stuff. I'll need your eye on what will look good where and what we'll need once we start hosting events. If it were me, I'd just put a recliner and a big screen in there and be done with it."

Where my eyes would have glazed over at the mention of sorting through antiques, Beth's lit up. "I'd love to see what she has."

"I'll pick you up a little after three, when school lets out. Now, I'd better see how Liam and Dave are getting on in there. They're doing the drywall, so you never know with those two if they're hanging it sideways or using it as flooring." He grimaced and headed back toward the house at the same clip he'd been moving at all morning. I felt tired just watching him. At half his age, I wished that I had even half his energy.

Beth seemed to be wearing out too, after all the painting. She stretched her back with a grimace, put down her brush, and lay flat in the green grass next to the gazebo with a sigh. Out of the corner of my eye, I saw Harmony toss a bundle of branches onto a brush pile and say something to her mom as she gestured toward Beth and laughed. As part of our circle of friends in high school, Harmony's main role had been to stir up gossip about everyone except the person she happened to be talking to at that particular moment. I had marveled at her ability to keep track of all the rumors she started. She and Ethan had dated briefly, so when Beth began seeing Ethan, Harmony talked about Beth with twice her normal fury.

In recent years, despite her disdain for what she'd termed the "smelly dump" back in high school, Harmony had become active in the Castle's restoration. She and her mom were now real-estate partners, and I suspected her continued enthusiasm had less to do with the Castle's historical value than the potential for development of the surrounding land. Beth had alluded to tension with Harmony, and I knew she avoided working at the Castle when Harmony was around.

Oblivious to Harmony's sneers, Beth sighed as she lay in the soft grass and looked toward the house. "This is finally coming together," she said as much to herself as to me. "We'll have the downstairs done by fall, and we can use our wedding pictures to market it. It will take some money to finish it off, but we could book small events as soon as November."

Reclining in the grass in her old overalls with a streak of white paint on her face, she looked as happy as I'd seen her in years—maybe ever. I could imagine her quietly directing people around the Castle and in the background making things lovely. "You'd be good at that," I said. I didn't say what we both had to be thinking—she would be good at it if her body would allow it.

"Thanks, Riley. That means a lot." Shading her eyes, she looked up toward the blue sky and wisps of clouds. "Sometimes I don't know . . ." She smiled a crooked little smile. "If I had a little more money and a lot less pain, I could do something big here."

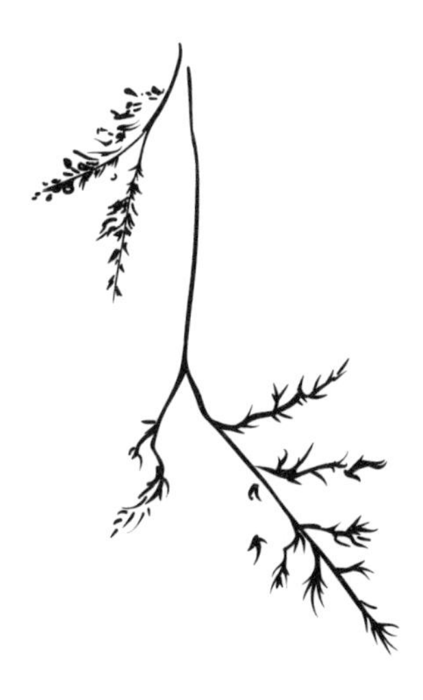

# CHAPTER SEVEN

*September 24, 2022*

The morning after Beth's murder, my reflection greeted me with glazed gray eyes, pallid skin, and pale blond hair that stuck out on one side. I had always figured that if I couldn't be beautiful, at least I could be neat, but today I gave up on even that. I needed to ration my energy.

I'd gotten home from Ethan's near two o'clock in the morning. Home was half of a Victorian house near downtown Wicksburg that I rented from a retired nurse named Beatrice, who lived in the other half. In the winter, the cold air seeped through the plaster walls, and in the summer the upstairs simmered, but I didn't mind. It reminded me of my parents'. The tall bay windows in the living room looked out onto the tree-lined street, and the galley kitchen had just enough space for a dinette table where I could sit and look out over the deep back yard. I furnished it with the bare necessities, thinking of it as a short-term stopover until I figured out what would come next for me.

When I'd gotten home, I'd let Bruno out to run gangly laps around the back yard, poured a scoop of kibble into his dish, and dropped into bed

feeling like my bones had turned to glass. Then, the moment I'd opened my eyes this morning, the weight of what had happened to Beth descended. As I pulled on jeans and a sweatshirt, my mind turned to unsettling questions: Who did this and why?

I scanned the roughly forty texts I'd received to make sure there was no news. Nothing. After returning a text from Sydney, I confirmed plans to meet Audra at Ethan's and ignored the rest. At some point I would need to email work to let them know I wouldn't be flying to England the next day. The dread that had ignited in my chest since I'd spoken with the police and Ethan had spread overnight like slow-burning fire. I'd known Ethan had been bottling something up and assumed it was grief, but in the quiet hours since, a little voice in my head kept speculating on what he would have said if Mom hadn't interrupted us.

At times like these, when everything seemed hopelessly wrong, I missed running so much that it hurt. I missed disappearing into the dark woods and pushing my body until all the parts synced up and the strength of my legs carried me along on autopilot. I missed the surging energy and clarity. I missed the sense of identity it gave me, someone with the steel to keep going beyond where others would quit. Since high school, I'd traveled all over the country to compete in marathons. But over the past eight months, my stamina had withered. The last race I'd run, only a 5K, had been over the summer. I'd fallen back farther and farther as my legs refused to cooperate and my breath came in gasps. I'd straggled across the finish line with the beginners and parents pushing strollers. The next day I'd barely been able to move. Now, instead of flying through the forest, my movements felt like plodding through pudding.

My phone buzzed again as I watched a pair of blue jays bobble across the yard and squawk with the musicality of two ancient smokers clearing their lungs. My vision blurred and then doubled until four blue jays hopped across the yard. I blinked at my phone until the text on my screen centered itself and held still. It was Audra telling me that she had arrived at Ethan's. Detective Osborne was asking when I would be there.

A couple of news vans from stations out of Cleveland were parked along the road in front of Ethan's. A blond newscaster in a tan wool coat spoke with her cameraman and gestured toward the house. I pulled around to the back of the house to avoid them. I'd brought Bruno along since he'd been on his own most of yesterday. He wagged his tail and woofed in the back seat.

The moment I opened the car door, he shot out like he'd been fired from a cannon and ran off toward the barn to sniff around. I hoped he wouldn't eat anything important.

A line of yellow tape fluttered in a perimeter around much of the back yard, and I recognized Detective Osborne with a tech squatting over the patio. Audra had gleaned a few details from Polly and texted to let me know that Beth's cell phone had still not turned up.

As I neared the house, Osborne caught my eye and waved me over. He ducked under the yellow tape and came toward me.

"Good morning, Ms. Svenson. Do you have a minute?" He was clean-shaven but had dark circles under his eyes. I wondered how much sleep he'd gotten, if any.

The thought of sitting down for more questions made my head pound. I glanced around for Ethan but didn't see him.

"Call me Riley, please." I said. "What do you need to know?"

"We just want to talk with you a little more about Beth's medical history."

"Yeah, fine." It came out sharper than I'd intended. I didn't relish answering more questions about Dr. Maclean and, more than anything, I wanted to find Ethan. But with the interest Osborne had shown in Ethan, our family needed to do whatever we could to stay in his good graces. "Of course," I said, aiming for a more cooperative tone.

Osborne led me through the back door and through the kitchen and pointed me to a chair at the dining-room table. I heard voices in the formal living room but couldn't make out if Ethan's was among them. "Let me get Polly," he said.

The pair returned a minute later, Polly looking at her watch. "I'll have to run over to get Liam's statement soon, but I can sit in for a bit." Seeing me, she stopped short.

She looked tired and drawn, her braid frayed and her uniform wrinkled, but something in my own face must have looked even worse, because she wrapped her arms around me in a quick hug. She smelled like sweat and coffee, but it was a comfort, nonetheless.

After a second, she released me, and we were back to business. As I settled in, I realized too late that my chair faced the dining-room windows, while Polly's and Osborne's backed up to the light.

I bounced my knee under the table as Osborne straightened a notebook. He got right to the point. "Riley, I was hoping you could tell me how Beth had been treating her pain."

I felt my shoulders relax marginally. At least he wasn't asking about Ethan this morning. "She did physical therapy and exercises at home, like stretching and strength training. But she had to be careful because she had a lot of nerve damage from the accident. She couldn't bend or sit for long periods. She took . . ." The word vanished. I looked between Osborne and Polly, my brain groping around. "People take it for headaches. It's over the counter." My cheeks warmed.

"Ibuprofen?" Osborne ventured. He raised his eyebrows and shot a look at Polly. He probably wondered if I was always this flaky.

"Yes, ibuprofen," I seized the word gratefully. "She also took an antidepressant that helped with pain."

Osborne wrote this down. "Anything else?"

I knew of at least one other thing she'd taken and suspected more. "I know she had a prescription for"—the word hovered in a blur at the edge of my brain before coming into focus—"for, uh, cannabis. I don't think that she used that too often because she said it made her tired. What's that have to do with what happened?"

Osborne plodded onward as if I hadn't spoken. "Was there anything else she ever mentioned or anything you saw her taking while you were around?"

I let out a sigh. "She never *mentioned* anything besides that. And I never saw her take anything else." That much was the truth, even if I guessed Beth may have found other ways to relieve her pain. I kept my expression blank and tried not to think about what Ethan may have suspected and how he would have reacted. "What exactly do you want to know?"

Osborne studied me for a moment. Again, I was struck by the illusion of concern in his tilted brown eyes. His neutral expression made it easy to project what you wanted to see. Twisting in his chair, he reached for a black shoulder bag that rested on the floor next to him. Opening it, he pulled out a clear plastic baggie that he set on the table. I kept my hands in my lap and leaned forward to look. Inside the bag was a blue plastic prescription bottle with no label. Lying on its side, it looked about half full of tablets. Polly glanced from the pills to my face.

"Does this look familiar to you, Riley?"

"No." I leaned forward to examine the bottle. "I haven't seen Beth with that . . . or, I *hadn't* seen her." I wasn't sure of the proper verb tense for this situation. "What is it?"

Osborne didn't answer. "It looks like someone tried to conceal this. Your brother told us you've had some health issues of your own lately. Have you ever been prescribed opioids?"

"No." It came out sharply, and I felt my brows pinch together in a scowl. Given that I'd forgotten how to speak a moment ago, would he believe me? I glanced at Polly, hoping she knew me well enough to take me at my word.

Osborne cleared his throat. "To your knowledge, has your brother ever had a problem with opioids?"

"My brother?" I arranged my face to let Osborne know that this question was even more ridiculous than the last. Like a lot of rural areas, North Haven had an opioid problem, but our immediate family was one of the few that had remained unscathed. "No. Polly knows how he is. He never even smoked weed and hardly drinks anymore. He's very . . ." I searched for the word. "Straightlaced, I guess." I nearly went on to say that Beth hadn't even told him about her prescription for cannabis but held off, knowing Osborne would probably interpret that as a sign of trouble in their relationship. *Would you say Beth kept a lot of secrets from your brother?*

"So, would you say this might belong to Beth?" Osborne probed.

I flicked my fingers impatiently. "Well, I don't think it's Ethan's. I guess if it's for pain, it makes sense that it's Beth's. They're opioids then?" I motioned to the pills and looked at Polly.

"We'll test them to see exactly what they are, but they are consistent with fentanyl," she answered. "Do you have any idea where Beth may have gotten something like this?" Her tone remained gentle, but she watched me closely. I felt keenly aware of the afternoon sun shining through the window like a spotlight on my face.

"I have no idea. You know how common that stuff is around here." I'd directed my comment toward Polly and immediately regretted it. Growing up, Polly had spent more time at our house than her own because of her mother's addiction. Audra had confided to me that one of the few times Polly had invited her to spend the night, it was clear from the vacuum lines on the stained carpet and the smell of cleaner that Polly had worked to make the place presentable. The girls had just settled in with a movie when Polly's mom stormed down from her bedroom, wasted and wearing nothing more than a dirty robe and screaming at the girls to shut the hell up. When her mom died a few years ago, Polly barely acknowledged her passing.

I couldn't read Polly's expression and shifted in my chair. "I mean, could it have come from a doctor?" I knew Beth's desperation to find relief. I remembered using her phone to take a picture of her next to a chair she'd reupholstered and noticing a cascade of browser tabs opened to alternative therapies and pain clinics.

"That's certainly a possibility," Polly said with a nod. "We do see that more often than we'd like." She glanced at her watch, pressed her palms on the table, and rose. "I'm sorry I have to run for an interview."

She patted my arm. "You'll be in good hands with this guy." With a last squeeze of my shoulder, she turned and left me with Osborne.

As her steps faded, the air in the room grew heavier. Osborne studied his notepad, flipping back a few pages, and frowned. I didn't know if his silence was intended to make me uncomfortable, but it did. The only sounds were the grandfather clock and the flipping of his notebook. My stomach gurgled and I held my hand to it. He didn't react. At last, he flipped to a fresh page, set his notebook on the table, and looked up at me.

"So, you said that opioids are common around here, Riley. Can you give me some names of people Beth might have gone to for this, assuming it wasn't her doctor?" He poked the baggie with the end of his pen. "You can see there's no prescription label."

Something about the nonchalant way he flicked at the pills touched a nerve. I leaned back in my chair and gestured sharply. "I only know that people get it because people OD and go to rehab. I'm not buying it myself, so I don't know *where* they get it."

Osborne leaned an elbow on the table. "Well, in a town this size, there must be rumors."

I hesitated, thinking about Liam and his duffel bag. I felt a sudden sense of panic that I still hadn't had a chance to tell Ethan the entire story. From the direction of the kitchen, I heard the outside door open and someone wipe their feet on the entryway rug.

Osborne's brown eyes stayed locked on me. I took a breath, readying myself to say, "Liam Hunt was here with Beth on Wednesday," when I heard a voice behind me say, "Riley, *there* you are!"

I looked over my shoulder. Audra stood in the doorway, her silky hair a gorgeous, blown-around mess. She rested her hands on her hips and smiled. "I saw your car, but I couldn't find you. Oh." She looked at Osborne across from me, who had leaned back in his chair. "I'm not interrupting?" It was obvious she was trying to extricate me from the interview with Osborne. That meant she must have news. After years of similar extractions from never-ending "heart-to-hearts" with our mom, Audra and I had a well-rehearsed routine. We were the Laurel and Hardy of getting out of difficult conversations.

"No, you're not interrupting," I answered on Osborne's behalf, welcoming the chance to talk with Ethan before finishing up with the police. "We're good?" I confirmed. As I stood up from the table, the room tilted and I clutched at the back of my chair to steady myself.

Osborne fiddled with the baggie of pills for a second and then looked at Audra. If Ethan's attention was like a warm sun, Audra's was like being in the path of a comet: big radiant smile, so white it emitted light, eyes like blue sparks. Osborne frowned and then nodded. "We'll finish up later."

"That would be great." I smiled so widely my cheeks hurt. It was possible I laid it on a little thick.

Audra motioned me to follow her into the kitchen and back outside. "Stop chewing your lip," she hissed.

Neither of us spoke another word until we reached the shelter of some tall evergreens that formed a canopy near the barn. We both sat on the soft carpet of needles, rustling up their piney smell. I breathed it in, trying to calm myself.

*Nothing says you're mine like pine.* The ridiculous slogan ricocheted around my nervous brain. *A candle for possessive Nordic lovers.* I took another deep breath and focused on Audra, the edges of my vision hazy.

"Did Osborne show you the pills?" she asked and, without waiting for my response, continued, "I think that's good for Ethan. They asked me all about him. And they were asking Marco about whether he could confirm where Ethan was all afternoon. Marco said he was hauling corn, but obviously no one is going to follow him around all day. It's clear they're looking at him as a suspect." Audra stopped to breathe.

My heart rate ratcheted back up. As usual, Audra had no reservations about blurting out what everyone was thinking. "What else did Marco say?" I asked.

"He was in Wicksburg and then milking, and Liam was in the combine harvesting corn. Osborne asked Marco whether Ethan had a temper. He said no, but it sounds like someone told the police that he used to get in fights. Marco told them that was a long time ago, before he settled down with Beth. They talked to Doug too, but I don't think Doug would have known about that."

"They asked me about Ethan yesterday too, but today Osborne seemed more interested in the pills."

"Yeah, that's good," Audra repeated and then amended. "Well, not *good* but better than focusing on Ethan. Polly said they found them under the trash bag in the office trash can, like between the bag and the bottom of the can." She shot me a furtive look. "Don't tell anyone I told you that. I saw them take the laptop out too. Polly said they haven't found Beth's phone, but they can pull her phone records, even without the phone. It's got to be the pills or else some random psycho."

I nodded and realized I'd clenched my fist around the pine needles I'd scooped from the ground. I opened my fist and let them sift through my fingers, a few sticking to my sweaty palm. "Who would have told them about Ethan getting in fights?" I asked. I tried to think who would know about it. "Maybe the guys at the farm. Or Polly."

The fights had started after high school, when Ethan's closest friends had gone off to college. Ethan had started hanging out with a new group of guys. The only thing they seemed to have in common was that they'd all stayed in North Haven.

On weekends, he and his new buddies, his Fight Club as he called it, would drive to concerts in Cleveland or Columbus, get drunk, and pick brawls with what they called "city guys." Ethan had routinely come home with a bruised face, a split lip, and skinned knuckles. He always claimed that the other guys provoked them, but I knew from experience that it wasn't hard for Ethan and his friends to feel provoked. They all carried chips on their shoulders, just waiting for a hint that someone judged them for staying in North Haven. I remember the withering look Ethan had given me my junior year of college when I'd commented on how run down Main Street was looking. He had barked back, "You think I can't see that? Just because

I stayed here doesn't mean I'm blind to the problems. Maybe I just care enough to help fix them."

I thought about who else would have known about Ethan's history of fighting. Audra must have been considering the same thing because she broke the silence. "Maybe Liam said something. Or Jeremy? I don't know who else the police have talked to."

"Speaking of Liam . . . I haven't mentioned this to anyone else, so don't say anything. You know how I came by to drop the flowers off for Beth on Wednesday?"

Audra nodded.

"Well, Beth wasn't alone. Liam was with her. Beth told me he was dropping off his rent, but they both acted like they were up to something." I explained Liam's guilty look and my conversation with Beth. "I don't think she would have something going on with Liam. I mean, I thought about it at first, but now I wonder if she might have been getting pills from him." I remembered her pinpoint pupils and languid movements.

"Why haven't you mentioned this?" Audra asked incredulously.

"Well, for one thing, it hasn't even been twenty-four hours since she died. But I haven't told Ethan yet either. He should know if Liam dropped off the rent. Maybe that's all it was and I'm reading too much into it." I shrugged.

"Stop that." Audra narrowed her eyes. "If you saw something, you saw it. It's that simple. After all this stuff with your doctors and your illness, it's like you don't trust yourself."

I didn't tell her how the memory of Beth and Liam had begun to flicker and warp the more I turned it over in my mind. I thought of the bumbling interview I'd just gone through with Osborne.

Why *should* I trust myself, when I couldn't complete a simple sentence, when my inner compass told me that perfectly solid rooms tilted under my feet?

Audra softened her voice. "Listen to your intuition. Tell Ethan the whole story, especially now that we know about the pills. He should have listened to you about Beth before, though," she added. "He gets blinders on when he doesn't want to see something."

Leaning my back against the thick trunk of the pine, I looked toward the old stone barn and the empty window from which Bibbs had watched me the previous night. I dropped the pine needles I'd been pouring through my hands, my palms sticky from the pine tar and sweat. "I will. I'll talk to him." The weight that had lodged in my chest told me I wasn't looking forward to it.

# CHAPTER EIGHT

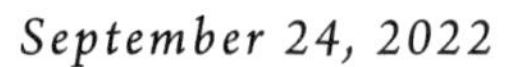

*September 24, 2022*

I watched for a chance to speak with Ethan, but no one wanted to leave him alone. Mom, Audra, Marco, Doug, and I spent most of the afternoon packed into the small parlor, everyone circling Ethan. The moment one person moved off, another moved in, as if he might self-destruct if left to his own devices for a full minute.

I'd seen Doug only briefly the night before; today, I saw how Beth's murder had decimated his normally unflappable exterior. He wore his customary sport coat, but his lively dark eyes had dimmed. His posture showed his age, pitching him forward like an old man worn down by gravity. When he hugged me, he gathered me in as if hanging on for dear life. "You meant so much to her, Riley. I'm so glad she found a friend like you."

"She meant a lot to me too," I said and realized how true this was.

Late in the afternoon, Polly returned from Liam's, and she and Osborne filtered in and out of the parlor, checking in with all of us individually and conferring with each other. A quirk of really old houses is that bathrooms tend to be situated wherever a few spare feet can be found. In Ethan's house,

this meant the half bath sat ignobly off the dining room, providing awkward background noise during dinner parties and game nights.

But sounds carried the other direction too. I happened to be drying my hands when Polly and Osborne crossed paths in the dining room late in the afternoon.

Footsteps sounded and a chair scooched along the hardwood. "Anything?" Polly asked.

Something solid clacked on the table, maybe a laptop. Osborne cleared his throat. "Doug checks out. Turnpike cameras caught him getting on near Chicago and off at the Sandusky exit. Not much left at the scene with all the rain. Still nothing on Beth's phone. Probably at the bottom of the river, but we're waiting on the records."

"Anything jumping out at you?"

"Just Ethan."

The heavy silence that followed roared like the ocean in my ears. Polly's voice was low and harder to hear. "Ethan, hmm . . . with the time of death. Yeah, well, we'll keep looking. I'm going out to talk to Aldridge before it gets any later or else he'll be too drunk to answer questions. I'll catch up with you at the office."

"Later."

I waited for Polly's heavy boots and Osborne's lighter tread to move off before I dared to exhale. Doubling over, I put my hands on my knees. When I stood, my hands shook so badly, it took three tries before I succeeded in turning the old lock and throwing open the door.

It was evening before I finally had the opportunity to talk with Ethan alone. I found him sitting on the back steps looking out across the fields toward a sunset that was beginning to burn orange and pink. The woods where Beth had been found also lay in that direction. I sat down on the steps next to him. The yellow caution tape rattled in the wind around the broken-up patio and leaves from the maple trees swirled each time the breeze picked up.

I looked at him squinting at the horizon and leaned my head on his shoulder. Before Ethan and I became so different, we had been completely alike. When we were little, no one else had ever had much time for us. Mom dashed from the catering business to the house and to the farm. Dad worked constantly, and Audra, a majestic five years older than us, had her own cares.

Old videos showed Ethan and me waddling around the yard having full conversations in toddler babble. I'd led Ethan by the hand toward the swing set and set him on one end. He'd trustingly gone along, knowing I'd never steered him wrong before. Later on, when we had finished feeding the calves on summer days, he would say to me, "Woods?" and I would anticipate an evening among the briars and the skinny undergrowth hauling scrap metal for the fort we were building. Or I'd say, "Bobber?" and we'd spend twilight at the pond, sitting on the rough wooden dock, casting for bluegill and slapping mosquitoes. I missed the clear views we'd once had into each other's heads without even trying.

Somewhere in the twenty years since, we had diverged from telepathic almost-twins to close acquaintances with little in common except a shared childhood. Still, those intense years, that jumble of games, physical work, fights, and running wild in the woods, forged the marrow of who we were. We had grown like plants pointed at two different suns—taking on separate interests, jobs, and beliefs—but still moored to each other, roots still twined together in the same soil.

Maybe it was because we had always communicated so easily that we struggled so much with it now: two inarticulate souls with no idea how to say the things we felt all the way to our bones.

After waiting all day for a chance to talk with him, I didn't know where to begin. The cold had seeped through my jeans and crept under my sweatshirt by the time I spoke.

"The police showed you the pills?"

He nodded, his lips colorless when he looked at me. "She didn't need to hide them from me. I would have understood. I know how much pain she's in."

I wondered how understanding he would have been in reality, but I could tell he was beating himself up already. "I know. She didn't tell me either." I paused and sat back to study him. "Did you see any signs that she was using?" Since Osborne had shown me the bottle of pills, I'd thought about her drowsy manner over the past months, her growing detachment from everyone.

He shook his head and then let out a heavy sigh. "I don't know what I saw, Ri." He looked like he was combing through a catalog of memories with Beth and evaluating them in a new light. As I watched him work through his grief, I felt ashamed of the worries that had flitted around my mind since the previous evening. But if I'd had fleeting doubts, that meant others surely would.

"What did you do when the police told you?" He scowled, and I held up my hand. "We can't pretend they aren't looking at you. I know you'd never do anything like this, but they don't know you like I do. We need to be careful."

I could tell from the way he looked away that he was listening to me and thinking back, probably visualizing how he had appeared to Osborne and Polly at a moment when Beth's secret had come crashing home.

After a minute, he said, "I didn't get angry, if that's what you mean. I'm sure they could tell I was surprised and hadn't known about it. I asked where the pills came from, but they didn't know. They seemed to think I might know more than they did." His shoulders tensed.

I filled my chest with air and then sighed it out. "Remember how I told you I thought something was going on with Beth?"

Ethan's withering look conveyed that he was in no mood for an I-told-you-so. I shook my head. "No, there was something else. Liam was here the day I dropped off the bouquet. He didn't look happy that I saw him. He had a bag with him—"

"What the hell, Riley? You're only sharing this now?"

My own anger rose instinctively. "Just listen. You ever think maybe people keep things back because you get pissed off about everything? Besides, I didn't know what Liam was doing. You were already telling me what a terrible friend I was to even imply that something could be wrong. You would have told me I was jumping to conclusions about Liam. Beth told me he was there to drop off the rent. Could that've been it?"

Ethan frowned. "I don't know, actually. I'd have to look at our deposits. Beth handled the rent, and Liam has been late before. About every month, actually. He might have been dropping it off, but last Wednesday would have been awfully late." He paused and looked at his shoes. "You don't think something was going on with *them*, do you? I mean, *Liam*?" His eyes crinkled in skepticism, and in a less dire situation, I would have laughed.

"No, I don't think that, and that's why I didn't want to bring it up. I figured it was nothing. But now we know about the pills. She was getting them somewhere. It had to either be a doctor or someone she would have seen regularly. Who else did she see? I mean, I don't think Charlotte was dealing." I pictured Charlotte with her permed gray hair and handsewn jumpers dropping off a bottle of fentanyl sewn into the bridesmaids' dresses.

"Did you know Liam went to rehab about a year ago? And you know how he talks. He's got his big plans in LA." Ethan rolled his eyes at the last bit. "He might need money."

"I didn't know about rehab. I only knew he'd had some personal stuff and left work for a while."

We both looked out in the direction of the woods where Beth had been found. "Do you think I should tell the police?" I asked.

"Hell yes, you should tell them." He took a breath and dropped his voice. "But thank you for coming to me first."

He picked at a ragged cuticle, and I could tell he had something more to say. "Did *you* know she was using?"

I shifted on the hard step and tried to sort out what I'd known about Beth versus what I'd suspected. "No, nothing certain. I thought she might be taking something, though. The way she looked when I saw her Wednesday . . . I didn't know if it was a new prescription or what, but she wasn't herself. She put on a good cover, but she hadn't been herself, at least for a couple of months."

Ethan turned away from me again and said nothing. He scratched at a worn spot on the knee of his jeans with his thumbnail, wearing the threadbare fabric even thinner. When he did speak, he sounded like the life had seeped out of him.

"Maybe I didn't want to see it." His Adam's apple bobbed. "I thought she was happy."

A lump rose in my throat. I put a hand on his shoulder, not sure what to say. As warm and solid as he felt, he shivered. "I think she *was* happy with you. But she was in pain too. One doesn't cancel out the other."

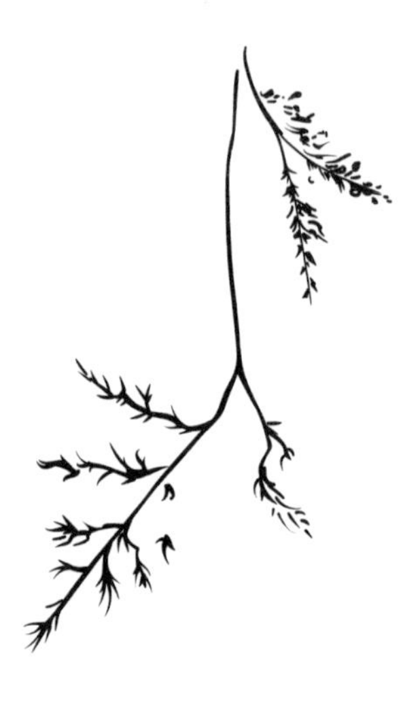

# CHAPTER NINE

*Two Months Earlier—July 23, 2022*

The summer party went very well that year, right up until the point that it went to hell. Mom started out the day nervous but determined not to let a piddling thing like our father's death interfere with the annual tradition of having our friends and neighbors over to celebrate the height of summer. The weather cooperated with a soft breeze stirring the heat of the day. The angular white farmhouse glowed in the evening light like something out of a fairy tale, and the old couples—which it seemed like most of our neighbors were—danced to "Moonlight Serenade" under the shade of the giant maples. All the people of North Haven whom we knew, loved, or simply tolerated were gathered.

Mom had made it clear to us kids since childhood that we were staff, not guests, at these parties. She barked orders throughout the day, but I knew the work she put in alongside us and why it meant so much to her for this one to go smoothly in Dad's absence. Now twelve years old, my niece Sophie was expected to pull her weight. When Mom spied her dancing awkwardly with a group of friends, she asked drily if Sophie thought this party

was for her enjoyment and handed her a crab-crisp-laden tray to circulate. But now that dinner had been served, even Mom was beginning to relax and make the rounds with a half glass of wine in her hand.

Ethan, Beth, and I had escaped to the swing on the front porch, which caught the evening breeze that blew across the pastures. Across the yard, I spotted Marco, Audra, and Polly sitting together at a table under the oak tree. Polly had finally purchased her dream house—one of the formerly grand Victorian houses on Main Street that would have cost a small fortune elsewhere. Audra and Marco had helped her move earlier that day, and the three of them looked worn out. Sophie leaned back against Polly, whose fingers moved automatically, French braiding her soft brown hair. Nearby, Franky screamed with laughter and cries of *again* as my cousin Brent held him in his arms and zoomed him around like an airplane.

Next to us, Doug and Mr. Perry each leaned against a porch post, soaking up the breeze. Doug had steered the discussion toward the potential of the land around the Castle. My mind had felt fuzzy all day, like a bank of fog was rolling through, obscuring people's words and gestures. My attention faded in and out as Doug and Mr. Perry bantered.

Doug propped one foot up on the porch step and made expansive gestures with his non-drink hand as he made his case. "I'm not talking McMansions, Al, just a line of townhomes along the river to start. Three-twos with river views, garages in the back. Young couples would kill each other to get in there."

"Well, I'm not sure we want *that,* Doug." Mr. Perry laughed. Polly had finished Sophie's hair and approached us on the porch. "Polly already has enough on her hands in this town. I get the appeal of that land—I mean, I love it there myself—but I'm not sure I want to see it developed. The reason it's so nice there is that it *hasn't* been developed."

Doug swirled the ice in his drink. "I get what you're saying, but think about the tax revenue it could bring in. Young professionals are looking for places exactly like this with the low cost of living. Plus, those folks want to see the natural environment maintained, so we'd keep the woods and add more paths along the river. It'd be good for quality of life all around." He fixed his dark eyes on Mr. Perry and gauged how his volley had landed.

"Walking paths would be nice," I agreed, mostly to fill the awkward silence. Beside me, Beth sighed.

Polly had kept her eyes on Doug as he gave his pitch. "The village could use the tax revenue. Maybe fix up Main Street a little."

Mr. Perry lifted his hat and rubbed his forehead. "Maybe I'm getting old, well I *am* getting old, but I would just hate to see the landscape disrupted that much. And I'm not sure this is the kind of town that Gen Zers or whatever are looking for. We don't have the trendy restaurants and whatever things that they would be used to. I don't think they'd be real excited about having to get their groceries from the Dollar Store."

Doug adjusted his stance and switched drink hands. "Well, that kind of thing is reciprocal. Restaurants and service economies only work where there's a population to support them, and right now we don't have that here. But we could. I've had investors tell me flat out that this place could be a gold mine if we could get the ball rolling. But Beth and I saw the promise here, even without shops and restaurants. Lots of people are looking for that same peace and quiet. And think of what you could do for the Castle itself with the capital the sale would generate."

Polly nodded. "There're plenty of vacant spaces downtown. It'd be great to see those put to use. Bring back a grocery store and some restaurants." She nudged Mr. Perry and grinned. "You're the one who used to go on about how we need to build the community we want. I'm fixing up a house in town and keeping the peace, but I can only do so much." Mr. Perry's lectures on civic responsibility were legendary. Polly's tone was playful, but I knew that in her work, she saw the ugly side of North Haven: the overdoses, domestic abuse, and child neglect. Increasing opportunities for people in the town mattered to her. I'd often thought that I could see her running for office someday. She certainly had the intelligence and ambition.

Mr. Perry crooked his thumb toward Doug but addressed Beth. "Seems I'm outnumbered here. Did you ever win an argument with this man? Every time I see him he chips away at me." He laughed but I sensed his growing irritation.

Turning back to Doug, Mr. Perry chose his words carefully. "Even if I was interested—and I'm not saying that I am—you'd need to convince every member of the Carlton Castle Association to sell, and I'm probably the least stubborn among them. Milly Carlton wants to be buried on that land, and I don't think she wants to share her eternal rest with a bunch of townhomes. Besides, I think the Castle will start generating its own income before long, especially with your daughter behind it." He smiled at Beth. "Now, if you'll excuse me, Doug, I'd better get going before you convince me to sign something."

Mr. Perry said his goodbyes and Doug patted him on the back. Polly walked off with Mr. Perry, their heads bent together in conversation. Doug watched them for a moment before he smiled at Beth. "I'm making some headway there."

She raised an eyebrow. "You think? Besides, it is nicer undeveloped. You said yourself that that's what makes it special." Her voice was soft but resolute.

Doug looked exasperated with his daughter. "Whose side are you on here? Besides, it's not one or the other, Beth, you know that. You can develop a piece of land and still conserve the environment."

Beth swayed on the porch swing as she formulated her argument, but Ethan was quicker. "That's exactly what I told Mom when we built the new barns. You've got to do both. We kept most of the old trees and the buffer strip along the river, but we almost doubled the capacity of the free stalls and can divide the herd into different holding groups based on production now. You should take a look, Doug."

Ethan admired Doug's entrepreneurial streak and was always looking for opportunities to talk business with him, especially with Dad gone. Doug looked like a man searching for an excuse as he looked down at the drink in his hand, when Beth chimed in. "You should see what Ethan's done, Dad. It's amazing." That sunlight smile warmed Ethan's face.

Doug's shoulders slumped and he agreed. We all set off toward the farm, which sat about a hundred yards behind the house. The chatter of the party and music faded and the hum and hustle of machinery and livestock grew louder. There were four barns on the farm, including an old barrel-roofed barn with two cupolas, and four-hundred-foot-tall concrete grain silos. On either side of the barns, pastures and ponds spread out, and beyond the barns ran the Vermillion River and eighty acres of woods. Ethan had financed the construction of the new barn and milking parlor on my parents' property despite Mom's wishes. She'd fought Dad's expansion of the farm, knowing that every new plot of land he bought meant more hours, more debt, and more pressure, but like Dad, Ethan knew that in the age of big agribusiness, family farms had to grow to keep up or disappear. The days were long gone where a family farm could survive with a few animals and forty acres of crops.

We passed the pasture where a dozen yearling heifers grazed. A few galloped up and followed us with their wide-set brown eyes as Beth told me about the work they'd been doing on the house. Ethan threw his arm around my shoulders. "We just finished the first spare room, so we have an actual bed for you now. Aunt Riley's official room—you can stay over whenever."

At the words "Aunt Riley," I glanced at Beth's flat stomach and then her face. She laughed and shook her head. "He's getting ahead of himself," but she smiled as she said it. I knew they both wanted to start a family, and I felt a rush of happy anticipation for them. I realized how much I would enjoy living nearby as their kids grew up. Living in Seattle, I'd missed so many firsts with Audra's kids, but I'd have the chance to be around for Ethan and Beth's.

Ethan led us through a covered passageway that connected the old barn to the new and stopped at a pen where a newborn calf lay in the fresh straw with its mother. "This guy was just born this morning." Ethan reached through the slats of the gate to stroke the soft white star on the calf's forehead. "Remember our first job, Ri, bottle-feeding the new calves?"

I smiled at the memory of us getting up in the dark hours before school to mix the milk formula. We would share the weight of the heavy bucket as we hauled it and some bottles to the eager, bleating calves.

The black-and-white calf had nestled its pink nose into its flank and stared up at us with enormous brown eyes. Beth and I said "aw" in unison and laughed. Doug stayed several feet behind the wooden gate. "He's quite a . . . handsome animal."

Ethan led us farther into the barn and explained to Doug how the new double-twelve milking parlor tracked milk production for each cow and adjusted milking times automatically.

I heard the pride in his voice and saw how he kept looking at Doug's face, like a kid looking for approval.

Huge fans ran in the parlor, but it smelled eternally of bleach, manure, and the warm, grainy scent of livestock. Doug nodded at everything but didn't ask any questions. I could tell he was trying not to breathe as Ethan showed him the new bulk tank that held 2,600 gallons of milk.

Outside of the parlor, Doug gratefully gulped the fresh air. Beth spoke in a low voice to Ethan and he squeezed her hand. She turned to her dad. "What do you think?"

Doug was looking at the bottom of his tan leather loafers. "Well, what I think, honey, is that I'm going to have to burn these shoes." He looked up and smiled, but Ethan's face flushed. Realizing that his joke had flopped, Doug backpedaled. "Quite an operation you have here, Ethan. Who would have thought that farmers needed all this technology?"

Ethan stiffened and Beth frowned. It was a quiet walk back to the house with Doug shuffling his loafers in the grass along the way. Doug's comment reminded me of when I was in middle school, and a friend's dad had stepped into the office at the back of the house to drop me off and declared with surprise that he'd never expected to see a computer on a farm. Mom had smiled and, without missing a beat, responded, "What an ignorant thing to say. How many multimillion-dollar businesses do you know of that don't use a computer? And Riley probably knows more about how it works than you would." My friend's dad had mumbled something inaudible and slunk back out the door.

Still, I never knew to be embarrassed about growing up on a farm until my first semester of college. There, during a discussion about classism in freshman sociology, a girl with passionate opinions about things I'd never before heard of declared that she didn't think people who came from poor urban neighborhoods should be embarrassed because of their roots—it wasn't like they'd grown up on farms or something.

If nothing else, Doug could read a room, and he left soon after, maybe to go home and burn his loafers. But Ethan's mood had turned. Adding to the new friction in the air, while we'd all been out at the barn, Audra had departed too. When I asked Polly what had happened, she'd shrugged. All she knew was that Audra had been talking with the family attorney one minute and storming off the next. I sighed and texted to ask if she was okay, but let it go when she didn't respond. I was too tired to push it, and my brain felt too sluggish for a conversation anyway.

Beth and I returned to the porch swing, where we rocked gently, listening to the wind in the maples and the hum of distant conversations. Though the party was winding down, Ethan was just getting started on a bottle of whiskey with Liam and Jeremy, who had finished the milking and joined the party. I watched as the level of the whiskey in the bottle dropped rapidly. Beth's breathing had slowed beside me, and I was pretty sure she had fallen asleep. Liam, who considered himself a film aficionado, was drunkenly explaining the merits of *Everything Everywhere All at Once* to a skeptical Ethan and Jeremy, who countered that it had been the weirdest movie they'd ever seen.

"It made absolutely no sense," Jeremy stated. "I mean, was the daughter evil? She was like a different person in every scene." He raised his hands, imploring someone to please explain it. He and Liam had come straight from the barn, and when Jeremy moved, I caught the smell of the milking parlor.

"No." Liam sighed. I couldn't see his face, but his eye roll was practically audible. "That was the multiverse—all the possible paths she could have taken." Liam shook his head, drained his Solo cup of whiskey, and refilled.

Ethan leaned against a porch post with the moonlight bathing one side of his body in silver. He turned to Jeremy. "In that case, I wish I lived in the multiverse where we'd watched *The Batman* instead." Jeremy and Ethan doubled over.

Liam waved a hand at them and sighed again. "You're so funny. Can't you see? It's about *possibility*. All the choices we make. Like, you don't have to just follow what your father did and his father did." I cringed at his wording. He wasn't referring to Ethan and our father, but I knew how my brother would take the comment.

In the dim light, I could see Ethan tilt his head. "Well, we're just a couple of dumb hicks stuck in our ruts, aren't we, Jeremy? We could never understand sophisticated things like film." He kept his voice light but jerked his arm back to finish off his whiskey.

"That's not what I said. You know what you like, and that's fine, but you haven't studied film. You don't get the choices a filmmaker . . . makes. That's why I need to get out to LA so that I can be around people who live this stuff." Liam sounded dreamy and completely oblivious to Ethan's souring mood.

"Oh, well, thanks, Liam. I'm glad to hear that I'm allowed to like what I like." Ethan laughed harshly. "But, seriously, I'm happy for you, bud. You know what you want and you're going for it. I'm sure you'll meet a lot of filmmakers when you make it to LA and start bussing at a gay club. I bet they'll have a lot to teach you out there." That had been a running joke at Liam's expense ever since he'd made the mistake of admitting he wanted to move to LA and make films, but I hadn't heard it in years and had hoped it had died with time. Ethan and Jeremy cracked up again.

I stared at them, a heaviness my chest. "Ethan, stop."

Liam nodded at me and then slurred at Ethan, "You should've learned by now not to be so homophobic. Stuff like that is why people think we're all intolerant rednecks around—"

Ethan, whose silhouette had been swaying, froze. "The fuck did you say?"

I stilled the porch swing and pressed my feet to the ground, readying myself to move. "Ethan, just stop!"

"Lighten up, Liam," Jeremy said over me. "He's joking with you."

"I'm just saying you're acting like a redneck. You need to get out of North Haven more."

Ethan moved out of the moonlight and under the porch roof toward Liam. "You should really learn to shut your mouth."

In the dark I couldn't tell who took the first swing, only that their bodies met in a drunken, ineffectual scuffle. I stumbled up, pitching forward into a porch post. Fortunately, Jeremy was more nimble and wedged himself between Liam and Ethan. By now Beth was wide awake, though I wasn't sure how much she had seen or heard. Liam held a hand to his nose where Ethan had connected. "What the hell, you psycho?"

The few people still left at the party had gathered to see what the commotion was about. Marco rushed over. "What's going on?"

"He's talkin' shit." Ethan motioned toward Liam, who stepped toward him again.

"You're the one talking shit, Ethan. Just stop." My hands shook and I felt sick to my stomach.

Marco put his arm around Liam's shoulders and steered him away, while Beth and I tried to calm Ethan. I didn't want him to do anything worse.

"You've had too much to drink. Let Beth drive you home."

"What did Liam say?" Beth asked me quietly.

"He said Ethan was acting like a redneck," I told her in a low voice. "Which he was."

Ethan had slipped away from us and was striding toward the driveway, where cars had pulled off onto the grass to park. As if to confirm Liam's words, he looked around and then walked unsteadily toward Liam's truck, raised his foot, and delivered a kick to the fender. It landed with a dull metallic thud.

Beth ran after him. "What's the matter with you? Stop it!" She grabbed his arm and yelled, "You're acting like a child." In all the years I'd known her, I'd never heard her yell, but I'd also never seen Ethan throw a tantrum around her that warranted it. She held out her hand.

"Keys."

Ethan stood stock-still for a moment and then dug in his pocket. Beth snatched the keys from his hand before he could extend his arm and turned on her heel toward Ethan's truck, got in, slammed the door, and pulled off without him. Ethan hadn't moved an inch. Only his head swiveled as he stared after Beth and the taillights receding down the long driveway.

The wind went out of Ethan after Beth departed, and he agreed to let me help him into the house to sleep it off. Mom had left the party to the younger generations and gone to bed already. The house was quiet, and the moonlight cast a milky pall across the kitchen as I poured a glass of water for Ethan, who sat with his head on the cool wood table.

By now, he had passed through his angry phase and had moved into the sloppy, maudlin stage that preceded passing out. I knew I had to get him up the stairs soon or he'd be dead weight. With his head on the table and his eyes closed, he asked plaintively, "Why did everyone leave?"

"I don't know. Maybe it had something to do with the fit you threw." I had more to say, but wasn't in the mood to waste my breath on words he wouldn't even remember. "Let's go upstairs. You'll feel better in the morning." He would feel awful tomorrow and deserved it.

I grabbed his thick arm and he let me guide him toward the stairs like a child. "Why did everyone leave?" he asked again, his voice soft.

"Because it's late and they know it's time to call it a night."

"Nooo," he drew it out in frustration. "I mean, why did everyone leave North Haven? I'm the only one who stayed." He sounded so young.

"I'm right here. Audra and I live less than an hour away. We didn't leave you." As quiet as I tried to be, every stair creaked as we climbed. Some part of me felt like we were sneaking in after a late night and couldn't wake Mom.

"Yeah, but you all went off to college and Wicksburg. I'm the only one that stayed right here." He pointed down and heaved a dramatic sigh. "Did you guys leave because of me?"

"It wasn't because of you," I said softly. While we certainly hadn't left to escape Ethan, in part we *had* left to escape behavior like he had just exhibited—the undercurrent of closed-mindedness, hostility, and violence that ran through North Haven. In Audra's case, the final straw had come when some boys in Sophie's class told her that she should go back to Mexico. Marco had shouldered plenty of hateful comments over the years, but he wouldn't have his daughter face the same thing. They had listed their house that week and enrolled Sophie in Wicksburg schools.

North Haven and my family made me who I was. Yet, from the time I was old enough to spin the globe that sat on my dad's desk and understand the size of the world, I'd wanted to live somewhere else. All my adult life had been a tug-of-war between that dream and my family. Still, I had never lived more than a cross-country flight away. Now, with the opportunity to head up IT in the company's new European headquarters in Bath, I knew I'd have to make a choice.

Ethan sagged heavily against my shoulder as I steered him to his childhood room. Climbing the stairs with him wobbling into me was hard enough, and with no central air, the upstairs baked like an oven. By the time we reached his room, I was so hot I couldn't stand his sweaty arm draped around my neck for another second. I pushed his arm off, and he crashed down onto the twin bed, the ancient box springs whining.

He winced and mumbled, "You didn't have to leave." A minute later, he was asleep. I looked at him with his mouth open and beads of sweat on his forehead.

"Well, I didn't have to stay either," I whispered.

I set a glass of water on his nightstand and left him lying on top of the covers of his childhood bed with his boots sticking over the footboard.

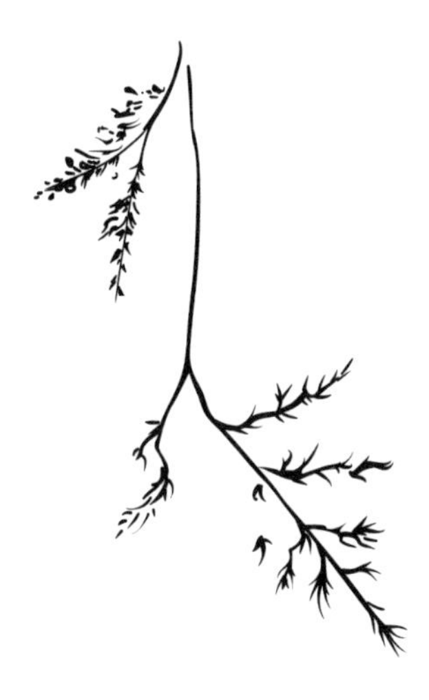

# CHAPTER TEN

*September 25, 2022*

I had fifteen minutes until I needed to leave for Beth's memorial. I was looking through search results for *how to get pillow marks off of your face quickly* when my friend Sydney's text came in. In typical Sydney fashion, she got right to the point. She instructed me to *watch this* and linked to a news story from a station out of Cleveland.

I'd lain down around noon just to rest for a second but ended up falling asleep for most of the afternoon. Now, I was hurrying to make myself presentable for Beth's hastily planned memorial. I had snagged my black stockings, found Bruno-sized teeth marks pocking my black heels, and my respectable black dress hung on me like a sack. Added to this, a brocade-patterned imprint from the throw pillow I'd slept on adorned the right side of my face.

Looking in the mirror, I accepted the fact that I was going to be late and sat down to watch the video Sydney had sent. The thumbnail of the story showed North Haven's empty main street and the caption *Quiet town rocked by brutal slaying of young woman about to be wed.* My first thought was

that this seemed like a lot of prepositional phrases to string together; my second thought was that this must be bad if Sydney insisted that I watch it.

I tapped play and the video opened with a wide view of Ethan's house and the reporter I'd seen there yesterday, Juliette Gundy. The camera closed in on Juliette's telegenic face as she began to tell the story of Beth's brutal slaying in a voice that dripped with gravitas.

*North Haven, a sleepy community of simple folks, has been shaken to its core by a horrific death. Beth Lauderdale was a beautiful young woman with her whole life ahead of her. She was engaged to be married in less than a month, but tragically yesterday, after a brief search, police located her body in a nearby woods.*

As Juliette spoke, footage played of cornfields and woods, the outside of Ethan's house, and yellow caution tape flapping near the broken rear patio. I recognized my car parked in the driveway and spied Bruno wandering through a shot of the police behind the house. A photograph flashed onto the screen of Ethan and Beth from a trip they had taken to Kelleys Island. Beth leaned into Ethan's arms, and they both smiled at the camera as the sun set into Lake Erie behind them. They looked young, beautiful, in love, and everything else that made for a compelling human interest story.

In the next shot, Juliette explained that the police were looking into foul play. The view widened to show Osborne standing next to her with a somber expression, his arms behind his back as he leaned toward her microphone. *The circumstances under which Ms. Lauderdale was found indicate that someone else was with her at the time of her death. We are looking into possible suspects, and her fiancé, Mr. Svenson, is cooperating with us fully.*

I cringed. Without uttering a single negative word, Osborne had made Ethan sound like a suspect.

The scene switched to Juliette standing on Main Street in front of a flat-fronted brick building where farming supplies and horse tack were sold. Next to her stood Dotty, a woman who had attended church with my parents since time began. Dotty was as pink and white and sweet as a powdered jelly doughnut. I had faith in Dotty to steer this story back on course. She beamed as Juliette Gundy tilted the microphone toward her. "Such a nice family, I can't believe a thing like this could happen to them." She twisted her wedding band on her plump pink hand. "And I'm certain this is all just nonsense about Ethan."

My heart pumped harder. "Why'd she have to add that last bit?" I asked Bruno, who sighed and rolled onto his side. I knew the police were looking at Ethan, but I hadn't had time to think about the court of public opinion. A headache began to thrum behind my eyes. As good-natured as Ethan could be, everyone in North Haven knew about his explosive temper.

Juliette was wrapping up: *The family and her fiancé are declining to comment at this time, but residents here are shocked and concerned. Police are asking the public to come forward with any information that could help in their investigation. If you know anything that could be of help, please call the tip line at the number shown below.*

The video ended and a pop-up filled my screen offering me three simple tips to get rid of belly fat fast. I shut down my phone, closed my eyes, and put my head in my hands. Under my black sack dress, I was suddenly cool and damp with sweat. What had promised to be a horrible evening had suddenly turned a hundred times worse.

In a small town, when someone in your family dies, your neighbors console you with their most magnificent food—the rich lightness of their puffed meringue, their jewel-colored fresh berry pies with sugared lattice tops. I remembered this kindness from when my dad died. Of course, you can't taste the food at the time, but knowing people around you care is still nice.

But when someone you love is murdered and, even worse, suspicion is cast on your family, they don't bring food. In fact, they keep a wide berth, as if what happened to you might be catching. That takes a different kind of toll: you still grieve the one who's gone, but you learn not to expose your vulnerabilities.

This atmosphere was further dampened given that a good share of North Haven had concluded that Ethan had done away with Beth himself, though no one seemed to blame him much. In the two days since Beth had been killed, theories had filtered back to us. Audra had heard speculation passed on from a friend of a friend that Beth cheated on Ethan with the lawyer from her car-accident settlement and Ethan found out. Marco's cousin's neighbor conjectured that Ethan had finally figured out that Beth was a gold digger and snapped after she turned into Bridezilla, planning the expensive wedding of her dreams. Even as our acquaintances charged Ethan with murder, Beth remained the villain. *It's always the boyfriend,* people whispered, and with Ethan's history of brawling and Beth's imagined faults, *of course.* It felt true.

My family all stayed close to one another at the memorial, seated around the card tables in the church basement like a phalanx of soldiers protecting our flank, a grim portrait in black, blue, and gray. The coroner still held Beth's body, awaiting autopsy. The police made it clear that it could be a while before a proper funeral could be held, so friends and extended family had organized this memorial to bring us all together to share awkward conversation in our time of grief.

Harmony, a high-school frenemy and one of Ethan's pre-Beth girlfriends, had staked out the door. She had gone all out in a form-fitting, off-the-shoulder black dress. Before I could get my coat off, she engulfed me in a crushing hug that smelled of tanner and hair product. Tall and—as her daily Instagram posts illustrated—a hard-core fitness junkie, the arms she wrapped around me were nearly as buff as Ethan's.

"Mom and I have been praying for you." She took my hands and looked across the room at Ethan, who wore a pale-blue dress shirt with the cuffs rolled up. A sheen of sweat glistened on his forehead. "He is so brave to show up tonight." Her spidery lashes fluttered as she scanned my reaction.

I extricated my hands, murmured thanks, and escaped. The encounter felt like an unwanted sequel to my dad's funeral less than a year ago—this time with more scandal—the same church basement with the same people offering their thoughts, prayers, and unwanted touching. Harmony had consoled me then by telling me how terrible it was that the doctors had said it was COVID that killed my dad. When I'd told her that COVID *had* killed him, she'd shrugged and said with a meaningful look, "Well, I know that's what they *said*." I didn't ask her to enlighten me.

I fought my way through a crowd of sympathetic smiles and long embraces to where my family had gathered. I sank into the folding chair next to Audra. She was fully occupied tending to Franky, who looked itchy in his little plaid dress shirt. Sophie, who had suddenly morphed into an adolescent now that she was in junior high, lowered her head over her phone and repeated the process of scrolling, glaring at her screen, and scrolling some more.

My mom was occupied with Charlotte, who had dropped the dresses off for Beth the day she died, making her the last known person to have seen Beth alive. Audra once described Charlotte as a barrel-bodied woman and I've never been able to unsee that image. In her sixties with curly gray hair, Charlotte was a woman with very few unexpressed thoughts. Currently she was unburdening herself to my mom.

"Well, I wish I could say that we had a nice visit the last time I saw her, but she practically grabbed the dresses from me and rushed me out the door. I know I told her that I'd be there by two, but it wasn't even half past two by the time I got there. She didn't even let me do the final fitting on her gown. I don't know what kind of bride does that. But it's just been so awful for me knowing that I was the last one, well, almost the last one"—she couldn't keep from flicking her eyes to Ethan—"to see that poor girl alive. The police wanted every little detail, and I've been a bundle of nerves. To think, the murderer could be in this very—"

"Yes, this must all be very hard for you," my mom cut her off and turned away, her blue eyes sparking. Charlotte nodded and moved on to Doug. Sitting next to my mom, he had dressed as sharply as usual in a navy sport coat, but his face was pale and starkly exhausted in the fluorescent lighting. He glanced up at Charlotte from the Styrofoam cup of coffee he'd been contemplating; the blank look behind his eyes told me he hadn't the slightest idea who she was.

Ethan sat at the end of the table with his hands in loose fists on his knees, his focus on nothing. I wondered if he had seen the news story yet or if—as rumors tended to do—it had just orbited around him without making contact. When friends stopped by to greet him, he would come to with a jolt, shake their hands without getting up, and drift off again once they left.

I numbly exchanged hugs with the friends, family, and neighbors who stopped by the table. Somehow my friends Jane and Kevin from work had heard about the memorial, and I was touched to see them, but I managed to keep my emotions in check until Sydney approached. She knew the vulnerabilities I guarded from everyone else, and the look of understanding in her sympathetic eyes did me in. I stood to accept her hug and then buried my face in her curly dark hair.

After a moment, I straightened up, wiped at my eyes, and blew my nose. "What a mess," I said, referring to myself as well as the larger situation.

"Yeah, I know that you cared about her, unlike half the creeps here."

Sydney and I moved away from my family to an unoccupied corner where we could talk. "Thanks for the warning," I said in reference to the news story she'd shared. "I'd say more than half are only here to claim rights to firsthand gossip. What are people saying?"

"Do you really want to know?" She knitted her eyebrows together. I nodded. "Nothing new. Some people suspect Ethan. Others think it was some psycho passing through town. Some think she was tied up in drugs. No one knows anything."

My eyes came to rest on Harmony and her mother, who'd huddled with a few of Mom's supposed friends near the coffeemaker. They all stood close and spoke behind their hands, like they were relishing the arrogant, sharp-tongued Lorna Svenson getting her comeuppance. I felt a tired anger at how quickly people we'd seen as friends had stepped into the role of eager spectators.

"What I'd really like to know is what *they* think." I inclined my head in the direction of Osborne and Polly, who stood by a table of bottled water and coffee. Polly had her hair in her usual tight braid but had donned a black suit for the occasion, and Osborne wore dark pants and a stiff white shirt with a navy tie. They were deep in discussion, and both kept scanning the room to keep an eye on who was where, with whom, doing what.

"I know they're looking at Ethan," I continued. "Audra gets what she can from Polly, but obviously she can't tell us everything." I nodded toward Osborne, who was making his way toward the door now. "Besides, he's the one I worry about. You and I know Ethan wouldn't do this, but he doesn't know us."

Sydney's gaze followed mine. She gave Osborne the once-over. "Why don't you get to know him then? Go after him and find out what he thinks. Let him know you're normal people . . . well, mostly." She grinned. "He's going to be around, whether you like it or not. Maybe you should work with him instead of against him."

"How'd you get to be so wise?"

"Just kinda happened. Now go on while he's on his own." She shooed me toward the door.

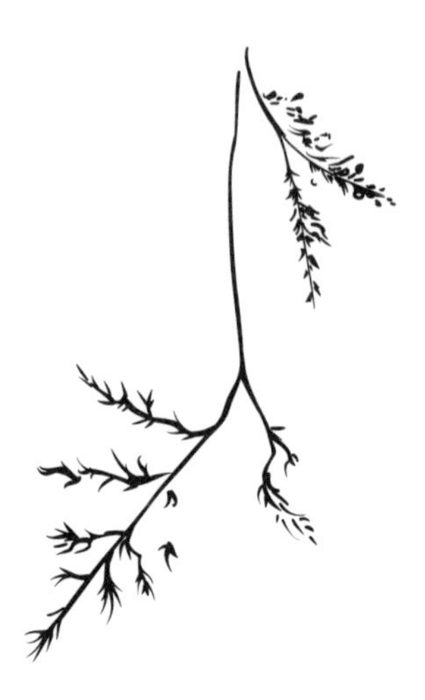

# CHAPTER ELEVEN

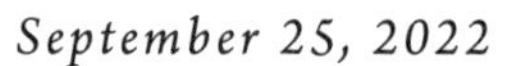

*September 25, 2022*

By some miracle, I made it out of the church basement without being waylaid by a sympathetic acquaintance. The night had cooled, and I crossed my arms, feeling the hard thump of my heart against my chest walls. Osborne sat alone at a plastic picnic table, his head bent over his phone. I sauntered toward him, feeling about as smooth as a kid at a junior-high dance.

He glanced up at me and tucked his phone away. "Riley," he said with a note of surprise. He motioned to a spot next to him with a kind of old-fashioned formality. "Please, have a seat. How are you holding up? It's quite the turnout for Beth."

"Yeah, I guess it is." I sat next to him and looked at all the cars crammed into the small parking lot. In my cynicism toward the gossips, I hadn't thought about it that way. "Small towns are good about that sort of thing. You're not from around here, right?" I didn't actually care where he came from at the moment, but I wanted to get him talking.

He let a quick breath out of his nose, a scoff. "No, not at all. Northern California, but I grew up in a pretty small town there."

"How'd you end up here?" I asked with genuine curiosity. "Not too many people move from Northern California to North Haven."

"The county needed a computer forensics investigator. It was a promotion, and that's what I want to do in the long run. It's only been a few months, so this"—he waved his hand to encompass the surrounding area—"is all new to me. Fall has been nice, and the woods remind me of home, but I can't say I'm looking forward to winter, though. I'll probably go back to California for Christmas. My mom is back there."

It struck me that he wasn't much older than I was, and I heard a more human note in his voice when he talked about home and his mom. I realized, suddenly, that he was probably lonely here and almost felt bad about my self-serving reasons for speaking with him. Still, I needed to turn the conversation to his job. "Yeah, I've actually done some forensics for work. Not a lot. Mostly I do network architecture, but sometimes people leave the company and take sales lists or proprietary information. Then, I have to process their laptops. You find all kinds of stuff, which I'm sure you know."

"That's right. You said you work at Wicks?" I expected him to pick up the thread about computer forensics, maybe even drop a hint about Beth's laptop. Instead he said, "My mom loves that stuff."

I frowned. "Oh, the candles?" I nearly sighed in exasperation. But I took a deep breath. This was an opportunity to ingratiate myself with the man who played a role in Ethan's fate—a man who missed home and his mom. "You know, I could order something for her at a discount. Just let me know what she would like. How many wicks do you want?"

He stared at me. "There's more than one option?"

"Oh, yeah. You can get anything from one to twenty." I felt compelled to warn him. "But they're not really safe beyond ten wicks. At least, you don't want to leave them unattended or near anything flammable."

He laughed. "Uh, well, I'm not trying to set my mom's house on fire. How about just one wick?"

"Okay, if you want to give me the address, I could have it shipped—or I suppose you'll be around?"

He had been leaning forward with his elbows on his knees, but at that question he straightened up, shifting back into his official capacity. "Yeah, I'll be around, at least until we wrap things up here."

"You're getting close?" My heart raced as I waited.

"Depends on what we find. I'm running forensics on the laptop. Still don't have a phone. We're waiting for toxicology, so we'll see where that takes us. And we're finishing up interviews."

"Oh. Do people have any theories?" I fought to keep my voice casual.

"You know I can't share that kind of thing." The admonishment was gentle, but I felt the door between us that had opened just a crack closing again. I rushed ahead.

"It's just that in small towns, people can take a little grain of half-truth and blow it up into something else. Like, when I was in college, I had to go into the hospital for mono. Next thing I knew, the story circulated that I was in a coma and might not survive. I moved to Seattle soon after that, but years later when I came home to visit, people would come up to me and tell me how they'd prayed for me to wake up." I took a deep breath. "It's like the rumors with Ethan and Beth. She kept to herself, and a lot of people couldn't understand what Ethan saw in her, so they filled in the blanks with gossip. But I *saw* how they were. Ethan loved her more than anything." My heart thudded in the long silence that followed.

"I told you I'm from a small town. I know how that goes."

Our conversation lagged as I tried to gauge his response. He seemed in no hurry to get back inside, and the idea that maybe I'd made him understand the rumor mill gave me hope. After all the people packed into the church basement, the cool air felt refreshing, and despite the damp cold, I didn't feel chilled. I watched my breath condense into a cloud with each exhalation and knew now was the moment to turn the conversation to Liam.

"You know, I've thought of something that happened a couple days before Beth died. Wednesday of last week." I recounted the story of finding Liam with his duffel bag at the house with Beth, how I'd gotten the impression he hadn't wanted to be seen and later found out about his history of addiction. I could feel the growing intensity of Osborne's attention as I spoke. "I'm not trying to start my own rumors, but it stuck out to me since I'd never known them to be close." I still couldn't quite wrap my mind around the idea of Liam harming Beth, but then, how well did I actually know him?

Osborne didn't say anything for a moment, and I began to worry. Maybe I'd come across as too blatant, too eager to steer suspicion away from Ethan. For a cold moment, I feared he wouldn't believe me.

When he spoke, his tone was flat. I couldn't see his expression. "Why didn't you mention this earlier?"

"You never asked if I'd seen anyone at the house, and there was nothing *that* weird about it. But after you showed me the pills the other day, I thought about seeing Liam and his history of using." I shrugged. "I mean, maybe it's nothing, but the pills had to come from someone."

He leaned a hand on his knee and pivoted toward me on the bench.

"Thanks for coming to me with this." I still couldn't make out his expression in the dark, but he sounded sincere. "This could help. At the very least, it's something new. We'll talk to Liam again. He's here tonight, isn't he?"

"Yeah, I saw him earlier." My thoughts flickered between hope and shame that I was throwing Liam into the line of fire to save Ethan. People were beginning to filter out of the basement to their cars by now, silhouetted against the security lights in the parking lot. Many of the figures stooped and lumbered against the pain of old age. It struck me again that it was good of so many people to come out, at least the half of them who weren't creeps.

Osborne cleared his throat and stood. "Thank you again for sharing this, Riley. I hope you feel like you can come to me or Polly with anything you think of. I'd better get back inside." With a slight inclination of his head, he rose and walked back toward the light of the open basement door.

I sat by myself, soaking up the silence before gathering the fortitude to go back inside. Relief poured into my bloodstream at the thought of Osborne's focus shifting from Ethan to Liam, and the adrenaline that had propelled me through the evening waned. I wondered if anyone would notice if I were to lie down on the picnic-table bench. The shooting pain on the side of my head and face throbbed. Since getting sick, I could rally myself to get through events, but the effort often left me destroyed the next day. The unceasing stress of the last few days was taking its toll.

By the time I returned, the basement had cleared out considerably. Across the wide room, I spotted Osborne speaking with Polly, who had her hands shoved into the pockets of her suit coat, her eyes boring into his.

Looking around for Liam, I saw him heading toward the table where my family sat. He approached Ethan and bent to speak to him. Liam's eyes flicked around as he spoke, resting on Polly and Osborne for a beat. I couldn't hear a word, but I could see the tension coil in Ethan's body, in the way his shoulders rose and he gripped the edge of the table.

My stomach turned. Before I could cover the distance to stop him, Ethan was up out of his chair and pressing himself into Liam's space, jabbing his finger into his chest. Liam took a step back, knocking into a folding chair. The eyes of everyone in the room, including Polly and Osborne, locked on them.

Liam retreated and had nearly made it to the doorway when Polly and Osborne intercepted him. Osborne addressed Liam and motioned outside. He shook his head but followed them out the door. Audra had positioned herself near Ethan during the exchange, but I saw her look up as the three of them walked out. She glanced my way and widened her eyes before turning her attention back to Ethan, who still stood near the table with his cheeks flushed and his fists curled.

I felt sick and shaky. Was this Ethan's response to what I'd told him about Liam and Beth? What was he thinking? I was so wrapped up in weaving through the tables and chairs to reach Ethan that I jumped when someone put a hand on my shoulder.

"Riley, I'm so sorry."

I turned to see Mr. Perry. He wore a tucked-in golf shirt and khakis, but he had dark circles under his eyes and had missed a spot shaving.

"I can't believe this. What a loss. You know, we were getting the team onto the bus for the scrimmage at Western when I heard the sirens, and I thought, 'Boy, something serious is going down somewhere.' But I never in a million years would have thought that—Beth was such a sweet girl and never into trouble—unlike so many kids around here." He shook his head. "How are you holding up? How's Ethan?" He glanced in his direction, and I wondered if he'd witnessed all that had just unfolded.

"As well as can be expected, I guess."

"Have you heard anything from the police?" Mr. Perry studied me. I shook my head and he continued. "Such a shame. So many addicts and deadbeats with no hope. I wish I could say that I couldn't imagine one of them doing this, but you never really know what desperate people are capable of."

I knew he didn't mean Ethan, but the words smacked me in the chest. I scanned his face, wondering who he did mean.

"Okay, sweetie." He wrapped me in a hug and cleared his throat. "You tell me if there's anything you need. Tell Ethan I'm rooting for him. I'm so sorry this has happened to you guys. You're good people." He gave my shoulder a squeeze before moving off toward the table where my family had been.

Mom now sat there alone, staring into space and twisting her wedding band, maybe pondering how Dad would handle this mess, or simply wishing for his calm presence the way I did.

I started in the direction where Ethan had stood a moment ago. He had to understand what it meant when he lost his cool like that in front of everyone, but as I neared the table, he wasn't there. I stopped and turned in a full circle. Scanning the room, I realized he was gone.

Neighbors were wrapping up trays of cold cuts and cheese by the time Simon Aldridge, the former owner of Ethan's property and eternal nuisance to our family, decided it was his duty to drop in. He wore an old dress shirt with a brown stain down the front and leaned heavily on a wooden cane. He stood in the doorway with his feet far apart, as if to keep his balance, ready himself for battle, or both. I hadn't seen him up close for years. He had arranged his hawkish face into a scowl and looked like he'd aged at least a decade.

"Well, if it isn't Riley. You're looking fine this evening." He glanced down at my legs.

"Hello, Simon. I didn't expect to see you here. I guess you're feeling better?"

"I still feel like hell," he snapped and sucked in a labored breath. "But I'm not seeing a doctor for COVID. They're the ones invented it. They'd probably smother me in my sleep for the Medicaid check. But I made a ventilator for myself just fine." He straightened his bony shoulders. "Parts from a fish tank and some tubing. Still don't feel right, though." He punctuated this point with a lung-rattling cough.

"Hmm, that's really something. You know, we're finishing up, but there's some food over there if you want to take some with you." It was my best Midwestern brush-off, sending someone home with food.

I was grateful to see Marco appear next to me with his arms crossed. "Simon, glad to see you're able to make it. Can I make up a plate for you to take with you?"

Simon eyed Marco and curled his lip. "Nah, I don't want any tacos, but thanks anyway." He narrowed his eyes. "I s'pose it was you that covered for him while he was gone that day? I guess you're a loyal people for all your faults."

I looked at Marco. He'd set his face into the mask of infinite patience I'd seen him use his whole life to deal with ignorance and ugliness, but he also had a baffled expression as he studied Simon. "Who exactly is it that I covered for?"

"Your amigo, Ethan. You work with him. You had to notice he was missing."

The door had been propped open as people carried trays of food out to their cars, and I noticed Osborne stood in the doorway now, watching the scene unfold.

Marco looked at me with concern and then at Osborne. "I don't know what he's talking about."

"I saw him there that day. He came from the cemetery. That's still my land, and it's my freedom to be there. I'm a sovereign citizen. Government has no right to take what's mine." Simon looked around at all of us. His face had turned a mottled gray and his chest heaved, but he had a brightness in his eyes like he was enjoying himself.

Osborne took a step closer. "Mr. Aldridge, are you saying you saw Ethan on the afternoon Beth died? Why didn't you mention this to Polly yesterday?"

"Well, I guess I'm telling you now. And I don't owe anything to her. She was one of 'em that turned me out of my own house. But I want them," he nodded at us with a sneer, "to know what their golden boy was up to that day."

Marco appealed to Osborne. "Ethan was hauling corn and fixing the silo belt. I told you that he was in and out, but that's because he had to go between the farm and the field."

Osborne put a hand on Simon's arm and Simon shook it off. Osborne held his hands out and stepped back. "Why don't you come with me, Mr. Aldridge, and we can sit down and talk about what you saw."

Simon was starting to teeter. He looked like he was about to argue and then shrugged. "I can talk with you, I guess."

My heart, which had been racing since I'd seen Liam and Osborne leave for a talk, now felt like it would explode. Osborne was motioning Simon toward an unoccupied table across the room. I grabbed his arm. "Please, you can't believe what he says. He's hated our family since my dad bought their land. Then when Ethan bought his house at auction . . . he's just saying this to get Ethan in trouble. He probably thinks he'll somehow get his house back."

Simon turned and looked down the crooked bridge of his nose at me. "You're not so smart, Riley, for all your education. You don't even know what your own family gets up to."

Osborne gently shook off my arm; I had the feeling of being very politely punched in the gut. "Come with me, Mr. Aldridge." He looked at Marco and me. "Please give us some space." Polly joined them at the table at the opposite end of the room and pulled out a folding chair for Simon. He coughed violently in Polly's face and settled into the chair with a grin.

After a moment, he caught his breath and started to tell his story as another deputy ushered the rest of us outside.

The next morning, I woke to see I'd missed a dozen calls, some from an unknown number and several from Mom. I decided to make some coffee before I called her back, but my phone buzzed before I had a chance. The word *Mother* popped up on my screen. I took a centering breath and answered.

"Hi, Mom."

"They've arrested Ethan." Her words were clipped and breathless. "Oh my God, Riley. What are we going to do?"

A bolt of electricity ran through me from my neck to my legs. I managed to set my mug on the counter and sat down. "Where is he?"

"In the Wicksburg jail. I called an attorney that Polly recommended, and he's going to see him. What will we do?" she asked again.

"How can they arrest him? Just based on Simon's word?"

"I don't know. I don't know anything else. The lawyer said they have to give him a bail hearing within three days."

I sluggishly tried to remember what day it was. I'd scheduled time off of work and the days had taken on a nightmarish pace where each one lasted an eternity, yet the shock was as fresh as if we had found out about Beth moments ago. It was Monday morning, so they could keep him until Thursday.

"I'll be right there," I told her, hung up, and grabbed my keys.

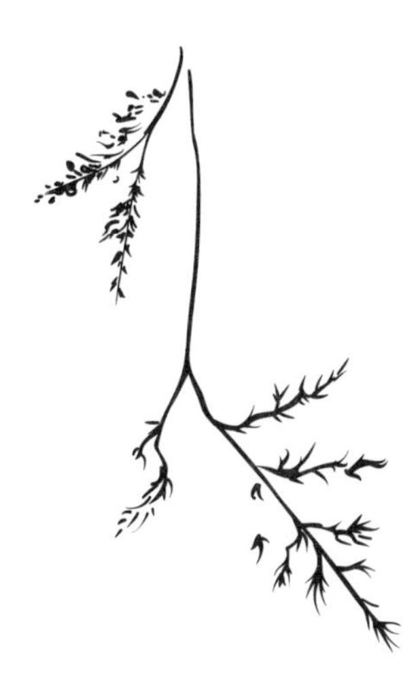

# CHAPTER TWELVE

*September 26, 2022*

The first thing Audra told me when she met me at Mom's front door was that Ethan would not be allowed visitors, aside from his lawyer, until tomorrow at the earliest. I heard the hollowness in my own voice when I assured her this would all be cleared up before then. The second thing Audra told me was to brace myself.

I walked into the living room to find Mom, deathly pale and pacing like a caged wolf. In a high, quaking voice, she erupted, first with how this was my fault for sleeping through Ethan's calls from jail this morning, then Audra and Marco's fault for moving to Wicksburg. Most of all, it was Beth's fault for getting herself killed. I told myself she didn't mean any of it, but the words still stung. After less than an hour, my Aunt Caroline—who, as my Dad's sister, possessed some of his Mom-whispering abilities—murmured in my ear that it might be best if we gave her some time.

Turned out from Mom's, Audra and I drove the half mile to Ethan's house, where the police had released the remaining cordoned-off rooms overnight. I unlocked the door with Audra at my side, the tense silence

between us a high-pitched hum. After being packed with police for the past few days, the house felt eerily empty and still. Stepping in from the bluster of wind and leaves, we stood uncertainly in the mudroom, like intruders in a stranger's house. I glanced at Audra, wondering where her mind was, and saw her gaze come to rest on a storage bin full of scrapers and wallpaper remover. I saw the wheels turning.

She clenched and unclenched her fists. "Maybe we should put our nervous energy to use."

I knew she meant we should finish Beth's last project for Ethan: removing the wallpaper in the spare room. A sound escaped me—half laugh, half sob—because it was exactly like something my dad would have said. *Take something bad and do something good.* I opened my mouth to say that was the last thing I felt like doing. Then, I realized I had no better ideas and that doing something constructive, however mundane, might dull my sense of helplessness.

That was how, on the day of my brother's arrest for murdering his fiancée, I found myself with shaking hands peeling a fingernail-sized shred of wallpaper from a spot that I'd been scratching at for two full minutes.

"This is not as cathartic as I'd hoped," I told Audra. The wallpaper had been applied over the original wood paneling and bonded to it like a coat of paint. Beth had done some prep work, scoring the paper along the edge of each wood panel, and completed about two-thirds of the room before her death. I shivered as I thought about her spending some of her last hours in this room as I followed the slow, repetitive process of scoring, soaking, chiseling, cleaning, soaking, chiseling a bit more, sponging up glue, and then drying the wood. As the shock of the news began to melt away, the gravity of Ethan's situation replaced it.

"What have you heard from Polly?" I asked Audra.

"She hasn't texted me back. You know, she can't tell me everything." Audra didn't look away from her scraping, but her breezy tone told me that Polly ghosting her bothered her, even if she could see the logic behind it. "But you know Sandra, that I worked with at Children's Services?"

"Sandra?" No picture emerged from the mist rolling around my brain. "You know I'm not good with names."

"Well, you're also not good with faces."

"That's true," I acknowledged.

Audra gave me a pitying look. "But you're good with dogs. You never forget a dog."

I accepted the meager compliment and gestured for Audra to get to the point.

"Anyway, Sandra's cousin is the office manager for the medical examiner, and she said the coroner found bruising on Beth's wrists and left cheek. The wound on her head is what killed her, like they thought, and that probably came from a fall on the patio. There was lots of blood there. But with the bruises, it looks like someone pushed her, or at least she fought with someone. Then, she was moved, obviously." Audra blew out a shaky breath after this otherwise clinical recitation of the facts.

As sick as I felt listening to the details of Beth's injuries, Audra's words brought Ethan's innocence into clearer focus. He would never have left her lying in her own blood to die.

The specifics about how Beth had been found had filtered out over the three days since. I remembered them all too well: at the edge of the woods northwest of here, about a hundred yards from the road, wrapped in a sheet and left in a pretty spot where the river bent to the west. The image of her swaddled in the sheet in the wet leaves seemed to have imprinted itself on my optic nerve and floated in from the darkness whenever I closed my eyes. I wondered if the sheet had just been a practical way to move her or if there had been more reason behind wrapping her up.

"I don't get why someone would bother moving her," I said. "What does that accomplish?"

"Maybe they didn't want her to be found here, or didn't want her to be found right away?" Audra didn't look at me as she spoke, and something in the way she said it made me wonder if she shared my certainty about Ethan's innocence.

Polly had helped to secure the scene and had hinted to Audra that the heavy rain had obliterated any footprints or tire tracks that would have been left. She'd also said the ground beneath Beth had been dry, which meant that by the time I'd stood on the porch waiting for the police and watching the rain cross the fields, Beth was already dead.

I imagined the rain wetting her senseless skin. "Do they know if it was quick?"

"I don't know. All I know is it was the wound on her head that killed her. They think somewhere between three and six o'clock. I'd guess she was unconscious, at least." Audra watched me out of the corner of her eye as she continued. "You know how the techs found blood on the patio in the back? I guess they found traces of blood in the bed of Ethan's truck too."

I looked sharply at her but didn't reply right away. My vision blurred as I dipped my sponge into the bucket of lukewarm water and wrung it out. This was news to me.

My first instinct was to dispute it.

"Did you get that from Polly or from Sandra's brother-in-law's third cousin?"

Audra scowled. "From Polly. And if you don't want me to tell you what I'm hearing, that's fine." She punished me with her silence for a full minute, scraping angrily at a remnant of wallpaper.

I felt the walls closing in on Ethan, and my thoughts whirled. Clearly the police had suspected him from the start given the personal nature of the crime, and now they had Simon's statement to back up their theory and blood in Ethan's truck.

How motivated would they be to look at other suspects now that they had their prime suspect in custody?

I mulled over what Audra had said. "Traces of blood? So, they don't even know if it's Beth's?" Audra shrugged and I continued. "That doesn't really prove anything. Blood could have gotten there lots of ways. Ethan bangs himself up all the time at work. I'd be more surprised if there *wasn't* blood somewhere in his truck."

"I wouldn't say it like that to too many people." Audra's gaze warmed the side of my face again. "Not that I think he did anything," she said after a beat.

We worked in silence for a few minutes before she asked, "Do you think Ethan was really here that afternoon?"

I almost snapped, *What are you trying to say, Audra?* But when I looked at her, I saw the fear written all over her face—the same fear of the unknown that I'd felt in my lowest moments over the past few days.

I took a deep breath and thought back to my conversation with Ethan on the porch the evening Beth went missing as the rain fell around us. "He told me he hadn't talked to her since that morning. I believe him over Simon." At least I wanted to believe him over Simon. At the moment, I couldn't hold a single thought in my head long enough to distinguish what I truly believed from what I wanted to believe.

A heavy silence fell over us again, broken by the sounds of our scraping and scrubbing. Outside the day was gray and unsettled. The timbers of the house creaked against the occasional gust of wind.

I ran my hand through my hair as I considered the timeline of Beth's last hours. "You know, I heard Charlotte talking to Mom at the memorial. She said Beth rushed her out of the house before she could do a fitting on her gown."

Audra gave me a smirk that said there was nothing unusual about wanting to escape Charlotte.

"I know," I acknowledged. "I mean, who hasn't wanted to get rid of Charlotte at some point, but I think Beth would have put up with her long enough to have her gown fitted. I mean, the wedding was in a few weeks, and Charlotte would have had to make alterations and bring it back. It doesn't make sense. Why wouldn't Beth let her fit her gown? She'd just have to do it some other time."

"Maybe she was having second thoughts about the wedding."

"But why would she still text me about picking up my gown if that was it? Charlotte mentioned she was late getting here. What if Beth was expecting someone else that afternoon, someone she didn't want Charlotte to see, so she had to rush her off?"

Audra wrung out her sponge and frowned. "You mean Liam?"

"I don't know who, but it wouldn't be Ethan. It wouldn't matter if Charlotte saw him—"

"You don't look good, Riley," Audra interrupted.

"Well, you don't look so great either, Audra," I retorted. Aside from her red-rimmed eyes, she looked fantastic.

Audra knitted her brows. "No, you're white as a sheet. Well, more so. Why don't you sit down?"

I realized I was winded from the effort of talking, squatting, and scrubbing. A year ago, I could run miles without losing my breath; now I couldn't strip wallpaper. My hands and feet felt fiery, tight, and itchy. Looking down, I saw my fingers were splotched an angry purplish-red. I flexed my swollen knuckles.

"Okay, let's take a break."

I sank down onto an upside-down bucket and looked at the room: we had made incremental progress. All that was left was a wall about three feet high, under the eaves, along the back of the house. While I caught my breath, Audra moved pieces of an old metal-frame bed out of the way and went to work wetting this last section.

I thought about who else Beth could have been expecting that day. Really, anyone other than Ethan or Doug would have set Charlotte off gossiping. Besides, Doug had been in Chicago that day. Liam seemed the most likely possibility. As one of the few people who still believed in Ethan, I had to consider who else might have had a reason or opportunity to harm Beth. But I needed Audra's perspective. While I had lived away from home for the past ten years, she had spent all but the last year of her life here. Unlike me, she still had connections to everyone from North Haven to Wicksburg.

"Liam was supposed to be combining that afternoon in the field on Old Bridge. Do you think he could have snuck away without anyone noticing?

Ethan was hauling corn from the field back to the farm, but he had to fix the conveyor belt too, so if Liam knew that . . ."

"Liam would know he had some extra time," Audra finished for me. "In fact, he probably would have had to wait if he filled the wagon before Ethan could get back. It's less than a mile from that field to Ethan's, so he could have slipped out and returned in the time Ethan was away. I wonder if anyone else was in the field with them. What did Osborne say when you told him that Liam visited Beth?"

"He said he'd talk to Liam, and he did at the memorial, but that's all I know. But then Simon showed up—it seems like the police should be looking at Simon too. I mean, if it's true that he saw Ethan, then he was obviously nearby as well."

"Yeah, but Simon can barely haul his own body around, let alone Beth's —unless you think he's faking. Maybe he's not as sick as he's letting on."

"As much as I would like to pin the blame on Simon, I don't think you can fake that kind of phlegm—" As I'd spoken, Audra had begun vigorously scraping away at the low wall and generating more racket than I'd thought possible. The wood paneling rattled and knocked with her motion. "How are you managing to make so much noise over there? What's with the thumping?"

"What is . . . oh? The paneling is loose here. I'd love to see *you* scrape this section without making noise. I know Ethan loves it, but this house is a wreck." She placed the edge of her scraper along the scored edge of a panel and angled it to show me a gap between it and the framing behind it. As she twisted the blade of her scraper, widening the gap to make her point, the entire section of paneling popped free from the wall and fell to the floor with a bang.

"Audra, did you break that off?" I stood up in surprise.

"No, I didn't! How can you break a wall? It was already like that." She caught her breath. "Oh my God, Riley, look! It's a little hideaway back there."

"What?" I picked up the piece of paneling that had broken free. On the back of it, a latch had been attached. Running my hand along the opening in the wall, I felt a little groove at the top of the rectangular opening left behind. "It's like a trap door."

The ceiling angled down at this end of the room and the wall was only a few feet high. I got down on my knees and peered into the rectangular opening. "It extends all along this wall. Look."

Audra shined the light from her phone into the opening. "It's about six feet across."

"Why was it paneled over?" I looked again at the latch on the back of the panel. Although the latch was metal and looked relatively new, there were marks on the old paneling where hinges must have once been attached to the side, allowing the piece to swing open like a door. "Do you think this is part of the Underground Railroad?"

"I have no idea. I suppose it could be. The house is old enough, and this paneling looks original, but I've never heard of this house being part of it." Audra ducked her head inside the space to get a better look inside.

"There's a storage container back here. It's one of those plastic bins, so it can't be that old. How could that have gotten there?" Audra looked at a scrap of the orange-and-brown flowered paper. "This wallpaper's been here since at least the seventies."

Audra pulled the bin closer to the opening.

"Wait, Audra, don't! Should we be touching this? I mean, who put it back there? And when?" I thought about how Beth had scored the wallpaper along the edges of each wood panel. With the edges precut, the piece of paneling could have been removed and put back without disturbing the surrounding wallpaper. "What if it was Beth? She's the one who was working in this room. She could have found this when she was prepping the wall. She cut around the panels." I traced around the edge of one with my finger to show Audra. "She could have taken this piece off and put it back on. Maybe the police should look at it?"

Audra eyed me steadily, a thread of dust clinging to her hair where she had ducked her head into the opening. She was uncharacteristically hesitant. "But what if *Ethan* put this back here and it makes things worse for him?"

I weighed her question and felt my stomach turn at the possibilities. A gust of wind rattled the leaves in the big oak outside the window, and the timbers of the house groaned some more.

"Okay," I answered. "Then let's look at it first, but don't touch it bare-handed. Use this cloth to pull it out. We can always put it back if it's nothing important and act like we never touched it. And let's clean up the wallpaper mess in front of the opening or else we'll get glue all over the bottom and they'll be able to tell we had it out."

"You're disturbingly good at this," Audra said as she took the cloth I handed her.

We tidied the floor in front of the opening, and Audra dragged out the storage container. It was blue with plastic latches on either end and had almost no dust on it. She looked at me, hesitating for only a second before popping up the latches and lifting the lid. We both peered in.

Stacked neatly on one side of the container were plastic bags full of blue pills and on the other side, stacks of cash. In a baggie in the middle was a cellphone.

"Fuck."

The room went still. Even the wind hushed. I sank back on my heels and looked at Audra, who had gone pale beneath her golden complexion.

"Is it Beth's or Ethan's?" She didn't look at me.

I ran my hands over my face, smelling the chemicals from the wallpaper remover and feeling the rough remnants of paste against my skin. I thought of the haunted looks I'd caught on Beth's face, the lies, and the promise not to hurt Ethan. This had to be at least part of what Beth had been keeping from everyone.

I uncovered my face and stared at the pills. "It has to have been Beth's," I answered finally. "I doubt Ethan knew—I'm pretty sure he didn't even know about the bottle of pills she had." I massaged my forehead. "What if we give it to the police and they test for fingerprints? If his prints aren't on it—"

"What if they are?" Audra kept her eyes on the bin. "And whether he was involved or not, it's in his house. It'll look like he was in on it."

I nodded, contemplating all the possible outcomes. Audra had a point. The discovery of drugs in his house would complicate his bail hearing, to say the least. "Okay. Nobody else sees this until we know more."

We both sat for a long time, looking at the bin, until Audra asked, "What if Ethan didn't know but then he found out?"

I felt a flash of anger. "Why don't you just say what you mean?"

"I'm not saying anything. I'm asking you."

Looking at her pinched expression, I took a deep breath. What *would* Ethan have done if he'd found that Beth had been hiding something like this? How angry would he have been?

I waved the possibility away. "There's no point thinking like that. We don't know whether he knew about it or not. The bigger question is where it came from. Someone had to be bringing all of this to Beth. She hardly left the house except for family things or doctor's appointments . . ." I trailed off.

"Dr. Maclean," Audra exclaimed.

"No, not Dr. Maclean."

"Why not Dr. Maclean? Beth was seeing her for chronic pain. She has all kinds of chronic-pain patients. *Refrain from pain.* It makes complete sense! She gave it to Beth, and Beth distributed it. Remember, she asked you about opioids when I was there."

"She asked if I used them. She didn't ask if I wanted some!"

"Well, she acted weird about it, like she was testing the waters to see if you might be interested."

I tried to think back to Dr. Maclean's face during the discussion, but all I could recall was her acknowledgment of the pain I'd been in and the anxiety of not knowing the cause. "No, Dr. Maclean wouldn't. She's been a good doctor so far."

"Well, she's not such a good doctor if she's dealing painkillers and murdered our future sister-in-law." Audra crossed her arms.

"Well, no doctor is perfect. At least she's in network."

Audra rolled her eyes. "It's something you need to consider."

I shook my head. "I don't see it. Plus, I don't think she could have moved Beth."

"Why not? She looks athletic. And could have had help, like a henchman," Audra suggested.

"A henchman? I'm not sure people keep henchmen anymore." I scanned the contents of the bin. "We should check the phone. Maybe there are contacts or messages." I pulled my sleeve over my hand and picked it up, careful not to touch it.

"Give me the cloth." Audra handed me a clean rag, which I laid on the floor. I slid the phone out of the baggie onto it. It was a cheap, black phone. I held my breath and pushed the power button. Nothing happened.

Audra, who watched me press the power button multiple times as she leaned over my shoulder, waited in silence as long as she could. "Is it on?"

I looked at her. "It's dead. We need a charger." I examined the bottom of the phone. "Mine should work."

I dug through my bag for my charger and checked it against the phone. It fit. I wiggled the other end of my charger into an ancient outlet, praying it wouldn't blow a fuse in the fragile electrical system. After a second, a red light illuminated the top of the phone.

"What now?" Audra asked.

I paced back and forth between the charger and the opening in the wall, checking the red light on the side of the phone with each pass.

"We wait."

# CHAPTER THIRTEEN

*One Month Earlier—August 27, 2022*

Ethan had just turned twenty-eight, which meant for the next month, he and I would be the same age. As kids we had dubbed this Twin Month and pretended for those four weeks that we were actual twins. We coordinated the colors we wore, invented secret words, and attempted to read each other's minds. During our seventh Twin Month, we conducted an experiment where I stuck a needle into the pad of my thumb to see if Ethan could feel the pain. He had doubled over and fallen to the ground, wailing and insisting that it had caused him great agony.

Although we'd mutually agreed that Twin Month was for babies by the time we were ten, Ethan and I still celebrated together whenever we could. This year, we'd gathered at the Haven, the only bar in North Haven, with a few of his friends. The Haven sat on Main Street along the river, wedged into a row of old flat-fronted buildings between the Pizza Barn and the closed hardware store. What had been a lively little town when I was growing up, with colorful Victorian houses, a soda fountain, shops, and a diner, had dwindled until even the grocery store had closed. Now, of all the

grand Victorian homes along Main Street, only Polly's sported a fresh coat of paint. Gaps, like missing teeth, had sprung up between businesses where buildings had burned or been demolished over the years and never rebuilt. A faceless investment company—presumably from out of town since they had money—had recently acquired a few of the remaining buildings that backed up to the river. For now, they still sat empty, their front windows boarded up or painted over.

The group celebrating Ethan's birthday pushed two sticky tables together and gathered beneath the glow of the year-round Christmas lights that were draped along the rafters of the Haven. Friends had drifted in and out all night, buying Ethan drinks. By now it was after midnight, and only a handful of us remained. Our drunken conversation had devolved from high-school memories, to who among our acquaintances was having extramarital affairs, to the Cleveland Browns, and, finally, aliens.

I listened as Jeremy, who was passionately Team Alien, tried to convince Ethan that extraterrestrials had visited North Haven. "The mayor told me himself. He saw something he couldn't explain behind the preserve. Like a football with dancing lights. It hovered there and then, *fwoop,* shot straight back up." Jeremy thrust his beer bottle up from the table to demonstrate. "Didn't make a sound. And he's the *mayor.*"

Ethan eyed Jeremy skeptically and rubbed his chin. "Sounds like the mayor saw a drone." He laughed and turned to Marco. "You ever see any dancing footballs around here?"

Marco had come but not Audra, who had stayed home with the kids. She hadn't attended many family gatherings since the summer party when she'd found out about Mom's plans to transfer ownership of the farm to Ethan over the next few years. She had put the freeze on Mom and Ethan, speaking to them only when it couldn't be avoided. Although Audra and I would inherit the equivalent value of the farm one day, we both knew it was wrong to exclude Marco from the business he'd worked so hard to grow.

I hadn't sensed any resentment from Marco but wondered if he just hid it better than Audra. Pretty much everyone hid their feelings better than

Audra. Marco smiled and shook his head at Ethan's question. "I've never seen anything myself, but you know my brother, Arnoldo? When we were little in Jalisco, he was out playing with his friends one night. He came running home and told my mom there was a giant silver saucer hovering over the mountains." Marco outlined the shape of a disc with a finger. "She said he'd had too much sun and just seen a cloud, but then the next day we heard from all kinds of people who saw the same thing."

"Thank you!" Jeremy gestured toward Marco. Then, to Ethan: "See, there's *stuff* out there—stuff we can't explain," he whispered.

Ethan smiled indulgently at Jeremy. "Everyone's got their own opinion." He shrugged as if nothing more could possibly be said on the topic.

"But it's not an *opinion,*" Jeremy protested. He'd matched Ethan drink for drink and wasn't backing down. "The mayor *saw* it!"

Ethan put his arm around Beth and frowned. "Okay, not an opinion, maybe, but people see it differently. Like I think it's a drone. The mayor and you believe it's a UFO." He shrugged again.

I laughed. "Yeah, but that's not a belief either. It either happened or it didn't." Ethan scowled at me as I took another sip of my wine, which tasted like grape juice mixed with vodka. Even as it destroyed my palate, it was growing on me. "All beliefs aren't equal. Some are based on evidence, and others . . ." I waved them away with my hand.

"Thank you! That's what I'm saying." Jeremy widened his eyes at me in gratitude.

Ethan took his arm off of Beth's shoulders and tilted his head. "Well, thanks for those kernels of wisdom, Riley. Since you know so much, why don't you enlighten us?" He propped his chin on his hands, like a child engrossed in story time. Beth rolled her eyes.

I could feel myself slipping into the toxic routine Ethan and I had developed over the past year: I disagreed with him, and he sneered that I thought I was so smart. Then I got offended and tried to prove just how smart I was, indeed. In my better moments, I resisted the tug to battle him, but that night, amped up on hard grape juice, was not one of those moments.

"Well, I don't know what happened behind the preserve, but I know that there are experts who study this stuff or have seen things that are unexplained—scientists at SETI who monitor space for radio waves and . . . things like that." It was only when I tried to articulate what I'd heard or read that it dawned on me how little I actually knew, but I powered on. "And there have been pilots who have caught videos of objects doing maneuvers that aviation experts can't explain. Or you can have multiple eyewitnesses, like Marco said. Even behind the preserve, people could put up cameras and try to record something if they really wanted to know. I'm not saying there *is* or is *not* something. I'm just saying that there are ways of finding out and looking for proof, not just opinions and beliefs." I drained my wine and placed my glass on the table with a clatter.

When I mentioned recordings, Beth shot me an odd look, but Jeremy's eyes had lit up. He started explaining to Marco how he'd seen the videos pilots had taken and they were exactly like what Mayor Hankins had described. I kept my eyes on Ethan. He'd been accepting drinks throughout the night, and looking at his flushed face and half-mast eyes, I realized how hammered he was and knew he was entering his aggrieved phase. Bumping his chair, he stood and clapped. "That's great, Ri. I'm glad that all those years of college taught you such a fancy way of telling us all that you don't know a damn thing. Yet, somehow, you still know better than all of us." He laughed, and Beth shot him a sharp look.

Jeremy and Marco were engrossed in their conversation, but Ethan kept his focus on me and leaned toward my ear. "If you put so much stock in evidence, you should listen to your doctors."

His words hit like a jab to my chest. I recoiled from his alcohol-soured breath. "What's that supposed to mean?"

"I mean, if there's no evidence of something, then . . ." He held his hands apart. "Maybe there's nothing there. You said so yourself."

Tears sprung to my eyes. "When did you become such an asshole?"

He shrugged lazily and fell back into his chair. The UFO conversation carried on without us. No one but Beth had noticed our exchange. Blindly,

I rose from my chair. Tears in my eyes, I kept my head down as I made my way to the ladies' room. Once inside, I leaned against the beat-up black door and caught my breath, trying to convince myself not to cry, which only made me want to cry more.

At my back, someone pushed on the door. "Riley?" Beth's voice was muffled. "Can I come in?"

I moved, and Beth crowded with me into the small space that smelled overpoweringly of whatever scent was being shot out of a plug-in air freshener. In her yellow sundress, she looked out of place in the grimy bathroom with its scuffed green walls. The fluorescent ceiling light blinked and buzzed. I noticed how thin Beth had become with the harsh light emphasizing the hollows in her cheeks.

"What did he say?"

I didn't want to repeat it. Ethan had verbalized my secret fears: that I was imagining my illness. That everybody could see this but me. Dr. Maclean's latest round of tests had found nothing more than low levels of antinuclear antibodies, which could signal autoimmune disease but could also be found in healthy people. Another nonanswer. She'd asked me to come back in for another appointment, but after so many tests showed that I was "fine," I'd begun to wonder. I wasn't afraid of the stigma of mental illness. I'd been through depression in college and—as hard as that was—I could accept that if it gave me some route toward getting better. What shook me was that I didn't *feel* that this was in my head. If I couldn't know my own body, what could I know?

I wasn't ready to say all of this to Beth. I gave her the short version. "He thinks I'm making too much of being sick . . . or whatever this is."

Beth raised her shoulders and let them drop. "He doesn't know what it's like. He's got the energy of ten people and has hardly been sick a day in his life. He can't understand. That's why I talk to you about my back more than I do with him."

"But he understands when you feel bad." I regretted saying it the moment it came out. I didn't want to make this a competition—the suffering

Olympics—but I also couldn't understand why Ethan so readily sympathized with Beth's limitations but not mine. I tried to smooth it over. "I just don't get why he can't believe me." My voice wavered.

Beth frowned as she considered my question. "I think it's because he was there in the hospital with me after the accident and *saw* it. I didn't have to tell him or explain it, because he was there through it all. He knew what bones were broken, and the doctor showed us my pinched nerves on the imaging. Other things"—she motioned to me—"aren't so easy to see. It's harder for him to understand, especially since he's never experienced anything like it himself." She paused. "But I know that what you're feeling is real. I know what it's like not being believed. To have doctors think you're just looking for attention or pills." She shook her head. "But nobody knows what you feel better than you."

"I'm just so tired of it."

"I know," she said, and I could tell from her pained expression that she knew better than anyone.

It wasn't Ethan's callousness but Beth's kindness that finally made me bawl. As I snuffled, Beth gathered me into a light hug. "It's okay. I know," she murmured again. When my tears began wetting her shoulder, she nudged me away, wrinkled her nose at the damp spot I'd left, and grabbed a handful of paper towels so we could clean ourselves up.

Although I still sniffled and hiccupped, I felt better, like I'd unburdened myself of a shameful secret. It was a relief to know that Beth understood. We didn't have to make excuses to each other for our smaller lives, for needing to go home early or not go out at all. These were the only lives we could manage right now. Looking at her hollow cheeks, at that moment, I sensed that we both felt a growing desperation that if we couldn't figure out how to get better, we might be constrained to these small lives forever.

I wiped my face and took some deep breaths. Beth handed me powder and lipstick from her purse, which I dutifully applied. With the strong red color on my lips, I didn't look like myself, but I liked the change.

"You look nice," she said with a small smile. "Let's go."

Back at the table, Marco sat with Ethan, who had his head bent over a plastic cup of water now instead of a beer.

Marco frowned at his phone and looked like he was deep in thought tapping out a text, but he tucked it into his pocket when he saw me and motioned me over. "You okay?" he asked with a smile.

"I'm all right." When his smile faded, his face looked sad and tired. As much time as Marco and I spent in each other's company, he and I seldom talked one to one, and then it was usually about the kids or stories about the farm, never about Marco himself. "How about you?" I asked.

"Ready to go whenever you are." The smile was back, and I wondered if I'd glimpsed anything at all. He and I were carpooling back to Wicksburg, and he'd insisted on being the designated driver. He'd had one beer to toast Ethan early in the night and nothing but water since then. Now he was helping Ethan sober up. More than once, I'd wondered where my family would be without Marco quietly holding things together.

Beside Marco, Ethan looked up at me sheepishly and patted the seat beside him. "C'mere." After a moment's hesitation, I sat next to him. He draped his arm roughly around my shoulders. "I don't wanna fight with you. Don't listen to me when I'm drunk."

It was a non-apology. "No, it's good to know how you really feel." I shrugged off his arm.

"Don't be like that."

"We'll talk tomorrow." Now wasn't the time. I was hurt and both of us were drunk.

"Ah man, tomorrow." He leaned his chair back on two legs and regarded me with a drunken grin. "My birthday party. What kind of cake do you think Mom will come up with this year?"

Annoyed as I was, I couldn't help but smile back. "Last year's will be hard to top." Mom had made an anatomically correct Holstein dairy cow. It had been remarkably accurate; so much so that no one had felt comfortable cutting into the pink udder. "Look, I'm tired. I'm going to head out, but I'll see you tomorrow. Happy birthday."

"You're always tired," Ethan complained. "See you tomorrow."

I sighed and glanced at Marco, who nodded. As he and Jeremy discussed staffing for the morning milking, I watched Ethan sip his water and cast glances at Beth, who studied her phone. His appearance struck me anew, like it was the first time I had really looked at him in a long time. Although he looked pretty much the same physically—a bit heavier in the jaw—I realized something in his expression had changed. He no longer looked like the kid with the infectious curiosity who found the good in everyone. Instead, I saw a man drawn into himself, his eyes scanning the room, on the lookout for slights. Spending that much time looking for something, he was bound to find it.

Audra had once informed me that about every seven years, we replace all of our cells and essentially become new people. By those calculations Ethan and I had created and discarded several versions of ourselves since that seventh Twin Month when he had writhed in pain at the needle in my finger.

I was pretty sure Audra's scientific fun fact wasn't true, or was at least an oversimplification, but as I looked at Ethan, it felt about right. Each day I recognized less and less of the kid from twenty-one years ago who swore he could feel the hurt that I felt.

We were all sitting down for Ethan's birthday dinner at Mom's the next day when we learned of Perk's overdose. Perk—or Priscilla as only her paychecks called her—was one of dozens of kids who cycled through as part-time help over the years and became like extended family to us, working side by side with us kids and joining us for meals, and then inviting us to celebrate their graduation parties and weddings as they grew up. Perk had made it to graduation but just barely.

Marco was the one to get the text. He whispered something to Audra, who cried out and let a serving bowl piled high with mashed potatoes clatter to the table. Audra told the rest of us, and the room went silent. Even Franky looked around at the hush and kept quiet, sensing something was deeply wrong. Across from me, Beth flushed and caught her breath.

Only eighteen years old, Perk had been a favorite. Despite her small, wiry frame, she threw herself into the physicality of farm work. She'd had a walk so full of bundled energy that she practically skipped. When she bottle-fed the baby calves, she sang to them, and after her shifts, she'd climb up into the haymow to coax out the wild kittens that hid out in the narrow gaps between bales. Following her graduation, everyone had been sorry to see her leave for a full-time job at the printing plant in Wicksburg. It was inconceivable that someone who had overflowed with life had suddenly, utterly ceased to be.

With all the warm food laid out on the table, we still ate, though without appetite, and sang to Ethan. He dutifully blew out his candles on the cake that Mom had made, this year in the shape of his house, complete with purple flowers in the window boxes.

At the conclusion of the subdued celebration, Beth and I left to walk in the woods, as we often did on Sunday afternoons at my mom's, escaping the post-dinner chatter and chaos of our family, the kids screeching around in circles, and whatever guests Mom had invited or the kids had brought along that particular week. The effort to follow the overlapping conversations and track the constant motion exhausted me. Once outside, my frenetic brain waves settled into a more regular rhythm.

Those Sunday walks were a bath of color and sound. North Haven could be brown and dull for long stretches, but during the six months that it was alive, it really lived. The green hills, clear streams, and light through the rustling forest canopy cast their own spell. Black branches and trunks, bright jagged leaves, and the sun, like something tangible and gold, dappled the paths. The broad shadow of an unseen hawk or vulture passed; the silky sparkle of spiderwebs draped like bunting across the path. Unknown birds trilled, living their lives and telling everyone about it. At bends, the creek sang along the stones, carrying what came from somewhere else toward what was next. Above it all, peeks of bright blue sky.

Beth and I seldom broke the sacred spell of these walks with speech, not wanting to interrupt the scattered, perfect order of it all. It filtered through us, like warm water through limestone. At least, it did for me, and I always thought it did for her, beside me on the path, with her head toward the ground or glancing at a shimmer or shadow.

This last Sunday afternoon I spent with her, we'd meandered through the paths, with the late summer bugs whining, our own thoughts layered in with the whisper of leaves. Beth walked slowly with her arms limp, her fingers occasionally twitching like she was flicking away a gnat. Far away in my own mind, I let her fall behind. Thinking about Perk, Ethan's words from the previous night, and the pain shooting from my neck down my back, I hadn't spared a thought as to where Beth's mind was until I heard her cry out behind me.

Turning, I saw her on her hands and knees on the path with her head down. Her long hair grazed the loamy ground and her shoulders shook. For a moment, I froze; something about her posture—on all fours with her head down and face away from me—seemed so private, so primitive and self-contained, that my instinct to check on her felt intrusive, like she was an injured animal who wanted nothing more than to be left alone. An instant later, I went to her, kneeling on the path.

I gripped her arm. "What's wrong?" I tried to see her face through the curtain of her hair. "Is it your back?"

She didn't answer, but when she sat back, I caught my breath. Tears streamed from her eyes, but she laughed without a sound, a stifled, bubbling laugh, like something that had long been trapped inside her had found an escape.

She pressed her hand to her mouth to stifle the laugh and then uncovered it to gulp air. As her breathing slowed, we both looked down at her bloodied hands. Leaves and dirt stuck to the scrapes.

I leaned back from her, uneasy, as if her familiar face suddenly belonged to a stranger. "What's wrong?" I repeated.

When she looked up at me, there was pleading in her brown eyes. Dirt and blood smudged her cheek where she'd pressed her hand to her mouth. For a second, she was about to say it, but then something behind her eyes shifted.

She nodded and smiled. "I'm sorry," she said. "I'm okay. Let's go back. It'll be dark soon anyway."

I wanted to say something else, but no words came to me. Finally, I held out my hand to help her up, and we turned to make our way home on the rough path through the whispering leaves. A dozen times on that slow walk back, I almost cut through the birdsong to ask again if she was okay, but I didn't. I wish I had.

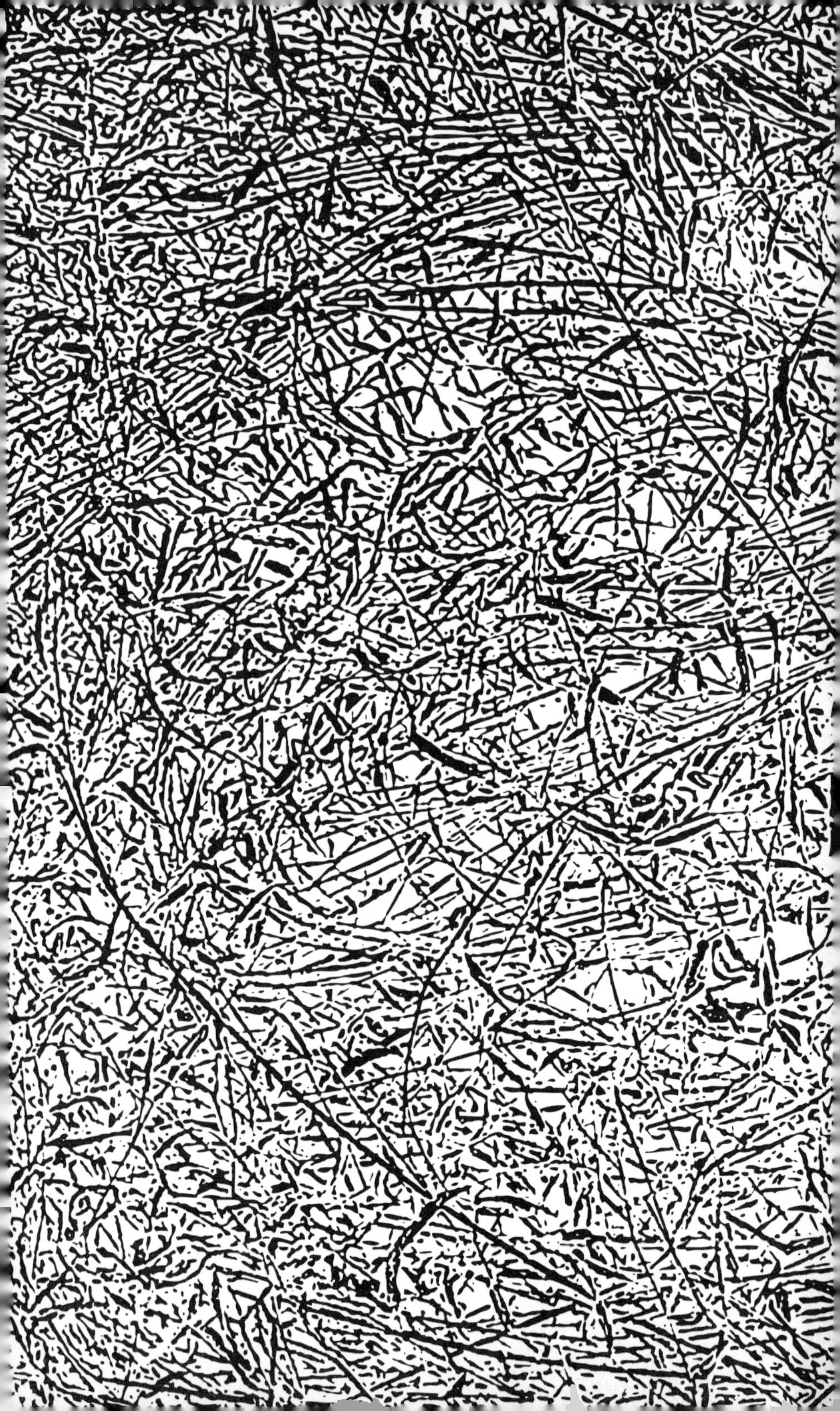

# PART TWO

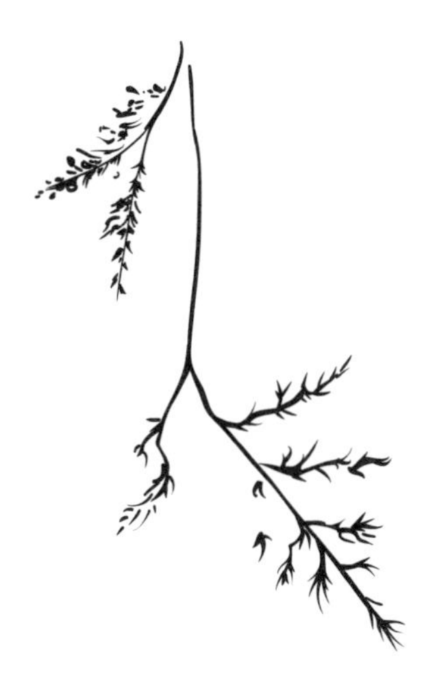

# CHAPTER FOURTEEN

*September 26, 2022*

While I waited for Beth's burner phone to charge, the tension built in my head, as pulsing and electric as a migraine before a violent summer storm. As worried as I'd been about Beth a week ago, I never would have imagined what was to come: her murder, Ethan's arrest, and now the discovery of what she had been hiding. I thought back to all the time I'd spent with her over the past couple of months, but I realized now how little she'd shared with me lately. I had been too beaten down by pain, illness, and keeping up with work to do much other than sprawl companionably on the couch with her and nod off to HGTV. I remembered how Beth had slept too, her breath so slow and shallow that once I'd put my hand in front of her mouth to check that she was still breathing. Looking out the window over the woods, I thought of that last walk we'd taken together, the terrible look on her face when she fell on the path. Whatever had happened to her—and whatever she had done—I owed it to her to find out.

Audra sat on the floor with her back against the wall next to the opening we'd uncovered. She wove her hand through her hair as she stared into

space. I picked up the cheap phone and tested the power button. With a chirpy trill, the screen lit up. A bright geometric pattern dissolved into pixels as it started up.

Audra sat up.

There was a single green bar on the battery indicator. "It's working."

We bent our heads over the phone. A few icons appeared as the screen brightened, just standard apps that would have been preloaded. Still, I flipped through them all. There were no contacts and nothing in the call history, but when I clicked on the message icon, a conversation popped up.

I clicked on it and scrolled to the earliest message to read through the whole conversation. From one month ago:

Beth: *I'm all out*

50871: *Hold tight. More coming soon*

*Can you move 40 units*

Beth: *Not by myself*

50871: *You'll have help*

Beth: *OK*

50871: *Will arrange drop off tomorrow pm and discuss details*

The next set of texts came from just over a week ago. It was clear that in the time between conversations, something had happened to change Beth's tone.

Beth: *I'm not doing this anymore*

*Not worth it*

*I'll leave everything at the tree for you but I'm done*

50871: *Do not leave it at the tree*

*Disappointing*

*We'll talk in person*

*Delete this*

Beth: *OK*

That was it.

Audra sat back on her heels and met my eyes. "That's it! Proof. Someone else was here that day."

"I don't know." I read the messages again. "It doesn't say that. It only says that someone was going to talk with her. We don't know *when* they planned to talk or that it even happened." I imagined how Osborne, or even Polly, would interpret the bin and the texts.

There was still nothing to prove that Ethan wasn't involved. If anything, the presence of drugs and money secreted away in his house could implicate him.

"None of this helps Ethan unless we can show that someone else was actually here that day, or at least figure out who she was talking with. We can't even prove Beth was the one sending these texts. For all the police know, it could have been Ethan."

We sat in silence for another minute. Something outside banged against the house with a gust of wind and set my heart racing.

"Maybe we should look around ourselves," Audra suggested. "Who knows what else might have been missed? There might be other hiding spots, or maybe we'll find something that fits with this."

I nodded. "We should put the bin back where we found it in case someone shows up. Let's make sure there's nothing else back there."

Audra crawled back into the hideaway and emerged a moment later with her nose wrinkled. "Just mouse poop. I need to wash my hands."

I pushed the bin toward her, folding my sleeves around my hands to keep from touching it. "Put this back first, and don't touch it."

With the bin back in place, we repositioned the panel, which snapped into place with a click. The slight gaps at the edge of the panel were more apparent with the wallpaper partially removed.

"Why don't we put that in front of it?" Audra pointed at the old metal bed frame.

We pushed the bed frame in front of the panel and quickly cleaned up the worst of our wallpaper mess. Adrenaline was beginning to surge through my arms and legs at the thought of searching the house. My fingers were clumsy as I tied off a garbage bag full of wallpaper scraps.

"Why don't you check the office and I'll check the bedroom?" I suggested.

Audra nodded and we split up.

Ethan and Beth's bedroom was painted a restful blue gray. Beth had covered the two tall windows with white Roman shades that she had made. On one side of the bed, the white duvet and sheets were still rumpled, as Ethan had left them. Beth's side appeared as untouched as when she had made it days earlier. I blinked, trying to erase the image of the bloody sheet on the line. I imagined Beth moving around this room changing sheets and making the bed in the hours before she died.

Next to Ethan's side of the bed, he'd strewn his socks and a T-shirt across the floor. His bedside table was bare aside from a lamp; Beth's held a matching lamp and a few books, including a volume of Mary Oliver poems, a book on healing pain through the mind-body connection, and a dull-looking library book on wedding venues. I flipped through the books and held each upside down to see if anything of interest fell out, aware that I was probably duplicating the work the detectives had done already. I put the library book back on the table but then picked it up again, figuring no one else would return it if I didn't.

The room had two small closets. I looked in Beth's first. Her dresses, blouses, and skirts hung neatly, organized by color. I felt around the back of the cedar-lined closet for loose boards and secret spaces. Nothing. At the end of her clothes rack, Beth had hung my puce gown that Charlotte had dropped off that day, still in its plastic cover. I removed it from the closet and looked it over. The rosettes around the boatneck collar and the puffy sleeves were flattened beneath the plastic.

I held the dress against me and looked in the mirror that hung on the back of the door, thinking about the wedding that was supposed to have happened in just weeks. My breath caught. I pictured Ethan and Beth on that day, exchanging vows in the gazebo with the autumn trees blazing behind them, taking their first dance, and then, all our family and friends joining in.

Swallowing hard, I put the dress back in the closet and moved on to the drawers. Beth's belongings were rumpled where someone else had already searched. She would have hated people rifling through her belongings, and I felt a pang of guilt for invading her tightly held privacy, but then I thought about all she had hidden and opened another drawer.

Downstairs something banged, and I froze, trying to quiet my breathing, waiting. Nothing but the wind buffeting the house and my heart pumping like crazy in my chest.

I went down the hall to check on Audra, who was sitting on the floor in front of a filing cabinet with several hanging folders beside her.

"Did you hear anything?"

She looked up and shook her head. "Nope, nothing but wind, and there's nothing here but utility bills and receipts for home-improvement stuff. Looks like the police already took most of it." She gestured to the few folders that remained in the filing cabinet. "I'm guessing anything interesting is with them."

"Have you looked through the craft materials?" Shelves on one side of the room were stacked with fabric, cans of paint, sandpaper, and countless other little gadgets whose purpose I didn't recognize.

Audra gave me a look. "You think someone got her with a hot glue gun?"

I ignored her and rummaged through a bin of measuring tapes, shears, a staple gun, a ring light, and a small white video camera. Although it didn't look like a typical webcam, I figured it was something Beth used to document her craft projects. I checked it for a memory card. Empty.

I sighed. I didn't know what I'd expected to find.

"When do you think we'll be able to talk to Ethan?" I asked Audra.

She shrugged. "We can't place calls to him. He has to call out to us. The next visiting hours are tomorrow evening. In the meantime, we keep this to ourselves?"

I nodded and sank into the desk chair, still clutching Beth's library book. Her belongings weren't telling us anything we didn't already know, but I had an idea who might be able to tell us something new.

"What do you think about paying Liam a visit?"

Audra cocked her eyebrows at my question. "You mean now?"

As anxious as I felt to do something, I knew it would be all I could do to get out of this chair and drive home. The events of the past few days had collided and exploded like a million hunks of space junk, orbiting in a chaotic cloud in my head. I needed time on my own to make sense of it all. I needed to go home, look into how bail worked, verify visiting hours, check on Mom—I needed time to wrap my brain around it all.

"How about tomorrow?"

Audra still sat near the filing cabinet, gazing at the sparse collection of hanging folders. She slowly nodded, stood, and straightened a kink out of her back. She squared her shoulders. She liked a good plan, and I knew she was on board before she spoke.

"I'll pick you up tomorrow morning." Her features took on a familiar look of determination. "Liam won't know what's coming."

## CHAPTER FIFTEEN

*September 26, 2022*

Fatigue dragged at me as I turned my key. Opening the thick leaded-glass front door and being greeted by Bruno's joyful wagging was usually enough to cheer me up after even the worst day, but the image of the bin full of pills and cash and the thought of Ethan in jail weighed me down.

After walking Bruno, I lay on my sofa, hoping to fall asleep. My bones felt like heavy irons, and my heart pounded in slow, forceful thuds, but my mind kept reconstructing memories and running through scenarios. Perk's overdose and Beth's breakdown on our walk that day kept surfacing. Had Beth played a role in Perk's death? I fiddled with my phone, wishing I could google an answer to all of this.

Restless, I got up again, ran a bucket of warm water, and poured in some lemon-scented cleaner. As much as my body ached, I knew the drudgery of cleaning would settle my mind. As I scrubbed at the kitchen tile, my shock at what Audra and I had found shifted to anger.

For all of Beth's ambitions for the future of North Haven, I didn't understand how she could have gotten involved in the opioids that were killing

the town. Every few days brought the news of another overdose, often the same people again and again until it was too late. Other times it was someone who had kept their substance abuse secret, even from the people closest to them, until an overdose gave it away. It bankrupted people financially and emotionally—living in fear of what their addicted relatives would do next, what they would lie about or steal, or what it meant when the phone rang in the middle of the night. People lived with their muscles tensed, ready to absorb the next blow from their brothers, daughters, parents, or whoever's life had been repossessed by addiction.

As I scrubbed at a rusty stain on the tile that never came clean, I kept drawing a blank as to what had possessed Beth. Had she needed money that badly or had she needed access to the drugs herself? I remembered her telling me about the expense of pain treatments and how insurance didn't cover them. Maybe that had driven her to desperation. My shoulders and neck ached as I wrung out my sponge, and for a split second, I thought of the bin full of fentanyl. The thought made me sick. But I could see how someone in as much pain as Beth would be tempted.

Rolling my shoulders, I narrowed my concerns to more immediate questions, namely who Beth had been expecting on that last day and who had been texting her. It seemed almost certain that they were the same person or at least tied together by the pills and cash we had found. Again, I thought about calling Detective Osborne and tried to anticipate how he would react. In roughly half the scenarios I played out in my head, the information blew back on Ethan. I needed to know more before I could trust him. Bruno's claws clicked as he made his way into the kitchen, turned in a circle, and then lay down on the section of tile I'd just cleaned. My breath was labored and I needed to stop anyway. Rising from my hands and knees, I surveyed the half-clean floor. As had been the case in recent months, I'd run out of energy before running out of dirt.

I was emptying the bucket of dirty water when the doorbell rang and cut through my thoughts. For an irrational moment, I feared that Osborne had somehow discovered what Audra and I had found and come to question me. I wiped my hands on my jeans and smoothed my hair behind my ears, hoping that whoever stood at the door wasn't the judgmental type. Peering through the leaded glass, I was surprised to see Beth's father standing on the porch with his shoulders hunched and a black peacoat wrapped around him against the chill.

I flipped on a light and opened the door. "Doug," I stopped short of asking how he was doing. The pleasantry seemed inane given recent events. Instead, I said, "I'm sorry I'm such a mess. Come in." Bruno's claws clicked on the floor behind me as he approached to see who was visiting and what food they might have brought.

Doug's eyes looked puffy, and when he spoke, his voice lacked its usual force. "Thanks, Riley, I hope I'm not interrupting—"

From the corner of my eye I saw a black blur. Suddenly Bruno was a foot from us, barking at Doug. His fur stood in a ridge along his back.

"Bruno, stop that!" I yelled in shock. Viciousness was not one of Bruno's many faults.

Doug spun in quick semicircles one way and then the other to try to keep his back to the whirl of black fur, but Bruno circled and barked, nimbly springing away as I tried to catch hold of his collar.

"I'm so sorry," I yelled to Doug over the barking.

"Why?" Doug yelled back. In all the commotion, I wasn't sure if he was asking why I was sorry or why Bruno was barking. Either way, the answer was that my dog was a jerk.

Finally, I got my hands around Bruno's collar, pulled eighty pounds of wriggling resistance up the stairs to my bedroom, and shut the door. I heard a *harumph* as he sighed and lay heavily against the other side of the door. I was winded and took a moment to pull myself together. I could see the tips of Bruno's paws poking out from beneath the bedroom door. "I'll let you out soon, buddy." His tail thumped once.

By the time I returned down the stairs, Doug had moved from the hallway to my small living room. He stood with his back to me and examined a picture on my bookcase of Ethan, Beth, and me at our high-school graduation ten years ago. It seemed like we had all been different people then—before Beth's accident, before I had moved away, returned home, and gotten sick. Before Ethan had cultivated his resentful streak.

"I'm so sorry about that, Doug. Please have a seat."

Doug jumped at my voice and then turned away from the picture.

"Oh, that's okay. Quite a protector you've got there." He forced a chuckle, but he looked even worse than he had at the memorial. He had always moved with purpose and confidence, as if he was headed somewhere important and knew exactly what to do once he got there. Today, he moved slowly; his gray hair fell over his forehead and he brought his eyebrows together as he looked around, perhaps wondering what the hell he was doing in my cramped living room.

What *was* he doing here?

I contrasted my apartment with his showplace of a house that backed up to the river. The first time I'd been there was to work with Beth on our senior project. We'd made a habit of working together at my house, but when my mom hosted her book group, she banished us for the evening.

In comparison to the constant motion and noise of my own home, the absolute stark stillness and open spaces at Beth's felt like an abandoned museum—a place designed to be seen but not touched. It was all sharp angles, clean lines and glass, razor edged and bright. There had been only one picture of Beth with her mom, from when Beth was a baby; I had studied it when she left the room. Beth looked like her mother—the same delicate features and big brown eyes.

Doug had been out of town that evening, so after we finished our homework, Beth and I made spaghetti and sat on the tall stools around the giant marble counter to eat, the only sound the mechanical hum of the stainless-steel appliances. Afterward, Beth had wiped down the counter and washed the dishes, while I dried. As she folded the dish towels and hung them, squaring up the corners, she looked more like a parent presiding over her kitchen than my seventeen-year-old classmate. I wondered how often she was on her own in this colossal, sharp-edged house.

Doug moved a scattering of decorative pillows out of the way and sank into my cheap sofa. He winced when he hit the concrete-hard seat and cleared his throat. "I'm so sorry to drop in on you like this. I was in Wicksburg for estate work and thought I'd stop by. I've just been thinking about your friendship with Beth and felt . . ." He shrugged. "I guess I wanted to see how you're doing. I'm not so well myself." He gave a weak smile to keep from sounding too self-pitying.

I sighed, not really sure myself. "I'm not so great either," I responded, only realizing it as the words came out of my mouth. "I keep forgetting that she's actually gone. I think about something we need to do for the wedding or something I want to tell her. Then it hits me, and it's so awful I can barely breathe."

He nodded. "I know exactly what you mean. And then this with Ethan. I hate to see the police looking at him. In all the time they were together, I never had any reason to believe Ethan would hurt her."

I was grateful to Doug for bringing it up and clearing the air. It was reassuring to know he saw it that way. "Yeah, Ethan would have done anything for her. He would never hurt her."

"I know. He's a good kid. Really, I can't think of anyone who *would* want to hurt her. Can you? I mean, I know she didn't quite fit in with everyone in North Haven, but I thought that she was making a life for herself here, with her work on the Castle. I really thought . . . I don't know. I mean, who could have done this?" He held his hands in front of him, palms up, like a plea.

*Maybe someone with a burner phone who's missing a storage bin full of drugs,* I thought. I couldn't help but feel for him and fought the urge to pour out my soul, to tell him what Audra and I had found. Part of me feared he would take the information straight to the police, regardless of how it might impact Ethan.

Beyond that, I realized that on some level, I had never fully trusted Doug, despite his charm. It wasn't that I believed the rumors that had circulated about why he had moved to North Haven from Austin—that he was running from debt or a financial scheme gone bad. It wasn't even the whispers from the tellers at the bank that, despite his big house and expensive car, he kept bouncing checks. No one in North Haven escaped the rumor mill, so it wasn't the stories of his murky past or financial woes that troubled me; it was more that I had always felt like he was playing me. His Texas accent came and went, depending on who he was talking to.

With me, he used it. He had the kind of ready smile and quick charm that seemed generated by some script that ran in his brain and spouted whatever was socially appropriate. I knew that this didn't necessarily mean that something sinister lay beneath the polished veneer, but it still left me with the uneasy impression that what I saw was not the same as what was there.

Deciding to keep the day's discovery to myself, I shook my head. "I don't know who would hurt her either. I keep wondering if it was just random, someone from out of town who found an isolated house."

Doug sat back on the couch. "That could be, I suppose. It's hard to think that it could be something so random. But then it's just as hard to think it may have been someone who knew her. The police seem to think it was someone who cared about her because she was found wrapped up so carefully. Did they tell you that?"

"Yeah." A mix of fatigue and curiosity made me ask, "Do you know if she and Liam were close at all? I saw him at the house a couple of times."

He leaned toward me and brought his gray eyebrows together.

"Liam?"

That was all he said. Then he stood.

Something in the air had changed. He paced toward the front window and back to the couch. Then he forced a laugh and sat back down. "I guess you would know better than I would. She never talked to me about Liam."

That was something. I watched him closely. Was it the mention of Liam that upset him or the fact that he hadn't known?

He wiped a hand across his forehead. "I'm afraid I'm learning more about her now that she's gone, things I should have known." His voice dropped off and he looked away. When he met my eyes again, his expression was blank. He angled his head so that his dark eyes penetrated mine.

It dawned on me why he was really here: to find out what I knew. Something I'd said had agitated him. I felt a prickling of fear along the back of my neck. It was natural enough that he would want answers, but suddenly I wished that I hadn't shut Bruno away upstairs. I thought of Bernice next door with her poor hearing and wondered how much noise it would take to get her attention.

I shrugged and kept my tone natural. "Well, I didn't know about her and Liam being close either. I guess it's all just such a shock." I paused. "Where were you when you found out?" I already knew that the police said he had been out of town, but I wondered if turnpike cameras were enough. Would they have captured his face or only his car? Would they check gas station cameras too?

Something flared in his eyes, but his expression didn't change. "I was in Chicago, on the outskirts. I was looking at property on the South Side and figured it was the agent calling." His eyes were pinned on me. "That was the worst moment of my life."

His grief was palpable in the small room. I felt a lump in my throat as I thought of that night. The tension I'd felt a moment earlier evaporated. My shoulders dropped, and I felt like a fool for my momentary paranoia. Was my mind playing tricks on me? Was it fatigue? I looked down at my feet. We sat for another moment, the wind buffeting the house.

Eventually Doug put his hands on his knees and pushed himself into a standing position. "I should be going. Sorry again for dropping in."

"Don't be." I stood with him. "It's good to be around people who cared about her."

We walked to the front hallway. I realized I had never offered to take his coat and how unwelcoming I must have seemed. He gave me a quick hug, opened the door to leave, and then turned toward me.

"Get in touch with me if you ever need to talk. We need to get through this together." He wrapped his coat tightly around himself.

I nodded and said good night. A gust of wind scuttled leaves across the porch. As I watched Doug walk away through the halo of porchlight and into the gloom, I wondered if he and I were after the same thing.

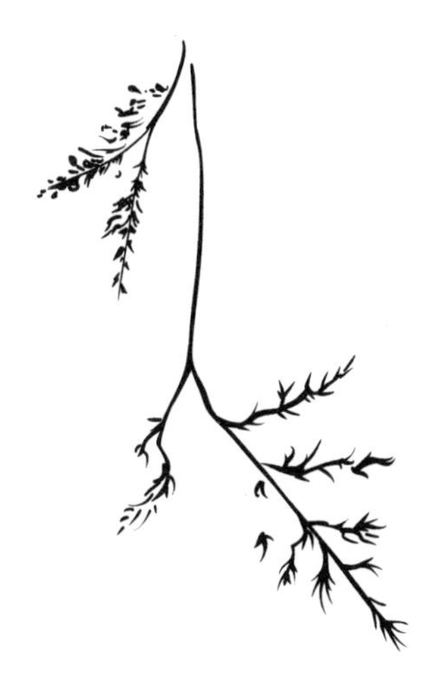

# CHAPTER SIXTEEN

*September 27, 2022*

Audra picked me up at eight the next morning in her ancient Jeep Cherokee that had been limping along on its last legs for years. I could hear the sputtering engine from inside the house. I stepped out to see it idling at the curb in a haze of blue exhaust, drawing worried glances from a group of ladies walking two fluffy white dogs.

I rolled my shoulders as I locked the front door, trying to ease the tension that kept creeping in. The wind from the previous day had died down, and it was a bright, still morning. Dew sparkled on the grass, wetting my shoes, and a squirrel scolded me from the oak tree along the curb. When I opened the passenger door, I was surprised to see Franky in the back seat, stuffing animal crackers into his mouth in wet fistfuls.

"You're bringing Franky?"

"The sitter is sick. What? He won't know what's going on. Besides, Liam will have to behave himself with Franky watching."

I buckled my seat belt, letting the contradictory logic of these two statements slide.

Audra pulled away from the curb into the sparse traffic of downtown Wicksburg, leaving a toxic haze of exhaust in our wake. I looked out the window at the well-tended Victorian houses flying by at the edge of town.

The space between houses grew the farther we went. Well-tended yards gave way to farm fields edged with bright woods as we neared North Haven. Queen Anne's lace and foxtails lined the roadside ditch. In the distance, between gaps in the woods, the river sparkled. On days like this, I understood why Ethan never wanted to leave the area. The image of him confined to a jail cell crashed down on me. Before Audra picked me up, I'd called the jail to see if I could talk with Ethan, but the officer I spoke to confirmed what Audra had told me: that inmates could only make outgoing calls. Aside from the morning of his arrest, he hadn't called. I turned the ringer on my phone up to full volume, just in case he tried again.

As we passed the road that led to Doug's house, I thought about his visit the previous evening.

"You'll never guess who came to see me last night," I told Audra.

She glanced at me sharply. "Osborne?"

"No, not Osborne. Doug. Supposedly, he was in the neighborhood and wanted to see how I was doing." I recounted our conversation, including the sensation I'd had that he was digging for information.

"Well, it wouldn't surprise me if he was poking around to see who knows what. That's what we're about to do," Audra pointed out. "I'm glad to hear he's not buying that Ethan has something to do with this. Maybe we should tell him about the storage bin, or at least try to find out what *he* knows. He's got connections to people who do business in the area and might know more than we would about the money flowing around North Haven."

I made a noncommittal sound, but she was right that it made sense to look for someone with an unexplained influx of cash. She turned off the highway onto the gravel road that led to Liam's drive. Liam lived in a dilapidated Greek Revival farmhouse that he rented from Ethan, who had bought it at auction, mainly for the adjoining farmland. It had been Ethan's first house, and he had replaced the furnace and some broken windows, but unlike the house he and Beth shared, he hadn't done much to improve the aesthetics of the place other than slathering a coat of white paint over the chipped wood siding. His main focus had been keeping the rodents out and improving the surrounding farmland. The lawn was clipped but full of weeds, and the front porch sagged to one side, like the effort of resisting gravity had finally overwhelmed it. Liam's truck was parked beneath a rusty metal carport that looked more hazardous than anything it might protect the truck from.

As we got out of the car, a fluffy black-and-tan shepherd mix came running up to sniff us. Smelling Bruno on me, he gave me a thorough nosing. I petted his soft head and he leaned happily into my legs. Franky tottered up and joined in bathing the dog in attention, grasping its long fur as the dog tried to lick Franky's cracker-coated fingers.

Audra got out of the car. "Are we here to play with the dog or talk to Liam?"

"Can't we do both?" Behind her briskness, I could tell Audra was tense. She rolled her shoulders and arranged her hair. The dog ran ahead and barked that new friends approached.

I took Franky's sticky hand as we climbed the slanting wooden stairs. Audra rang the doorbell, and a chime sounded faintly from within the house. Out of the corner of my eye, I saw the edge of a blind move. No one came to the door. The dog sat beside us patiently, glancing around with his mouth open and tail wagging.

"He's in there," I told Audra and pointed at the window where the blind had twitched.

Audra rapped loudly on the door. "Liam, we know you're in there. We just want to talk with you." There was an air of authority in her tone. She'd been a social worker in Wicksburg until Franky came along, so I trusted her to handle the formalities.

The blind flicked again and a second later footsteps sounded on the other side of the door. A lock clicked and the door opened a few inches. I could only see a sliver of Liam's face. His long dark lashes shadowed his eyes as he looked at our feet.

"What?"

Audra's gentle expression told me she was about to slip into the soft, consoling tone that usually got her whatever she wanted. "We just want to talk to you about Ethan," she lilted, as if she was reciting a bedtime story. "You know he's been arrested, right?"

Liam said nothing. Perhaps he was immune to Audra.

"I know you were harvesting the corn with him that day. We just want to know if you might be able to help. Maybe you can vouch for him that he was hauling grain that afternoon."

"I already talked to Polly and that guy." Liam still gazed down at our feet. I glanced down to make sure there was nothing remarkable on my shoes.

The dog had grown bored with our back-and-forth and nudged his nose against the door, ready to go inside. Liam stepped back and Audra took advantage, wedging herself into the opening. Liam would have to forcibly remove her if he wanted to get rid of us.

"Just give us five minutes," Audra pleaded, somehow maintaining her child therapist tone as she forcibly held open the door.

"The police aren't telling us anything. We just want to know what's going on," I added.

"Ha!" Franky chimed in and shoved his hand in his mouth.

Liam glanced at my face. I thought I saw a hint of sympathy in his eyes. He inclined his head and moved to let us in.

As we filed in, I noticed the same old-house smell as when Ethan had lived there—a bouquet of dust, wood, and wet—but Liam had fixed the place up to look as inviting as possible on his minimum-wage income. He led us to the living room, where charcoal gray curtains were drawn back to let in the morning sun. A pair of abstract landscapes hung on the walls and two built-in shelves were filled with paperbacks and thick books about filmmaking. Liam had thrown a blanket over a sectional couch, and the dog jumped up and plunked down in what seemed to be his usual spot. Liam sank into a chair opposite the couch and gestured for us to sit. Audra, Franky, and I arranged ourselves on either side of the dog, who couldn't have been more delighted at our company and laid his head on my leg.

"Well, what do you want to know?" He glanced at his phone. "I have to leave for work soon." I doubted this was true, since he usually worked afternoons and nights. Even if it was, Liam had never been one to worry about punctuality.

Audra eased into the topic of Ethan. "We know you were working in the field on Old Bridge the other day when everything happened. We're thinking that you could tell us about how Ethan was hauling grain with you that afternoon. Maybe you could vouch for him—say that he couldn't have gone anywhere near Beth." She nodded encouragingly at the end.

Liam stared at his own foot now, curling and uncurling his toes. The furnace turned on with a mechanical sigh and circulated the smell of hot dust around the room. Liam cleared his throat. "I didn't tell them right away. I didn't even think about it the first time they talked to me."

Audra narrowed her eyes and sat forward. "What do you mean? What didn't you tell?"

"I didn't tell Polly what I saw when I first talked with her, but when she and that guy talked to me the second time, they asked. See, they'd been to the field we'd been working on, so they knew I had a good view from up in the combine. You know, that rise in the field on Old Bridge Road? You can see pretty much everything from up there, especially from up in the combine. They already knew from Simon that Ethan had gone to the house that day. So they asked what I saw. Ethan timed it so that I'd be going the other way, but I saw him plain enough in the rearview mirror."

"What are you talking about?" Audra dropped her coaxing tone. "He timed what?"

"Ethan went back toward his house—after going to the farm. He was gone for at least an hour. Jeremy and I even had to stop because the wagon was full and Ethan still hadn't come back. When he did, he told us he'd been fixing the conveyor belt. Jeremy never saw anything because he'd been pulling the wagon behind him, but I knew that wasn't the direction Ethan had gone." Liam shrugged, still talking to his foot. "At the time, I just figured he went home to see Beth and didn't want us to know he'd been slacking, but then when the cops asked if he could have gone home—when I actually had time to think about it . . . I mean, I have convictions for possession. I had to be honest."

Blood thrummed in my ears. I pictured the field on Old Bridge Road. That field did sit up higher than the land around it, and it ran along the road that connected Ethan's road to my parents' farm, where the grain was stored.

From his vantage point in the tall combine, Liam would have had a good view of everyone's comings and goings, while Jeremy, down in the truck pulling the wagon to catch the grain shooting out of the unloader, wouldn't have been able to see behind him.

Audra had gone still. "You told this to the police?"

Liam nodded and stared miserably at his sock.

Audra looked at me. "That's why they believed Simon."

"What time of the day was this?" I asked.

Liam cocked his head. "A little before three maybe. I know he was back by around four."

I shook my head. This wasn't how it was meant to go. The hot air in the room felt thick. Liam's news spun like a whirlwind through my mind, upending everything. I tried to focus on the question that had brought us here.

"Why should we believe you? You visited Beth last week. What was that about?"

Liam flinched. "I was dropping off my rent." The answer had a rehearsed quality to it. Hopefully Liam's Hollywood ambitions did not include acting. He held my eyes for a beat and then went back to the sock.

"You were paying rent in the middle of the month?"

"Well, it was late, but Beth and Ethan had been good about it. They knew I'd pay eventually."

I huffed. "Then why were you so eager to get out of there?" I remembered him slinking off toward his truck. "You looked like you couldn't get away fast enough."

Liam sighed and threw up his hands. "Look, I didn't do anything wrong here, so you can either believe me or not. I'm sorry that I had to be the one who saw where Ethan went that day, but that's what happened. I wouldn't lie about something like that. I'm telling you the truth."

The dog swiveled his gaze from Liam to me. My muscles had gone rigid. Sensing the rising tension, the dog jumped down from the couch, wandered over to a bed under the window, turned a few times, and settled. While the grownups talked, Franky had gotten up to explore the living room and stood near the window, bouncing the way he did when he had to go to the bathroom.

I motioned toward Franky. "He needs to use your bathroom."

Liam and Audra both looked at Franky, who was doing a good job of selling it, clutching his crotch now while bouncing.

"Fine, but I need to get going, so after that . . ."

"Yeah, I know." I looked at Audra. "Such a model employee."

Liam rolled his eyes and flopped back in his chair.

I took Franky by the hand and led him down the dim hallway into the small bathroom. I had been in the house plenty of times when Ethan lived here, and I knew the bathroom was in the front next to the bedroom, where I'd seen the blinds twitch before we'd arrived. I sat Franky on the toilet and told him, "You stay put here, okay? Go potty. I'll be back to help you wash your hands, okay?"

Franky nodded solemnly as I held a finger to my lips and closed the door.

I was pretty sure Audra knew what I was up to. Her voice carried from the living room and I hoped whatever she talked about with Liam would cover any noise I might make. I crept across the hall into the bedroom and took a quick inventory. The neatly made bed had an upholstered headboard. A mid-century modern bedside table and matching dresser filled the space perfectly. I felt a flush of inadequacy, realizing that Liam's decorating skills put mine to shame.

I headed for the night table and rifled through the shallow drawers. The top drawer held condoms, a glass pipe, and a ceiling fan remote; the bottom drawer was empty except for rolling papers.

I crept back to the door. Franky was still in the bathroom. I could hear Liam's voice from down the hall. I had time to check the dresser. I silently slid the top drawer open, thankful that Liam had splurged for soft-close drawers. With reluctance, I sifted through his underwear, then his socks, undershirts, and sweaters. It wasn't until the bottom drawer that I hit something interesting. I lifted the jeans to examine what I'd felt: a small black phone, identical to the burner we'd found at Ethan and Beth's. I pressed the power button, but nothing happened. Dead. As I lifted my own phone to take a picture, I heard a soft footfall behind me. I jumped and turned, adrenaline surging through me.

Franky stood behind me holding his hands out toward me. "Wash," he said accusingly before putting his finger in his nose.

I put my hand to my chest and tried to breathe. "Get your finger out of your nose, Franky. Always, but especially now. I'll be right there." I snapped a quick picture of the phone, arranged the jeans as they'd been, and stood. A wave of blackness flooded my vision and I leaned over, trying to follow Franky back across the hall in my bent-over position. I couldn't pass out in Liam's bedroom.

With my sight narrowed to a gray pinhole, I felt my way across the hall to the bathroom and waited for my head to clear. After a moment, I helped Franky with his much-needed handwashing and we returned to the living room. I wondered if Audra and Liam could hear the blood roaring in my ears.

Audra was talking about her memories of Liam's father, who had worked at the farm years ago. She glanced up as Franky and I returned and put her hands on her knees to stand.

"Well, we should let you get to work, Liam. Thanks for talking with us."

I inclined my head toward Liam but I couldn't bring myself to thank him. Liam and the dog walked us to the door, and as we went back out into the bright morning, I heard it close behind us. Then the lock clicked.

Back in the car, the only sounds were the tires whirring on the road and Franky's intermittent humming. Finally, Audra broke the silence and summed things up. "Ethan might be fucked."

"He might be." I rubbed my temples, hoping to massage away what Liam had shared. "Ethan told me specifically that he wasn't there that day. He told me he didn't have time to go home for lunch."

"Well, it sounds like he lied to you," Audra responded flatly. "But don't feel bad. He lied to all of us."

"You believe Liam and Simon over him?"

"They're both telling the same story. I don't know why they would both lie, but we know why Ethan might lie."

Audra and Ethan had never been close. Whatever one believed, the other believed the opposite. I didn't know if this made Audra more or less objective than me when it came to considering the evidence. "Even if Ethan was there, it doesn't mean that he hurt her. There could be lots of reasons why he went home, and someone could easily have been there after him. Besides," I pulled out my phone to show Audra the picture I'd taken of the phone in Liam's drawer. "Liam might have his own reasons to lie."

Audra glanced at the picture. "Is that a burner phone?"

"Yep, just like Beth's. It was hidden in his dresser under his clothes. Liam knows something he's not telling us. I'm pretty sure he was seeing Beth about something more than rent. He could be the one that pulled Beth into all this."

Audra sighed. "I don't know, Riley. If we're talking about someone bringing in drugs and selling them, it's got to be somebody with connections. I don't see Liam putting all that together. Besides, whatever he's involved in—it doesn't matter, as long as Liam and Simon still say Ethan was at the house that afternoon."

"Yeah, but Ethan was back in the field before four, and you said Beth could have been killed any time before six. That's plenty of time for someone else to have gone there after Ethan. Besides, we don't even know that Ethan saw Beth. Liam just said he saw Ethan going in that direction. It's only Simon saying that he actually went home." I chewed my lip and thought. "Has Polly told you what Simon told them?"

Audra frowned. "She hasn't gotten back to me since they took Ethan in, but she's swamped right now."

I understood Audra's discomfort. As different as she and Polly were, they had been like sisters most of their lives. In my memories, she and Audra were a single blur of long braids, pumping arms, and bare feet whirling around the periphery of my childhood.

It would hurt Audra to admit that she and her best friend were now on separate sides of this investigation.

"I think we need to talk to Simon." I glanced back at Franky. "Maybe Franky would be better off with Mom for that one. We could drop him off on the way."

I had texted with Mom the night before to check on her, but I supposed Audra hadn't talked with her since yesterday's blowup. As difficult as she could be, I worried about my mom.

With Dad gone, she spent too much time on her own in the big, creaking house and in her own head. Dad hadn't been perfect, but at least he'd been steady and slower to anger. He'd kept her delicately balanced, like a touchstone she used to get her bearings a few times a day. Part of the reason I'd stayed in the area was because I knew she needed family around her, but I didn't always have my dad's calm patience with her. Audra almost never did.

I could see her calculating the cost-benefit analysis of leaving Franky but having to interact with Mom. Finally, she sighed. "I suppose."

She jerked the wheel and turned off the highway onto Old Bridge Road.

"So, I'm just supposed to drop everything and babysit?" My mom's tone left no doubt that this was an accusation rather than a question. She had arranged herself in her most obstinate stance, all 110 pounds of her squared up with her hands on her hips. Although still formidable, she looked more fragile than usual today. Capillaries showed through the paper-thin skin under her eyes.

When Audra and I had arrived, Mom had been chatting with Traci, a loan officer at the bank in town. Traci, who was a couple of years older than Audra, stood about five feet tall in heels and had a lot of blond hair that she piled high on top of her head to gain a few more inches. In her rattan platforms, she teetered at the kitchen island, holding on to a thick manila folder and flicking glances between Mom and Audra.

With Traci present, no one mentioned Ethan, but the toll of his arrest permeated everything. She wasn't a malicious gossip, but she couldn't keep a secret to save her life, so Audra and I were faced with convincing Mom of the importance of taking Franky without telling her of our plans to visit Simon.

"What is it that you girls are doing that's so important?" Mom flicked her eyes between us. "You know, I managed to accomplish quite a bit with three kids in tow. It seems like the two of you could manage one." She looked at Franky, who played with the suede fringe on Traci's purse, blissfully unaware that he was the subject of contention.

Audra curled her lip. "I guess someone didn't raise us all that well," she countered.

Traci's smile grew tighter each time Mom glanced at her for agreement. Rather than taking a side, she focused on Franky. "Oh, he is just a little sweetie. I'd take him back to the bank with me if I could," she cooed. "I'm not sure Clark would be thrilled about that, though." She gave a weak laugh. Clark, the longtime manager of the bank, was a dry, dour man of about sixty. I couldn't imagine he'd ever been thrilled about anything.

Audra, who mirrored Mom's obstinate stance, sighed and tried again. "It will only be an hour or so. He can watch a show for that long." Audra gestured at the tablet she'd placed on the island.

"That's fine," Mom martyred. "Just leave him here. I'll handle it, and we won't be needing that." She fluttered a finger to dismiss the tablet. "It's a beautiful day. We'll play outside, the way kids used to. You girls go ahead and run off to whatever it is you're doing." She flicked her eyes back and forth between us again.

I could see Audra wrestling with whether to take issue with Mom's critique of her parenting or walk away now that she had agreed to keep Franky. I tried to head off the former. "Thanks, Mom. We really won't be long." I turned Audra toward the door. "Just say thanks," I told her quietly.

"No," she said through gritted teeth, but she didn't fight as I put my hand on the small of her back and propelled her toward the car.

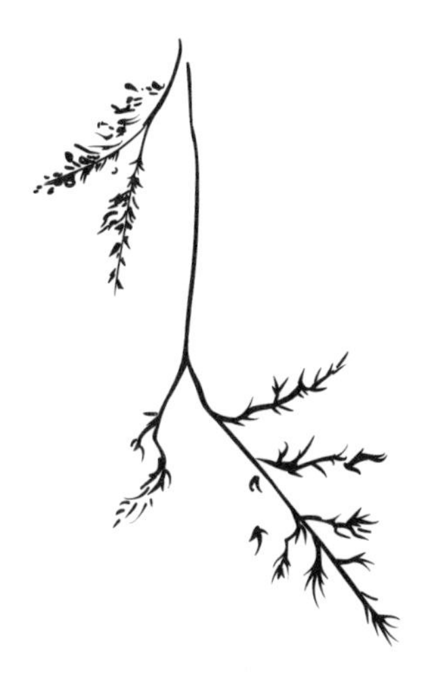

# CHAPTER SEVENTEEN

*September 27, 2022*

The drive from Mom's to Simon's took us past the field where Ethan and Liam had been working the day Beth was killed. My parents' farm backed up to Ethan's property through a maze of fields and woods, and a branch of the Vermillion River divided the two properties. When Ethan had bought his property, he and Dad had constructed a footbridge to span the river so that our two families could walk through the woods to visit.

By road, the two properties were connected by Old Bridge Road, so named for the covered bridge that had long ago been replaced by a more structurally sound but uglier steel-girder construction. Going south, Audra slowed as we passed the field Ethan and Liam had been working.

Although I couldn't see Ethan's house from the road, I could picture how Liam would have had a bird's-eye view of his surroundings from the top of the rise.

Still, I didn't see how he could say for certain that Ethan had gone home, because the house wouldn't be visible from that vantage point. That left only Simon's word to place Ethan at the house that afternoon.

"Are you sure you're up for this?" Audra glanced from the road to me and back again. "You didn't seem so good yesterday when we were doing the wallpaper. And you look a little . . ."

I straightened up from my slouch. "I'm okay. You know, I have good days and bad." That was the baffling truth. Some days I felt almost like my old self, and on others I felt so depleted that the capable person I'd once been seemed like a stranger. Today I hovered somewhere between those extremes.

Audra turned right onto Aldridge Road, which took us past Ethan's. She kept her eyes straight ahead, but I couldn't help looking at Ethan's quiet white house up on the rise with the neat lawn and horseshoe driveway. The pots of mums Beth had planted still brightened the front steps. It looked like happy people lived there.

Simon lived about a mile farther down the road named after his family, in a dented white-and-aqua trailer half hidden by weeds. He'd inherited his family's farm but not their inclination for farmwork, so he had survived for most of his adult life by renting out the tillable land to my dad and selling off small parcels as needed. Apparently, that income had not been sufficient to cover Simon's cost of living, mainly bourbon, cigarettes, and taxes. Naturally, he'd let the taxes go first and, after repeated notices from the sheriff's office, was forced to sell the property to cover what he owed.

Now he lived in the rusted-out trailer he'd once rented out to a series of junkies, but Simon still considered himself an Aldridge and therefore superior to the upstart Svensons. He had gone from calling my dad "the dirt farmer," whatever that meant, to "the land baron" as my dad purchased more and more of the surrounding small farms that came up at auctions.

A faded blue Ford was parked near a metal outbuilding in Simon's driveway, and a green side-by-side UTV sat near the broken lattice of Simon's entryway. Simon favored the UTV over his truck since he could take it off road and avoid drunk driving arrests. Even after Ethan and Beth had moved in, Simon had made frequent visits in his UTV to "check on his property," which consisted of him riding around in the fields and snooping around the outbuildings. Ethan had told him he was welcome to visit his family's cemetery, which sat about a hundred yards down the road from the house, and to ride around the edges of the fields, but he drew the line at allowing Simon to poke around near the house and barns. A bad case of COVID had kept Simon at home for a few months, but if he was telling the truth about seeing Ethan, he had begun venturing out again.

I looked at Audra, who was already frowning in anticipation of the unpleasantness we were about to encounter. "Well, are you ready?"

Audra eyed the grimy trailer, grabbed a bottle of hand sanitizer from the center console, and nodded.

The day had warmed under the midday sun. As we walked toward Simon's trailer, grasshoppers flung themselves out of the dried weeds and across our path. The dying sounds of summer—katydids and crickets—seemed to press in on us from the tall grasses.

I walked ahead of Audra up to Simon's porch, grasping the rough wood railing that swayed as if the slightest pressure would send it tumbling into the yard. Simon's front door was made of a textured plastic composite and coated in mildew. It made a hollow sound when I knocked.

I was pretty sure Simon would have heard the racket from Audra's Jeep pulling in, but it still took him a full minute to come to the door. I imagined him standing on the other side of the junky door savoring the fact that he was making us wait.

Finally, the door opened with a creaky protestation and we were treated to Simon's tobacco-stained smile. "Well, my my, what pretty visitors. An old man like me doesn't get such lovely ladies stopping by very often." He looked us both up and down with his cloudy blue eyes.

I couldn't gauge if Simon honestly thought we might find this charming or if it was his intention to creep us out. Audra had played good cop at Liam's, so it was my turn. I swallowed my bile.

"Hey, Simon. We were hoping to talk to you about what you were saying at the memorial." I tried to think how long ago that had been. Only two days? It seemed like at least a week. "We just want to know more about what you saw that day." I kept my voice level, not pleading but not anywhere near as hostile as I felt either.

Simon hacked and cleared phlegm from his throat for a full minute. Audra and I both leaned back. Finally, he wheezed, "I don't know. I'm not sure I'm really feeling up for visitors right now, at least not two ladies at a time." He wiped a shiny spot at the corner of his mouth and smiled.

From the corner of my eye, I saw Audra reach into her giant purse. For a moment I was certain Simon was about to be treated to a face full of pepper spray. Instead, she pulled out a pint of Wild Turkey. "We brought you a peace offering, Simon. We don't want to give you any trouble. We just want to hear your side of things." It wasn't quite the story-time voice she had used with Liam, but it was close.

Simon's face lit up at the sight of the bourbon. He put on a show of struggling with the decision, but after a second of pretense, clumped away from the door to let us in.

"Do you always carry a pint of bourbon with you?" I asked Audra.

"Know thine enemy," she whispered, waving the bottle at me.

The inside of the trailer was hot, dim, and smelled of a sweet rot, like fermenting garbage. Suddenly, as the door banged closed behind us and the walls of the tight, dark space closed in, I realized how isolated we were, with nothing but fields and woods all around. Simon led us just a few steps to a sitting room and collapsed into a green recliner with a raspy exhalation. Every surface, from the kitchen counter to the coffee table, was covered with layers of papers, food wrappers, precarious ashtrays, cups, and the other odds and ends of a misspent life. While he closed his eyes and caught his breath, Audra and I moved a jacket out of the way and seated ourselves on the brown floral sofa. I tried not to think about the years of wear that had rubbed the velveteen fabric smooth.

As soon as I sat, Simon regained the ability to speak and motioned to the bottle of bourbon. "You wanna pour me a glass of that, hon?" His beady eyes were focused on me, so I took the bottle from Audra, rose, and dug a green glass out of a sticky kitchenette cupboard. I filled it as close to the top as I could without spilling and carried it carefully back to Simon, who accepted it with a glow in his eyes.

"That'll wet my whistle." He winked at me and reached to pat my arm. I dodged his wrinkled claw and settled back on the worn couch.

"I'm glad," I said. "We just wanted to hear from you what you saw that day." I hoped to steer Simon to the task at hand and go. I'd been uneasy around the man for as long as I could remember. My first memory of him was from when I still had training wheels on my bike and he sat in his truck watching me ride up and down our driveway. He had always found some reason to come to our house to harass Dad and watch Audra and me.

Simon sipped his bourbon for a full minute before setting it on the paper-strewn end table with a shaking hand. He cleared his throat. "I was checking out my fields along the river," he began. The fields he referred to were Ethan's fields now, but we let that go. "I'd been cooped up for months with my illness, you know. I was riding along the tree line to the west of my house, near the cemetery, making sure he's treatin' the ground right."

I pictured the spot Simon described. He would have been behind Ethan's house on the side away from the barn. The field on that side of the house backed up to some woods, which ran to the river. Beth and I had walked in that area often, and it was near where her body had been left. I knew the view Simon would have had from there across the cemetery to the side yard and back of the house.

"I stopped up there for a smoke and was looking toward the house when I noticed Ethan's truck. It was parked in the pull-off beside the family cemetery, but then I could see Ethan on the back porch. Now, doesn't that seem kind of strange that he would park over by the cemetery rather than in his own driveway?" He looked from Audra to me, hamming up a puzzled expression. "So naturally I wanted to see what he was up to, and sure enough, there he was, peeking in the windows around the back of the house, like a peeping Tom on his own woman. At first I thought, well, maybe that's what those two kids like, you know? I'm not a man to judge others for their proclivities." He wrinkled his face into something like a smile. "Didn't think too much of it, but then when I heard the girl turned up dead that same day, I thought, well . . ." Apparently his thoughts hadn't extended much past *well* because he just shrugged one bony shoulder and picked up his glass of bourbon.

I could feel Audra tensing next to me, but I ignored it. Although my shoulders slumped at Simon's words, Ethan's presence at his own house didn't make him guilty. "What window was this?" I asked.

"Oh, he looked all over the place, in the back door and the kitchen window and then the window along the back porch into the dining room." Simon motioned as he described the position of the window and slopped some bourbon onto his hand. He looked at it mournfully.

"How long did you watch this?"

"Only a few minutes. Not a peeping Tom myself, but I couldn't help noticing. After a minute, your brother sat himself down on the porch, like so." Simon mimicked a posture I'd seen Ethan take when he was distressed, leaning forward, holding his head in his hands. "Looked upset. I figured it was just a lovers' spat until I found out what happened. Then," he tapped his temple, "I put two and two together, you know. Seemed to me like what I saw must have been him gearing up to go after her, or maybe he'd already done it and the shock was settin' in. I don't know the whole sequence, but I knew enough that I had to do my duty and come forward."

"Right." As a self-proclaimed sovereign citizen, I knew that Simon didn't hold the police in high esteem. That he had come forward at all was a testament to how much he disliked Ethan.

"So he never went into the house from what you saw?" Audra asked, a note of hope in her voice.

"I just told you that I only watched for a few minutes," he spat. "When I left him, he was heading back to his truck, and I was going the opposite direction along the tree line. I headed into town from there to do some errands—"

Suddenly, the unmistakable sound of a gunshot rang out, and the metal front of the trailer pinged as something—either a bullet or flak—hit it. For an instant, I saw the narrow slits of Simon's eyes widen and felt Audra slide to the floor next to me. I dove onto the brown shag carpet as another shot rang out from what sounded like the direction of the road. Audra lay beside me with her hands covering her head in tornado-drill position. Pressing myself into the floor, I registered food crumbs nestled deep in the brown loops of carpet.

"What was that?" Audra's voice was breathless.

"Are you okay? Did you get hit?" I hissed at her. From the road, I could hear an engine rev and then fade into the distance.

"I'm fine! You?"

"I think so." My limbs surged with electricity and blood thrummed in my ears, but I was all in one piece.

Still in his chair Simon wheezed, "Don't nobody worry about me." He had crouched down as far as his arthritic back would allow but hadn't been able to make it to the floor.

"What the hell *was* that?" Audra repeated, her voice high with panic.

"A shot. Two shots." I was only now recovering my senses enough to state the obvious. Keeping low, I crept toward the window that faced the road and ventured a quick look out. Nothing but tall sunlit grasses and the empty road. I quickly ducked back down, my scalp tingling. "There's no one out front. I heard someone drive off." I cautiously crept to a side window while Audra looked out back.

"Nothing," Audra confirmed. "We should call the police."

"Could it be an accident? Maybe a hunter?" I asked. Audra shook her head and Simon looked at me like that was the stupidest thing he'd heard in quite some time.

"That'd be quite a coincidence since it's never happened before, and here you two are today, poking around a murder." His eyes were still wider than normal and his hand shook as he reached for his glass of bourbon. "I may not be the most popular man in town, but I'm not in the habit of being shot at." He tried to pick up his glass and sloshed the amber liquid onto the pile of newspapers strewn across the end table. After another try, he gave up, though he continued to gaze at the cloudy green glass.

"Then what was it?" I asked. "Ethan's in jail, so don't try to pin this on him."

"Could be one of his friends," Simon suggested but without much conviction.

Audra had pushed herself up from the grubby carpet and was coating herself with hand sanitizer from the elbows down as she spoke. "I'll call Polly."

Simon scowled. "No, you will not. I don't need the authorities coming onto my property. No thank you. Last time that friend of yours was on my land, she and her goons turned me out of my own house."

I tried to picture Polly with an entourage of goons and failed. "Wouldn't you like to know who just tried to kill you?" I asked incredulously.

Simon waved the idea away. "No one was trying to kill me. Those were only warning shots. And I'd wager they were aimed at you girls." Simon's hands still trembled, but something in his expression had changed from shock to caginess. A smug look was layered in with the fear, and I could tell he was done sharing. "Now if you girls are finished stirring up trouble, you might be on your way. I'm an old man and I need my rest."

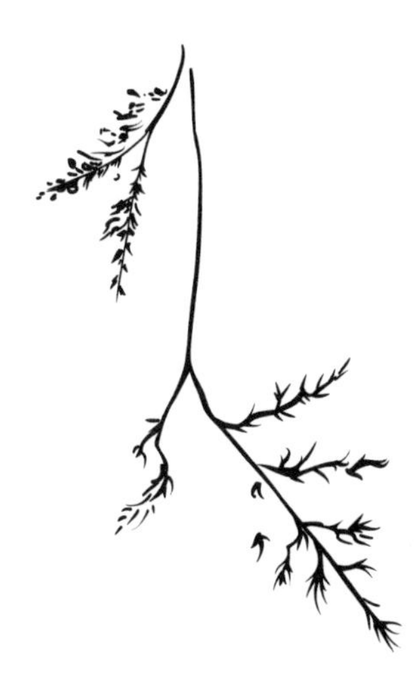

# CHAPTER EIGHTEEN

*September 27, 2022*

Audra and I left Simon to his much-needed beauty sleep. I had heard the fading rumble of a vehicle's engine immediately after the shots and felt certain that the shooter had gone, but we scanned the road, the woods, and the fields again as we crept from Simon's with our heads low. My heart still raced and Audra's hands shook as she fished her keys out of her purse. On our way to the Jeep, we examined the outside of his trailer and found a hole, about the size of a quarter, along the bottom of the metal skirting that faced the road. The bullet had passed through the aluminum, searing paint off the surface surrounding the hole and leaving a smooth circle of metal in its wake. Audra put her finger to it and then looked out at the road, where someone had fired at us.

"At least we didn't have Franky with us," I said, shivering. Audra ignored me.

In fact, she had been uncharacteristically quiet as we'd left Simon's. I didn't press her to talk. I felt weak and tired as I leaned back in the afternoon sun.

My adrenaline was waning, leaving behind a marrow-deep fatigue. I closed my eyes and felt the now-familiar sensation of spinning. I heard Audra signal and slow for the turn back onto Old Bridge Road.

She let out a shaky breath. "Polly needs to know about this. Something bigger is going on."

I opened one eye to peer at her. "Bigger? Bigger than Beth getting killed and Ethan getting arrested and us getting shot at? Is that not big enough?"

Audra shook her head and drummed her fingers on the steering wheel. "I mean, there's something more . . . complicated going on. Something someone doesn't want us looking into. I don't see some random person from out of town doing this. It's someone we know. I mean, who would know to look for us at Simon's, or even that Simon was mixed up in this?"

I thought about who might fire shots at us—just a dark silhouette in my mind—and felt chilled at the thought that the anonymous figure belonged to someone we knew.

"You think someone followed us from Mom's or Liam's?"

"Maybe, or else someone was watching Simon's." She signaled to pull into the long driveway at Mom's. "Either way, I think someone wants us to stop asking questions."

Audra called Polly from the Jeep as we sat outside Mom's. The line rang through the speakers, and Polly answered on the second ring.

"Hey, Audra. What's up?" From the tinny background noise, it sounded like she was on the road too.

"Oh, not much," Audra answered, building up momentum, "other than being shot at in Simon Aldridge's trailer this afternoon." She proceeded to dramatically reenact our experience for Polly, complete with sound effects (*boom* and *ping, ping*) and the details of her inner monologue in which she visualized what would happen to her children if she bled out on the floor of Simon's trailer.

Polly cut her off. "What were you doing at Simon's in the first place?"

That stopped Audra short. She adjusted her hands on the steering wheel.

"We were following up on his story about seeing Ethan. You know he's not reli—"

"Audra, you need to leave this to the police." I hadn't heard Polly this exasperated since their freshman year when Audra had cut Polly's bangs while she slept. "If anyone finds out you and Riley are going around talking to witnesses, that's going to look an awful lot like witness tampering to a prosecutor."

Audra stared stonily ahead, her jaw jutted forward.

"Do you hear me, Audra? I'll check out the damage at Simon's, if he'll cooperate, but I'm not overly optimistic that he'll roll out the red carpet. I'll see what I can find, though. I'm on my way to speak with Doug right now, actually." There was a staticky pause. "I'll see where he's been this afternoon, if he's been anywhere near Simon's." She added, "I'm not happy you were out there, but I'm glad you let me know about it."

Audra chewed on her lip and I wondered if she was going to tell Polly that Doug had paid me a strangely unsettling visit the evening before, or worse, that we'd visited with Liam earlier in the day, but for once in her life, she stemmed the stream of consciousness that normally poured uninterrupted from her brain through her mouth. Instead, she asked Polly to update her on her trip to Simon's. Polly agreed, as long as Audra promised to stay away from witnesses.

On that uneasy truce, they ended the call. Audra blew out a frustrated breath. "I told you this was a bad idea."

"No, you didn't."

"Well, I'm sure I thought it."

"I don't think you did. Anyway, it doesn't matter. Polly has to say those things." I leaned back in the seat and closed my eyes against a wave of dizziness. "It's her job to look out for us, but it's our responsibility to look out for Ethan."

When we arrived at Mom's, Audra and I found Franky alone at the kitchen table eating a piece of chocolate cake the size of his head.

"So much for him sleeping tonight," Audra muttered and set to coaxing the remaining cake away from him with the temerity of a lion tamer.

Without discussing it, I knew that Audra and I would not share our experience at Simon's with Mom. From the living room, I could hear her voice alternating with a deeper voice. I paused outside the doorway trying to determine if it was a conversation I should join.

"I don't see why bail would be in question. It should only be a matter of how much."

I remembered Traci's presence this morning and the stack of papers she and Mom had been reviewing. Was she getting funds together for bail? I wondered how much money Mom had available and felt guilty that Audra and I had left her to deal with that on her own.

I crept back a few paces and made some noise as I approached the living room anew. "Mom?" I called. "Audra and I are back."

"Well, I hear you clomping, don't I?" Mom answered. "Like a Clydesdale."

As I entered the living room, a tall man in a dark suit stood and smiled at me. He looked to be around eighty, with a stooped posture and just a few wisps of gray hair remaining. He shuffled toward me to introduce himself. I stepped forward to save him a few shuffles.

"You must be one of Ethan's sisters. I'm Carson Applebaum. I'll be representing Ethan at his bail hearing." He smiled warmly, showing me his very white dentures.

"I'm Riley. It's nice to meet you." He commenced the long journey back to the love seat. I wasn't sure if I should be reassured by the extent of Carson's life experience or concerned.

Mom turned toward me. She wore a pale yellow sweater set and slim gray pants, a picture of respectability aside from a smear of chocolate frosting on one sleeve. “It’s set for tomorrow, Riley. The arraignment and bail hearing. We’ll all be there to support him. Make sure you wear something nice.” Her pinched expression indicated that she worried about my ability to do that.

I sat next to her on the couch. “Is there anything you need from us?” I looked at Carson. He smiled again warmly and shook his head as if we were all having a very pleasant time.

“If you and your family can just be there, that would be a nice show of support for your brother.”

“Wear your hair up tomorrow, Riley. And earrings.” Mom’s voice was high like she was afraid she might forget to impart something vital.

I leaned forward to get up and she caught my arm and brushed my cheek with the tips of her fingers on her other hand.

“And bronzer.”

I rolled my eyes and rose. “It was nice to meet you, Mr. Applebaum. I’ll see you in the morning, Mom.”

“Did you eat? Take some food.”

I could hear Audra and Franky still battling in the kitchen. Mom called out one last urgent piece of advice behind me: “And don’t slouch like that tomorrow. You look like you’re half dead.”

As Audra worked on buckling a sugar-berserk Franky into his car seat, I walked in the direction of the barn that sat about a hundred yards behind my parents’ house. Liam’s black truck was parked in its usual spot.

A faint dent still pocked the right rear fender where Ethan had kicked it the summer before. Glancing around me, I rested my hand on the cool hood.

Walking back to the Jeep, I thought about any other vehicles Liam would have access to. I settled in next to Audra and glanced at Franky, who stared back with wide eyes. I kept my voice low. “Liam’s truck is out by the barn now, but that doesn't mean he was there *all* afternoon. The engine didn't feel warm, but he could have taken one of the farm trucks."

Audra nodded as we crunched down the long gravel driveway. "He could have followed us here from his place and then over to Simon's."

"Can you check with Marco on when Liam came in to work or if he left at all? And it's interesting that Polly thought to check on where Doug's been this afternoon."

Audra turned onto the road and gave me a sidelong look. "I'll check with Marco about Liam. But Doug?"

I shrugged. "Polly's the one who mentioned Doug, not me."

"You think Beth's own father might have had something to do with this? Is there anyone you don't suspect?"

I looked out the window at the familiar fields and thought about her question. "I've nearly ruled out Franky."

Audra didn't even smile.

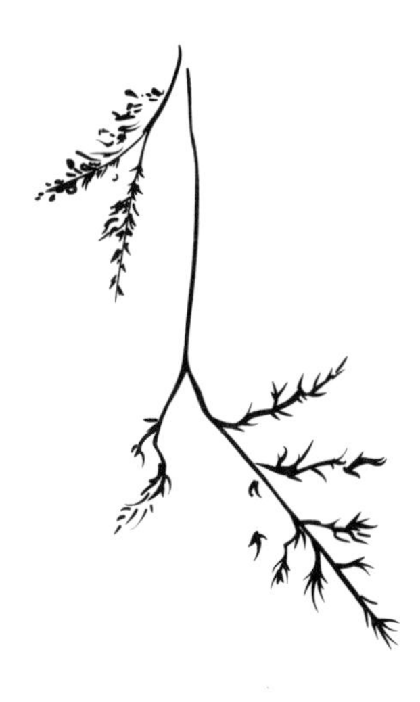

# CHAPTER NINETEEN

*September 27, 2022*

The sun had nearly set by the time I got home. Visiting hours at the jail ended at half past five, and I'd missed the chance to see Ethan. On our way back to Wicksburg, I could have hurried Audra, but I hadn't. As desperate as I'd felt to talk with Ethan only this morning, after listening to Liam and Simon expose his lies, I didn't know how to face him. In some unexplored corner of my mind, a shapeless fear gnawed as to what Ethan might tell me if I really pressed him.

Bruno met me at the door, wagging his tail and sniffing my pants where Liam's dog had brushed against me. As I snapped the leash onto his collar, I enjoyed that moment of simple, uncomplicated goodness. Still jumpy from Simon's, I checked the locks and closed the curtains. Then we were off into the autumn evening, the air smelling of woodsmoke and leaves scuttling at our feet. My knees wobbled now and then, but Bruno was happy for the slow pace that allowed him to sniff every leaf, tree, and lamppost to his heart's content. Like everything else that had happened over the past week, being fired upon in Simon's trailer took on a surreal quality, as if I'd lost my

anchor to reality. This was only heightened by my exhaustion, which had been building so steadily that tonight I could feel it seeping from my pores. But what choice did I have but to keep going? Everything I had done, day in, day out, for months now—from showering to having a simple conversation—required a monumental effort.

This fatigue was the hardest to explain. Being tired was normal, I could see people think if I mentioned it, and just something to power through. I'd been sick before and tired before, but this was something different: a constant, unrelenting gravity dragging at every action, casting a dense haze over my thoughts.

As I crossed at an intersection, a streetlight doubled in my field of vision and then merged back together, something that had been happening more and more. After Ethan's hearing tomorrow, I would call Dr. Maclean to get my test results from my last visit with her. I realized that, with Beth's endorsement, I had ventured to hope that Dr. Maclean would be the one to find what my other doctors had missed. At the same time, I feared getting my hopes up, like someone jaded by a series of disastrous relationships. After so many assurances from doctors that I was a healthy young woman, I was beginning to believe that this thing—whatever it was—was palpable only to me and that I would be cursed to carry its invisible weight with me forever.

Then, there were the doubts Audra had raised about Dr. Maclean and Beth's stash of opioids. Sydney had assumed her practice was a pill mill, and I remembered how Polly had smirked when I mentioned Dr. Maclean's name. Maybe desperation to find an answer for my ailment was skewing my judgment and I was in denial about obvious connections.

By the time Bruno and I meandered back home, the evening had turned dark. Pinpricks of stars blinked against the slate-blue sky. An owl sounded its rich *hooo hoo-hoo* from a stand of tall trees. Trudging up the driveway, I removed Bruno's leash and he loped ahead of me into the back yard through the open gate. My mind was occupied with thoughts of getting food, a shower, and appropriate clothing for the hearing tomorrow, when a few steps ahead of me, Bruno froze. The fur on his back stood into a ridge, and a low growl rumbled from his chest.

I froze too and peered into the deep back yard. The sheer terror that had overtaken me in Simon's trailer surged up from my stomach. As my eyes adjusted from the streetlights, I struggled to make out anything. Bruno faced the direction of the back fence, which was about four feet tall and separated Bernice's property from an elementary schoolyard. A dense row of arborvitae ran behind the fence with occasional gaps where trees had died and been removed over the years.

Bruno's rumbling growl continued and he took one stiff, stalking step toward the fence, keeping his head level. In one of the gaps between trees, against the dark sky, something stirred, just a darker smudge in the corner of my vision. I'd seen deer in this field before, but this was the wrong shape—too tall. As my eyes adjusted, I could make out what looked like a shoulder and a head, like the silhouette of a person half concealed behind a tree, half peering out in my direction.

A jolt shot through me and I grabbed for Bruno but found nothing but air. He'd bolted in the direction of the shadow, letting loose a ferocious racket. I took a step in his direction but knew I had little hope of catching him—a black dog in the dark yard. I ran to the back deck and felt along the rough brick until I touched a switch. I flipped on a security light and a white glow bathed the yard.

The sudden glare illuminated Bruno, his front paws up on the fence and his head craning over the pickets. He was barking after something as if his life depended on it, pointed exactly at the now-empty space where I swore someone had been watching.

Coaxing an agitated Bruno back into the house was no small task. Finally, the offer of his favorite peanut-butter treats overrode his instinct to protect me and he came sprinting in. I locked the door after him and double-checked all the curtains and blinds. As I caught my breath and waited for my heart to stop hammering, I pulled out my phone to call Polly. Pacing the hallway from my living room to my kitchen and gulping air, I stared at her number. Then I put my phone back in my pocket.

What would I tell her? That I thought I saw something? That Bruno barked at what looked like a shadow? Bruno barked at everything. I wasn't sure what I had seen myself. I had just watched a single streetlight split in two and then merge together. People often walked their dogs in the schoolyard beyond the fence. It could have been a neighbor, for all I knew. I couldn't face the prospect of Polly's doubt.

I kept hearing *Are you sure?* in her concerned tone. In my memory, the dark form grew fainter and more blurred until I was half convinced I'd imagined it altogether. I paced my kitchen, talking myself in and out of making the call.

By the time I'd showered, ironed a dress for Ethan's hearing, and readied myself for bed, I'd mentally slotted the shadowy figure away alongside my fatigue, dizziness, and pain—things my mind sensed quite vividly but that left no tangible mark on the world.

The next morning dawned gray and rainy. When I let Bruno into the back yard, he immediately returned to sniff the spot at the fence. With my umbrella and a cup of coffee, I followed him. As I peered over the fence, the tall weeds and dead leaves between the trees did look trampled, as if someone had stood there. But with the early-morning rain, the entire area looked fairly trodden. Still, Bruno's noisy sniffing reminded me that he had also sensed something.

Returning to the kitchen, I dried Bruno and considered if I should tell my landlady, Bernice, what I'd seen, since it was her house. My phone rang, and I picked up without looking at the display, expecting Mom or Audra with news about Ethan's hearing. Instead, I heard a voice I knew but couldn't place.

"Hi, Riley. This is Dr. Maclean. I hope I'm not calling too early. I wanted to catch you up on the results of the tests I ordered. Is now a good time?"

Glancing at the clock, I readied myself for the news of no news, for the frustration of learning that I'd paid for another round of futile tests.

"Yeah, now's fine."

Papers rattled on the other end of the line. "So, most everything came back within normal ranges, but there was one result that I wanted to discuss with you." More paper shuffling and breathing. "Here we are. Now, if you remember, I ordered an ELISA for Lyme disease, *borrelia burgdorferi*? You and I discussed that you don't recall ever having had a bull's-eye rash, but what's interesting is that your test results show that you *do* have Lyme antibodies." She released a sigh like she was sitting down. "Now, I don't want to get too far ahead of myself, but that could go a long way in explaining your symptoms. There's a second round of tests I'd like to order before I have you come into the office again, a Western blot, that can confirm the results of the first test and some other tests for tick-borne illnesses. I'm also going to call in a prescription for doxycycline. I want you to start taking that today if possible. Ideally, we would have gotten you on that long ago, but we can start it now, at least. Now, I know that's a lot of information. Do you have any questions for me?"

My brain sputtered as I tried to wrap my mind around what Dr. Maclean had said. The image of the tiny tick on my ankle after a run in the woods the previous autumn flashed in my brain. I'd tweezed it off and thought nothing of it.

"Lyme disease?" I repeated. I remembered how my neurologist had dismissed the possibility when I had raised it months ago. People with Lyme often found a red, bull's-eye-shaped rash. I'd never seen a rash, but people frequently didn't.

"Yes," Dr. Maclean responded as if I'd asked a coherent question. "It looks like you've had exposure to it at some point. And it's known to have devastating lingering effects on everything from your joints to the nervous system, particularly when it's not treated right away. I'd like to get you back to the office. If you can get the labs today, then we can expect the results in a week or two. Does that all sound okay?"

I carefully set my coffee mug on the counter. "Yeah, uh, yeah. Huh . . ."

The silence on the line lasted so long, I began to think we'd been disconnected. I heard Dr. Maclean take a breath. "There's one other thing I wanted to mention. I remember that you were referred to me by Beth Lauderdale, so you're aware that she was a patient of mine." My heart sank at the mention of her name. "I wanted to give you and your family my condolences."

"I appreciate that." I thought of what Dr. Maclean must be hearing about Ethan as well. She didn't leave me wondering.

"Of course, the arrest has been in the news too. I can only imagine the stress. I told you before, I don't think your symptoms are psychosomatic, but serious strain can worsen the symptoms you've been having—the autonomic dysfunction and pain. The stress activates your fight-or-flight response, which raises cortisol, which raises inflammation—and with your nervous system on high alert, you can get into a toxic feedback loop." She cleared her throat. "So, I guess all of this is just my way of saying that I hope you'll look after yourself."

It took me a while to respond around the lump in my throat. Where Dr. Thorpe's references to my mental state had made me feel as if I were looking for attention or faking illness, Dr. Maclean didn't dismiss the physical reality of my symptoms. What she described felt more like life as I knew it. "Okay," I said. "I will. Thank you."

Dr. Maclean transferred me to schedule a follow-up appointment, which I added to my calendar.

I stared at my phone, recalling Dr. Maclean's decision to order the test for Lyme. But it had been the end of our last appointment that had stuck with me. After she'd gone through the long list of diseases my first round of blood work had eliminated, I'd ventured to ask her the question that had been gnawing at me for months, one I'd been afraid to voice: *Could this all be in my head?*

She'd been typing up her notes and hadn't turned to face me, but I saw her smile and prepared myself for the blow. She launched into a story.

"I had a young guy come in here once, about your age, the picture of health. Handsome, athletic, built like an Adonis." She laughed to herself. "For a year or so he'd been having weakness, fatigue, joint pain, brain fog. You name it. He'd been through test after test with every specialist imaginable, and it all looked fine. His family kept telling him he was depressed. Well, he told me he'd had depression, and he knew what that felt like, and this was different. So he kept trying. Long story short, we finally tested him for an autoimmune disease that pretty much never affects men his age, and—boom—it came back positive. He'd been listing the exact symptoms for months, but nobody bothered to test him because he didn't fit the profile or it wasn't their specialty."

She'd stretched her legs out in front of her and leaned toward me. "What I'm saying, Riley, is that there are so many rare illnesses in the world and diseases where there's no definitive diagnostic testing. We know so much about the body, but there's a need to respect all we don't know too." She'd adjusted the top of her knee brace as she spoke. "Don't get me wrong. The mind can certainly contribute to physical symptoms, but when we can't explain physical symptoms with test results, it doesn't necessarily mean they're coming from the mind. That's one possibility of many, but I don't think that's the case with you."

I'd hung on her words. "How can you know?"

"Do you remember at your first appointment when I had you stand and close your eyes and you fell to the side? We talked about your impaired proprioception—that sense of your body in space. Well, that tells me you have some dorsal column dysfunction going on. So, yes, that's coming from your brain, but not in the way you're asking about." She smiled.

I'd nodded. The last thing she'd said was, "We'll figure this out, Riley."

I'd replayed that story and her promise countless times since that appointment, hoping they weren't just kind words. Now, after so many months, I was beginning to believe.

Glancing at the time, I saw I was running late. As I hurried to get ready, I thought of all that had happened since that appointment, and the word

Dr. Maclean had used, *proprioception,* echoed in my mind. I recalled the sudden jolt of falling in the darkness after I'd closed my eyes. I'd felt like that since Beth died, only now—with everything I thought I knew about my world in question—opening my eyes was no help. I'd lost the fixed points I'd always used to moor myself and my sense of who I could trust or where my steps would take me. Still, I had to keep moving forward.

I grabbed my keys and jogged to the car. As for minimizing stress, I knew it was excellent advice. I promised myself I'd consider it right after Ethan's bail hearing.

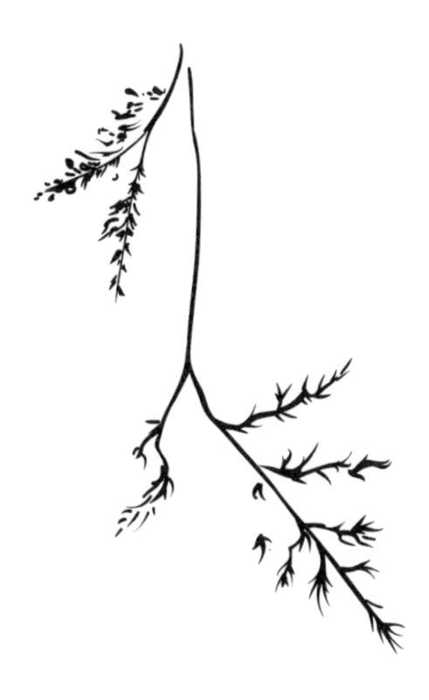

# CHAPTER TWENTY

*September 28, 2022*

The cold rain that I'd woken to hung on throughout the morning. Mom, Marco, Audra, and I all hunched under one umbrella as we climbed the wide stairway and passed through the blocky limestone pillars into the county courthouse. With the drips rolling off of the lip of the umbrella onto my head, I ended up wetter than if I'd had no umbrella at all. I kept running through the timeline of Ethan's bail hearing, posting bail, and his release—anticipating that, as early as this afternoon, he'd be out. I'd have some questions for him, and I had to be ready for the answers. As we made our way down the marble hallway to the main courtroom, the wet soles of our shoes squeaked and set my nerves further on edge. Outside the courtroom doorway, I recognized Juliette Gundy amid a huddle of cameramen and reporters. A buzz of conversation animated their hive.

We had no sooner found seats together in the third row than Marco excused himself.

"Liam didn't make it into work this morning. I need to get someone there to cover."

He shook his head in irritation and scrolled through the contacts in his phone, looking for someone who might be able to fill in. I tried to keep my expression blank at the mention of Liam as Marco sidled back down the row of seats. Marco had always been remarkable for his ability to let negativity roll off of him, but with Ethan's arrest, the full responsibility of managing the farm now fell on his shoulders. This morning he looked weary, the toll of it all carving a furrow between his eyebrows.

At the front of the courtroom, Carson Applebaum spoke with a younger man in a suit. Whatever the man was saying seemed to cause Carson's shoulders to stoop a few more degrees. He turned toward us and greeted us with a wave before motioning for my mom to join him. I noticed that he either wore the same dark suit and navy tie from the previous afternoon again today or else he owned an exact duplicate. He tilted his head near Mom's to tell her something. Whatever it was, my mom winced and said something sharp in return. Carson shook his head and Mom returned to us with her mouth set so tight that her lips disappeared. She sat back down with her back ramrod straight and stared at the front of the courtroom. "What is it?" Audra leaned across me to ask.

Mom swiveled her whole body toward us, her posture still rigidly upright. "Carson tells me there's an outstanding warrant against Ethan from Cuyahoga County. Assault. It's several years old. Probably from that phase he went through with those hooligans." She tried to wave it away, but it came off as more of a spasm. "But that's not it." She took a breath and paused so long I wasn't sure she'd continue. "Liam was in an accident early this morning. It looks like someone fired at him and ran him off the road. He survived, but he's in critical condition. Carson tells me that Liam had . . . placed Ethan at the house on the afternoon of the murder, so he's considered a witness against him. So . . . all of that looks bad for Ethan."

"Oh my God." Audra's mouth dropped open, and I took a gulp of air. Something sharp wedged its way inside my chest, making it hard to breathe. The edges of the courtroom wavered and I focused on not falling out of my chair. Had our visit to Liam had anything to do with what happened?

First the gunfire at Simon's, and now this? It was like Beth's murder had set off a chain reaction. The more we tried to combat it, the faster the chaos expanded.

Audra recovered first. "How can they blame Ethan? He's been locked up."

Mom held a hand to the side, palm up, as if to say she didn't know. Her eyes darted to her trembling hand, and she dropped it back into her lap. "I guess they think someone did it on his behalf. I don't know, but Carson said that if there's even a *hint* of a threat to a witness, then . . ." She trailed off, as if she had neither the energy nor the heart to finish the statement. We'd gotten the gist. Ethan might not be coming home anytime soon.

Marco had returned and stood at the edge of the row next to Mom. He scanned our grim faces with his own look of wariness, as if bracing himself for the inevitable bombshell that was about to explode next. "What?" he asked with a tone of dread. "What did I miss?"

The hearing went as poorly as expected. Doug arrived at the last minute and seemed conflicted as to where to sit. After taking a step toward us, he veered in the other direction and took a seat across the aisle, where he gave us a sheepish wave. I noticed Polly and Osborne seated in the back row by the door. I tried to catch Polly's eye, but she had her head bent over her phone.

The bailiff told us to "all rise," and then the judge came out.

"Oh no." Audra ducked her head. I followed her eyes: Doris Lorenzen, Audra's former classmate, was the judge. When she had moved to North Haven in seventh grade, with her flame-orange hair and hangdog eyes, the kids in her grade had nicknamed Doris the Lorax. By eighth grade, having endured their torment long enough, Doris decided to reinvent herself as a platinum blonde. Unfortunately, the resulting color had been more of a yellow-orange, and the bleach had turned the texture of her fine hair into that of fiberglass insulation.

Although my school usually fell near the bottom on state tests for reading and math, when it came to inflicting petty cruelty on one another, we were in the ninetieth percentile across the board. Within the first few hours of the new school year, the boys in her class crafted the taunt *Doris the Lorax dipped her head in Clorox.* Never mind the slant rhyme; it took off. Doris spent the remainder of the school year sharing a lonely lunch table with Rat Boy.

In the same grade as Doris but at the other end of the high-school food chain, Audra had been obscenely popular—homecoming queen, head cheerleader, prom queen, and class president. Polly once described her as loved, feared, and hated in equal parts. By the expression Audra wore as she shielded her face, I guessed that she had not been as noble as she should have been in defending Doris. I had no idea if someone who had come as far as Doris might hold a grudge against the little twerps who made her life so miserable long ago. But now, she would be deciding my brother's fate.

Ethan looked as insubstantial as a ghost when the bailiff led him into the courtroom. His glassy eyes passed over all of us only for a second before he was turned away. Despite the dread piling up in my chest, I tried to look optimistic for his sake. Judge Lorenzon studied Ethan over her glasses as she read the charges. He showed no response to her words and kept his head down with his eyes on the table in front of him. I wondered if he was even listening. Phrases were uttered that I'd never expected to hear outside of a courtroom drama. The choreography of rising, talking, and sitting went on, almost comical as I watched without the least ability to actually follow the meaning. At last, Judge Lorenzon said something that penetrated my thoughts, conceding that as a lifelong resident of the community, Ethan posed little risk of flight. For a split second, a tiny spark of hope flared. Then she kept talking.

"However, in light of the threat Mr. Svenson poses to the community, particularly potential witnesses, his history of alleged assault, and the circumstances surrounding the unfortunate injury to a witness this morning, it is my decision to deny bail."

Acid surged in my throat. Next to me, my mom's superhuman posture finally gave out and she slumped back in her seat, resigned to the fact that flawless comportment could no longer save her son. The hearing proceeded rapidly from there: Carson noted his intention to appeal the denial of bail, and Ethan was remanded into custody.

A bailiff approached Ethan, who stood, had his hands cuffed, and was led from the courtroom. As the bailiff steered him, Ethan met my eyes with a look of despair. Then he was gone.

Afterward, Carson huddled with my mom and tried to soothe her with words like *appeal* and *character witness,* but the fight had gone out of her. After a moment, he moved off, and we filed out of the courtroom in a daze, funneling through the narrow doorway. In the hallway, a knot of reporters waited, firing questions at us.

Juliette Gundy positioned herself near my mom's shoulder amid the frenzy and asked, "Do you believe your son killed Beth Lauderdale?" Mom's head swiveled slowly and ominously toward Juliette, but Audra was quick to put an arm on her shoulder and maneuver her past. A moment later, we were all greatly relieved to be back out in the drizzle and to have removed Mom from the tumult before she'd had a chance to dig her nails into Juliette's smooth face.

On the way back to the car, we didn't bother with the umbrella, but I hardly noticed the rain hitting me. I had driven separately and needed to go get my blood test, but before I split off, I whispered to Audra: "We need to talk about Liam."

Her eyes were solemn as she nodded. I could tell that, like me, she was thinking about the visit we'd paid him less than twenty-four hours before someone had tried to kill him.

"Call me later."

# CHAPTER TWENTY-ONE

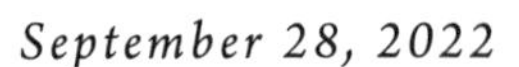

*September 28, 2022*

As I watched my blood fill the tube, my vision blurred, and for a moment, two overlapping garnet-red tubes hovered over the crook of my arm. A few blinks and the tubes of blood merged back into one. The phlebotomist taped a cotton ball to my arm and called after me to drink water as I tottered out the door. In the parking lot, I switched my radio off and sat in my car for a few minutes trying to catch my breath. In the five days since Beth's murder, I'd been carried along on alternating waves of jittery adrenaline and stupefying exhaustion. Sitting in my quiet car with my hands trembling, I felt like a rubber band that had been stretched too far for too long.

The rain had stopped, but midday traffic was heavy as I pulled out of the lab parking lot. I shook my head to clear it. Outside of a preschool, a crossing guard stopped me to release a stream of cars from the parking lot and my thoughts turned to the bail hearing, replaying the broken look on Ethan's face as he was led away in cuffs and the sharp stab in my chest at the news of the attack on Liam. I couldn't help but wonder if Audra and I had put a target on him yesterday.

Someone honking behind me brought me back to the present. The crossing guard was waving me on impatiently, and I accelerated. With all the traffic, I took the turn for Route 20 rather than Main Street—a bit longer but with fewer lights. Once I was home, I'd call Audra and talk through our next steps. I grimaced at the thought that we might have to tell Polly about our conversation with Liam.

I was rounding a curve and merging into the left-turn lane for Route 20 when the dense smoke began to creep in at the edges of my vision. I blinked my eyes, willing it away. Not now. For a moment, the road ahead of me shimmered and then the single turn lane drifted from the center out. Two wavering, overlapping lanes stretched out in front of me.

I jerked the wheel, pure panic firing through my veins. Cars buzzed by on either side, horns blasting. My heart fought its way up my throat as I squinted at the two hoods of my car in two possible lanes, no idea which one was real. Traffic whizzed by. Fast. I had to keep going.

I heard the sound of tires screeching and the slam of metal on metal before I even saw the SUV. The impact jerked me to the side. My head whipped forward and my teeth bore down into my lower lip.

The next thing I knew, I was gasping for air. More horns chorused, but they sounded far away over the ringing in my ears. I shook my head and eased my door open. Then I heard it, a wailing little voice.

A black SUV was now attached to my front bumper. The driver's-side door flew open and a tall, thickly built man with red hair jumped out. He strode toward me like he wanted to wring my neck. "What the hell are you doing? You could've killed someone!"

From there, my impressions came in fragments: the volume of the wailing increased when the little girl was lifted from her car seat—her red curls, red face with a shine of snot under her nose. A blue plush bear on a plastic ring dangled from her fingers.

Someone led me to the damp grass on the side of the road, and I watched a police officer direct traffic around my car and the SUV. Drivers craned their necks as they passed me. A medic gave me a bottle of water to rinse my mouth, and I spat blood into the grass. Wiping the blood from my face, she examined my lip and shook her head. No stitches. Aside from my minor cuts, no one was injured. With my heart still lodged in my throat I felt grateful for that, at least. I knew this was my fault.

The red-haired man was giving a statement to the officers, and I caught snippets. "Could've killed someone . . . on drugs, or something." The man held his daughter protectively on his hip away from me, keeping the bulk of his body between us, glaring at me as if I could still harm her.

I began to shiver so hard my teeth chattered. The man and his daughter wove in and out of focus. When I closed my eyes, it was no better, because I saw Liam, crystal clear in a hospital bed, hooked up to machines—maybe because of me.

The man was absolutely right. I could have killed someone. What the hell was I doing?

After I passed a sobriety test, the police let me go with a ticket for driving left of center. The officer who wrote out the citation raised his eyebrows when he read the name "Svenson" off of my license.

I'd just gotten home, kicked off my shoes, and let Bruno into the back yard with his tennis ball when the doorbell rang. My first thought was to wonder if it might be Doug again, since I knew he'd been in Wicksburg for the hearing.

Instead it was Detective Osborne's blurred face that I saw through the leaded glass. I felt a surge of irritation as I swung the door open. This guy standing on my welcome mat was the one responsible for putting my family through hell and adding to the tragedy of Beth's murder. On top of this grief, while Ethan remained locked up, someone else was out there terrorizing Simon, Audra, me, and now Liam. My brain weakly objected that Osborne was just doing his job by following up with me, but the swell of anger in my chest told my brain to shut the hell up.

I leaned across the doorway and crossed my arms.

"Hi, Riley. I'm glad I caught you at home. Do you mind if I come in?" He held a trench coat folded over his arm.

I searched for the right words to tell him to get lost, but decades of habitual politeness battled with my resentment. In the end, the best I could come up with was, "What do you need?"

"I was hoping we could talk. I'm sure you've heard about what happened to Liam this morning. I'm trying to get a picture of what he's been up to these last few days." He paused and asked again, "May I come in?"

"Fine, but I need to head out before long," I lied. I considered elaborating on my fake plans but then thought better of weaving unnecessarily complicated lies for a detective.

Turning my back to him, I touched my lip to ensure it wasn't still bleeding. I motioned him to my uncomfortable couch and noticed with satisfaction that the afternoon sun blasted him in the face as he sat. The day had cleared and the sun shone forcefully. In the fierce light, Osborne's brown eyes looked almost amber and he leaned forward to avoid the worst of the glare. Sitting across from him, I studied his regular features and noticed fine lines across his forehead and a faint white scar above his right eyebrow.

"How have you been holding up?" was his first question. I realized that he thought we could pick up where we'd left off, recapture the camaraderie we'd shared the night of the memorial. The only problem was that he'd arrested my brother since then.

"Fine," I answered shortly. "Where's Polly?"

"Polly has recused herself from this case in light of Ethan's arrest and her ties to your family." I could feel the searchlight of his eyes on my face and tried to hide my dismay. "It was purely her decision, but don't worry. Another detective will be assigned."

My shoulders sagged. Another detective would not know Ethan like Polly did. I supposed that was the point, but I wondered at the wisdom of a policy that discouraged actually knowing the people you were investigating. Polly's presence had been a spot of hope for me. It wasn't that I expected her to sweep things under the rug or do us favors, but she understood on a personal level what this case meant to us and cared enough to keep looking for answers. With her gone, I worried more than ever about the detectives' willingness to look at other possibilities with Ethan, the fiancé and prime suspect, already sitting in jail to take the blame.

Osborne shifted his weight on the unforgiving sofa. "I'm sorry. I know this has been hard on your family." I nodded. "But with the developments this morning, I'd like to ask you a few questions."

Liam. I held my breath and when I didn't answer, he continued. "Do you happen to own a gun?"

I exhaled a sharp laugh. As worried as I was about him asking about Audra and me visiting Liam, I hadn't expected this. The question actually came as a relief. "Are you seriously asking me if I'm involved in what happened to Liam?"

"I'm not saying that, Riley. I'm just covering the bases. I wouldn't be doing my job if I didn't talk to you and Ethan's associates."

"As long as you have Ethan locked up for this, then you're not doing your job. Why start now?" The words left my mouth before I could think.

He blinked, but the rest of his face remained immobile.

"No," I answered finally as the silence wore on. "I don't own a gun."

"Do you know of anyone close to Ethan who might?"

I couldn't help but laugh again. "About every guy and half of the women. It would be a lot easier if I could just name the people in North Haven who *don't* have guns. That'd be quicker."

The corner of his mouth twitched. "Fair enough. Well, we're actually looking for two different guns, a hunting rifle—which, again, I know might not narrow it down—and a handgun. Could you tell me who you know that might have something like that?"

"In the country, probably more people than not, at least with the hunting rifle. I wouldn't really know about a handgun. Look, I'm sorry I can't help. I hate what happened to Liam, and I really hope he'll be okay. Once he recovers, he can tell you what happened himself, but my family and I were all getting ready for Ethan's hearing this morning. That's where our focus is." I had intended for the last part to sound stern, but it came out sad.

Osborne pushed up the cuffs of his dress shirt and cleared his throat before meeting my eyes. "I'm not just here to . . . Look, Polly tells me that you and Audra paid a visit to Simon Aldridge yesterday and that someone fired at his residence while you were there."

I nodded and my heart beat a little faster. I knew Audra had not told Polly about our visit to Liam, but I still didn't like Osborne knowing what we'd been up to the previous day.

"Can you tell me what you and Audra were doing there?"

I focused on a spot on the wall behind Osborne's head as I mentally paged through a variety of responses. Ultimately, I settled with the simplest version of the truth: "We wanted to know what he saw, or what he *says* he saw, at least. Simon's not the most reliable person, and he's had a grudge against my family for as long as I can remember. But even *he* says he never saw Ethan go into the house that day." My voice was rising. "There's no proof Ethan hurt Beth."

Osborne frowned and looked down at his folded hands. "Then why do you think he would lie to us about being at the house that day?" He held up a hand to stop me before I could respond. "And why were there traces of Beth's blood in the bed of his truck?"

This last part silenced me far more effectively than his hand had. Audra had told me that traces of blood had been found, but I hadn't heard that they had been matched to Beth. My cheeks felt icy as the blood drained from my face. Part of me wanted to lie down right there on the couch and ask Osborne to see himself out. How long could I keep arguing against the mounting evidence? I didn't know if love or stubbornness kept me fighting. Would a video of Ethan committing the crime even change my mind? I'd probably call it a deep fake and keep on arguing.

I closed my eyes, sensing Osborne's gaze but no longer caring. The truck. I thought about all the trips Beth and Ethan had taken to the garden center, all the antiques she had dragged home to restore.

I opened my eyes. "Beth used the truck all the time for gardening and work at the Castle. She could have cut herself on a rosebush or on a nail in a piece of trim. There's a million ways it could have happened that don't involve Ethan doing anything wrong." I said the words to myself as much as to Osborne.

He laced his fingers together with a deep sigh, as if I was a particularly exhausting child. I wondered if I was wearing him down or if he was just losing patience.

"Look, Riley. I appreciate that you want to help your brother. I know you're an intelligent woman, so I hope after what happened to Liam you'll have realized this already, but you need to steer clear of this investigation. If there is something else to find, we'll find it, but you and your sister . . . it not only looks bad for Ethan to have you interfering, but it puts you in danger. The last thing your family needs is for something else to happen to one of you. I'm saying this to you as a friend."

The sun had lowered while we spoke. Only a portion of Osborne's face was still brightly illuminated—I could see the faint shadow where he had shaved and an irritated patch on his neck where his collar rubbed. I tried to read him, but he wore the same genial, unflappable expression as he did the terrible day I'd met him. Something about this conversation nagged at me, but I couldn't identify what.

I put my hands on my knees, preparing to stand. "Well, if that's all, I should get going."

Osborne regarded me and then nodded. I stood and took a few brisk steps in the direction of the door and, feeling the familiar, sudden blackness crowd my vision—the roaring of blood in my ears—staggered into the doorway.

I backed up and bent over, still blind, and waited for gravity to carry blood back into my brain.

"Are you okay?" I heard faintly over the white-water noise in my ears. As I tried to coax my body into gear, I recalled that Osborne had witnessed me passing out the night Beth went missing. I was determined he wouldn't see me like that again—not that my determination had much say in the matter.

"Fine," I got out. "I had some blood tests this afternoon. Probably dizzy from that." He didn't need to know about the accident. I straightened up and looked for Osborne through the dark curtain that still hung in front of my vision.

His brown eyebrows tilted. "Let me get you some water, at least. Sit back down."

"I'm okay," I repeated, but he was already on his way toward my kitchen, so I lurched toward the chair. Might as well sit.

Sounds drifted to me from the kitchen: a cupboard opening and closing, a rustle of plastic, and running water. The tap shut off and Osborne called to me. "There's a dog in the yard?" It sounded like a question. "And it's really digging."

Perfect. "Can you tap on the window? He'll come in if you open the back door."

"Let me bring you the water first." He was already returning with a coffee mug of water. "It also looks like he may have shredded your library book." Osborne handed me a book dented with canine tooth marks and a torn plastic cover. *Creating a Suitable Venue for Every Wedding.* It was the one I had intended to return for Beth.

Wonderful. I took the book in one hand and the water in the other. "Thanks."

Osborne nodded briefly before pivoting back to the kitchen to let Bruno in. I sipped the water and examined the book. The protective plastic cover the library had wrapped the book in had done little to ward off Bruno's wrath; it hung on by a millimeter of tape and the dust jacket beneath was shredded. The plastic cover had a library barcode affixed to it, so I finished Bruno's destruction and pulled the plastic cover off, intending to wedge it in the pages of the book for safekeeping—not that I expected to get away with returning the book in this state. I was *so* going to get a fine for this. As I pulled the plastic cover away from the book, something small fell from beneath the dust jacket and clattered onto the floor. I set my water on the end table and reached down. My vision clouded, but I felt along the cool hardwood until I touched a small square of plastic.

I could hear Bruno's claws clicking on the kitchen tile and Osborne closing the kitchen door. I quickly palmed the piece of plastic and instinctively tucked it into my pocket. A split second later, Bruno was upon me, nuzzling and licking my hands like he hadn't seen me in years. Osborne followed.

"He's a nice dog," he said, despite having just witnessed Bruno's swath of destruction. I didn't know Osborne well enough to tell if he was being sarcastic or not, but he looked serious.

"He has his moments," I replied, scratching Bruno's silky head. In reality, as ill-behaved as he was, he had kept me sane with his simple-minded affection through my dad's death, my illness, and now all of this. Bruno clicked across the floor toward Osborne, leaving dirty paw prints in his wake, and sat at Osborne's feet, expecting affection.

Osborne obliged and rubbed Bruno's ears but kept his eyes on me. "Are you doing better?"

I nodded.

"Good, but I don't think you should be going anywhere right away."

"I'm not planning to."

He tilted his head. "I thought you had to go somewhere?" A faint smile.

"Right." I sipped my water thoughtfully. "Yeah, I'm going to . . . reschedule . . . that." I felt myself blush. At least some blood was returning to my head.

Osborne didn't bother to hide his grin, and I realized I hadn't seen him smile before. There hadn't been much occasion for it over the past week, but it was a pleasant, open smile—or maybe it was simply that it was nice to see a smile at all.

For a moment, with him smiling and petting Bruno, I felt almost relaxed.

Then, I remembered the plastic square I'd hidden in my pocket.

"But I know you have things to do. Thanks for stopping by. I hope you don't mind if I don't walk you out." I raised the mug of water to show I was dutifully working on my hydration.

"Oh, of course." He gave Bruno a final ear scratch. "Take good care of her," he addressed Bruno lightly.

I laughed. "Oh, he'll take care of me all right."

Still grinning, Osborne grabbed the coat he'd thrown over the sofa and made his way toward the front door. With his hand on the doorknob, he looked over his shoulder. "Please think about what I said. Let the police handle this. I promise that if there's something to find, we'll find it."

I thought of the square of plastic hidden in my pocket. *Not necessarily.* "Okay, as long as you think about what I said too. Ethan didn't do this."

He looked down at the jacket tucked over his arm and nodded. He gave me a half wave and the door clicked closed behind him. From the front window, I watched him walk to his car. Before he had even pulled away from the curb, I was reaching into my pocket to look at what had fallen from the book. Wafer thin, black plastic, and less than an inch either way, it was a small SD memory card. It looked much like the type that would go in a camera, like the one I'd seen among Beth's crafting supplies. A bit of tape still clung to the memory card where it had been secured to the book. I felt a giddy anticipation. I had no idea what the card might hold, but I would be damned if I'd give it to the police before I had a chance to preview it.

I picked up *Creating a Suitable Venue for Every Wedding* from the end table beside me and removed the remnants of the mangled dust cover, which pictured a happy couple in front of a mansion and loads of hydrangeas. I hadn't expected to find anything more, but there, taped to the dark-green surface of the hardbound book was a neatly folded pink piece of paper. I peeled at the clear tape with my thumbnail and lifted the paper away from the cover. Holding it up to the light from the front window, I unfolded it.

Immediately, I recognized the delicate loops and arcs of the penmanship. The small, pink piece of paper was covered margin-to-margin with Beth's writing.

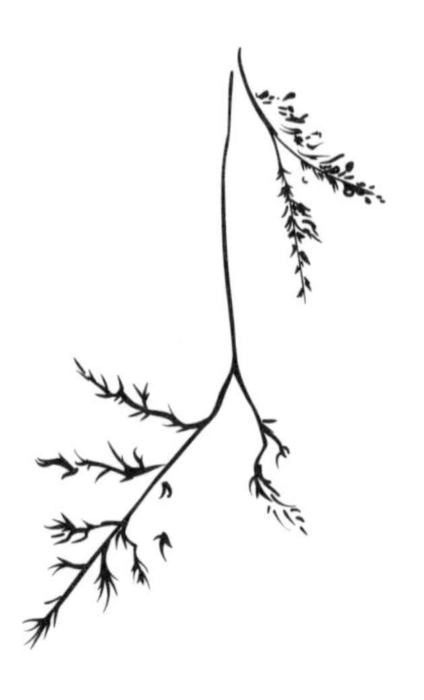

## CHAPTER TWENTY-TWO

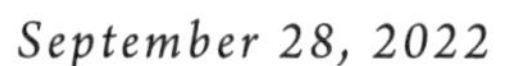

*September 28, 2022*

After ensuring Osborne's black SUV had disappeared down the street behind a screen of a fire-orange maples, I closed the front curtains tightly. I laid the piece of paper I'd found in the book flat on my sofa, snapped a picture, and texted it to Audra.

Setting the memory card aside for the moment, I focused on the paper. At first glance, it was simple enough. It looked like journaling or creative writing, but skimming over the words, it made little sense. Unconnected ideas ran in all directions across the small rectangle of paper. I focused first on a long passage that filled the center of the page, two paragraphs, the first written in cursive and the second printed:

> *A thing doesn't exist until you know about it. If it never got back to Ethan, if he never knew and the thought—the image of it—never even entered his mind, then it couldn't hurt him. It wouldn't even exist for him. But I underestimated the ripples of my actions in this quiet little pond. My every step into the water displaced something that was*

*already there, sent up a dusty plume of sediment that had lain for decades or rocked a tiny swell that lapped up somewhere else.*

Only now it's reversed. Now someone is moving in my direction, spurring a new tide that's rising against me. What used to be warm and easy has turned cold and rough. It's become all I can do to keep my head above water, my arms and legs too heavy to keep fighting. I need to make a choice—get out or take a deep breath and go under. Whatever I choose, Ethan will see me differently. Or, maybe he won't see me at all.

My heart hammered as I read Beth's words. Scanning the first two lines again, I thought about the last day I saw her, when she told me how she would "never do anything to hurt Ethan." Did she think that if he never found out about the drugs, it would all be okay? Did she really think that she could keep a secret of that magnitude without hurting him?

My phone buzzed. I picked up Audra's call.

Her questions came rapid fire. "Is that Beth's writing? Where'd you find it?"

I explained Osborne's visit, Bruno's destruction of the book, and my subsequent find. "I don't know what it is, though. Can you read the writing in the picture I texted?"

I could practically hear her squinting at her phone. "Mostly, but it's hard to make out the edges. It looks like creative writing or something." I could hear her mumbling the opening lines under her breath before she gave up. "Read it to me," she ordered.

I cleared my throat and read the two paragraphs from the center of the page. When I finished, the last words hung over the line between us. *Ethan will see me differently. Or, maybe he won't see me at all.* I shivered.

Audra was first to speak. "The beginning part has got to be about the pills, don't you think? Like, she thinks if Ethan doesn't know, it won't hurt him, right? That shows he didn't know what was going on."

"That's what I thought. Unless she had another secret. What about the second part where she talks about someone else—someone moving in her direction? It's like she knew she was in danger."

"Maybe things started to go sour. The first paragraph is cursive and the second is printed, like she wrote them at different times. Maybe things were going well enough at first, but then it changed."

The line went quiet as we both considered the few words Beth had left behind.

"Do you think she was going to tell Ethan? That part where it says he'll see her differently?" Audra asked.

I read the last lines again. "I think she was considering it. I mean, she talks about a choice, so I don't know what she would have done . . ." I remembered my last walk with Beth in the woods and the feeling that she'd been on the verge of confiding in me. I wondered if we'd had more time, what choice she would have made.

Along the top of the paper, more text ran perpendicular to the long passage. "What does the sideways part say? It's blurry on my phone."

I had only glanced at these lines myself. I rotated the paper, cleared my throat again, and read:

Plunged into the water
a buoyant armor of bubbles
suspends me, weightless, warm, my hair
snakes around me like a halo
Every joint loosens until I flow freely
pain disconnected as the current
Sun divvies the water into wavering panes
1 could float right through this silver net
shimmering sunlit, directly into heaven!

"What the hell is that?" Audra asked. "Why couldn't she tell us whatever it was she wanted us to know?"

"I don't know that she wanted *us* to know anything. We're just the ones that found it." I read the lines again. "Do you think it's about taking the pills for her pain, finally finding some relief?"

I thought of Beth's eyes and her loose bearing the day I'd seen her with Liam. I knew how desperate she'd been to find a way to keep functioning despite her pain. Anger and sorrow surged in my chest.

I held the paper more closely to study the closing lines. "Is that a number *1* or an *I* at the beginning of the second-to-last line?"

"Who knows? Maybe she was high out of her mind and expressing herself freely."

I cleared my throat again. "Here's the rest from the side of the page."

In smaller cursive, along the right margin, Beth had written two lines:

*Tend to your brother's house, your sister's home; tend to the river, the boatswain who carries them through the silver sycamores, beneath the sliver of moon. Dead trees light the way to the river on the other side.*

"Oh my God." Audra's frustration boiled over. "Like a metaphorical river or the real river? What's with all the water?"

"I don't know. Maybe both? That reminds me of something I've heard before, the dead trees. It sounds like a hymnal."

"Or maybe a poem? This doesn't tell us anything. Why did Beth have to be an English major?" Audra lamented.

I tried to think of where I'd heard similar words before, but my brain felt about as nimble as a lump of oatmeal. "I can't remember. Whatever it is, it's got to mean something if she bothered to hide it along with the memory card."

"What *about* the memory card? Is that any help?"

"I don't know yet. My laptop doesn't have a card reader." Audra lived only five minutes from me. "Does yours?"

"Let me check." I heard steps, shuffling, and a bang as she set down the phone. A second later I heard her breath again. "What am I looking for?"

After a detailed discussion of the various openings on her laptop, we concluded that none of them matched the narrow inch-long slot we needed.

I thought for a moment. "I have a card reader at work." As much as I wanted to jump into my car immediately, I knew I wasn't well enough to drive. The father's accusation that I could've killed someone still echoed in my ears. After some food and sleep I'd be better. "I'll go in tomorrow to check it out."

Among the many disorienting events of the past week, being away from work for so long had thrown me out of my routine. As eager as I was to return to normalcy, I knew that returning to work would not feel normal, at least not right away.

"Have you heard anything else about Liam?" I asked Audra. "Do you think anyone knows we were there yesterday?"

"Oh God. What a nightmare. Well, I don't think it's a coincidence that someone shot at us and then went after him the next morning. They could have seen us at Liam's and followed us to Simon's, and then forced Liam off the road this morning."

Somewhere in the back of my brain, the issue that had been nagging at me during my conversation with Osborne clicked into place: he had mentioned two different guns. "Osborne asked whether I knew someone with a rifle *and* a handgun. It sounded like a rifle at Simon's, so someone must have used a handgun with Liam."

Audra responded with a drawn-out sigh. "So, does that mean it's two different people or one person with multiple guns?"

"I don't know." I lay back on the couch as I considered the possibilities. Neither option was comforting.

I woke just as exhausted as when I'd lain down but relieved to be able to see straight. After the tumultuous past six days, the normalcy of readying myself for work came as a relief. My mind clicked into autopilot as I pulled out of the driveway and drove the familiar roads, but a sense of dread hung over me as I anticipated my coworkers' whispers and pitying looks.

I entered Wicks headquarters through the heavy glass doors, the air smelling like apples and cedar. The morning sun shining in seemed to infuse the particles of dust that hung in the light with a low hum. I'd arrived early to avoid causing a scene, but there turned out to be no reason to worry. In the quiet halls, no one spoke to me.

Few people were in yet, but those I did pass slid their eyes away from mine, suddenly interested in the pattern on the carpet or the view out the window. I didn't blame them. I wouldn't have known what to say to someone in my situation either. *So sorry to hear about your friend and future-sister-in-law's murder. Oh, and* also *sorry to hear that your brother may have done it. Thoughts and prayers.*

I settled back into my office. It took all my self-control to leave my door slightly cracked to allow Jane to stop in before I checked the memory card. Somehow, Jane managed to hold down the position of chief copywriter, even though she spent most of her time drifting from office to office, accumulating an encyclopedic knowledge of what everyone in the building was up to. Although I wanted nothing more than to check the card immediately, a closed door was no match for Jane, and I didn't want to be interrupted. I would get our visit out of the way and then have the privacy I needed. I started in on an enormous backlog of emails and, like clockwork, Jane silently materialized at a quarter after eight in a sky-blue peasant blouse and diaphanous white skirt that hid her feet, making her appear to hover in my doorway.

"Hey, sweetie." She slid into the chair across from my desk. After a second of awkward silence, she continued. "So . . . anything new with you?"

I smiled. Maybe a visit from Jane was exactly what I needed. "Nothing that you wouldn't have read in the newspaper," I replied.

Jane smoothed her skirt and shook her head. "I'm so sorry to hear about Ethan." Behind her big glasses, her magnified eyes did look truly sorry. "Your family has been through the wringer. Does he have a good attorney?"

"Well, he has an experienced attorney. I guess we'll find out how good he is." Jane's longtime partner was an estate lawyer and, consequently, Jane had absorbed a good deal of knowledge about the legal system over the years. I considered confiding in her, but as much as I loved Jane, I was reluctant to share. She was, after all, an accomplished gossip. I had trusted her with secrets before, but nothing of this magnitude.

Jane slid a bangle bracelet around her wrist. She always played with her jewelry when she was working up to something; I waited. "So, what does this all mean for the position in Bath?"

I sighed. "I can't even think about that right now. I don't need to decide until November."

"Well, you might not want my opinion, but I think you should do it. You're young, and it's only for a year. I would do it if they would send a copywriter." Reading the concern on my face, she added, "Your family will still be here when you get back."

I raised an eyebrow. "The way things have been going, I'm not so sure." Her words touched a nerve. I'd always dreaded what might happen if I wasn't around to smooth things over between Mom and Audra, then Mom and Beth. And what would happen now with Ethan? I imagined coming home after a year abroad to find Mom and Audra not speaking, Ethan in prison—all of us a family in name only.

I steered the conversation back to more surface-level office affairs. After catching me up on the latest news, Jane sensed I was not in a talkative mood, rose from her chair, and floated back out my door.

No sooner was she gone than I was up and closing the door behind her. As the door clicked softly shut, I heard the tail end of my eternally patient coworker Kevin counseling his wife Marian. *Think of your anger like stones. Throw them into the ocean. Toss them away.*

I took the card reader from my desk drawer and plugged the cable into my desktop computer. Digging around the small side pocket of my purse, I located the memory card. I took a deep breath and slipped it into the card reader.

The drive appeared on my screen and I clicked. A single folder popped up with a little lock icon on it. When I clicked on the folder, a box for a password appeared.

"Crap." I rose from my chair and paced. Maybe it was something simple. I never recalled Beth being especially technical. She had asked for my help fixing everything from her cell phone to the vacuum over the years. I sat back down, crossed my fingers on one hand, and with the other typed in *1116*, the month and day of Beth's birthday.

A little beep sounded and a warning under the password box told me, "Incorrect password. Nine attempts remain."

"Double crap." Keeping my fingers crossed, I tried Ethan's birthday, then their wedding date. Still no luck. My crossed fingers were cramping up. Seven attempts left. A whisper of panic began to creep in. I rolled my shoulders and stretched my neck side to side. What other numbers or words might Beth have found memorable? I tried her initials, Ethan's name, and his initials.

Sweat dampened my forehead. I texted Audra, *Need a password to access the file. Already tried birthdays, wedding date, and names.*

She texted right back. *Did you try* password? *That's what I usually use.*

I rolled my eyes. Then I tried it anyway.

*Nope, guess Beth had better security practices than you. 3 tries left*

Another text appeared. *Sometimes I add a 1 to the end of it.*

I shook my head in despair, but I was getting desperate; I tried *password1*. The same unsatisfying beep warned me that only two attempts remained.

Shoving my chair back, I got up and paced my small office. The thought of losing access to this file made me clammy. Maybe I should turn the memory card over to the police. The folder could be set to delete after ten unsuccessful attempts. But what would the police do that I couldn't do? There were password-cracking softwares out there, but those relied on generating random combinations until they found the right one. With only ten attempts permitted, that wouldn't work. This required an educated guess from someone who knew her. Then I remembered the piece of paper in the library book. Why would Beth hide it with the memory card?

I pulled the paper from my purse and scanned the text. My eyes paused on the cryptic poem. Why did Beth break those lines up like she had? I skimmed the passage again.

Plunged into the water
a buoyant armor of bubbles
suspends me, weightless, warm, my hair
snakes around me like a halo
Every joint loosens until I flow freely
pain disconnected as the current
Sun divvies the water into wavering panes
1 could float right through this silver net
shimmering sunlit, directly into heaven!

"Oh my God." I traced my fingers down the first letters of the first four lines. "P-a-s-s," I muttered. Maybe Beth was almost as bad at passwords as Audra. The password could be the first letter of every line. That would explain her use of the number 1 in the second-to-last line. I laughed. She had added a one, like Audra.

My heart jackhammered as I sat back down. Looking between the paper and the keyboard, I typed *P-a-s-s-E-p-S-1-s* and paused. I held my breath, and hit enter.

*Beep.* "Incorrect password. One attempt remains."

"Crap, crap, crap!" I hoped Kevin couldn't hear me. My shirt stuck to me with sweat. Kevin would tell me to think of my panic like stones and throw them into the ocean. I tried, but the panic-stones settled in my stomach instead.

I stood and paced again. The poem *had* to relate to the password. It was too much of a coincidence for it to be hidden with the card and have *Pass* in the first four lines. I sat down again and skimmed the lines with my finger.

The exclamation mark at the end of the last line! Passwords often required a special character, and Beth hadn't used any other end punctuation in the poem. Maybe it was *PassEpS1s!*

Or maybe I should skip the *s* in the last line and only use the exclamation point. I wrote out *PassEpS1s!* and then *PassEpS1!* on a sticky note and stared at them both. If I was right, then Beth was using one character from each line for her password, which meant I should omit the *s* from the last line.

This was it. My last shot. The contents of this card could hold the key to Ethan's freedom or indicate his guilt. At this point, I needed to know one way or the other.

I typed in *P-a-s-s-E-p-S-1-!* and hovered my finger above the enter key, nerves buzzing with anticipation. I turned my head away, took a long breath, and pressed it.

No beep.

I whipped my head around so quickly my neck cracked. It worked! The folder unlocked. I let out a breath, elated with relief, and pumped my fist. I got up and paced again—this time to celebrate. I texted Audra: *Success! Looking at it now.*

Sitting back down, I clicked to open the folder. Inside was a single video file. My hands shook as I put on my headphones.

The player that popped up on my screen showed a blurry, dark view with a faint light coming from one corner. I maximized the window and leaned forward, trying to make sense of what I was seeing. Then something in the frame oriented me: the edge of the gazebo, with its distinctive curlicue trim that Beth and I had painted. The footage showed the view from the back of the Castle out toward the river. The light in the corner of the screen must have come from a security light near the old stables. But nothing moved on the screen, so what had triggered the camera to start recording?

I moved the video back to the beginning and restarted it. This time I saw the movement. Beyond the gazebo at the edge of the river, a grainy shadow slid into frame.

I tried to remember my discussion with Beth and Mr. Perry from months back. This would be near the spot on the bank where the weeds had been flattened by a boat coming ashore. In the boat, the shadow lingered for a minute before it got out and came into clearer view: the figure was about average height and moved briskly. A baseball cap obscured any distinguishing features—not that the grainy resolution and lighting would have helped.

Carrying what looked like a large duffel bag, the figure strode out of frame in the direction of the stables. After a minute of nothing, the video clicked off and then back on as what looked like a floodlight or headlights bathed the trees along the river in light. Against the light on the trees, a shadow passed in front of the lights. I went back again but could decipher nothing from it.

A minute later, the lights swung across the trees and then left the area in darkness again. Nothing happened for a few minutes, and the recording clicked off again.

When it came back on, the dark figure from before was moving back into frame, this time without the duffel bag. I moved the video back to study the silhouette of the person: taller than I'd thought at first and fairly slim, but the hat and a loose jacket obscured anything further.

From there, the figure moved away from the camera, turning to nothing more than a dark, pixelated blob that got back into the boat, pushed off from the shore, and was absorbed into the darkness.

I sat back in my chair, thinking of the spring workday at the Castle and Beth's concerns about trespassers. Had she decided to take matters into her own hands by recording this?

Why hadn't Mr. Perry followed through with a trap camera like he'd said he would? Most of all, I wondered if something in this recording had cost Beth her life.

I must have watched the video a dozen times, trying to piece together more. Something about the figure's movements looked familiar to me, but there was nothing that remarkable about it either, even after I adjusted and brightened the footage. The trees in the video were thick with leaves, but that could have put the recording anywhere from late spring to just recently. The figure wore what looked like a loose, light jacket that hit below the hips. Summer evenings could cool down, especially along the river, but not usually enough to require a jacket. I guessed that Beth had recorded this either in the late spring or quite recently, but there was nothing more in the frame to tell me which it might be.

I uploaded the file to my personal drive. Then I forwarded it to Audra with the text, *Now we know why Beth was writing about the river. Does the figure look familiar?*

Less than ten minutes later, my phone buzzed with an incoming call. Audra. "It just looks like a blob. Can you enhance it?" Audra demanded.

"Hello to you too. I already lightened it and sharpened it as much as I could. It's a low-quality recording. Did you notice the duffel bag?"

"Yeah, are you thinking drugs? Or maybe money?"

"One or the other. Or guns?" I ventured. "What else would you smuggle over the river in the middle of the night? And did you notice the headlights a few minutes into the video? Someone else was there."

There was silence on the line as we both watched the video again and considered what it might tell us.

"I think we should go out to the Castle and have a look around. Beth had keys for everything out there, didn't she?"

"Yes, but personal belongings like that were taken as evidence."

Audra thought for a moment. "What about Mr. Perry? He could loan you his. If you can get them this afternoon, I could meet you out there before I pick Franky up from preschool."

"Why can't you get the keys?" I asked. "I'm at work."

"Mr. Perry likes you better and you were closer to Beth."

I sighed and agreed. My supervisor had urged me to take as much bereavement time as I needed. He wouldn't mind if I worked a half day and left at lunch. It wasn't as if I would be able to accomplish much. Closing the video on my screen, I stared blankly at data logs until the text danced in front of my eyes, then closed that tab and struggled to compose a basic response to an email. I couldn't put together a single coherent sentence.

The cursor on my screen blinked at me, and I sat back in my chair. I wondered if the shadowy figure had looked familiar to Beth too.

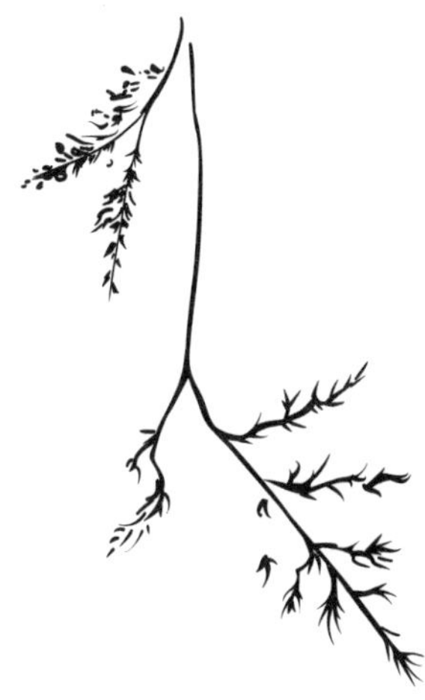

# CHAPTER TWENTY-THREE

*September 29, 2022*

Ms. Hanson, who had been the high-school secretary for as long as I could remember, asked surprisingly few questions when I said I needed to see Mr. Perry. She only requested that I sign in and give my mom a hug for her before she pinned a visitor's badge to my shirt and patted my cheek. She smelled like chamomile. Part of me wanted to stay in the office with her forever, drinking tea and reminiscing about shared acquaintances and better times.

Instead, I made my way down the long hallway toward Mr. Perry's classroom, my shoes squeaking on the terrazzo floor. I don't know if it was the wax the custodian used or what, but the school hallways had always been a chorus of squeaking shoes overlaid with teenage conversations and slamming locker doors. The familiar smells of industrial-strength cleaners, adolescence, and cafeteria food still hung in the air. The same gray-brown lockers lined the walls like soldiers as I turned down Mr. Perry's hallway. I spied my old locker and wondered what poor kid it belonged to now and if they felt as stifled by these walls as I had.

In our town, you became what people thought you were. Everyone knew everyone's parents and their parents so well that from the day you were conceived, it was plain who you would be. Like a chalk outline just waiting to be filled in.

In my case, I was the quiet, pale Svenson, the runner with the sneaky sense of humor. I was someone who could be relied upon because the rest of my family could be relied upon. It was far from the worst thing one could be branded.

But all the same, I wanted the chance to be loud, to yell and be stupid, to be unreliable. Just to see how it felt to be someone other than the person I'd been cast as since before my birth. So the week after high-school graduation, I'd left to be that new person, to try on and discard identities until I found one that fit.

Yet here I was again, in my old town, in my old school, slipping right back into old patterns—doing what Audra told me to do, appeasing Mom and Ethan. The sense of self I'd built up over the past decade eroded away the more I slipped into old habits.

Well before I reached his door, Mr. Perry's deep voice drifted down the hall, rising and falling like the modulated tones of an actor onstage. He was a natural storyteller. This had made history and social studies a favorite for many of us, but for the kids he didn't like, his class could be a special kind of hell. His was not the kind of classroom where you could quietly put your head down and fail; he expected kids not only to do their work but to get excited about it.

The current class sounded like senior civics. Chalk clattered on the blackboard as Mr. Perry peppered his students with questions about the responsibilities of citizens in a democracy. I heard him respond to a student. "Yes, obeying laws is part of it, but that's a pretty low bar." He clapped his hands. "What else?"

I checked the time on my phone. This could be a while. I could picture him crossing his arms and scanning the class. I closed my eyes and leaned against a locker until at last I heard what sounded like a break. "I want you to get back into your groups and revisit the list you put together at the beginning of the period."

After the scraping of desks quieted, I stepped into the doorway and waited for a lull in the action. Mr. Perry circulated around the groups, bending over and pointing as he commented on students' work. He frowned as he approached a pair of boys, one with unkempt brown locks that fell in waves over his eyes and the other with bristly blond hair and acne-pocked cheeks. Both slumped over their desks as if gravity weighed extra heavily on them.

In contrast to the other students, the pair had no textbook in sight, and their laptops were closed. I could see Mr. Perry's displeasure piling up like a thundercloud with each step he took toward them. He stopped and silently loomed behind one student. The boy with the longer hair noticed him, popped up in his seat, and opened his laptop.

As if to make a point, the other boy glanced at his teacher, curled his lip, and slumped down further.

Mr. Perry jabbed his finger toward the boy with the bristly hair. The boy recoiled. The teacher hadn't touched him, but he'd hissed something at him in a low voice. Having overheard many of these diatribes during my high-school years, I imagined it had something to do with the boy's future and the importance of gumption. A pair of girls in their cheerleading uniforms paused what they were working on and craned their necks to watch. Leaning in close to the boy's face, Mr. Perry kept talking. One of the eavesdropping girls put her hand to her mouth and looked at her friend with shock before bursting into laughter. A moment later, Mr. Perry straightened up and walked away from the boy, whose face was now pink. I remembered how Mr. Perry could act like your best friend or your worst enemy—depending on how well you followed his rules—and felt for the kid, who looked as if he'd been punched.

After checking in with a few more groups, Mr. Perry spotted me and smiled. He took a few long steps toward me and clapped a hand on my shoulder.

"Why, Riley! What a pleasure to see you here. What can I do for you? You're not here to argue about that A minus I gave you on that research paper, are you?" He lowered his voice. "You know, if you'd been in here with this group, I would have given you an A. Kids aren't what they used to be."

"I've moved on, but who knows what I could have done with my life if I hadn't had that A minus holding me back?" I smiled at him. "Actually, I'm here about the Castle."

He clasped his hands in front of his chest, a move that would have looked childish from anyone else. "Well, that makes my day. What is it that you need?"

I'd considered how to broach the issue of getting into the Castle. While I didn't think Mr. Perry would mind letting me look around, I also needed to give him a plausible reason. Not knowing what Beth would have told him about the recording, I didn't want to introduce the topic.

"I've been thinking about all the time Beth spent there, and I haven't been out there since this past summer. I guess with her gone, I'm just looking for any connection, and I know the Castle and the work she did there meant a lot . . ." I trailed off, not needing to feign embarrassment at my sentimentality. In reality, I *had* been thinking about all the time that Beth had spent at the Castle and wanted to see what she had been doing in the months before her death.

A quick line flashed between Mr. Perry's bushy eyebrows, and he shook his head. For a moment, I thought he was going to say no, but then he cleared his throat. "I can't be out there myself without thinking of her." He stared at the terrazzo floor. When he looked up, his eyes were damp. "Yeah, of course. She'd be proud for you to see it. I know she wanted to surprise everyone at the wedding rehearsal, but now . . ." He shrugged. "Hold on, I'll grab my keys."

He strode off again to his desk, opened a drawer, and rifled through a keyring that would put a custodian to shame before removing one. Returning, he said, "This will get you into the Castle itself through the front door. You know, I was thinking we should submit something to the *Wicksburg*

*Gazette* if you want to take some pictures while you're there. It'd be nice to show the public our progress and honor Beth that way. We'll have to keep it going for her. She was my marketing genius, so I can use any help I can get." Although he kept his tone light, I knew how much he had cared about her too.

I tried to smile, but the heaviness of the conversation weighed on me. I thanked Mr. Perry and promised to take pictures. I had squeaked about halfway back down the hallway when some magnetic pull on the back of my neck made me turn and look. Mr. Perry still stood where I'd left him in the doorway, backlit by the fluorescent classroom lights and watching me. He lifted his shoulders, gave me a little wave, and then turned back to his students. I could hear him clap and say, "All right, friends, I'm excited to see what you all have put together for me."

I wondered where he found the enthusiasm.

As I turned into the Castle, the tunnel of bright yellow trees lining the drive enveloped my car, and the road disappeared behind me. I was reminded why the people of North Haven had used the site to avoid the prying eyes of neighbors for more than a hundred years—first, helping people escape slavery on their way north, and in ensuing years for less-righteous ventures. And now, for whatever seedy endeavor Beth had uncovered. I wondered how many activities had taken place on these grounds that would forever remain unknown, and would go—or had already gone—with people to their graves. At a fundraiser for the Castle, Mr. Perry had once spoken about how little was known about the site's history with the Underground Railroad due to the secrecy surrounding such ventures. He'd explained that reconstructing the past was about arranging the few things we knew and filling in the gaps in a way that made sense. I was starting to think the present was no different, with all of us taking all the small things we saw and heard every day and weaving them into coherent stories in our heads. We all assumed the stories we made up for ourselves reflected reality, until something like Beth's murder came along and showed us differently.

As I crested the rise near the house, I was surprised to see a massive white SUV trimmed in chrome parked by the front porch. Pulling up behind it, I read the vanity plate: RLS T8.

"Arrels Tate?" I mouthed.

The fallen leaves had muffled my approach on the gravel drive, and before she noticed me, I spotted Harmony at the river's edge with her phone held out in front of her as if she was taking pictures.

"Oh, *real estate*." I could be a dolt.

It was only after I got out and closed my door that Harmony glanced over her shoulder and shielded her eyes from the sun with a sour expression. In a quick motion, she tapped the screen of her phone and turned to face me. By then, she had plastered a wide smile on her face. Rather than her usual glamorous attire, Harmony wore black yoga pants, hiking boots, and a dark pullover, into which she tucked her phone.

"Riillleeeey!" she squealed and let her hands fall limply in front of her chest like a helpless baby animal. I doubted anyone had ever been that happy to see me and, judging from the expression I'd caught on her face when she'd first spotted me, Harmony certainly wasn't.

"Hi, Harmony. What are you doing here?"

"Oh, you know. Real-estate stuff." She pulled her hair away from her face and held it with one hand in a ponytail. "It's getting warm, huh?" She fanned her flushed face.

"Hmm, real estate? Is the association selling some of the land?" The last I'd heard, they had committed to keeping the parcel intact, although Doug had been working tirelessly to change their minds. I knew Doug had collaborated with Harmony and her mom in the past when he purchased farmland that he'd converted into a soulless subdivision, but I didn't think he'd be pursuing deals at the moment, just days after his daughter's death.

"Well, no, I guess it's not real estate, *exactly*." She chuckled and waved the idea away. "I was taking pictures of the Castle like I would do for a listing. I figure we need to promote it, and it's not that different from marketing real estate. I know marketing was kind of Beth's thing." She nodded. "So I wanted to help out Mr. Perry however I could. You know, I've been pretty involved in the restoration too." She shrugged as if she did altruistic things like this every day.

I'd never known Harmony to do anything that did not directly benefit her own interests, but I couldn't tell which part of what she was saying was bullshit, or if all of it was. As I wondered if Mr. Perry knew she was out here, I recalled his request for me to take some pictures.

"This is perfect, actually. I just spoke with Mr. Perry, and he wants photos to share with the *Gazette*. You should send him the ones you took." I would be interested to see if any pictures materialized. I'd ask Mr. Perry when I returned the key.

Harmony's lips compressed into a thin line that she muscled into a smile. "I should do that. Yeah, that's a great idea." She was already walking toward her SUV and digging out her keys. "I'm so glad I ran into you. We need to get together now that you're back. Oh, and tell your family everyone is thinking of them."

"Thanks, I know they are," I said as she pointed her key fob at her SUV, which chirped in response. "Byeeee." I gave a limp, kittenish wave as she pulled away.

No sooner had Harmony pulled out of one side of the circular drive than Audra pulled in the other. She climbed out of her Jeep and took long steps toward me. "I don't have much time. I need to get Franky by four. Was that Harmony? What's she doing here?"

"That's a good question. She *said* she was taking pictures to promote the Castle, but I think she's lying. She was kinda sweaty about the whole thing."

Audra quirked a corner of her mouth. "That's interesting. She volunteers here, doesn't she?" Audra looked toward the river. "You know, I assumed it was a man in the video, but Harmony is tall enough . . ."

Without discussing it, we both set off toward the back of the house near where the camera would have been positioned. "I was thinking the same thing, but would she have access to a boat? She and Dave live in a condo, so if they had one, they'd have to store it somewhere."

"You think it's someone who lives on the river then?"

"Not necessarily. I mean, there are plenty of places to pull off and launch a boat. There's a launch just that way." I motioned to the west in the direction the boat had come from in the video. "But you'd have a lot more risk of being seen if you had to haul your boat somewhere, park your car with a trailer, and launch the boat. At that point, why wouldn't you just drive instead?"

Audra considered this and then her eyes widened. "You know Tomás? He and Marco were talking about walleye fishing at his daughter's party last spring. I was only half listening, but I remember him saying that he keeps his fishing boat near the public access because he doesn't have a trailer to haul it. Just puts a tarp over it." Audra mimed throwing a tarp over something. "Doesn't even lock it up."

"How has nobody stolen it by now?"

"That's what Marco asked him. Tomás said he knows people take it out. But he doesn't care as long as they return it in good shape and top off the gas."

I groaned. "That doesn't help. That means it could be basically anyone who knows the boat is there."

Audra crossed her arms. "Well, I'm sorry I didn't help you crack the mystery, Ms. Marple. I'm just telling you what I know."

I sighed. "Thank you. I'm only saying that we're not really narrowing down the possibilities."

I leaned against the railing of the back porch and shook my head. "I feel like we're going in circles. We know about the drugs and Liam being involved. We know Beth recorded *someone* dropping something off here, but I don't know if any of this is getting us closer to what happened to her. Or to exonerating Ethan." I rubbed my eyes and sighed.

Audra was staring over my shoulder and pointed. "Look at that."

"Did you hear a word I said?"

I turned to look at the porch post where she pointed, prepared to marvel at a large spider or an interesting bug. Instead, I saw a small smudge above my head, roughly rectangular and gray with dirt. Putting my finger to it, it felt faintly sticky and held little pieces of foamy white material.

"It's like what's left behind from one of those adhesive squares."

I turned my back to stand directly in front of the spot and looked out at the river. From where we stood, the position of the gazebo and the river matched up with the view in the video.

"That's where Beth put the camera." I looked at the spot on the post again. The small white camera I'd seen among her craft supplies wouldn't have been very noticeable against the white post in the shadow of the porch overhang.

Audra looked out at the river from the same position and nodded. "How would she know to point it at that spot?"

I recalled the conversation between Beth and Mr. Perry during the spring workday about people coming ashore from the river and the tramped-down weeds on the bank. "She knew people had been pulling their boats up there. I guess she wanted to know more about what they were doing. Mr. Perry had said he'd look for a trap camera, but I guess he didn't follow through."

We walked toward the river. The tall grasses and weeds along the bank had been neatly trimmed back in preparation for the wedding, but near a large tree, the bank was still scuffed where a boat had been dragged ashore.

The river was full from recent rains, and the rushing water brought on a wave of dizziness. I put my hand against the ancient tree to steady myself, feeling the loose, papery bark. As I regained my equilibrium, I noticed a metal plate, just above eye level, nailed to the tree trunk, facing the river. My heart skipped and I brought my hand to my forehead.

"Audra! I remember where I heard that thing about the sycamore and dead trees. Do you remember Mr. Perry telling us about how the conductors on the Underground Railroad used sycamores and dead trees to guide them? They glow white in the moonlight. And then people would bang on pieces of metal like this one to signal to each other when they were here. Those lines that Beth wrote were like an old song that people used to sing. Beth put something like that on a poster for our senior project."

"Oh my gosh, Riley." She grabbed my arm in excitement. "Thank God you're such a nerd! I don't remember any of that. But what does it mean?"

I frowned. "I don't know." I flipped through the pictures on my phone to find the photo I'd taken of the note. I read the words aloud again:

*Tend to your brother's house, your sister's home; Tend to the river, the boatswain who carries them through the silver sycamores, beneath the sliver of moon. Dead trees light the way to the river on the other side.*

"Maybe Beth was hinting that the person in the boat was someone connected to the Castle, or someone who took Mr. Perry's history class," I ventured.

"That narrows it down to about every person in North Haven under forty."

"It could just be her describing how the pills were moved along the river too." I thought about how few people would have gotten that reference to the moonlit trees and the lines Beth and I put on our poster back in high school. Harmony and her husband, Dave, had been in that class, but so had Sydney and twenty other people. I wondered if Beth had somehow known this note would find its way to me, if she really meant *my* brother's house and *my* sister's home. We had found the drugs in my brother's house. How literally should I read the line about my sister's home? I shook my head. I was truly losing my mind to even have the thought.

Still, I glanced at Audra, who was checking the time on her phone. "Let's look at the stables and barns," I said. "They're in the direction where the person in the video was headed." Without waiting for her, I walked ahead.

Aside from the Castle itself, the surrounding grounds were home to an old stone stable, a one-room schoolhouse with a collapsed roof, and a couple of small outbuildings used for storage. The first outbuilding was about the size of an outhouse. The gray wooden door creaked as Audra pushed it open. Sunlight filtered through the gaps between the wooden slats and illuminated flecks of dust. Stripes of light and shadow fell across a bag of potting soil, a weed trimmer, and a jumble of rakes, shovels, axes, and pruners. There seemed to be no more space to hide anything in the simple structure, but I looked behind the mess of tools just in case. Nothing more than the packed-dirt floor and spiderwebs.

Further east, a slightly larger but otherwise similar outbuilding held a push mower, gas cans, drills, and a toolbox. "I'm surprised Mr. Perry doesn't keep this locked." I eyed the collection of tools, which was probably worth hundreds of dollars, not even including the lawn mower. "Of course, Liam does the mowing here, and he probably couldn't be trusted to remember a key or a combination—"

Audra grabbed my wrist so suddenly that I flinched. "Oh my God, I forgot to tell you. I just heard on the way. Liam's awake."

I stared at her. "How are you only now telling me this?"

"Well, I meant to tell you earlier, but there's been kind of a lot going on here. Marco called me right before I came over. I don't know if he's talking, but it's looking better for him, at least."

"Thank God for that." I'd avoided mentioning our visit to Liam's house when I'd spoken with Osborne the previous afternoon. Though I was relieved that Liam had regained consciousness, I wasn't in a huge hurry for him to start talking. He might tell Osbourne of our visit.

Audra's mention of Marco reminded me of something that had been knocking around in the back of my mind. I wasn't sure if it was idle curiosity or the lines about tending to my sister's home that made me ask, "How much have you told Marco about our . . . adventures?"

Audra looked down at her hands and wiped dust from them as she answered. "Not much." She frowned. "He's been consumed with the farm since Ethan's arrest. It used to be him, Ethan, and Dad. Now it's just him managing it all on his own. I don't want to stress him more. He hasn't been sleeping as it is." There was a trace of guilt or regret in her voice. I couldn't tell if it was due to keeping secrets from Marco or something more.

Ahead of me, Audra glanced toward the sun, which was already nearing the treetops. With the glare behind her, I couldn't read her face. "C'mon, let's check out the stable. I'm on the clock. If I'm late to get Franky again, he's going to get a complex."

The stables, nestled in a stand of tall white pines on the eastern edge of the property, predated the house and had served as shelter in the Underground Railroad until the mansion with its hidden quarters in the basement had been completed. Arched openings to horse stalls and short wooden doors ran along one side of the old stone building. Something about the cavernous dark space had always given me the chills, as if the fears and anxieties of the people who had spent sleepless nights in the structure still remained. It had been a while since I'd seen the inside of the stables, and I was curious how much work had been done. As we approached the wooden double doors, I saw that where the other buildings had been wide open, a heavy padlock with a dial secured these doors.

Audra examined the lock. "Did Mr. Perry give you a combination for this?"

"No," I answered.

Audra pulled down on the lock. It didn't budge.

She walked over to a dark window, shaded her eyes, and put her face to the glass. "It's too dark to see much. There are some wooden pallets against the near wall. Dirt. Drop cloths over some furniture. Nothing too exciting."

I walked over to where she stood, peered in the window, and struggled to see anything more than blurry shapes through the wavy glass. "Maybe I can get the combination when I return the key." I straightened up and looked at Audra. "The good news is that now you have time to come into the house with me."

Audra frowned, but I could hear her following me as I approached the Castle.

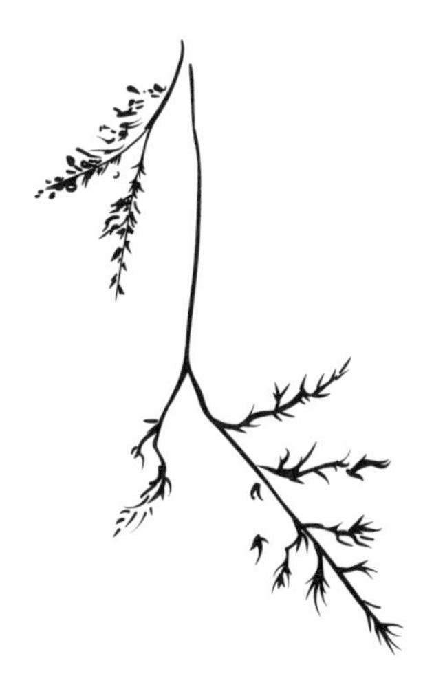

# CHAPTER TWENTY-FOUR

*September 29, 2022*

In the still, quiet clearing with trees whispering on all sides, the Castle looked like it had been waiting for us. The afternoon sun slid behind the building as Audra and I approached, giving the tower and sloping roof the look of a patient perched vulture.

A wide porch supported by improbably delicate white posts ran along the entire front of the house, framing the tall, dark double doors that led inside. The last time I'd been inside the mansion had been a few months prior with Beth; with excitement in her voice, she had shown me the area near the fireplace where the wedding party would sit for the reception, the nook by the bay windows where she and Ethan would cut the cake, and the sparkling ballroom where we would all dance late into the night. At that time, half of the floors had still been hidden beneath paper, and the dust of construction covered everything, but I could see it as she described it. She made it beautiful.

The brass key Mr. Perry loaned me slid into the ornate lock, and after a little coaxing, turned with a click. As I pulled the heavy wooden door open,

a cool draft from inside mingled with the warm afternoon air. Stepping into the dim, hushed foyer felt like entering a church, as if we were in a sacred place that was due some respect. The grand stairway to the second floor loomed in front of us, its wide steps padded with a runner and the thick walnut banisters curving out to each side at the bottom, like arms stretched out in embrace. Beth had described to me on our last visit how we would drape the stairway with garlands of flowers and ribbon. To the right was the dining room, with its high molded ceiling and paneled trim. My shoulders slumped as I took in the tables and folding chairs that stood ready for the reception that would never come.

Audra took a few tentative steps toward the imposing stairway and whispered, "What are we looking for?"

"You don't need to whisper." I willed myself to speak at a normal volume. "Beth said last spring that someone had been coming into the mansion, so we should look for signs of that." We entered the dining room, and I ran my hand over an antique buffet that sat against one wall, remembering that's where the punch bowl and drinks were to have sat. In truth, I had little idea what I was looking for, but I knew Beth had spent much of her time here in the last months of her life. I just needed to look around, to see what she had seen.

The transformation of the Castle since my last visit was remarkable. The new drywall that had been put up on the first floor had been finished and painted a cream color that glowed in the afternoon light, and the dusty paper that had covered the floors in the unfinished rooms had been removed to reveal the warm hardwood. In the previous mess, I had never noticed the dark woodwork along the rounded doorways and the tall baseboards in every room, but today they shone with polish. An old-fashioned but functional galley kitchen had been restored in the back of the house. The rest of the rooms were furnished and decorated with antiques loaned out from members of the Carlton Castle Association. It all looked perfect and ready to host a wedding. As I thought about all the work involved, I wondered how much Beth and volunteers had done themselves and how much they had hired out. Beth had always given me the impression that the Castle didn't have much of a budget, but I couldn't imagine Beth and a few volunteers pulling this off on their own.

In the ballroom, Audra craned her neck to look at a ceiling medallion painted a deep blue around the heavy chandelier. "I can't believe this is the same place that Marco and I used to sneak off to for—"

"Stop. Got the idea." I couldn't talk, though. My friends and I had ventured into these rooms a few times ourselves. On one trip on a dark winter evening, with our nerves jumping, we'd all asked a Ouija board what the future held for each of us. As creative as we'd gotten in our predictions, no one had anticipated the events of the past week.

I recalled Beth's complaints to Mr. Perry during the spring cleanup about someone entering the Castle and tracking in mud. Even though I knew Mr. Perry kept it locked now, I still held my breath as we entered each room. Every inch of the downstairs gleamed, showing no signs of unwanted visitors trekking through it. Audra and I ascended the wide stairway and surveyed the second floor. Here the hallway, which opened to the downstairs, had been partially restored. Old landscape paintings and photographs hung on the patched plaster walls and runners covered the floors, but off the hallway, the rooms themselves were still works in progress. Audra and I split up to explore.

Inside what must have once been bedrooms, I found cracked plaster and floors dulled beneath a century of dust. The rooms still showed promise, with a giant stone fireplace in one room and detailed woodwork beneath the dust and cobwebs, but corners were jammed full of antique furniture, brass candleholders, wall sconces, and any other old thing that might find a new life here someday. In another room, a dusty claw-foot tub sat in the middle of the scuffed floor, surrounded by peeling pink-flowered wallpaper.

Audra poked out of a doorway at the end of the hall as I exited another. I jumped and held my hand over my racing heart. "Find anything?"

"Just spiders and junk." She scrunched her nose.

At the end of the hallway, more stairs led to the third floor, which we found in still rougher condition. Each room was littered with junk and debris where someone might conceal themselves. Paranoia crawled up my spine. I moved through the rooms cautiously, swiveling my head, until I stumbled into a sheet of cobwebs.

Beneath the slanted mansard roof, water stains bloomed along the ceiling like sepia-toned maps. Mint-green paint peeled from the walls and the plaster had crumbled away or been ripped off in spots, revealing dusty wood lath behind it. As beautiful as Beth had made the downstairs, the rooms out of public view were as grim as ever.

"Oh, this is a mess." Audra looked around the room at the piles of moldering plaster. "It would take a fortune to finish this place off. It just keeps going."

"And it gets worse as it goes." I peered out a cracked window that looked out over the rear of the property. From there, I could see for a distance in both directions down the river before the trees closed in. "But the view gets better." I straightened up and nodded in the direction of a narrow door that led to the fourth floor. "Speaking of which, we should check the tower. It looks like it's unlocked."

In my previous visits to the Castle, the door that led to this narrow passage had always been locked for liability reasons. Mr. Perry had warned us that the stairway that led to the tower was a death trap. But now, with secure locks on the outside of the Castle, the padlock that had barred the door to the tower for so many years had been removed.

Audra retreated a step and pressed her back into the wall. "I'm not going up there," she asserted. "This is high enough for me. I have children who need me."

I rolled my eyes. For a moment I had forgotten Audra's fear of heights, which was remarkable considering how often she reminded everyone. On a farm with hundred-foot-tall silos and a hayloft that could only be accessed up a precarious ladder, it had gotten her out of all kinds of unpleasant, hot tasks. Someone needed to climb a silo to fix the blower? Audra was excused.

"Oh, so you're going to make the woman with vertigo go up alone," I retorted. I didn't actually mind going up, but habit compelled me to argue.

"You'll be fine." She sounded remarkably cavalier about something she was determined not to do herself. "I'll be right here, and if something goes wrong, I'll be able to hear you fall or scream."

"That's very comforting. You're a good sister."

"So are you. I'll say so in your eulogy." She smiled sweetly and brushed dust from her sleeve.

I shook my head as I opened the tower door. A spiral of rough wooden steps with open slats coiled upward. I placed a foot on the first step to test it: it gave a little but held. I gripped the loose wooden railing, put my head down, and climbed.

The higher I climbed, the warmer it got. Looking at my feet as I went, I noticed dead bugs and cobwebs festooned the space between steps. At the top of the stairway, I stepped onto a plywood floor, tested it, and then raised my head to look around.

The room itself was a perfect square, about eight feet across. In the middle of each of wall was a narrow window with a rounded top that offered expansive views in every direction. I crept cautiously around the room on the plywood floor, which bounced a little under my feet. Although the paint and trim were as dilapidated as that on the third floor, the windows here were less coated in dust and cobwebs, as if someone else had been up here enjoying the view.

From out the front window, the driveway wound through the rows of trees out to the road and farm fields beyond. To the east and west, there was nothing but trees, fields, and glimpses of river. The best view was out the rear window, where I could see down the river in both directions and the treetops across the way.

This room was the perfect lookout.

My mind raced as I hurried back down the stairs to share my idea with Audra. Paying attention to my thoughts but not my feet on the narrow planks, my foot slipped out from under me on the second-to-last step and I landed hard on my butt on the bottom stair with an *oof*.

Audra rushed toward me from across the room. “Are you okay?”

I extended my legs. They still worked. “Never better,” I said to Audra. “And I have an idea.”

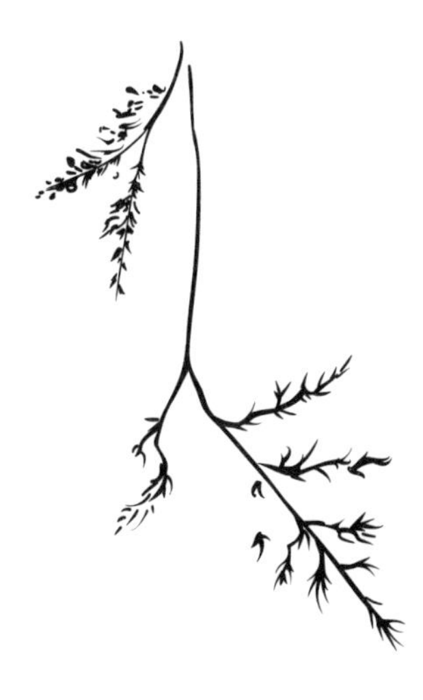

# CHAPTER TWENTY-FIVE

*September 29, 2022*

"This is a terrible idea," Audra said for at least the third time in the past hour, but the important thing was that she had come along. She and Franky were parked beside me in Liam's driveway. I had scouted the yard and knocked on the door to ensure no one was home, but Audra had yet to get out of her Jeep.

I stood at her driver's-side window. "Marco said Liam won't be coming home until tomorrow at the earliest. Nobody's going to see us. All I'm asking you to do is wait here and text me if someone pulls in."

"What if that someone is the police and they want to know why I'm keeping watch with my child while my sister is breaking and entering?"

"That's why I have the casserole." I crooked my thumb behind me to the casserole that I'd set on the roof of my car.

"Ah, yes, the old casserole defense," Audra responded. "Works every time."

"We are just aggressively nice people who are determined that Liam will come home to a well-stocked fridge. Dotty did the same thing for Mom

when Dad was in the hospital. Mom said she even loaded the dishwasher. Walked right in. Mom came home and Dotty was in the kitchen drying dishes and singing like it was her own house."

"Yes, but I think we can agree that Dotty doesn't always show the best judgment."

I thought of Dotty's unwitting implication of Ethan's guilt in the video Sydney had sent me the night of the memorial. I couldn't argue with Audra there. Instead, I tried a different tack, one more suited to Audra's inherent impatience. "I'd have been in and out by now if you would stop talking. Can I go? Are we good?"

Audra pursed her lips and then heaved the world's most aggrieved sigh but nodded. "Go on. Just don't get caught. I can't handle all of Mom's crazy by myself if you and Ethan both go to prison."

I grabbed the casserole and set off toward Liam's front porch. The zucchini casserole came courtesy of an inexhaustible supply that Mom kept in a chest freezer in the garage. While Audra picked Franky up from day care, I had muttered something to Mom about needing a dish for a work potluck and prepared myself to be peppered with admonitions about how a woman should be able to whip up a dish for a potluck with her eyes closed. Instead, Mom had just narrowed her eyes at me. Not knowing if I should be concerned for her, myself, or both of us, I took the casserole and backed away.

I approached Liam's familiar front entry, but instead of climbing the slanted steps, I set the casserole down and veered toward the window to the left of the porch, the one that went to Liam's bedroom. Any window would work, but I figured I had the best shot of finding this one unlocked since the old house had no central air and Liam probably opened it at night to let the cool air in.

The white paint on the window casing was cracked and flaking. I pulled on a thin pair of gloves I'd found in the trunk of my car. While I thought I might get away with entering Liam's house uninvited to drop off a casserole, I didn't particularly want anyone to find that I'd gotten in through the window.

The old screen on the outside of the window was loose and lifted easily. I gripped the lower window along the top of the sash and gave it an exploratory jiggle. It inched up, and I could see that the lock wasn't fastened. Thank God for Liam's absentmindedness. I probably should have just checked the front door. Still, this seemed to be working. I continued jiggling and the window opened incrementally until I could fit my fingers under it and pull it open entirely. Aside from some horizontal blinds, I had a clear entry into Liam's room.

The bottom of the window hit right around my chest. I considered the best way to climb through the opening. Since only Audra was watching, I settled on going headlong, using one hand to push the blinds out of my way and the other to keep myself from crashing to the floor of Liam's bedroom.

A few curses and bruises later, I slid onto the bedroom floor headfirst. After dusting myself off, I went straight for the dresser. I hoped the burner phone would be right where he'd left it, in his bottom drawer beneath some jeans. The irony of praying while I slid the drawer open to steal a near-comatose man's phone was not lost on me, but I did it anyway. Whether through the power of prayer or Liam's inattention, the phone was still there, nestled at the bottom of the drawer. I grabbed it and felt around for a charger but found nothing more. Not wanting to press my luck, I decided to take the phone and go. I figured my charger would do the job as it had for Beth's.

As I held Liam's phone in my hand, I heard a chirp. For a moment, I looked at Liam's phone in confusion before I realized the sound came from my pocket. My heart pounded in my throat. I hadn't heard anyone pull in out front. Was it Audra or a random text?

It was Audra, and the text was simple: *Get out of there now.*

I shoved Liam's drawer shut, leaving his jeans in disarray and took a step toward the window. How would it look if the police—or whoever it was—saw me coming out the window? After a moment of indecision, I headed for the front door, down the narrow dark hallway and past the living room, where Audra and I had sat with Liam. At the front door, I peeked around the curtain to see who awaited me outside, but I couldn't see around the corner of the house from this angle. I took a few deep breaths and willed my heart rate to slow to a semi-normal pace. I turned the lock on the front door, shoved my gloves in my pocket, and walked out onto the porch as nonchalantly as I could. It was only then that I noticed I'd left the casserole sitting on the front step.

Oops. With any luck, whoever was here would not even know I'd been in the house. I picked up the casserole and sauntered down the sidewalk toward the driveway. I could see Audra out of her Jeep now, gesturing angrily. I swallowed and kept walking, trying not to look as scared as I felt. When I saw the black Ford Explorer idling, I could feel the blood drain from my face. I knew that vehicle all too well.

I tried to smile pleasantly. "Mom, what are you doing out here?"

Mom stood next to Audra with her hands on her hips. I swear that the air above her head looked wavy from the white-hot anger emanating from the top of her skull. "If one of you girls doesn't tell me what's going on here . . ." She searched around for a consequence befitting her rage but couldn't come up with anything that was both suitably dire and appropriate for a mother to say to her daughters.

Thoughts ping-ponged around my head, but nothing came out of my mouth. Perhaps deciding that the best defense was a good offense, Audra countered, "I can't believe you followed us out here." She turned to me. "I saw her drive by a minute ago and turn around. She just pulled in. I told her we're only being neighborly."

"Neighborly? Please, girls. I am your mother. I know when you are lying. Now, you need to tell me what you two are really up to before I say things in front of Franky that you'll regret."

There was so much Mom-voodoo in that statement that I couldn't begin to unravel it. Thankfully, Franky seemed oblivious to the drama; he had gotten out of the Jeep and was picking up pieces of gravel from Liam's driveway and examining each of them like they might be mastodon teeth. It struck me that we hadn't run into Liam's friendly dog, and I hoped someone was taking good care of him while Liam was away.

I looked up again. Mom was still there. I knew there was no getting away from having this conversation, but I needed to regroup. "Why don't we all go back to the house and talk there. I don't think we want anyone driving past and seeing us all hanging out here."

Her instinct to disagree warred with her desire to keep up appearances. Given that Liam was a witness against Ethan, our presence here would raise eyebrows. She poked a finger at me and then at Audra. "You go straight to the house. I need to know what you girls have been off doing this past week, because you sure haven't been with me. Or Ethan."

Satisfied that she'd made herself clear, she turned, got into her car, and pulled out, never doubting Audra and I would be right behind her.

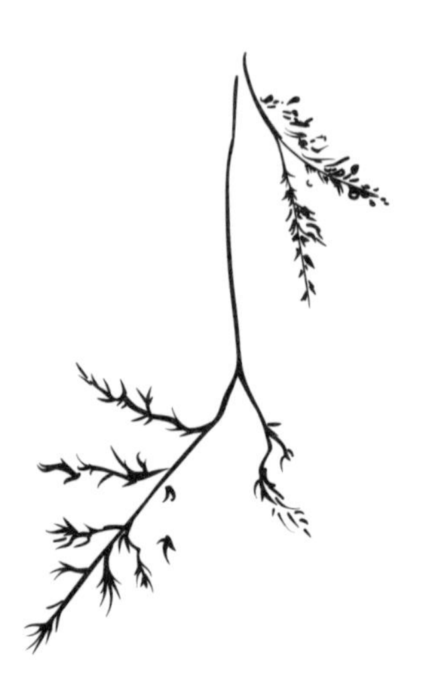

# CHAPTER TWENTY-SIX

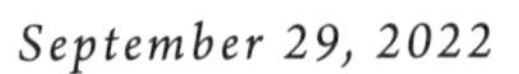

*September 29, 2022*

Something with a buckle banged around in the dryer from the laundry room down the hall. The smells of fabric softener and baking hung in the air, and the oven hummed as it preheated. Mom had announced that the casserole could cook while we talked, and Audra would take it home for dinner; no food shall be wasted.

Mom, Audra, and I sat around the kitchen table, and Franky sprawled on a blanket in the living room watching *Frozen* for the hundredth time, which meant he would remain reliably transfixed for the next two hours.

During the drive from Liam's to Mom's, Audra and I had spoken on the phone to run through our options, ranging from telling Mom nothing to telling her the full truth. Audra had even ventured to suggest that we both just go home and forget about stopping at Mom's at all. Maybe forever. Failing that, her strategy was to stick to our story of dropping off food, to dig in, and resist. But we both knew that Mom wasn't buying it. In the end, Audra had conceded that we'd tell Mom about the storage bin of pills, Liam's hidden phone, and the video Beth recorded but avoid any mention of what had

happened at Simon's. For all of Mom's issues, I trusted her when it came to looking out for Ethan's best interest.

She remained remarkably calm, her hands folded and resting on the table, while Audra and I took turns explaining the discoveries of the past few days. The overhead light cast harsh shadows on her face, which somehow remained girlish no matter her age, and illuminated the smudges of mascara beneath her long lashes, a hint of blush on her cheeks, and webs of fine lines fanning out around her eyes and mouth. It struck me that despite everything we were all going through, she had almost been more composed over the past week than she had been in the months since Dad's death. It was as if all that time she had been anticipating that another shoe would drop. Now that it had, she could breathe again and, knowing what the disaster was, face it. I felt a surge of guilt that Audra and I had cut her out over the past few days when she had needed us.

As I finished telling her about finding Liam's burner phone, I realized I needed to share a bit more—to explain the rest of my plan and why we needed the phone. I glanced at Audra, who shrugged as if to tell me it was my dumb idea, so good luck. I closed my eyes for a few seconds and took a deep breath.

"Even with all that, we're not any closer to knowing who really killed Beth." I glanced at Liam's phone, where it sat connected to my charger. "But, if we can link Liam's phone to Beth's, maybe we can use his phone to text the number that we found on her phone." On the way to Mom's, I had stopped by Ethan's and removed Beth's phone from the storage bin behind the wall panel. I set her phone on the table next to Liam's.

The silence in the room was unnerving. "Whoever Beth was texting told her what to do. I think Beth wanted out and that person didn't want to let her go. Or maybe she even threatened to expose them since she had the video. Do you remember how upset she was about Perk's death? I think that she knew she had to get out then."

Audra's fists were clenched, her knuckles white. "Well, how do we connect the phones?"

I picked up Liam's phone and checked the text and call logs. Both were blank, but there was one number stored in the contacts. It was time to test my hunch that his visit to Beth had been about something more than rent.

I selected the number and typed out the message, *Test.* Taking a shaky breath, I hit send.

Beth's phone let out a tinny chirp, and I felt a jolt of energy in my chest.

Audra picked up the phone and checked the message. "Now we know," she said, her voice quiet.

I nodded. I didn't know if I'd expected to feel vindicated, but the reality was more complicated. I was saddened by Liam and Beth's desperation—their lies—and underlying that, a nervy excitement vibrated. Knowing the two were connected gave us a path forward. I barreled ahead.

"So, we have the number of the person who was bringing the drugs in from Beth's phone. Once Liam is out of the hospital, we can use his phone to set up a meeting with this person at the Castle. Act like he's trying to make contact with his boss. Then, at least, we'll know who's running things."

Mom folded her hands. She'd been silent, her lips tightening as I'd explained everything. I waited for her to tell me she had told me so about Beth. But she didn't. Instead, she nodded and met my eyes.

"It's a good idea." She turned to Audra. "Should we involve Polly—or is she too conflicted as a deputy? We could use someone who knows what they're doing with a gun."

Audra widened her eyes, too stunned to speak for the first time that I could remember.

"Don't look at me that way," Mom admonished. "It's about time someone did something to find out what really happened. *We* all know Ethan didn't do this, but with him in jail taking the fall, who else is going to keep looking? For all of Beth's flaws—and there were many—I figured it was some random out-of-towner passing through, but hearing this, we have a chance of proving it's someone else. It's got to be related to the drugs."

Audra had recovered enough to answer Mom's question about Polly. "Of course I trust her, but I don't think we should tell her until we know we've got something worth sharing. Otherwise, she'll try to stop us. She already told us to stay out of it."

"Osborne said the same to me. First, we need some evidence. We can call the police from the Castle the second we know someone is showing up. But if we tell them beforehand, then they'll stop all of this before we have a chance to find out anything."

Audra raised an eyebrow and blew out a slow breath. "So, when are we doing this? Tomorrow night? I need to make sure Marco can be home with the kids. Franky can't ride along on this one."

"We need to wait until Liam is discharged first. If he's still in the hospital, then it won't make sense for him to set up a meeting."

"Why do you think this person will meet us at the Castle?"

"Well, I'm sure they'd like the money and the drugs Beth still had. One of Beth's texts mentioned leaving everything by the tree, and there's a big sycamore by the river at the Castle with a metal plate on it. I think that tree and the Castle were some kind of meeting spot. It's hidden, you can get to it from the road or the river, and you have a good vantage point of everything around."

Mom nodded. "Someone should cover the Castle itself and the crypt in the stables."

Audra and I both swung our heads toward Mom. "The crypt?"

"You don't know about the crypt? Beneath the stables?" Mom swiveled her gaze from me to Audra and back again. "All those projects you did on the Castle, and you didn't know there's a cellar in the stables? That was the original site for the Underground Railroad." Mom sat up an inch taller, pleased to have told us something we didn't know.

"First of all, I did one project on the Castle a long time ago. And second, doesn't a crypt have human remains in it? You mean the cellar?"

"I don't know." She shrugged, as if the actual meaning of words was a matter of personal preference. "Crypt sounds better. Anyway, I'll wait by the crypt and, Riley, since Audra is scared of heights, you'll wait in the tower."

"I wouldn't say I'm scared of them. I'm just not fond of them."

"Oh," I said. "Really? You want to take the tower then?"

Audra narrowed her eyes. "We should probably spread out. I could go somewhere else."

I was considering if there was a place where Audra might pull off along the road to warn us of an approaching car when Mom chimed in: "You could wait by the other tree at the boat launch."

"*Other* tree?" Audra asked.

"Yeah, there's a big sycamore at the boat launch with a metal plate, like Riley was talking about."

Audra shook her head.

"You're just a wealth of information."

"That's what I've been trying to tell you all these years." One corner of her mouth crept up.

"That would work," I said. "Then if someone approaches on the river, you can let us know. There's a path through the woods between the boat launch and the Castle, so we can get to each other on foot.

"But we need to think about having a car ready in case . . . well, in case of a lot of things. I could cover all of the Castle, Mom, if you could wait nearby with the car. We'll all be close, and we can call or text each other depending on what happens."

Mom narrowed her eyes. "What about the crypt?"

"I can cover the . . . crypt. It's less than a hundred yards from the house."

"Is this an age thing? Because I'm at least as capable as you girls." She looked me up and down. "Maybe more so."

"No, as I said, it's a *car* thing. We need a car." I emphasized each word.

"You don't need to get snotty, Riley. That's fine. I can be the getaway driver."

The buzzer on the dryer made us all jump. Mom rose from the table and returned a moment later with a full laundry basket. Without further discussion of the plan, we each grabbed a warm item from the basket and began folding.

"So, who do we think it is?" Mom asked conversationally, as if we were speculating about a PBS mystery. "It could still be Liam. Then someone else went after him to keep him quiet about the drugs."

I thought about the question. Actually, I hadn't stopped thinking about it since I'd seen the video Beth had recorded, imagining different faces on the dark figure striding from the boat to the barn. The problem was that almost any face could fit on a dark blob in loose clothing.

"I could see Harmony and her mom being involved," Audra interjected. She recounted my encounter with Harmony at the Castle, and Mom clucked her tongue.

I nodded and pulled another towel from the laundry basket. I wouldn't put many things past Harmony or her mom, and together they could move Beth. But something about the two of them didn't add up for me. Maybe it was the way Beth was found.

I frowned. "Why would they wrap Beth in a sheet like that? And then go to the trouble of moving and arranging her? It seems like if it was one of them, they would just get away from Ethan's as quickly as possible."

"Maybe they panicked and wanted to buy time before she was found." Audra shrugged. "The same with Liam, if it was him. Anyone really. The way she fell, it sounds like it was more of an accident than someone setting out to kill her, so whoever did it probably freaked out."

I nodded again. I couldn't find a reason to disagree, but I also couldn't shake an uneasiness that had been brewing in some part of my brain that didn't adhere to reason and logic. Audra would have called it my instinct, and she would have told me to follow it. And she might have been right, but that wasn't me. I couldn't voice something so awful without being sure.

I needed more than instinct; I needed evidence. I needed someone to show up at the Castle—to respond to a text from Liam's phone—and put a face to the shadow.

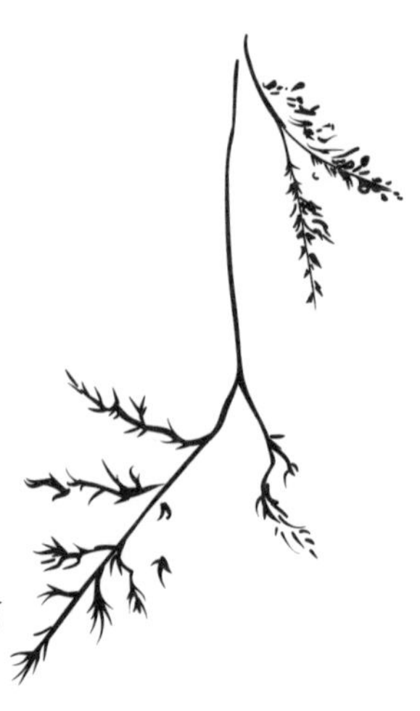

# CHAPTER TWENTY-SEVEN

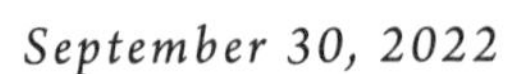

*September 30, 2022*

The next morning was Friday, one week since Beth's murder. Ethan had been in jail for four full days now, but with any luck, tonight Mom, Audra, and I would have the evidence to get him out.

Time would drag until I heard about Liam's release from the hospital, so I decided to go to work, where catching up would prevent me from checking my phone every thirty seconds, but I moved in slow motion. My right leg had spasmed all night and felt rigid and heavy when I woke. As I got ready for work, it lagged as if loaded with weights. Eight months back and in ordinary circumstances, this would have had me on the phone with Dr. Thorpe. But the strain of the past week had only heightened the dizziness, brain fog, and pain that had been building for so long. But as long as I could drag my leg along, I had to keep moving.

By the time I headed for my car, I was on the verge of running late. The big green garbage can sat in the driveway, reminding me that it was trash day. I sighed, set my purse and travel mug in my car, grabbed the wheeled plastic can, and pulled it out to the curb. As the can clattered down the drive

behind me, I mentally rehearsed the text Audra, Mom, and I had agreed to send from Liam's phone. It had been running through my head all morning as I tried to determine if it struck the right tone to lure someone out to the Castle in the middle of the night.

About halfway down the drive, I stopped short. In the grass a few feet from the driveway lay a roundish mass with light brown fur, about the size of a football. I figured it must be a sick animal or a squirrel that had fallen from a tree, but whatever it was, it wasn't moving. I took a few tentative steps toward it and tried to work out what I was looking at. It didn't look like any animal I recognized, but then the fluffy cottontail gave it away. It had to be a rabbit, but it was nearly unrecognizable since it was missing its head.

Heeding some long-dormant, primitive instinct, I looked up. I don't know if I was expecting an eagle or a pterodactyl, but scanning the sharp blue sky, I found nothing, not even a vulture. The grass around the bunny looked undisturbed, but I doubted a fox or coyote would leave traces in a yard. I edged around the bunny, irrationally concerned that it might spring to life and lash out. I didn't want to look, but I forced myself: Where its head should have been was nothing but a clean wound. I didn't see any blood on the grass.

Fighting the urge to gag, I considered what the normal response would be to this situation. I looked from the bunny to the garbage can, and thought about Bernice, probably happily sipping her tea on the other side of the house. I didn't want to disturb her, especially since a fear nagged at me that this may not have been the work of a fox or an eagle.

The persistent beeping of the garbage truck down the block added to the mounting sense of urgency. Leaving the can in the driveway, I limped back to the garage—my heavy leg scuffing the asphalt—grabbed my purse, a shovel, and a black garbage bag. I would document the scene as I'd found it, put the bunny in the bag, and then figure out what to do next. Just another event in a long series over the past week for which there was no script.

Walking around the bunny, I snapped a few pictures. Should I do anything else before moving it? Collect fibers? I briefly wondered if tiny cones or reels of yellow caution tape existed for situations like this. Gripping the wooden handle of the shovel, I slid the blade under the remains of the bunny and dumped it into the garbage bag. It landed with a soft thud and the bag released a powdery whiff of mountain freshness. Using the shovel as a cane, I shambled back up the driveway to return it to the garage. I'd hose it off later. It didn't really matter if I was late since I was still supposed to be taking bereavement time, but running behind added another layer to my stress.

As I turned toward the street, the garbage truck hissed to a stop at the house next door. I hurried back down the driveway to drag the can and the bag the rest of the way to the curb, where I clenched and unclenched my fists, as the garbage truck clattered and squeaked to a stop in front of me. A burly kid with beefy arms and a reflective vest jumped out of the truck and greeted me with a friendly wave before grabbing the trash from our can and tossing it in the back of the truck. He didn't seem fazed that I was standing at the end of my driveway holding another garbage bag and watching him collect my trash. His was the kind of clear mind I needed.

I took an awkward step toward him, still clutching the bag. "I found a rabbit this morning with no head." I wagered this was the weirdest thing he'd heard so far today, but he didn't react, so I continued. "I put it in the bag, but what do you suppose could have—"

The kid smiled at me, a lump of chew pouching out his lower lip. He had light blue eyes in a round face. "Aw, that's no problem. We'll take it."

With one fluid motion, he grabbed the bag, tossed it in the truck, and before I could utter a word, pulled off in a cloud of diesel exhaust with my forensic evidence. My mouth hung open as I watched the truck progress down the street, hauling the scraps and broken junk of people's lives—and one unavenged dead bunny—out of sight.

Even though I'd gone to work to distract myself, I had been exchanging texts with Audra all morning. After the garbage man had hauled off the bunny, I'd texted to ask if she had encountered anything weird this morning and if she could ask Marco—who knew all things wildlife-related—what kind of animal might take the head off a bunny. Audra's first response had been an emoji with round, horrified eyes. A few minutes later, she responded that, according to Marco, almost any predator the size of a raccoon or bigger could kill a bunny but that most would eat more than the head. I wondered what Marco had thought about Audra's question. Maybe he was too busy on the farm to find it odd. Sitting at my desk, my motions felt jerky. Electricity pulsed from my neck to my shoulder as I pecked away at my keyboard. I accepted a request for a meeting the next day and realized with a jolt that it was my birthday, one month after Ethan's, making today the final day of Twin Month. With everything else going on, turning twenty-nine had been the last thing on my mind.

An hour later, I was replying to an email about security settings on a customer database when Audra called. "Liam was released from the hospital," she said without preamble. "Are you going to send the text?"

My hand that rested on my desk began to shake. "Yes, should I do it right away?" I took Liam's phone from the side pocket of my purse and set it on my desk. I kept replaying the scene of Liam leaving the house with Beth, a duffel bag slung over his shoulder. My instincts screamed that this little phone was the key to finding out what had really happened to Beth.

"If you're going to do it, do it now. I'm losing my mind here."

"Me too. Okay." I grabbed the phone. With my hands shaking, it took me several tries but I typed out the messages and hit send.

*Someone is after me*
*Can we meet at the castle tonight at 10*
*I can bring what you're missing*

We'd debated whether to include the last line but ultimately decided it would sweeten the deal if we hinted at the return of Beth's stash of pills and cash.

I picked up my own phone. "Sent it," I told Audra.

Her impatience reared. "When do you think we'll hear back?"

"No idea. Who knows if this person even has the same phone anymore? They're called burners for a reason." I had alternated all morning between despair that the plan wouldn't work and fear that it would.

I ended the call with Audra and went back to the motions of work. Somehow, I made it through small talk with Jane and a two-hour team meeting. I looked at the phone every moment I had to myself.

The response came at 3:30. *OK* was all it said. My heart hammering in my chest, I texted Mom and Audra.

*We're on for tonight.*

# CHAPTER TWENTY-EIGHT

*September 30, 2022*

The visitation room at the jail was a wide-open space with a dozen locked black doors and four round tables spaced about ten feet apart. I hadn't said a word to Mom or Audra that I was going. I hadn't even realized I was planning it until after work, when I'd found myself pulling into the gravel parking lot with the tall chain-link fence. Maybe I'd run out of excuses.

Visiting hours were brief, just 5:00–5:30, and it was already ten after by the time the guard seated me at the plastic table where I waited for Ethan. My chest zinged with anxiety as I thought about the questions I'd played over in my mind. Most of all, I needed him to explain why he had gone to see Beth the afternoon she'd been killed. I'd come to terms with the fact that he'd been there and lied about it, but I had to know why. Aside from that, I needed to see my brother.

Over the past week, I'd tried to avoid thinking about his existence in his jail cell—cramped quarters with nothing but his own thoughts for company. I couldn't think of many days that he hadn't spent at least partially outdoors, in a field, pasture, or the woods. The land we grew up on was a

part of him—the iron in his blood came from the dirt at his feet, the oxygen from the trees over his head.

Sitting on the hard plastic bench in the recirculated air, I thought back to the first time Ethan and I had found an arrowhead, a spring day when we were about five or six. We'd been given the job of picking up rocks in a field about to be planted so that they didn't bust up the equipment. A fresh rain had washed back the top layer of dirt the night before, and in the glaring midday sun, we each carried a two-gallon bucket about half full that banged against our legs. Our eyes were peeled for the shine of stone in the upturned earth when Ethan spotted something.

"Riley, look at this!" He peered into his hand, wiping away dirt with the tail of his red T-ball shirt. His eyes were wide as he held out a triangular piece of rose flint, about half the size of his hand and shaped like a spade on a playing card. I took it and examined it, running my finger along the delicate notched edges.

"What is it?" he asked me.

We called to our dad who had been walking up ahead of us. At that age, Ethan and I still half believed our dad was an omniscient giant: tall, tan, capable of anything. On that bright day, as he approached, his head seemed to brush the sun.

I remember the low whistle and the note of excitement. "Look at that. You two found an arrowhead." He poured some water on it from his thermos, rubbed it with his thumb, and held it back out for us to see.

"You know where this came from?" We shook our heads. "From people who lived here before, the tribes, hundreds and hundreds of years back. They hunted in these woods." Dad squatted down to our height and showed us.

Ethan's eyes widened as Dad spoke, and when he returned the arrowhead and told Ethan to keep it somewhere safe, he whispered, "Wow."

After my dad walked away, Ethan looked up at me. "Here, you can have it."

"No, you keep it. You found it."

"Nah, I want to give it to you. Maybe I'll find another one." He had already turned his eyes to the ground to scan for more.

From that day, Ethan had been hooked on finding clues to who had come before us. He explored the falling-down barns that littered the countryside to collect peg nails. When he discovered what used to be a dump down an overgrown hillside near a creek, he spent days sifting through it for little bits of bright glass: blue, brown, and green medicine bottles that he brought home, cleaned up, and placed along the windowsill of his room to catch the light.

That was why I thought he and Beth made such a good match; they found beauty in what looked like rubble to the rest of us.

A sharp buzz sounded from one of the black doors that lined the walls and a heavy lock clicked. I glanced at the time, already a quarter after. The door opened, and out came Ethan in his beige jumpsuit. Hands shackled, he was escorted by a guard. If he had looked bad at his hearing, the past day and a half had drained what little life remained. His hair stuck out from the side of his head and pink bumps splotched the rough stubble on his cheeks and neck. Veins in his arms were newly visible, like all the fat and muscle had shrunk away from his skin, and his eyes, which used to spark and flash, were red-rimmed and sunken.

He sat down like it hurt. The guard fastened his cuffs to a ring on the table, checked the chain with a tug, and left us.

Ethan looked at me without expression. "Riley," he said.

My plans to ask him about his whereabouts the afternoon of Beth's murder evaporated for the moment. I scanned through a mental Rolodex of inane and inadequate things to say. Finding nothing better, I asked, "How are you holding up?"

He raised a shoulder a fraction of an inch and stared at a spot on the wall behind me. "I'm fine."

As far from fine as he looked, I figured there was little use pointing it out. A sudden desire to get up and leave overtook me, to be anywhere but in this sterile room with the buzzing lights and my broken brother.

All the reasons I'd avoided visiting emerged from the dark attic of my mind where I'd scuttled them, chief among them, not wanting to see him like this.

But as much as I hated to, I had to ask the questions I came for. If I was going to do anything to get him out of here, I had to know everything, and I didn't have much time.

I straightened my spine and looked at him squarely. "Why didn't you tell me you were at the house that day?"

He cocked his head and met my gaze for a second. My bluntness seemed to ignite something deep behind his eyes, and I saw a flicker of the person I knew. Then he returned his gaze to the spot over my shoulder.

"Where'd you hear that?"

"The police, Simon, Liam." I ticked them off on my fingers for his benefit. He shifted in his seat, about to protest. "And don't tell me you weren't there."

He took a slow breath in. I could see his chest rising and falling. I was beginning to think he was going to ignore me until visiting hours ended, when he finally spoke.

"It was because of what you told me. That something was wrong with Beth." His expression was wounded. "After we talked, I wondered what she did all day at the house. It dawned on me. What did I really know about how she spent her time, aside from working on the house and the Castle?" He huffed a short, bitter laugh. "So that afternoon, in between trips from the field to the farm, I went home. I don't know if I wanted to find something or see her doing nothing and prove you wrong. I parked down the road by the cemetery so she wouldn't hear me. I didn't want her to . . ." He shrugged. "It's not that I really expected I'd catch her in something, but I didn't want her to pretend or put on an act for me. I just wanted to see her when she didn't have her guard up."

That bitter laugh again. "It makes me sound like a weirdo, like I wanted to spy on the woman I was about to marry, but what you'd said to me just planted that doubt. You know? I mean, I've known her for ten years, we lived together, but I knew there's always been a piece of herself that she kept from me. Honestly, I think that was part of what I liked about her." He glanced at me and looked away. "She took care of her own garbage. She didn't expect me to *fix* the way she felt about things the way Mom always does. She just dealt with it. I know it makes me sound like an asshole, but I thought that's who she was and that it made us a good match. She didn't need something from me that I was no good at."

He looked up at the ceiling, nodding a bit, and I was glad now to avoid his eyes. He did sound craven and shallow, but he didn't need me to tell him. He swallowed and went on.

"I walked down behind the house. We were harvesting the corn, you know, it was a nice sunny afternoon. The inside of the house was dark, so I couldn't really see anything at first. I went up to the back porch, where the windows were in the shade. I thought, if she sees me, it won't look too weird for me to be out on the porch." He lifted a corner of his mouth. "So, I looked into the kitchen, under those little frilly curtains, nothing. Not even a spoon out of place. Just clean and neat, the way she kept it. Then I moved around to the dining room and looked. That's where I saw her." He shifted in his seat, the chain on his cuffs jingling lightly.

"I didn't even spot her at first. She was lying there on the dining-room floor on her yoga mat stretching her back. Doing those ridiculous hip tilts. You know, like she would do when we watched TV together and her back acted up?" He shook his head and smiled, as if this was the most absurd thing he could imagine, and then fell silent.

I waited a minute for him to go on, glanced at the wall clock, and then asked, "Why didn't you *say* this to Polly? Tell her you saw Beth that afternoon and she was fine."

He rested his cuffed wrists on the edge of the table and drummed his fingers. His whole body rocked forward and back like energy was building inside of him and had nowhere else to go. His blue eyes locked on to mine. "Well, because that's not all I saw."

I froze. I didn't even breathe, just waited.

"She was on the floor, but up on the dining-room table, stacked up nice and neat with rubber bands, were piles of money. I don't know how much or what the bills were, but there were piles. I guess there was enough that she wore her back out counting it. All I know is that I couldn't think of a single good reason why Beth would have cash like that."

In the silence of the room, I could hear him swallow before he continued. "I don't know how long I stood there and stared at it. Then, not even thinking, I backed away from the window, went back down the lawn, and just sat in my truck.

"I don't know for how long and then I came to my senses. I knew I had to get back to the field or else call Liam and Jeremy to let them know I'd be late. That's what I should've done, but I thought I'd use the afternoon to think and then talk to her about it that evening. I didn't know—" He lowered his cuffed hands to his lap and shrugged again.

I could hear the ticking of the wall clock and Ethan's rapid breath. I wanted to touch his arm, to thank him for telling me the truth. The guard stood on the far side of the room, far enough that Ethan and I could talk without being overheard, but he still watched our every move.

I kept my voice low. "You could still tell the police. Whatever Beth was into, *you* didn't do anything wrong. If anything, this explains why you didn't want to tell them about being there in the first place. You were protecting her, at least until you knew what was going on—"

Ethan blew out an impatient breath and curled his lip. "More like I was protecting myself. You think I want to be the dumbass who didn't know what the woman I was about to marry was up to? I still don't know what she was doing, but I can guess it had to do with the pills they found. All I know is that she kept about a million secrets from me, and I never saw it."

"You want to be the dumbass that sits in jail for something he didn't do then?"

"Look, Riley, you think the cops will believe me now? If the money was still at the house, they would have found it, and for all they know, I was in on whatever she was up to. I mean, I lived there right along with her. I could be the ringleader as far as they're concerned. I'm sure they'll think it's pretty rich that I didn't know anything the whole time. It's hard to credit someone for being that stupid."

"Shut up, Ethan. It's hardly stupid to trust the person you were about to marry." Out of the corner of my vision, I noticed the guard approaching. I glanced up at the clock. Half past. Our time was up.

"I'm sorry, ma'am. Visiting hours are ending. If you'll please say your goodbyes, I need to escort the inmate back to his cell." The guard's intonation told me he'd said those words enough times for them to have lost all meaning. Pleading for more time would get me nowhere.

I nodded and he took a few mechanical steps back to his place on the wall. I leaned a little closer to Ethan. "I think we can figure out what Beth was doing and who was involved, but you've got to speak up when the time comes. Okay? Audra and I have a plan."

Ethan's eyebrows shot up. "You have a plan? With Audra?" He leaned his elbows on the table. "Oh God. Don't do something stupid, Riley." He glanced at the guard who was approaching again and then shook his head at me.

The guard reached him, and Ethan held out his hands cooperatively. After unclipping the chain that held his cuffs to the table, the guard placed a hand on Ethan's back to shepherd him back through the black door to his little cell.

Ethan locked eyes with me. "Take care of yourself, Ri. Love you."

"Love you too."

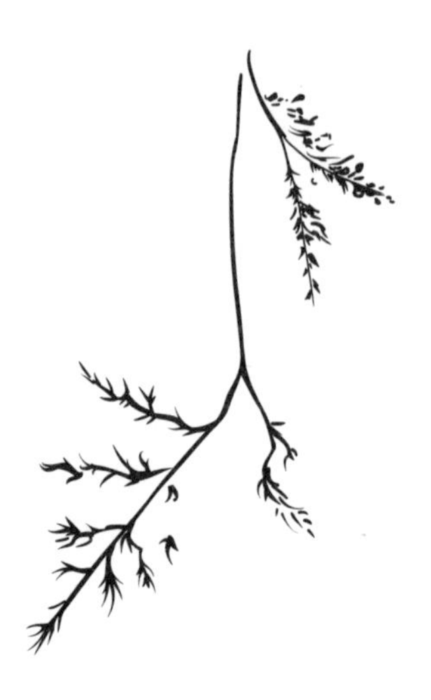

# CHAPTER TWENTY-NINE

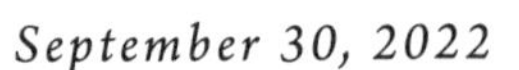

*September 30, 2022*

The three of us dressed in black. Whereas I wore sweats, an old hoodie, and running shoes, Audra had taken style into consideration. In her dark skinny jeans, short black jacket, and Doc Martens, she looked like she was on break between runway shows. I guess if we were going to get ourselves arrested or killed tonight, she wanted to look good doing it.

After visiting Ethan, I'd gone home to change and prepare for the upcoming night. I'd lain down to rest, the world spinning when I closed my eyes. But part of me felt more confident than I had in a long time—my renewed certainty of Ethan's innocence like a steady focal point to get me through the night.

Although I tried to rest, my mind raced, and on impulse, I'd pulled out my phone and searched for the county where Doug and Beth had lived in Texas. I knew they had moved from Austin, which I found was in Travis County. Going to the county website, I scanned the pages, chasing the drifting text across my screen as I read, and found a directory for online case information. Even though I knew Doug had been in Chicago the day Beth

was killed, I couldn't shake the feeling that he was hiding something. Maybe it was the image Ethan had left in my mind of Beth with the piles of cash, and Doug was one of the few people in North Haven who might have that kind of money. I wondered if it all really came from real estate or if maybe he'd been bringing something else back from all his business trips.

When I entered "Lauderdale" into the search bar, I didn't expect anything. I was being paranoid; I should know better than to listen to the small-town rumors about Doug's shady past.

Only one line of results came back: *January 2010, Felony, Dismissed.* That would have been right before Beth and Doug relocated to North Haven. I clicked on the case number. A case summary page opened up for one Doug Lauderdale, charged with bank fraud and tax evasion.

My breathing quickened as I scanned the lines of bail hearings and other court proceedings. At the bottom of the page, it said the case had been dismissed with the note RESTITUTION MADE + DEF DISCHARGED.

No wonder Beth and Doug didn't talk about their past. I remembered how tight-lipped she had been when my friends and I had asked her about Austin and her dad's business. Eventually we'd all given up asking, which must have been a relief for her. Even though the case had been dismissed, he would have had to plead guilty if he made restitution. It had been out there for anyone to find this whole time. I just never cared to look.

Feeling too unsteady to drive the dark roads, I hitched a ride with Audra to Mom's. The gravity of what we were about to do settled over me when we walked in to find her sitting at the kitchen island with Dad's handgun on the granite. Armed with only a flashlight and pepper spray, I felt underprepared.

Mom had the most reliable vehicle, so we set off just before nine in the Ford Explorer. A steady drizzle pattered the windshield and blurred the dark edges of the road. We were all too tense for conversation, too wrapped up in our own pieces of the plan, in our scenarios of what could go wrong or gloriously right.

I sat in the back seat and glanced at Mom and Audra, their faces dotted with the shadows of raindrops. I weighed whether to tell them about Doug and decided not to. There was no mention of drugs in the case summary, and surely the police would have looked into his past already. Polly and Osborne would know more about it than I did. Raising the possibility of Doug's involvement in Beth's murder felt out-of-bounds somehow. Maybe because murder was quite a step up from tax evasion—or maybe accusing a man of killing his own daughter just carried a particularly high burden of proof.

As the pull-off to the boat launch came into view, Mom tapped the brakes. She eased down the steep driveway through the woods, gravel springing up under the tires and dinging the bottom of the car, and pulled off into the grass near the spot we had discussed. Audra grabbed a small backpack. I got out of the car with her and we made our way across the uneven ground. I steadied myself on the trees we passed and carefully lifted my leaden leg over roots and branches. I followed until we reached a small opening in the undergrowth between two massive silver maples, near enough to the river for Audra to see an approaching boat, but far back enough to duck behind the trees and remain unseen. From the hiding spot, we gazed west. The light rain pocked the surface of the river in random concentric circles like schools of feeding fish.

"The rain will help," I said, to encourage myself as much as Audra. "You'll be able to see someone on the water, but it will be hard for them to see into the woods."

She pulled the hood of her jacket over her hair but didn't respond. I wondered if she was having second thoughts. I could understand. After all, she had kids at home, and a husband. I only had Bruno.

"Will you be okay here? You can get to your phone?"

She gave me a half smile. "You sound like the big sister. I'll be fine. Now go, before Mom starts blowing the horn and gives us away."

She gave me a wet hug and then pushed me toward the waiting car. I heard a sniff behind me but couldn't see her face when I glanced back.

The wipers screeched across the windshield and spattered me as I climbed back into the Explorer. Without a word, Mom backed up and pulled around, pointing the car back toward the street. Before leaving, we took a second to look into the trees where Audra waited, but in the rain and the gloom, there was nothing to see.

We pulled into the Castle drive at a quarter past nine. I'd arranged the meeting for ten, but I wanted plenty of time to get into position and didn't want Mom to be seen arriving. The dizziness that had hit me earlier had not let up, and on top of all my other concerns about what could go wrong, I was beginning to worry whether my body would see me through the night. The rain had lightened to a mist and the wipers skidded across the dry windshield, fraying my nerves.

"Can you turn those off?" I asked Mom.

She did so without argument, which told me she was equally nervous. The night was perfectly dark, aside from a few solar lanterns that cast dim yellow puddles of light along the base of the front porch. The Explorer's headlights swung across the Castle, illuminating its brooding silhouette on the hill against the dark sky.

Mom pulled up to the front porch to let me out. It felt somehow like being dropped off for the first day of kindergarten: momentous, scary. Neither of us had spoken on the drive, which was normal for me and abnormal for her. She leaned over in her seat and gave me a tight hug.

"Be careful, Riley," she said and let me go.

"I'll text you once I'm in the tower." I gathered up my things and got out. Taking a moment to steady myself, I turned to close the door. "Love you," I said at the last moment.

As the door slammed, I heard her muffled "Love you too."

Using Mr. Perry's key, I unlocked the front door. After a moment's hesitation, I locked it behind me. I didn't know if the person I was meeting would have a key or not, but forcing them to unlock the door would at least give me a few more seconds to call up reinforcements. My legs felt rubbery as I wiped my wet shoes on the entryway rug. What had seemed like a fair idea in theory was beginning to feel impossibly crazy as I turned on my flashlight and climbed the grand stairway. I told myself that Mom and Audra were just a phone call away. I had Polly's number and even Osborne's ready as well.

The yellow circle of my flashlight seemed puny against the vast darkness of the mansion. I told myself not to focus on all the things I couldn't see. With my hand on the railing, I made my way down the second-floor hallway and ascended the next set of stairs. The dampness of the night intensified the smell of age and mustiness that rose from the old house, especially on the unfinished upper floors, where the thick dust clung to surfaces like coral on a shipwreck. Something old and precarious shifted and settled inside a wall and a veil of dust plumed out, dazzling in the beam of my flashlight. I remembered someone telling me once that a portion of household dust came from people's dead skin. I thought of the century and a half of people who had trod through this house, and I tried not to breathe.

On the third story, the floors creaked with every footfall. I navigated through the piles of rubble, drop cloths, and plaster with my narrow beam, my heart skipping as each dark shape seemed to take on vaguely human contours. As I approached the door to the tower, I noticed it stood open, a gaping black rectangle. I struggled to remember if I had left it that way after rushing down the stairs in excitement to tell Audra my brilliant idea—an idea that was feeling less brilliant by the moment.

Clutching the loose railing in one hand and the flashlight in the other, I climbed the winding stairway to the tower, focusing my light on the narrow steps and concentrating on my balance. The screws that held the railing in place rattled in the wall, and the treads bounced and creaked beneath me. I counted the steps as I climbed and reached fifteen before finally placing my foot on the firm floor of the tower room.

I clicked off my light to allow my eyes to adjust. Without the light to give me a sense of my own position, dizziness washed over me. I steadied myself against the rough wooden railing. In the pure blackness, the room felt somehow smaller, more enclosed and airless than I remembered. As I tried to account for this, I sensed a movement in the far corner. I didn't hear or see a thing, but I knew beyond a doubt something or someone was there.

Then it rose and stood. The shadow from Beth's recording.

I still couldn't see the face, but I clearly saw the gun pointed at me.

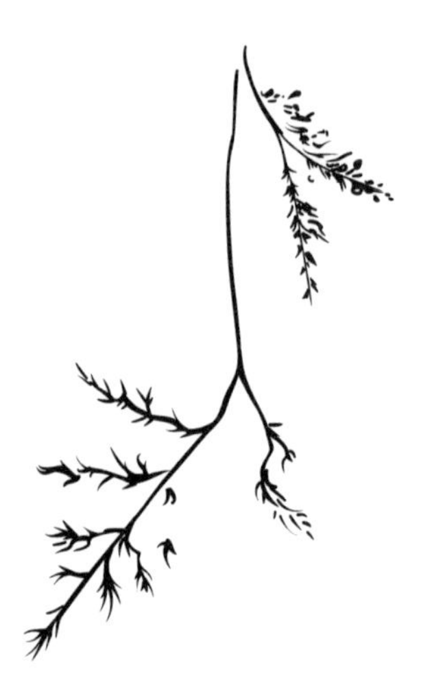

# CHAPTER THIRTY

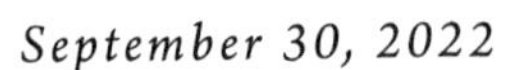

*September 30, 2022*

"Stay still now, Riley."

I recognized the voice before I made sense of what it said. The soothing inflection, the easy smile behind the words. I knew that tone—maybe even those words—from as far back as childhood. She and Audra babysitting, and her wiping disinfectant on my scraped knee.

*Stay still, Riley.*

Polly.

In the dark tower of the Castle, only a sliver of light fell across the side of Polly's face, gilding the little flyaways that had escaped her braid. It took my breath away. I'd prepared myself for a lot of possibilities—Doug or even Mr. Perry—but not this. I'd trusted her nearly as much as I'd trusted Audra for as long as I could remember.

"So, you found Liam's phone." She crooked the corner of her mouth. "I should've taken care of that myself. I guess you found Beth's too?"

I forced a dry swallow and nodded.

"The cash too?"

"Yeah." My voice rasped and I cleared my throat. "And the pills."

She barked a laugh. "I looked through that whole damn house, every corner of the barn. Where the hell were they?"

I ran my tongue over my teeth. One of Beth's last acts had been to hide the bin behind the wall sometime after Ethan had seen her with the money. I wasn't about to hand it over to Polly and undo Beth's last act that easily.

"It's someplace safe. I can take you there," I offered, looking for an excuse to get out onto the road where Mom might see us.

"Nah, we won't be going anywhere." She stepped closer. I took a step back.

"Why are you doing this?"

"Which part, Riley? The pills or screwing over your family? I guess one for money and the other . . . well, that's just the way things shook out. But I can't say I didn't take a little satisfaction in it. As much as I loved you guys, you always had it so good—the beautiful, golden Svensons. I'd be scraping my mom off the floor after a rough night, patching up a fat lip, like it was my fault she was strung out, and Audra would be the one complaining to *me*." Polly laughed. "About nothing. About having to do chores or not getting the earrings she wanted or your mom being difficult. As if you'd know what a difficult mother is. Audra never had a real problem her whole life. Everyone needs some kind of problem. So maybe this is it, to finally balance things out."

There was no hint of tension in her voice, no hurry. I wondered how long she had been waiting for me to walk up these stairs like an idiot into her trap and how many years she'd been waiting to say these things.

"How long have you been waiting up here?" I had no plan but figured the longer I kept her talking, the better chance I had to come up with something resembling a plan.

"Long enough to see you get dropped off. Was that your Mom? That's sweet. It's a shame she couldn't stick around. We could all have a nice party, a little cake." She shifted her weight. "Not that I'm enjoying this. I'd rather build things up, not tear them down."

I scoffed. "Selling pills was your way of building things up?"

"Don't be stupid, Riley. You think junkies weren't gonna get their hands on it anyway? I grew up with one, remember? I know what they're capable of, the shit they can live in as long as they get the one thing they need. I made sure that they had a clean supply and that the money stayed here, instead of some out-of-town lowlifes making money off our backs." There was an unmistakable note of pride in her voice as she finished—a satisfaction in finally sharing how resourceful she'd been, how she'd taken on a rotten situation and made the best of it. It made me sick.

"Right, so the money was for the good of North Haven? That's awfully generous of you." I took a step back so that I was fully in the shadow of the wall. As Polly talked, inch by inch, I'd moved my hand toward my pocket. I felt around for a button.

"C'mon, what do you see me spending it on? You know me, Riley. You see me driving around in a Ferrari? I've had the same damn car for ten years. I take my cut, but that's only fair. I saw right away after my first few busts. Anyone with half a brain could sell this shit if they had the contacts, and boy did I have contacts—with this job in this town. Do you know the disgusting shit I see every day? Generations of it, same as back when I was in school. Now it's their kids having more trash kids to fuck things up. One after another. Just history repeating itself in different clothes. The same stealing, the same sponging off everyone else while they let their own house fall down around them. If junkies wanna kill themselves, that's one thing, but I'm not gonna let them take the whole town down around them. If they're throwing their money away, I might as well catch it and build a place where decent people want to be, where they can raise their kids and their kids actually want to stay. We *were* building it. Beth saw that. For all her dreams, she could be practical."

I pictured the massive Victorian house Polly had purchased on Main Street and knew she was deluding herself. She cared about her own ego at least as much as the town, but I supposed the story she spun let her sleep at night.

A rectangle of light lit up from within the folds of her clothes. The screen of her phone. She glanced down and clicked her tongue.

"That'd probably be your sister asking me to check on you. Always needing something." She waved the gun, and I noticed the long barrel, a silencer. "How about you keep your hands where I can see them?"

I moved my hands away from my pockets. I had half of what I needed. Now I needed to keep Polly going.

I didn't think that part would be hard. She seemed energized by the chance to finally tell someone how smart she'd been, how she'd fooled all of us.

"Beth went to you about someone trespassing here, didn't she?"

Polly smiled. "Good work, Riley. Did Audra get it?"

I shook my head. I wasn't about to admit to Polly I hadn't known either until she had the gun on me.

"Didn't think so. Yeah, Beth came to me. Told me she knew something was going on here, and she said Perry wasn't doing anything about it, but it was the *way* she talked to me—she wasn't all flowy dresses and doe eyes. She knew something was going on. She'd seen me 'patrolling' the Castle on my own time, she said, when she was here late and just wanted me to know." Polly gave a grudging laugh. "Didn't want to get anyone in trouble, of course, but she didn't want to see someone blow up all the hard work she'd put into the restoration. She was sharp beneath all the pretty. Plus, she had the knack for disappearing in plain sight. The type of person no one suspects. First she just did a few favors in exchange for some pills for herself, but she saw the potential soon enough."

Polly gestured with the barrel of her gun around at the walls of the Castle.

"You think this grand transformation was just elbow grease? Crippled Beth and old Mr. Perry plugging away? Beth pictured herself making something of the place but knew it needed bankrolling. I'd been putting the money into the buildings downtown, but Perry and the association were only too happy to have an anonymous benefactor."

As much as I didn't want to believe Polly, I knew Beth saw her shot at a meaningful career in North Haven as tied to the restoration of this crumbling wreck—her chance to find a purpose, despite her pain.

Polly's voice turned boastful. "I could've had this place named after me for all the money I put into it. But all I want is the place I'm from not to be a shithole." She quieted. "Not to live with squalor my *whole* damn life. I mean, be honest, Riley, you didn't want to come back here and you weren't gonna stick around long. And that's what happens. Even Audra took the kids and hightailed it to Wicksburg for the precious schools. Most people with dreams leave. But not me, and not Beth. She and Ethan wanted to make *this* place their dream."

"Ethan." I felt a weight in my chest.

"Ethan? Oh, nah." She waved her free hand dismissively. "He helped with the Castle, but he didn't know anything more. Nothing against your brother. He's cute, but he wasn't . . . oh, the philosophical type to see the big picture."

Even with the gun still pointed at me, the relief made me dizzy—well, dizzier. Ethan had been honest with me about that much. He hadn't known. Inch by inch, I eased my left hand back toward my other pocket.

"So, if things were going so well, what happened? Why's Beth dead?"

A muscle in Polly's jaw clenched and she shifted her weight again. My eyes were adjusting.

"Well, believe me, that's not what I'd planned. She was getting cold feet, was tired of the secrets. Keeping it from Ethan, from you too. I stopped in to talk with her, to remind her *why* we were doing this—gave her a dozen reasons why—but she was worked up. She said it wasn't worth it, that the damage outweighed the good. She was making noise about the sheriff—" A quick shake of her head. "I was just trying to get her back under control when she ran out the back. Trying to calm her down . . . but she wouldn't listen to reason. She lost her wits just 'cause a few people OD'd who would've done it anyway." Her jaw flexed again. "Like people who steal from their own families would be missed."

A shiver of rage ran up my spine, not only for Beth but for Perk and the other lives wasted, the families left to pick up the shards. But I swallowed, steadied my voice.

"I know it was an accident with Beth." The bruises on her face and arm told me that there had been more to it, but I needed Polly to keep talking. "But what about Liam? And shooting at Audra and me at Simon's?"

"Liam?" Polly chuckled. "That wasn't me. That was just a happy coincidence. I was in the middle of recusing myself with Sheriff Klein when that happened. Pretty good alibi. I'd steered things the way I needed and it was time to bow out gracefully. And that with Simon." The corner of her mouth turned down. "That piece of trash was harassing Beth. He'd seen enough folks going in and out of the house that he suspected something and was threatening to blackmail her or tell Ethan. He didn't know the details, but his kind always thinks they know more than they do." She gestured dismissively with the gun.

"The shot was just to warn you off and keep him quiet. It was never close to hitting anything other than Simon's rusted-out trailer. 'Course, I should've known better than anyone that you and bullheaded Audra would just double down."

I thought about my bullheaded sister and mother, both waiting for me to let them know I'd made it to the tower safely. My only hope was that given their impatient natures, one or both of them had already contacted someone other than Polly.

She took another step toward me now, and I flattened myself against the wall, searching for space that wasn't there. "I get what you and Beth were doing." I kept my voice conciliatory. "I don't even disagree with it. You had good intentions, but I don't want to see Ethan go to prison for something he didn't do. You said yourself that he's the type of person we need in this town. Couldn't someone else take the fall? I won't get in the way of what you're doing. All we need to do is pin what happened to Beth on someone else."

She cocked her head.

I wondered if she was buying it or if she simply enjoyed watching me squirm. "What about Doug?" I asked. "He was involved, wasn't he?"

Polly sighed. "You think I haven't thought this through, Riley? Doug won't work. I mean, don't get me wrong. He's a useful idiot and he knows how to wash money. But if any pressure came down on him, he'd crack in a second, which would lead to Liam, which would lead to me." A half smile. "Besides, Doug hasn't been thinking clearly this past week. Who do you think went after Liam?"

"*That* was Doug?" I swallowed, remembering Doug's reaction when I'd told him about Liam visiting Beth.

"They knew each other from the money drops, so Doug got it in his head that Liam must've killed Beth. I don't know what scenario he cooked up in his head and didn't care as long as he wasn't looking my way." She shrugged.

All at once, it hit me how expertly Polly had played all of us, from being part of the team that processed the crime scene, to arranging to conduct Liam's initial interview without Osborne—then recusing herself once it was clear Ethan would take the fall. No wonder she thought she could get away with this.

The gun, which had hovered around the level of my abdomen, came up a few inches and pointed squarely at my chest. "Yeah, you guys have turned this into a real mess." She said it as easily as if she were talking about a craft project gone bad. "I hate to do this, Riley. You guys were like my family—at least the family I wished I had. But I can't trust you to keep your mouth shut as long as Ethan's in jail, and I can't get Ethan out of jail without getting myself caught up. So . . ." Another shrug. "You see where that leaves us."

"You can't shoot me here. People know I'm here. Beth took a video of you making a drop one night. She mounted the camera on a column on the back porch." I pointed behind her toward the river.

"Nice try, but if you had a video that actually showed me, I'm pretty sure you would have turned it over to Osborne by now." Still, for a split second, she flicked her gaze toward the window where I'd gestured. It was now or never. Gripping my canister of pepper spray, I brought my hand up from my pocket, held my breath, and blasted her directly in the face.

Polly screamed like an injured animal, making noises I never would have guessed her capable of. As she brought one hand to her face, the gun dangled in her other hand. I brought my heavy flashlight up above my head and swung hard at her hand. The gun went flying into a dark corner, and I heard a satisfying crunch when my flashlight smashed into her fingers.

I couldn't savor my moment of victory. Pepper spray filled the small room, burning my eyes and face. Still holding my breath and with tears streaming from my closed eyes, I felt for the loose banister at the top of the stairs and shuffled toward the first step. Polly still moaned and cursed at me through clenched teeth, but I knew she would be on my heels.

With my hand, I followed the turn in the banister that led to the stairs and eased blindly down to the first step. I felt a surge of relief as my foot found a tread, and I sped up. I'd made my way about halfway down the spiraling stairway when I took a step and felt only air beneath my foot.

Unable to recover my balance, I pitched headlong down the remaining stairs, crashing into risers, the newel post, and then the floor, my arms and shoulder taking the brunt of the damage. The flashlight clattered out of my hand and across the room. I heard Polly pawing around on the stairway above, trying to blindly find her way down. I didn't know if she'd found her gun in her distress or not, and I didn't want to stick around to find out.

Pain radiated from my shoulder as I pushed myself up from the floor. I blinked tears from my burning eyes and looked around blearily, the darkness of the third floor morphing in and out of focus. I ran toward the doorway, Polly's boots heavy on the steps behind me.

"You little bitch!" she bellowed after me, but I was already on the stairs down to the third floor. The idea of concealing myself in one of the jumbled piles of furniture in a room on this floor sprang to mind, but instinct told me to keep moving. My best chance was to get out of the house entirely.

As I rushed down the hallway and stairs, the noise of Polly behind me felt like a hot laser targeted at my back and propelled me forward. Despite the gallons of adrenaline coursing through me, I moved as quickly and quietly as I could so that she wouldn't know where to look. I heard doors to the rooms on the third floor opening and closing and knew I had bought myself some time.

I took the steps down the grand stairway as rapidly as my shaky balance allowed. The front door was visible now, but in the entry hallway, with my eyes still blurry, my equilibrium careened again. My dragging foot caught on the hall rug, and I fell forward, landing with a thud. So much for quiet. I scrambled up, the front door within reach now, but I regretted locking it behind me on my way in. What I'd thought would stall someone on the way in, now slowed me down.

My fingers felt like blocks of wood as I unbolted the door, but I got it open as I heard Polly's boots hit the second floor above me. Slipping out and closing the door behind me, I scrambled down the front steps and made for the outbuildings, praying the smaller one was still unlocked. The night had cleared enough that a pale sliver of moon shone on the wet grass. From the corner of my eye, I saw fog rising like a horde of ghosts off the warm river. The old wooden door to the smaller outbuilding was unlocked. It let out a soft creak as I slipped inside. In the dim light, I scanned the assortment of tools leaning against the back wall. I pulled a sturdy axe with a long wooden handle from the tangle of rakes and shovels and took an experimental chop at the air. The memory of Harald the axe murderer, who had protected his family, flashed through my head. I wondered how I'd explain my way out of killing a police officer with an axe if it came to that.

I pulled my phone from my pocket and dialed *911*.

"Nine one one, what is your emergency?" The woman sounded impossibly bored.

I kept my voice low. "Send police to Carlton Castle."

An exasperated sigh. "Ma'am, I can hardly hear you. You're going to need to speak up."

I held the phone to my mouth and cupped my hand around it. "Send help to Carlton Castle," I enunciated quietly.

A sound came from the direction of the mansion. I muted my phone and put it back in my pocket but stayed on the line. Part of me wanted to cower here in a dark corner, but I knew Polly would check the outbuildings. Adrenaline kept me moving.

I slipped out the wooden door and stumbled toward the river and the beacon of the white sycamores. The crescent moon cast just enough light to guide me, but it would guide Polly too. Again, I felt the sensation of a laser following me as I hurried across the open lawn toward cover. The heavy axe slowed me, but I didn't drop it for fear of needing to defend myself. At last, reaching the shelter of the trees, I slowed, lowered myself to the ground, and listened. The sounds of the night were remarkably undisturbed despite the horror unfolding. Crickets chirred, and a bullfrog belted its two-note croak. The river rushed steadily behind me. Far out on the main road, I could hear the tires of a passing car on the wet pavement. I considered yelling for help, but I knew Polly would reach me before anyone else. My own breath came in heaves and I tried to quiet myself. Under my nose, the earth smelled sharp and clean, like minerals.

Across the musical night, I heard the front door of the Castle open and close and slow footsteps on the wooden porch.

Every part of me shivered. The grass soaked my shoes and pant legs, and drips from the trees fell onto my head. Crouching as low as my shaking legs would allow, I crept toward the woods, where I knew paths would lead me toward the boat launch and Audra.

Suddenly the night illuminated, a blinding brightness emanating from the side of the Castle. After the near pitch dark, my eyes were dazzled. Too blind to be sure where to run, I flattened myself against the ground and crept in the direction of the woods on my elbows, my injured shoulder protesting every movement.

"I know you're out there, Riley," Polly called from the direction of the light. "It's only a matter of time. I know this place like the back of my hand, and I think you'll find those woods aren't so friendly tonight to people who don't know them like I do."

What did that mean? For the first time, I wondered just how prepared she had been for this. Obviously, she had turned the tables on my attempt to lure her here. Had she gone so far as to lay traps in the woods? Could she have backup waiting out there? I wondered if the 911 operator was still on the line, but I didn't dare speak for fear of drawing Polly's attention, and there was no way to text Audra or Mom without the light of my phone giving away my location.

The spotlight went out and, again, I was blind in the darkness. Noises came from all directions. Tree limbs rubbed and squealed against the wind, and a small animal made a rattling sound as it stirred beneath a pile of dead leaves. I felt exposed on the ground and feared that Polly and her searchlight would find me if she came closer. Dragging my axe along, I crawled further off the path and into the brambles. As a trained police officer, Polly would be patient. But she didn't have forever. Between Audra, Mom, and the 911 operator, surely someone had sent for reinforcements.

A flicker of movement came from the far side of the lawn in the direction of the outbuildings, opposite of where I had last seen Polly with the light. Was she checking the outbuildings for me? Maybe she had a helper.

I reached a pocket of tall weeds and curled my body behind them. Over my gulps of air, I listened—the bullfrog, crickets, drips of rain. Then something large crackled through the brush in the woods behind me.

*Please be a deer,* I prayed, a nice little spotted fawn and not some sidekick of Polly's. Then it whispered *fuck.*

Polly had brought support. Time to move.

I edged back from where I'd hidden myself and slowly rose, scanning the dark grounds. The fog drifting along the river blocked then revealed areas along the bank in turns. I'd seen movement across the lawn. Maybe I had a sliver of opportunity to make it to the driveway.

I took off, running blindly, clumsily, as fast as I could with my spinning head, a leaden foot, and an axe tucked under my arm. I knew I was making more noise than I wanted, but reaching the driveway and the road beyond it seemed my best hope with who-knew-what behind me in the woods.

Another burst of light lit up the night, rapidly coming toward me from the direction of the outbuildings. Blinded by the sudden glare, I lost my bearings again and lurched but kept moving. A muffled *ping* of a gunshot sounded from the direction of the light. Then another *ping* and a sharp sting burned through my lower leg. I took another stride, but my leg buckled. I fell hard into the wet grass, my teeth cutting into my tongue, the axe flying from my grasp.

"Stay down," Polly ordered. I marveled at her arrogance to tell me to hold still and make killing me easier on her, but as I tried to rise, pain shot through my leg. Again, it gave out.

The spotlight drew closer. From the ground where I lay, all I could see were mud-spattered pant legs and a glare of light where Polly's upper body was.

"Stop fighting, Riley . . . I don't have time for this." Above the pounding of my heart, I caught the far-off sound of sirens. I just needed a little more time. I edged away from her as much as I could with a useless leg and injured shoulder, but she easily stayed with me. At last, my shoulder gave out, and I fell back, pinned down like an insect beneath the harsh light.

My senses had never been so sharp as in that moment. I watched her extend her arm and point the long-barreled pistol down at my head. I smelled the sweet spicy clover in the grass where I lay and heard the rustle of Polly's clothes as she shifted. "I'm really sorry it had to come to this, Riley." She set her feet like someone who knew what she was doing and squared her aim. I kicked out my good leg at nothing and then closed my eyes. My thoughts turned to Audra and Mom hearing the news. I regretted not staying alive for them.

The crack of a shot split the air, and I heard a cry. In the course of a split second, a dozen thoughts and images cascaded through my brain, first that the silencer didn't really live up to its name. And where was the pain? Maybe that's what dying felt like, I thought, the absence of pain. Then I wondered, *Why am I still thinking?* I opened my eyes. The spotlight swung in a wild arc across the lawn. Had Polly somehow missed at such close range? Figuring

I remained alive for the moment at least, I pulled myself in the direction of the road, praying the police would make it in time. Then I heard a matter-of-fact voice behind me.

"Is she dead?"

I looked back over my shoulder in confusion. Polly's spotlight had fallen a few feet away, and the sideways beam slanted across a scene that made no sense: a diminutive figure with a gun in one hand stood over a gurgling, crumpled body on the ground.

"I think I got her," my mom said. "Maybe I should finish her off."

I pushed myself up into a sitting position and stared.

"Kick her gun away," I managed to say. Mom daintily kicked at the gun twice, missed twice, and then finally just bent to pick it up from where it lay, a few feet from Polly's outstretched arm.

Polly didn't move, but wet moans came from where she had fallen. The sirens grew louder. Through the trees, red and blue lights flickered on the drive.

"Are you okay?" came a panicked voice from behind me.

I twisted. Audra limped toward me from the direction of the woods. "What happened?"

"I shot her," Mom said simply.

"I fell in a hole and cut my foot," Audra said by way of explanation.

"It was you in the woods?"

"Yeah, who'd you think it was?" Audra peered at the figure on the ground and froze. She brought her hand to her mouth. "Oh my God." She dropped down beside me. "Polly?"

She looked at me, and I nodded. I knew Audra was going to learn things that would hurt her. "Oh God, Polly. What did you do?"

As the sirens grew closer, I tried to rise, but my leg gave out again.

My mom stood over us both. "Are you hurt, Riley? Stay there. Did she hit you?"

"She got my leg." Blood soaked my pant leg, but I felt surprisingly little pain with all the adrenaline coursing through me.

On the ground next to me, Audra crushed me in a hug as a police car skidded to a halt on the gravel drive. Osborne climbed out and raced over to us as more vehicles flew up the lane behind him.

Audra let go. I dug into the pocket of my sweatshirt and pulled out the small audio recorder she had loaned me. It was still recording. Audra let out a laugh of amazement as I showed her the display.

Before climbing the stairs to the tower, I'd readied the recorder. In the dark room with Polly, all I'd had to do was reach into my pocket and tap a button.

I didn't know how much of the last hour it had picked up, but I hoped it would be enough to get Ethan out and put Polly away in his place for a very long time.

# CHAPTER THIRTY-ONE

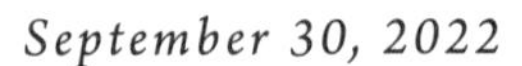

*September 30, 2022*

As it turned out, the acoustics in the pocket of my old hoodie were pretty good.

My recording had captured Polly monologuing about her grand scheme to revitalize North Haven with drug money and her confrontation with Beth, along with Doug's involvement.

As the EMTs tended to Polly, I played the recording for Osborne and Audra. Listening to her again, I heard the self-satisfaction in her voice; she'd been proud of what she was doing. At the part where she described how no one would miss people who stole from their own families to get high, Audra gasped. Osborne shook his head.

The officers who stood nearby wore heavy expressions. Osborne's face told me he'd heard enough to realize how seriously he'd messed up by arresting Ethan and missing what his own partner had been up to. To be fair, none of us had seen it, except Beth.

After being patched up, Polly was cuffed and carted off in the first ambulance with a pair of uniformed police officers in tow. Judging by their

scowls, she would not be receiving special treatment. Paramedics helped me onto a stretcher and into an ambulance next. In the quiet of the back of the ambulance, I closed my eyes, waiting to hear the slam of the rear door before we moved off. When I opened my eyes again, Osborne stood in front of me, leaning against the open door. The flashing red and blue lights reflected in his unreadable eyes. When he saw me watching him, he leaned in.

He kept his voice low. "That was stupid, Riley. You should have stayed away from this like I told you." He paused, seeming to weigh his next words. "But all that considered, you didn't do too badly."

I swore I caught a half grin on his face before he turned away.

In the ER a harried-looking doctor told me that I'd separated my shoulder. The bullet to my leg had nicked my tibia and passed through but would not likely require surgery. As one nurse fitted a sling for my shoulder, another cleaned and wrapped my leg in thick white bandages.

The detective I'd seen alongside Osborne earlier in the night, Detective Towson, visited me next to get my account of all that had happened with Polly. I was grateful the recording backed up my word against hers. As I described how she'd held me at gunpoint, first in the Castle and then later in the yard, it struck me how lucky I was to have come out of the night alive.

Towson, who had a salt-and-pepper beard and black-framed glasses, wore a permanent expression of disapproval, as if the endless parade of criminals he'd seen over the years had been a great disappointment to him. He said little while I spoke, but at the end, offered his professional assessment: "That was a pretty stupid thing to do." It seemed he and Osborne agreed on that point. They would hit it off. He clicked his pen and glanced up at me. "But I suppose your brother will thank you."

I looked up at him, trying not to get my hopes up too high. "Will he be released now?"

"Charges should be dropped once we get Polly processed, so probably in the morning."

The nurse who had wrapped my leg returned and shooed Towson away before giving me a couple of pills to swallow, which she told me "should help."

They did, along with the news that Ethan would be released. I could feel a sleepy smile on my face by the time Mom and Audra joined me.

"You're still a free woman?" I said to my mom, my voice curiously slow. Although my tone was light, after the detective and nurses had left me, I had begun to worry about the consequences she might face for shooting Polly.

"I told the police I was defending my daughter *and* neutralizing a dangerous criminal that had worked right under their noses. If anything, I should get a commendation."

I don't know what I'd been thinking, doubting her ability to win an argument. She approached the side of my bed and took my hand. "Besides, Polly isn't denying it."

Audra limped over and stood beside Mom. She looked weighed down, and I knew it wasn't from her injury. Her red eyes told me she was reeling from the discovery that she'd never really known the woman she'd considered her best friend most of her life.

"She tried denying it at first, but Osborne said when she heard the recording . . ." She raised a shoulder. "She knew it was over. Now she's bragging about how she operated right under everyone's noses, telling how she kept the drugs in a building on the riverside in town and transported them to the Castle for Beth to distribute." Audra's tone was bitter, like the words stung in her mouth.

According to Polly's statement and the gaps that Osborne had filled in for Mom and Audra, Polly had stopped in to talk with Beth about her text around four thirty that afternoon, when they had begun arguing. Facing Simon's blackmail and my suspicions, Beth wanted out. In Polly's words, "she became hysterical" and threatened to go public.

At some point, the argument moved from the kitchen to the back yard, probably around the time Polly left the bruises on Beth's face and arm. According to Polly's statement, Beth had been backing away when she'd stumbled and struck her head on the jutting concrete of the broken patio. I wondered if we would ever really know if she'd had help falling.

Realizing it would only be a matter of time before Ethan returned home, Polly used a sheet from the clothesline to wrap Beth and moved her to the woods to buy herself a few hours until the rain could come along and degrade the physical evidence. But in her haste moving Beth, she had left the blood on the remaining sheet with her gloved hand—a print I'd assumed had come from Beth. But Beth had never moved from where she'd fallen. The same nurse who had chased off Detective Towson overheard Mom and Audra's chatter and reappeared to escort them away. Then she closed a curtain around my bed so no one else could find me.

As I waited to be discharged and the pills took hold, I wondered again about the sheet—if wrapping Beth up had been for expediency or if there had been something more tender behind it. Polly and Beth had both been family to us. The way I had found Beth, in the woods facing the river she loved and with the sheet around her like she was sleeping, made me think that maybe Polly's fondness for our family had played a part. But then I thought of Polly on the porch with Ethan and me that same evening, calmly probing us about Beth's plans for the day, and then steering the investigation toward Ethan as he and I were out calling her name and looking for her body in the rain-soaked fields. I figured, then, that the sheet was just a convenient way to move her. I went back and forth in my thinking. As waves of chemical calm washed over me, I realized that the only thing I knew was that, after all the years I'd known Polly, I had no idea who she really was, deep down.

The next morning, I turned twenty-nine and, for once, there was no cake. No one minded except Mom, who fussed that it wasn't a birthday without cake and that she would make it up to me. I told her that since she'd pretty much saved my life the previous night, we could call it even. Watching her light up with a smile in that moment was more than enough. Besides, all of us, including her, were too excited about Ethan's release from jail to care about cake.

She and I rode together to pick up Ethan and take him to Audra and Marco's, where we would all gather for a quiet celebratory lunch. I fidgeted and bounced my good leg in anticipation.

As we pulled into the lot behind the jail to await Ethan's release, I balanced on my crutch and told Mom I had a quick errand to run.

"What's in the bag?" She eyed the Wicks bag I'd grabbed from the back seat.

"Just something I owe someone."

"Hmm," was all she said, but she smiled, and her eyebrows rose behind her big sunglasses.

The sheriff's office sat one building over from the jail, and even though it was Saturday, I felt pretty certain that Osborne would be in, with all the work surrounding Polly's arrest and the allegations against Doug and Liam.

It took me a while to make the short journey with my crutch and slinged shoulder. I attracted some glances as I hobbled my way toward Osborne across the open room of desks. When he looked up, his jaw dropped and, at that moment, my labored ambush was worth it. He stood up from his desk chair, patted some papers, then sat back down.

"Delivery." I held out the Wicks bag. "The candle you ordered for your mom."

"Oh yeah." He blew out a breath as he took the bag from me. "I'd almost forgotten. Thank you. You didn't need to bring it by."

"Well, I had to get it to you somehow, and I was just down the street to pick up Ethan." I left the statement hanging, hoping the mention of Ethan might spur an acknowledgment that he had been wrong all along.

He set the bag on his desk, where all the papers and folders sat at precise right angles. "What do I owe you?"

I almost told him not to worry about it, and then I remembered what Ethan's arrest had put my family through. "Twenty-four dollars and ninety-five cents." That was the price without my Wicks discount.

He rifled through his wallet for some bills. "Here's twenty-five and you owe me a nickel."

I smiled but vowed he would never get that nickel from me.

I noticed his wrinkled clothes and wondered if he'd slept at all since I'd seen him. "Did you bring Doug in last night too?" I asked.

Osborne nodded. "Yeah, he's looking at significant time for money laundering and the attempt on Liam, but I don't think he'll be much help with Polly. Liam was the go-between. Doug says he never knew who was behind it all and swears he didn't know Beth was involved. Says he only dealt with Liam, so I guess when he found out Liam had been paying visits to Beth, he thought he'd put it all together—he just put it together the wrong way."

Looking down, I felt a sinking feeling, knowing I'd been the one to send Doug down that path. I felt Osborne's gaze on me.

"Don't blame yourself for what Doug did," he told me. "I know you mentioned Liam to him, but I questioned him about it too. Doug's the one who made the decision to hurt him. There were a million other ways he could have handled it, and he chose the worst one."

I nodded. I appreciated his kindness, but guilt still nagged at me for the small part I'd played.

He scratched his temple and looked to the side. He harrumphed like he had something stuck in his throat. "You know, once things have settled down a little bit, I'd love to talk with you some more about your work in IT security, the forensics work you mentioned. Maybe we could get a coffee?"

I narrowed my eyes. What? Was this truly about work, or was he asking me out?

After everything, would he do that?

As much as I told myself he'd been doing his job, I couldn't tamp down the anger that flared every time I thought of Ethan sitting in jail. I knew it was unfair to fault him for believing what, at times, I'd feared myself, but I couldn't reason my way out of it. Not quite yet.

I blew out a puff of air that indicated the prospects were not promising, but then answered honestly. "I don't know. We'll see. Right now, I need to get back for Ethan."

"Okay." He let out a deep sigh, relief and something else. "I'll follow up with him once he's had some time." He looked down at the Wicks bag and nudged it with his index finger. "I know I owe all of you an apology."

That was a start. "You do."

He held my gaze as I nodded goodbye and maneuvered around on my crutch to go.

I made it back to the parking lot just as Ethan emerged from the door at the back of the jail. He held the metal railing as he came toward us down the steps, still a thinner, sallower version of himself, but when his habitual grin widened across his face, I smiled in return. Seeing him walk toward me in that moment eclipsed the worry, doubt, and grief of the past week. He, Mom, and I all converged right there, group-hugging in the gravel parking lot like a bunch of saps. Mom even cried for something like the third time in her life.

On the car ride over to Audra and Marco's, Mom peppered Ethan with questions about what he had eaten, what food he had missed, and how good it would feel to sleep in his own bed. Ethan tried to meet her enthusiasm, nodding and dimpling when she promised to bring his favorite, chicken and scalloped potatoes, over to him tomorrow. But at the mention of his house, his expression tightened.

As we pulled into Marco and Audra's driveway, I saw him swallow and caught a look of pure weariness flit across his face. I wondered if he was ready for this. All of it. As ecstatic as we all were to have him out, I worried about him going home and being alone in the place where Beth had been killed. The place where they'd loved and made a home together, and where, every day, she had lied to his face.

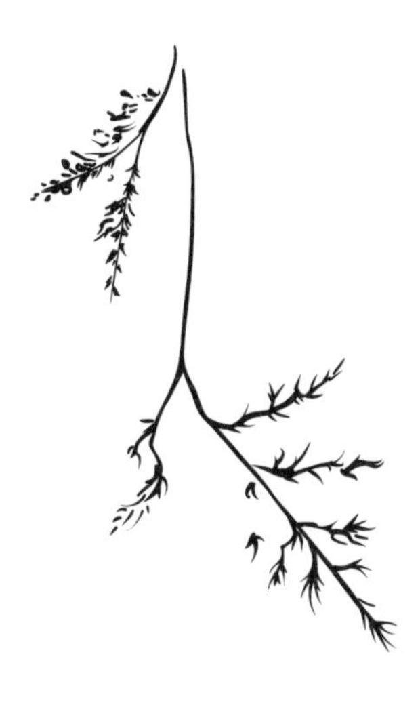

# CHAPTER THIRTY-TWO

*October 4, 2022*

The Tuesday after Ethan came home, Dr. Maclean called to tell me my Western blot—the second Lyme test—had come back positive. I had Lyme disease. I sank back into my couch as she spoke. A diagnosis, at last. But it still wasn't simple. In fact, the more she talked, the less clear it became. With the news of an actual word for all this—Lyme—reverberating in my head, I struggled to keep up with all she was telling me.

". . . Can't say for absolute certain that Lyme is the culprit. All we can tell is that you've been exposed to Lyme bacteria and coinfections in the past. But your symptoms are spot-on for what a subset of people experience with Lyme, particularly when it's left untreated."

She gave me the name of an infectious disease specialist in Cleveland and sighed into the phone. "You're going to learn a lot about this illness, whether you want to or not. I'll have Jodi send you some links to good information through the patient portal, but you'll see that there are a lot of parallels to long COVID, or any post-infectious syndrome, in that there's a lot still unknown about the disease etiology and the best course of treatment."

My head began to throb on top of the headache I already had. Was it possible to have two headaches at once? All this time looking for a diagnosis, I had never expected the answer to be so complicated.

"So, there's . . . no treatment for it?" I asked.

"There are treatments, but no quick fixes, I would say. To be honest, a condition like this can be life-changing, particularly when it's caught so late. You'll probably have to make adjustments to your activity level, at least for a time. And you're going to need a good team—I'll be a part of it—to find a plan that works for you. We *are* going to get you feeling better." She enunciated each word. "In a way, it's fortunate to get these results and identify what you're dealing with. Lyme is notoriously hard to catch with testing. I know you didn't want to be sick in the first place, but think of this diagnosis as the start of your recovery. Okay?"

"Okay," I echoed. I thanked her and we wrapped up the call, but I remained motionless on the couch after I hung up. The little piece of paper in my hand on which I'd taken notes held a jumbled mess of new vocabulary. *Borrelia, babesia, bartonella. Autonomic dysfunction, autoimmune, post-Lyme.* My eyes jumped from word to word, sparking sporadic connections in my disorganized brain. They looked like a poem, the distillation of my condition, my symptoms. Words that would help me to think about and talk about what I'd been experiencing all this time.

What I couldn't see clearly, though, in any of the underlined phrases and asterisked notes, was the road ahead. I closed my eyes as I ran through all that had unfolded over the past two weeks—the secrets that had emerged and taken on solid form. The surfaces of my world had wavered and then fallen away. Now, somehow, I had to find a way to rebuild them.

On my way over to Ethan's, I called Audra. I wanted to tell her about my diagnosis, but she didn't pick up. I knew she was still dealing with the fallout from Polly. Audra's nature was to bounce back, but that would take time.

It would take time for all of us to grapple with the idea that the people we had gravitated to in our lives had kept such grave secrets. Audra had barely known her lifelong best friend. And, in her desperation, Beth had entangled herself with Polly rather than coming to Ethan or me for help. On the surface, Polly and Beth had little in common, except for how self-contained they were. Both were good listeners but not ones to talk about themselves. With that distance we'd so readily given, they'd had room to concoct whole other lives. Even Marco, who had been the calm center of our family over the past months, kept his feelings to himself. I vowed to talk with Mom again about the farm paperwork and then realized maybe Marco was the one I needed to talk to first.

As for Mom herself—I'd kept her in the dark about my illness, telling myself I was shielding her, but I recognized, now, that keeping so much from her had only added to her concerns. Just as I'd needed her help with Polly, I would need my mom's help getting through this illness. For all her faults, I never doubted that she loved me. I could already picture her freaking out when I told her about my diagnosis, but I knew she could handle it. She'd been through worse and come out the other side. We all had.

I saw the column of dark smoke rising from behind Ethan's house as soon as I turned onto Aldridge Road. I stepped on the accelerator with my non-bandaged leg and pulled in behind the house.

Dressed in a loose flannel shirt and old jeans, Ethan stood next to a barrel from which flames licked and smoke billowed. He looked from the flames to me. Beth's things lay scattered at his feet.

I got out and limped toward him. He made no move toward me, just watched me approach with no expression.

When I got close, he held up a hand to halt me and shook his head. "I don't wanna hear it."

"Don't do something you can't take back, Ethan. You're grieving right now—"

He laughed and tossed a book into the flames, watching them jump and shimmy in response.

"I can't grieve for someone I never actually knew." He spat the words out, but his eyes looked raw and hurt rather than angry.

"Sit with me, okay? Let it burn and leave the rest for now. It'll be there."

I moved to sit on the back step and leaned my crutch beside me. After a moment, he followed me and sank down next to me, every movement looking like an effort. He smelled of the toxic smoke from things that weren't meant to be burned. He put his elbows on his knees and his hands over his face, rubbing his forehead and pushing his hair back so that it shot up in points. Sitting with him on the step reminded me of the day after Beth died, when we'd sat together in the same spot, both mourning her in our own ways then and now—mourning the Beth we'd thought we knew and the one we were still figuring out.

I didn't have the words he needed. Even less now than back then. Yet, this felt like all the hundreds of other times we'd sat together since we were little, thinking along the same lines, surrounded by the same old trees and houses, tethered to our weird, loving, sometimes-crazy family.

As we watched the flames flicker in the barrel, I caught a streak of gray near the barn. Bibbs shot from one hiding place to another, vanishing into some tall weeds. I looked at the bowl sitting on the porch, expecting to find it empty, and saw food piled high in it. Had Ethan filled it? Something about that small act gave me hope.

When I took his hand in mine, he didn't pull away. The edges of his fingernails were rimmed in black from the fire. With his other hand he rubbed his temple, like he was trying to ease some strong emotion on its way through. My own chest felt full watching him. We'd both lost our sense of certainty about so much, but we had walked away, still with each other to moor ourselves. I wouldn't let him retreat within himself.

Emotions flittered and played across his face. Some I knew and some I didn't. I couldn't read his thoughts, just like he couldn't feel what it was like for me to ache every day.

But it was okay. He was my brother, not my twin. We would just have to find the words.

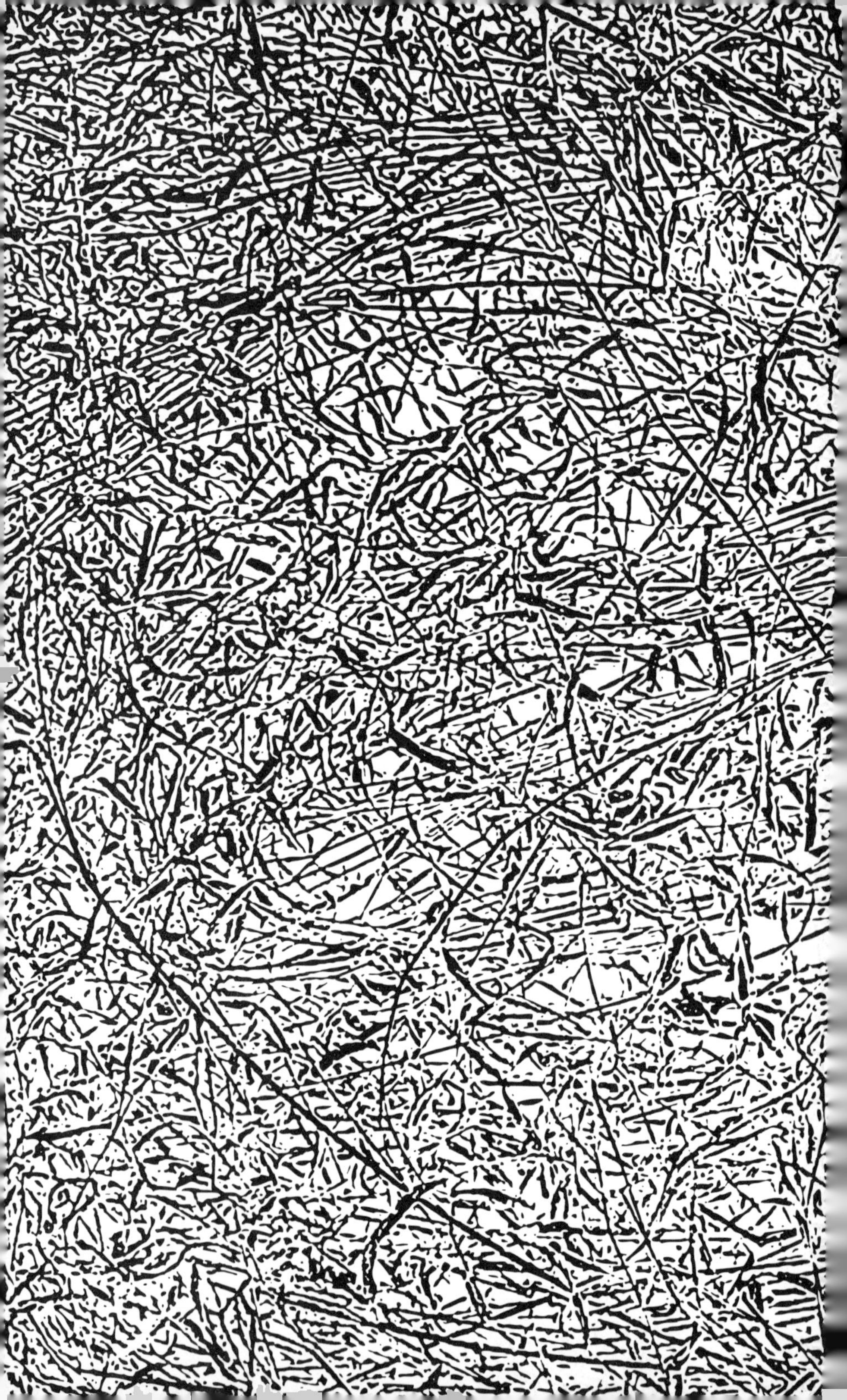

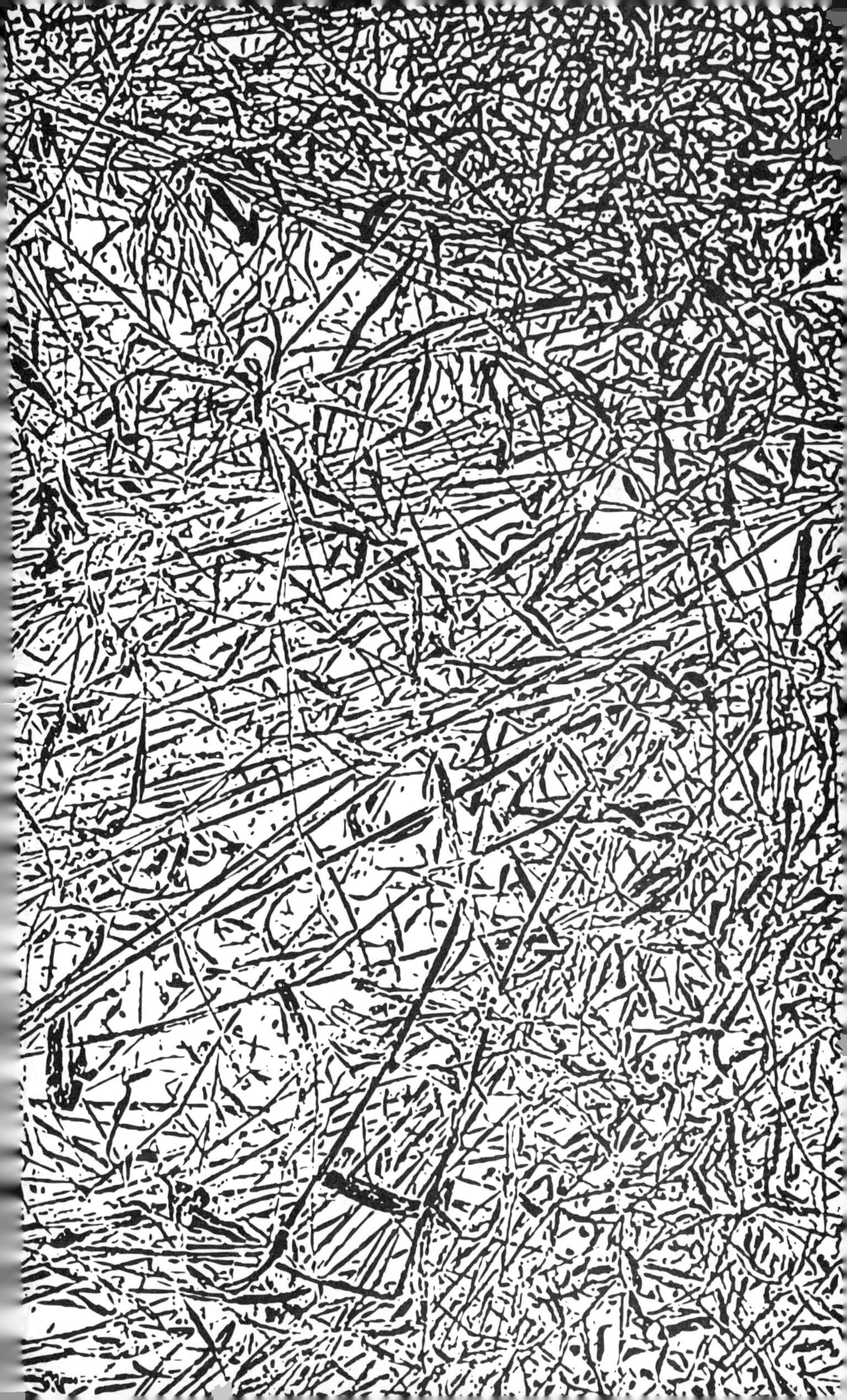

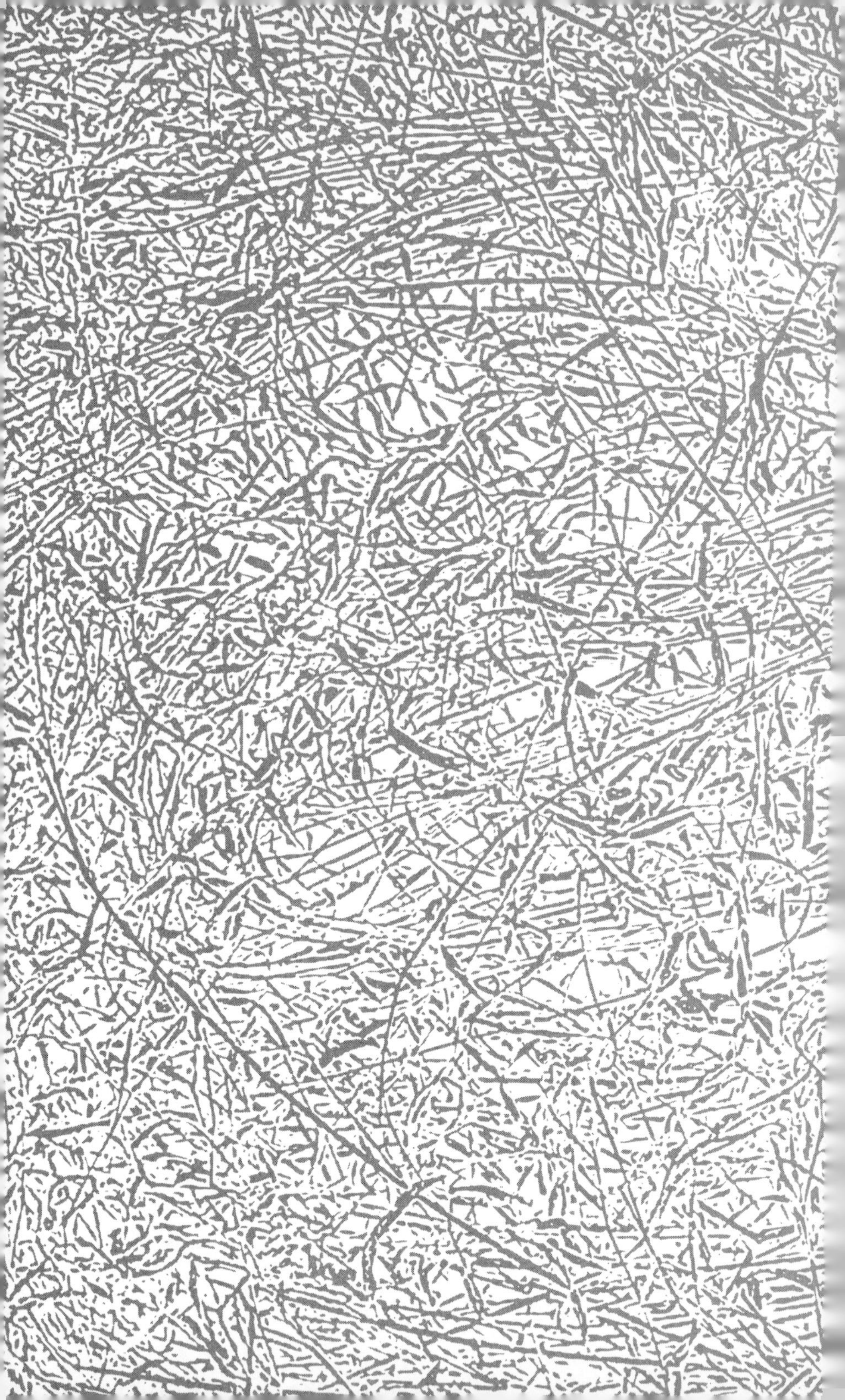

# ACKNOWLEDGMENTS

I never understood how many people contribute to the creation of a book until I wrote one myself. Now, every time I finish a novel, I read the acknowledgments with a new understanding of the community that goes into writing, editing, and publishing a novel.

I have tremendous gratitude to everyone at CamCat Publishing, particularly Bill Lehto and Sue Arroyo for seeing promise in my manuscript, and Helga Schier for guiding me through the editorial process. I feel fortunate to have been able to work with such amazing professionals on my first book and to be in the company of the many talented authors at CamCat.

It would be impossible to name all of the writers in the mystery community whose kindness has helped me along the way, but I have to thank Sisters in Crime for introducing me to so many fellow writers and serving as a repository of wisdom, support, and advice. I'm so grateful to the Guppies Chapter, in particular, for awarding me the 2023 Dorothy Cannell scholarship, which allowed me to attend Malice Domestic. There I met still more wonderful writers and readers and soaked up wisdom from my favorite authors. Among the many takeaways was my "support group," Sally Milliken and Sue Anger, whose stories and advice I look forward to every week. Thank you, also, to my online critique group, Judy, L. C., and Mary, for keeping me on track as I continue writing and for being such fantastic human beings. It's always a pleasure reading your work and learning from you. Finally, thank you to the Midwest Chapter of the Mystery Writers of America for the 2022 Hugh Holton Award, which recognized *Hidden Rooms* as one of the best unpublished mysteries by a Midwest writer. (I'm still pleasantly shocked every time I say that!) As a new fiction writer, this recognition means everything to me. Thank you for what you do to encourage and support emerging mystery writers.

I am so grateful to the Toledo Writers Workshop for welcoming me into their group, introducing me to a local community of writers, and telling me in the kindest way possible that my mystery should not begin with my main character waking up and going to work. Your good advice saved me! The Toledo area is full of talented writers, and I'm lucky to have the chance to learn from some of them every Tuesday night. Before turning to fiction, I wrote poetry, and many (many, many) years ago, I was fortunate to go through the Ohio State MFA program for poetry. I want to thank the amazingly talented classmates and professors who shaped my love of language.

A number of brave souls were kind enough to read an early draft of this book, including Lois Berkowitz, Janet Biblewski, Tom Biblewski, Jamie Fletcher, Leslie Gulvas, Joyce Rupley, Nicole Starkey, and Kateri Walsh. Thank you to all of you for taking the time to read my manuscript and for being such kind and discerning readers. Your constructive feedback and encouragement helped me take *Hidden Rooms* from a draft to something resembling a book. I feel very lucky to have benefited from your perspectives.

I could never have written this book without some help with my research. Thanks to Lyme Village, particularly Tim Rife, for the wonderful tour of Wright Mansion and the information on the Underground Railroad in northern Ohio. I would also like to thank those in law enforcement who took the time to answer my questions. I am indebted to nonfiction writers, such as Megan O'Rourke and Maya Dusenbery, who have so wisely and empathetically written about women's experiences with poorly understood illnesses. I know I can never fully represent the spectrum of experiences with chronic pain and illness, and I'm sorry for where I have fallen short, but I hope I have captured some portion of the truth.

I'm lucky to have a wonderfully supportive family, who offered encouragement throughout the writing and publishing process—and sometimes just listened to me go on about my characters and the plot for far longer than I probably should have. Very special thanks go to my mom for reading my drafts as I wrote them and for being the person who cultivated my love of books and mysteries in the first place. Thank you to my dad for answering questions about all the details about farming that I should have already known, considering where I grew up. Thank you to my mother-in-law for being an encouraging early reader and my father-in-law for his hilarious stories (one of which may have made its way into the book). Thanks to my siblings for reading early versions of the book and their enthusiasm. I'm not sure what I did to be rewarded with such an amazing family and in-laws, but I'm glad I did it.

Finally, "thank you" doesn't begin to cover how grateful I am to my husband for everything. Thanks for being there for me during the lows and celebrating the highs. No matter what kind of day I've had, spending time with you makes it better. Here's to more of all of it with you.

# ABOUT THE AUTHOR

Kate Michaelson lives with her husband and pets in Ohio. She has worked as a technical writer, English instructor, and curriculum developer. *Hidden Rooms* is her debut novel.

You can connect with her online at
www.katemichaelson.com

If you enjoyed
Kate Michaelson's
*Hidden Rooms,*
please consider leaving us a review
to help our authors.

And check out
Marcy McCreary's
*The Summer of Love and Death.*

# 1

## FRIDAY | AUGUST 16, 2019

**I FUMBLED** with the zipper of my yellow slicker as I stood in front of the framed poster—an illustration of a white dove perched on a blue guitar neck, gripped by ivory fingers against a bright red background. Band names cascading down the left side. Usually, I paid it no mind. But today was different. Exactly fifty years ago, four hundred thousand teenagers and young adults descended upon this town. The so-called summer of love.

The poster, touting three days of peace and music, hung (slightly askew) in our entranceway. The Woodstock Music and Art Fair didn't take place in Woodstock, NY. The residents of Woodstock were not keen on having the initially projected fifty thousand hippies traipsing through its town. The concert promoters eventually secured Max Yasgur's farm in Bethel, NY—fifty-eight miles from Woodstock and six miles from where I live now. I was four at the time.

I have no memory of it. Mom said I was sicker than sick that weekend. Ear infection. Fever escalating to one hundred and four degrees. She tried to take me to a doctor, but the roads were clogged with festival revelers, so she had to postpone my appointment until Tuesday. But by then, the worst of it was over.

Fifty years. Those teenagers were in their sixties and seventies now. The older ones in their eighties. How many of them were still idealistic? How many were still into peace, love, and understanding? How many "dropped out" and berated "the man," only later to find themselves the beneficiaries of capitalism? They themselves becoming "the man."

I leaned over slightly as I reached for the handle on the front door. It swung open, smacking me in the forehead. "Whoa." I ran my fingertips along my head. No bump. For now.

"Sorry, babe. Didn't realize you were standing there."

Ray's voice drew Moxie's attention. Our thirteen-year-old lab-mix moseyed into the foyer, tail in full swing. Moseying was really all Moxie could muster these days.

Ray had left the house over an hour ago. I peered over his shoulder at the running Jeep. "Forget something?"

"Yeah. My wallet." Ray stepped inside, dripping. Moxie stared up at him, waiting. He squatted and rubbed her ears. "Raining cats and dogs out there. No offense, Moxie." He glanced up at the poster. "Just like fifty years ago." He sighed.

Ray's parents were married at the festival by a traveling minister. One-year-old Ray in tow (earning him bragging rights as one of the youngest people to attend Woodstock). Tomorrow would have been their fiftieth wedding anniversary.

Their death, at the hand of a drunk driver twelve years ago, spawned a program called Better Mad Than Sad—a class baked into the local drivers-ed curriculum that Ray (and the drunk driver's girlfriend, Marisa) created ten years ago. Parents would join their kids for a fifty-minute session in which they pledged to pick up their kids or their kids' friends, no questions asked, no judgment passed.

Last month, Ray reached out to a few of his and his parents' friends asking if they would be up for a "celebration of life" vigil at the Woodstock

Festival site this evening. Nothing formal. Just twenty or so folks standing around, reminiscing and shooting the shit about his parents.

Ray shook the rain off his jacket. "Met your new partner this morning."

"Yeah?"

"He's very good-looking." Then added, "Movie-star good-looking."

I leaned back and gave Ray the once-over. "I'm more into the rough-around-the-edges look."

"So I got nothing to worry about?"

"Not as long as you treat me right." I smiled coyly.

I had been without an official partner for a little over a year, since July 2018. My ex-partner bought a small farm in Vermont. He told me not to take it personally, but he was on the verge of a nervous breakdown. I still wondered if I contributed to his anxiety in some small way. Then I got shot in the thigh that August. So hiring a new partner got put on hold. Upon my return to active duty in October of 2018, I was assigned an under-the-radar cold case with my dad brought on as consulting partner. By the time the Trudy Solomon cold case was resolved in December 2018, Chief Eldridge still hadn't found a suitable replacement. Small-town policing isn't everyone's cup of tea. So for the better part of 2019, I was flying solo. Dad and Ray assisted on the Madison Garcia case, but the Chief made it clear that protocol called for two detectives working a case, and my partnerless days were numbered. Don't get me wrong. It's not like I didn't want a partner. I did. I just wished I had a say in who it was.

THE DREADED handshake awaited me as I walked into the precinct. I thought about using the "I-have-a-cold" excuse, but lying to Detective John Tomelli on Day One seemed like a dishonest way to kick off what should be a trusted partnership.

"There she is," Eldridge called out, motioning me over to where he and Detective Tomelli were standing.

John thrust his right hand forward.

"Ford doesn't do handshakes," Eldridge said.

"Oh, oh," John said, furrowing his brow and drawing his hand back to his side.

"Just getting over a cold," I said with wavering conviction. Which wasn't entirely a lie, as I spent all of July on antibiotics for a sinus infection.

"Well, I'll let you two get to know each other," Eldridge said, backing away toward his office.

"So, John—"

"Jack."

"Jack?"

"Yeah, everyone calls me Jack."

I nodded. "Okay."

"My dad's name was John. So to avoid confusion . . . y'know." He eyed my right hand. "What's with the no handshakes."

"Well, *Jack,* I have a weird medical malady called *palmar hyperhidrosis.* Ever hear of it?"

He shook his head.

I held up my palms. "Sweaty palms. Uncontrollably clammy hands."

"Does it affect your ability to handle a gun?"

And this was why I didn't tell anyone.

"No," I said curtly. "It doesn't," I added for good measure.

"Ford! Tomelli!" Eldridge shouted before *Jack* had a chance to say anything else on the matter. Nothing like getting off on the wrong foot on the first day.

Jack led the way. At the door, he stepped aside and waved me in. Instead of being appreciative of the gesture, I wondered if he would have proffered the same courtesy if I was a guy. Was this a "ladies first" move or was he merely deferring to my seniority.

I didn't know what was pissing me off most—his Hollywood good looks, that gun remark, or the fact that he just treated me like his date. *Shake it off, Susan.*

"I just got a call from dispatch," Eldridge said as we lingered in front of his desk. "Possible homicide at The Monticello Playhouse. Paramedics are there now. Pronounced dead at the scene. Mike and Gloria are on their way. As is CSI."

"Mark and Gloria?" Jack asked.

"Mark Sheffield is the county's medical examiner and Gloria Weinberg is our crime scene photographer," I explained.

Jack turned to Eldridge. "Who's the victim?"

Eldridge peered down at the paper on his desk. "The woman who called it in said it was one of the actors. Didn't say which one."

Jack turned to me and smirked. "I'll drive."

My blood started to boil.

THE MONTICELLO Playhouse was situated a mile down the road from the Holiday Mountain Ski & Fun Park—a seven-slope ski area, with an elevation of thirteen hundred feet and a vertical drop of four hundred feet. I spent many youthful days zipping down their trails. Back then, you had to rely on Mother Nature for a good coating, and most winters delivered what was needed. These days, the owners relied on snowmaking machines—it was the only way for the ski area to survive the warming winters of climate change.

Jack lifted his hand from the steering wheel and pointed toward the windshield. "Ski area?" he asked as we passed the entrance sign. "Looks open."

"Yeah. It doubles as an amusement park in the summer. Arcades, rock-climbing wall, bumper boats. That kinda thing." I side-eyed Jack. "You should take your kids."

He frowned and shook his head. "Don't have kids. You? You have kids?"

"One kid. Adult kid. Natalie."

I waited for him to ask a follow-up question. *How old? What does she do for a living? Grandkids?* But he just tapped his thumbs on the leather-encased steering wheel of his fancy Volvo. I thought about volunteering more info, get a conversation going, get to know each other better, but he seemed tucked away in his own thoughts. Neither of us said another word.

We pulled into the parking lot of the theater. Jack swiveled his head from side to side, then swung his car to the right and parked below a canopy of trees, a good ways away from the hubbub of activity. Above our heads, birds tweeted in melodious call-and-response chirps.

I spotted Mark's silver Honda Accord and Gloria's Ford pickup truck. "Gang's all here."

Jack popped open the trunk and grabbed his crime scene kit, a duffel containing personal protective gear, evidence markers, and evidence collection equipment.

As Jack and I strode up the stone walkway toward the entrance of the playhouse, Officer Sally McIvers and her partner appeared from around the side of the building. Sally jogged over to us.

"You must be the new guy," Sally said. "Detective John Tomelli?"

"You can call me Jack."

"Jack it is." Sally held out her hand and Jack shook it firmly. She turned to her right. "This is my partner, Officer Ron Wallace."

Ron stepped forward. "About time they filled the position," he said, pumping Jack's hand.

"You guys first on scene?" I asked.

"Yeah. I just surveyed the ground under the windows," Ron said, twisting around toward the theater. "Nothing obvious, but I took photos, just in case. Hopefully, Gloria can get some pro shots before the rain starts up again." He paused. "All the windows lock from the inside."

Sally picked up the thread. "I checked inside the building and all the windows were locked. Doesn't mean someone didn't crawl through an open window, lock it, and then use the front door to leave, but that's for you two to figure out."

I glanced over at the old rectory building, now the actor's dormitory, situated about twenty yards from the theater. A small crowd had gathered outside, craning their necks and whispering among themselves. Three officers stood between them and us, keeping them at bay.

"Mounted cameras anywhere?" I asked Ron and Sally, remembering how an obscure CCTV camera helped get my ass out of trouble last year.

"Nothing obvious," Sally replied. "But they could be hidden. I'll look around."

"Let's get a perimeter going," I said to Ron, scanning the vast outdoor area around the theater. "Fifteen yards out from the theater. Also, set up a single entry/exit point over there. I'll get one of the other officers to log who comes and goes."

I turned to Sally. "Who found the victim?"

Sally flipped open her notebook. "Jean Cranmore, the woman in charge of costumes. She's over there." Sally pointed to a fifty-something, red-headed woman sitting on a nearby bench, her hands tucked between her knees, rocking back and forth. Her blue windbreaker zipped up to her chin. "I took her statement when I first arrived. She said she's seen enough cop shows to know not to let anyone near the body or say anything to anyone, so at least we know the crime scene hasn't been contaminated."

"Eldridge said it's one of the actors," Jack said. "Did she say which one?"

"Actually, the director." Sally scanned her notes. "Adam Kincaid. She said she was freaked out and must have said actor by mistake when she called 911."

"Let her know I'll speak to her after I've surveyed the crime scene." I noted a scowl form on Jack's face when I used the word *I* instead of *we*. Should I explain it was merely a habit from not having a partner for a while?

Sally jutted her chin toward the walkway that separated the dormitory from the theater. "What about the lookie-loos over there?"

"Interview them as well. That'll help me sort out who I need to talk to first." Oops. Did it again.

Sally flipped her notebook closed. "Will do."

"You saw the body?" I asked.

"Yeah. It's a weird one," Sally hinted, knowing full well that I preferred to assess the crime scene without exposition. "You'll see."

THE MONTICELLO Playhouse used to be a Catholic church. It sat abandoned for about fifteen years until Malcolm Slater bought it five years ago. Yeah, that Malcolm Slater . . . lead singer of Blueberry Fields, an alternative rock band that dominated the radio airwaves in the nineties. Three of his albums went platinum. After calling it quits with his bandmates in the mid aughts, he drifted over to the production side of the business and opened a recording studio in the neighboring town of Forestburgh, New York. He also founded an indie label, Slater Records, and launched the career of several indie rock artists. So the guy was a bit of a celebrity around here. Rumor had it he was also a prima donna.

Malcolm Slater not only invested in the property, but he installed himself as the theater's Executive Director, providing the bulk of the funding for the summer stock productions. Some called it philanthropy, a gift to revitalize the area. Others believed he had an ulterior motive . . . to give his girlfriend, Shana Lowry, a stage and a starring role.

I gazed up at the white gable-roofed building, the narrow bell tower shooting straight up over the entrance. Slater did a heck of a job transforming it from rundown church to refurbished theater. I'll give him that. Jack raced by me, taking two steps at a time as he ascended the ten steps to the porch landing. He stood in front of the wooden double doors. I sucked in my breath, then slowly exhaled before climbing the stairs. Fuck, he was getting on my nerves.

He unzipped the duffel and extracted two plastic bags containing Tyvek coveralls, booties, and a pair of blue latex gloves. He tossed one in my direction. We quickly donned our PPE. Jack opened the door and, once again, stepped aside and waved me through. With a tightlipped smile, I hurried into the foyer, then up the aisle to the stage. Mark was center stage, leaning over the body. Gloria was in the orchestra pit, hunched over her camera equipment. She looked up and waved me over. I glanced over my shoulder and saw Jack making his way up the aisle.

"Ready?" I asked Gloria.

"Just took the global photos. Waiting on you for mid-range and close-up." Gloria tipped her head toward the dead body. "I've photographed a lot of crime scenes in my day, but this one takes the proverbial cake."

As I mounted the steps to the stage, I heard Jack introduce himself to Gloria.

When Jack caught up to me, I initiated the introductions. "Jack, meet Mark Sheffield, Sullivan County's death investigator and medical examiner and, in my nobody-gives-a-shit opinion, one of the best in the business."

"Good to meet you, Mark."

"Likewise. Ready?"

I walked to the center of the stage where the body was situated. Jack remained behind me, but close on my heels. Was this deference or a case of nerves?

I wasn't sure what to expect, but it wasn't this. No one prepares you for this.

A MAN, roughly late twenties, laid in a narrow platform bed. His wrists and ankles bound by rough-hewn rope. Fancy nautical knots. Naked. And that wasn't the worst part of this tableau. His face was caked in smeared makeup. Lips bright red. Cheeks pink with blush. Eyelids powdery blue. A white pillow—placed below the feet of the deceased—was also smeared in makeup, looking like a second-rate Vasily Kandinsky knockoff. A large makeup bag, partially open, lay on the floor at the side of the bed. I looked around for his clothes, but there was not a stitch of discarded clothing anywhere on the stage.

Jack swayed, shifting his weight from his right foot to his left. “What the—?”

I turned to face Mark. “Approximate time of death?”

“Well, it was called in at nine-fifteen this morning. Based on rigor and lividity, I’d say between eight last night and and eight this morning. Hopefully someone can tell you when he was last seen alive . . . help you narrow that down.”

“Cause of death?”

“Possible asphyxiation,” he said, pointing to the pillow. “There’s some bruising around his nose and mouth. But until I get him back to the morgue I won’t know for sure. Didn’t put up much of a fight, so I’m thinking drugged, then smothered. Tox panel will give a fuller picture.”

“Is this bed part of the set?” Jack asked, peering over my shoulder.

“Yeah,” Gloria chimed in, then turned to me. “You’re gonna love this, Susan . . . they’ve been rehearsing Agatha Christie’s *Murder on the Orient Express*. Supposed to open tonight.”

“*Murder on the Orient Express* is a play?”

Mark straightened up. All six foot six of him in full view now. “Yeah, in fact I had tickets to the Sunday show.”

“Well, I hope you can get a refund, because I’m pretty sure there won’t be a Sunday show. It’s going to take a while to process and clear the scene.” I surveyed the stage for anything out of the ordinary. But nothing leapt out at me. “They’ll be lucky if they open on Monday . . . if at all.”

My phone rang. It was Sally. I walked to stage right. Or was it stage left? I could never remember if the wings were from the actor’s perspective or the audience’s perspective.“Yeah.”

“I got Malcolm Slater out here. He’s demanding to go inside.”

“He can demand until the cows come home. Tell him I’ll be out to talk to him when I’m done in here.”

A man’s voice erupted through the line. “Give me the phone!”

Sally abruptly ended the call. She’s no shrinking violet. If anyone can handle that guy, she can. An aging rocker versus a no-nonsense police officer with two tours in Iraq under her belt. I got my money on Sally. Even so, I did not appreciate being rushed, but now felt somewhat obliged to speak with Malcolm Slater sooner rather than later.

I rejoined our little group and conferred with Gloria on the mid-range and close-up shots. Jack simply nodded as I spoke. The side door opened and a sudden burst of light illuminated the stage. Three county CSIs entered and strode toward us.

"Let's use this pathway for getting on and off the stage," I said, motioning with my arms a narrow passage from where we were all standing to the steps. "Jack, can you mark the path with the cones? There should be some in the CSK. And while you're at it, can you bring me back a stack of evidence markers? I'm going outside to chat with the theater's Executive Director."

He nodded.

I flashed a smile at Gloria and she winked back. She knew exactly what I was doing. Establishing my dominance. Making sure he knew who was in charge.

BEFORE LEAVING the theater, I lingered in the lobby. I had hurried through this area when first arriving with Jack and didn't get a chance to see if anything was amiss in here. There were wooden benches along the wall to my right. On the wall to my left hung 9x12 framed photographs of all the troupes—cast and crew—who had performed in the theater. I walked over to the photograph closest to the door, the first troupe to perform in 2014.

I moseyed down to the last photograph. Engraved on a gold-plated plaque above this photograph were the words: Cast and Crew of Mousetrap and Murder On The Orient Express, Summer 2019

I examined the faces of the people who were about to be shocked to hear the news about their director. When I exited the theater, I beelined it to Sally, who was standing at the designated entry/exit point. Pacing behind the yellow crime tape was none other than Malcolm Slater—tall and wiry, with hair too dark and too long for a man his age. He charged toward me.

"I've been standing out here in the rain for a fucking hour!" he screamed, tilting his large black umbrella slightly backward. "I'll have your badge! Your supervisor will be hearing about this. Chief Cliff Eldridge, right?"

"You're free to file a complaint," I said, doing my best to sound cordial. Well, somewhat cordial. I glanced around looking for shelter and spotted a barn at the edge of the tree line. "We haven't cleared that barn over there, but we can talk under the overhang."

As we strode toward the barn, plump droplets replaced the gentle mist. By the time we reached the overhang, the rain intensified and all I could think about was all the outdoor evidence being washed away. Sally said she had taken pictures with her phone around and below all the windows before Gloria arrived, so at least there was that.

"I have a right to know what's going on in my theater." Malcolm lowered his umbrella, shook off the water, and pulled it shut. "Was there an accident? Or something . . . worse?"

"There's been a murder. Until we notify next of kin and get a positive ID, there is not much more I can tell you."

He stepped closer to me. "That's bullshit! Utter bullshit!" He shook the umbrella, causing it to open slightly. He grabbed the little strap and secured it around the middle. "Was it a member of the cast or crew? At least tell me that much."

"Mr. Slater, I have an investigation to run. I will not risk fucking this up just because you threaten to 'speak to my superior' or 'have my badge.' Got it?"

Malcolm stepped back. He opened his mouth, but quickly snapped it shut.

"Who has access to your theater at night?" I asked.

"Ricky is responsible for locking the front and side doors after rehearsals and shows, but there are a few people who have keys to the side door."

"Ricky?"

"Ricky Saunders. Our maintenance guy."

"Okay. I'll need a list of everyone who has a key."

"Sure."

"Are there security cameras on premises?"

Malcolm shook his head. "I find them to be invasions of privacy. And I don't want my actors to think I'm spying on them."

That's understandable, given his previous profession. In his heyday, the paparazzi were relentless. He leaned heavily into the sex, drugs, and rock 'n' roll stereotype. Although, I always felt some of his shenanigans seemed manufactured, played up for publicity.

"Who lives in the old rectory?"

Malcolm tilted his head to the right, craning over my shoulder to glimpse the building. "The equity actors and a few department heads live on the first and second floors. The non-equity actors live on the third, fourth, and fifth floors. There's a smaller building behind the rectory that houses the crew."

"And those bungalows?" I asked, pointing to the edge of the property near the road.

"That's where the musicians live."

"So, the entire cast and crew live on-site?"

"No. Not everyone. Some department heads are scattered around the area. I bought a few small bungalows around Smallwood and Sackett Lake to house them during the summer. This way I can attract top talent." He cleared his throat. "Now that I've given you the lay of the land, I would appreciate you telling me who has been murdered."

"I've already told you more than I should have. So, I suggest you keep that under your hat until we've had a chance to interview folks. The more you cooperate with me, the more I will cooperate with you. Do I make myself clear?"

Malcolm whipped open his umbrella and stormed away just as a crack of lightning lit up the gray mid-morning sky.

TO SHIELD our witness from the rain, Sally had escorted Jean Cranmore, the costume director, to the gift shop—a one-story stand-alone building about thirty feet from the theater's side exit door. Sally had asked Malcolm to unlock it when he arrived on scene so CSI could do a sweep of the place. When given the all-clear, Sally asked Jean to wait in there.

A tinkle announced my entrance. Jean was seated on a stool amongst the Monticello Playhouse–branded mugs, T-shirts, keychains, refrigerator magnets and other touristy tchotchkes.

"How are you holding up?" I looked around for another stool or chair, but there was none, so I leaned against the glass counter.

She sniffled and ran her sleeve across her nose. Her eyelashes were moist and mascara smudges lined the area beneath her eyes. She inhaled deeply, then let out a long breath.